THE NEW NELLY

What would the old Nelly have done in this situation? Easy. She would have disappeared into the woodwork, making no fuss at all, but not the new Nelly. Not Anyella Devin Lure. She knew how to end an argument—her way.

"Come on," she said to Mac, who sat glaring at her. "Forget those dark thoughts. Let's dance."

"But that's rock they're playing."

"So? What have you got against rock?" She grabbed his hand and led him out onto the tiny dance floor and began moving to the music. "Smile, droopy," she said. "It only hurts for a minute. Shake your booty on this one, Mac. You can do a minuet later."

He began to move to the music, stiffly at first.

"Come on. Loosen up," she said, but then the combo segued into a ballad she loved, "Memories." He pulled her to him for a slow dance. Nelly boldly pushed closer and nestled her head against his neck. They moved in a kind of trance; it was easy to follow when your bodies were glued together this way.

It was dark, and nobody was looking. Tenderly his lips found hers, and he gave her a kiss so sweet and gentle that when he let her go, she ached for more.

"Loosen up?" he whispered in her ear. "That wasn't a bad idea, Anyella."

IT'S NEVER TOO LATE FOR LOVE AND ROMANCE

JUST IN TIME   (4188, $4.50/$5.50)
by Peggy Roberts

Constantly taking care of everyone around her has earned Remy Dupre the affectionate nickname "Ma." Then, with Remy's husband gone and oil discovered on her Louisiana farm, her sons and their wives decide it's time to take care of her. But Remy knows how to take care of herself. She starts by checking into a beauty spa, buying some classy new clothes and shoes, discovering an antique vase, and moving on to a fine plantation. Next, not one, but two men attempt to sweep her off her well-shod feet. The right man offers her the opportunity to love again.

LOVE AT LAST   (4158, $4.50/$5.50)
by Garda Parker

Fifty, slim, and attractive, Gail Bricker still hadn't found the love of her life. Friends convince her to take an Adventure Tour during the summer vacation she enjoys as an English teacher. At a Cheyenne Indian school in need of teachers, Gail finds her calling. In rancher Slater Kincaid, she finds her match. Gail discovers that it's never too late to fall in love . . . for the very first time.

LOVE LESSONS   (3959, $4.50/$5.50)
by Marian Oaks

After almost forty years of marriage, Carolyn Ames certainly hadn't been looking for a divorce. But the ink is barely dry, and here she is already living an exhilarating life as a single woman. First, she lands an exciting and challenging job. Now Jason, the handsome architect, offers her a fairy-tale romance. Carolyn doesn't care that her ultra-conservative neighbors gossip about her and Jason, but she is afraid to give up her independent life-style. She struggles with the balance while she learns to love again.

A KISS TO REMEMBER   (4129, $4.50/$5.50)
by Helen Playfair

For the past ten years Lucia Morgan hasn't had time for love or romance. Since her husband's death, she has been raising her two sons, working at a dead-end office job, and designing boutique clothes to make ends meet. Then one night, Mitch Colton comes looking for his daughter, out late with one of her sons. The look in Mitch's eye brings back a host of long-forgotten feelings. When the kids come home and spoil the enchantment, Lucia wonders if she will get the chance to love again.

COME HOME TO LOVE   (3930, $4.50/$5.50)
by Jane Bierce

Julia Delaine says good-bye to her skirt-chasing husband Phillip and hello to a whole new life. Julia capably rises to the challenges of her reawakened sexuality, the young man who comes courting, and her new position as the head of her local television station. Her new independence teaches Julia that maybe her time-tested values were right all along and maybe Phillip does belong in her life, with her new terms.

Available wherever paperbacks are sold, or order direct from the Publisher. Send cover price plus 50¢ per copy for mailing and handling to Zebra Books, Dept. 4401, 475 Park Avenue South, New York, N.Y. 10016. Residents of New York and Tennessee must include sales tax. DO NOT SEND CASH. For a free Zebra/Pinnacle catalog please write to the above address.

ONE KISS

MARTHA GROSS

ZEBRA BOOKS
KENSINGTON PUBLISHING CORP.

To my daughter, Jennifer Gross
My best critic
My best proofreader
My best friend.

ZEBRA BOOKS are published by

Kensington Publishing Corp.
475 Park Avenue South
New York, NY 10016

First Printing: December, 1993

Printed in the United States of America

Prologue

Something was ready to happen. Something momentous, mind-boggling. In some way she would change forever. She felt it, almost as physically as she might feel a breeze or the pelting of rain. That subtle tingling in the air, that slowing of time, that keen, sharp awareness of everybody and everything around her.

Like her mother, Nelly was psychic. Wordless messages would often warn her of something wonderful or something terrible. She *knew* as surely as she knew her name, that a crucial turning point was imminent in the chilly air. And that somehow, her life would never be the same again.

She felt it the moment she woke with Albert's hand groping clumsily at her breast, just before he crashed onto her bed, all but shaking her out of it. He lie there, unconscious, breathing in loud, foul-smelling snorts. The stench was always the same after an all-night poker orgy—sweat, beer, salami, and sour breath.

After poker, fortunately, was the only time he approached her bed anymore. He was always so comatose that he could forget that sex was the one area where Nelly refused, after twenty-eight years, to obey his orders.

She knew that instant, thanks to the heightened awareness that went hand in hand with her premonitions. Over Albert's noise she could hear the morning's every sound so clearly—the kitchen clock ticking, the air conditioner whirring, a bicycle whizzing by in the street outside. Because of that subtle slowing of time, she seemed to be crawling from the bed in slow motion. And because of the charged aura in the room, she felt the same sensations she'd had right after Hurricane Doreen when she told Albert that somehow she *knew* a tornado was coming. And it did.

They were the same feelings she'd had the night she suddenly insisted, for no apparent reason, they go down and stay overnight in her mother's apartment on Miami Beach. That was the night lightning struck the old oak tree out back, and the whole tree crashed through the roof of their Florida room.

Well, whatever was going to happen, whatever change it would bring—to Albert, snoring on the bed, or to the drab, almost invisible little shadow she had become—Nelly knew it could only be a change for the better.

One

Actually, awesome signals of portent had been nagging at Nelly on and off for a week, though not as acutely. She sometimes got lesser premonitions before an intense one, preceding a major happening. Like warning tremors before an earthquake.

She felt the first surge on Wednesday at the luncheon with Mac Britton and Claire Clemency-Graves, known as C.G., who was now her boss at the accounting firm of Raymond, Schlesser, McKinnon & Goldberg. C.G. had set it up—at the Down Under. Britton, Llewellen, and McVey was the New York law firm that was opening offices in Fort Lauderdale. "They're big time," C.G. explained as the waiter showed them to their table. "But hiring local accountants and PR people is the thing to do if they want to make friends and become part of the community as quickly as possible."

They had just begun studying the menu when the waiter returned, followed by a lean, tired-looking man in his fifties. He was impeccably dressed and well-groomed except for an unruly shock of wiry grey hair.

"Ah, Mrs. Clemency-Graves. Am I late?" He took C.G.'s hand, gave it one shake, and released it. "Three important calls from New York came in just as I was leaving. It's still a madhouse—our office. So much to work out and we're already taking cases here."

"No, Mr. Britton, you're right on time," said C.G. graciously. "We just arrived a minute ago. I thought an Intracoastal view might be a pleasant change. We've done the Sky Club to death lately. This is my assistant, Nelly Holachek. Your people will be dealing directly with her."

"Mrs. Holachek," he repeated, nodding and giving Nelly's hand that same brief but firm shake.

"She'll visit you on a regular basis once you're set up, and guide your system—or rather guide your personnel in implementing it," said C.G. with a broad smile. Britton nodded and C.G. went on. "Mr. Raymond said you would appreciate any suggestions that would help integrate your company into the community more quickly."

"Yes. That, of course, is one of our major aims."

C.G. smiled. "Well, there's one thing we do for many of our clients that might be very useful. How to explain it? You might say we trade experts around town. We do the books for a couple dozen condo associations and if one needs a speaker for a meeting, we get someone from the library to talk about what services are available. Or someone who can talk about a medical specialty in the news today—Alzheimer's or breast cancer or AIDS. If the Medical Wives group wants entertainment at their luncheon, we find a retired comedian or vocalist from one of the condos. We're in touch with so many different companies and groups and people that we're able to help them all out."

Nelly choked. C.G. knew very well that it was she, Nelly, who did all that, *on her own,* for their clients and anyone else who asked. It was Nelly who heard, two years ago, that condo associations loved speakers on useful, practical subjects, and got someone from the fire department to lecture on fire safety for every association client on their list. Next she provided lectures on security from the Sheriff's office. When the Cancer Society needed some kind of entertainment to rev up a fundraiser luncheon, Nelly got them a bunch of retired clowns from various condos. And she had been helping their clients this way ever since.

Then C.G. had come to work for Raymond, Schlesser, to do the same work Nelly had been doing, and had somehow taken over. She had been bossing Nelly around so much and taking credit for anything she could, that by now nobody seemed to realize anymore that C.G. simply took requests and handed them to Nelly. Or Selma, the office manager, or Georgia, the receptionist, would take requests and give them to C.G., who gave them to Nelly, but one way or another, it was Nelly who did the actual work. Ben Schlesser was the only partner who seemed to realize that C.G. had never once booked a speaker or entertainer and wouldn't know where to begin.

Yet here she was, acting as though she ran it all!

Nelly was furious, but predictably, she said nothing. Her face revealed no anger. She sat there, her usual invisible self, while C.G. cozied up to Britton. Surely C.G. wasn't hoping for any personal response. Why, she was at least five years older than he!

But then Nelly noted Britton's beautifully cut, obviously custom-tailored suit. English, she guessed. His watch—gold, but simple. One ring, gold, no diamonds. Just a large cabochon sapphire. Nothing flashy. No bracelets. And that hint of weariness, almost sadness, in those blue, blue eyes. Somehow, he didn't look like the kind of man who would mix business with his personal life. C.G., Nelly guessed, was wasting her time.

He did seem a trifle impatient, though. He started drumming his fingers twice, but quickly stopped.

At one point, when C.G. paused to take a breath, he turned to Nelly. "Mrs. Holachek. I'll tell the office to expect you. I suggest you call my secretary and set up your first visit, and I'll introduce you to the people you'll be working with."

10

Nelly nodded. "Yes. I'll talk to whomever handles record-keeping for you. To see what you do. And we'll go from there."

The waiter interrupted. "Are you ready to order yet?"

"No, come back in one minute," said C.G. "Shall we look at the menu, Mr. Britton? The swordfish is delicious here."

"Sounds good," said Britton, closing the menu. He obviously didn't like to waste a lot of time deciding what to eat. He was probably decisive, and liked to work things out quickly and get on to the next project or problem. The best kind of person to work with, thought Nelly.

"Oh, Nelly, dear," cooed C.G. "if you're very rushed, you don't have to stay and eat."

Nelly looked at her, stunned. She was being dismissed! Told she shouldn't stay for lunch. She felt another rush of anger.

But Britton shook his head. "Oh, please stay," he said in a friendly tone. "If you have time. I'm sure I'll have a dozen questions before we're through."

He doesn't think that's very nice, either, realized Nelly, looking up at eyes that now looked kindly instead of sad. And that was when she felt it the first time, overlying her anger at C.G.—a blanket of warmth, of awareness. She could suddenly see every line and wrinkle in his face. She could hear his breath, see the pulse throbbing in his temple. The

11

clink of every fork and spoon in the room played like a Walkman in her ear. Time slowed. C.G. turned to her in slow motion, and gave her a pointed look. Nelly mumbled an excuse and slowly stood up, as Mac Britton did the same, to reach over and pull out her chair.

And then like a rubber band snapping, time clicked back into its normal speed slot. She nodded at them and left. The urgent feeling—the aware- ness—was fading. She got its message. Something important was going to happen, but maybe not right away. C.G. was a viper. And Mac Britton, Nelly was certain, could tell.

It happened again later, at the drug store, when she tried to write a check for her vitamins and the pharmacy clerk spoke up.

"Do you have a check cashing card with us?"

Nelly had only been buying toothpaste and filling prescriptions there for ten years, and this clerk had only waited on her about twice a week for half that time. This girl *never* remembered her.

But then, who did? Nelly's own mother, Lauren, after urging her for years to wear some make-up and dress with a little more pizazz, once advised her, "You should join the CIA, dear. You'd make a mar- velous spy. You're totally invisible."

Nelly had long ago accepted that. But at the drug store

checkout, she was furious. And with her anger she felt again, that rush of awareness, that slowing of time.

She felt it Friday, too—in the office, when she came in after visiting four different clients that morning and the receptionist, Georgia Peel, merely glanced up and asked who she wanted to see. But this time, totally out of character, Nelly bent down and said right in Georgia's face, "I'm Nelly. Remember me, Georgie? I work here. For three years, now. I help the clients keep records. And what do *you* do?" Georgia stared, aghast, as Nelly turned smartly and marched off. Nelly was moving in slow motion again. She could hear every pencil scratching in the offices she passed.

Something big *must* be about to happen, but what? Would it have to do with the fact that nobody ever recognized or remembered her? And why, at the age of forty-nine, was that suddenly so irritating?

Of course, her mother always said it was her own fault. "You have wonderful bones. That's the bottom line for looks, dear. You could be a knockout. A little make-up. Some decent clothes. Why do you deliberately choose to look like the downstairs maid?" But then again, Nelly told herself, Lauren thought every woman should have her nose redone and her hips lipo-sucked and run around imitating Cher.

Two

Emmet never had to take their orders. The partners from Raymond, Schlesser ate breakfast together here in the Sky Club every Monday, week in and week out, and invariably wanted the same food. Jack McKinnon, the huge rolling tank of a man, always had Eggs Benedict. Ben Schlesser got Nova on a bagel. Mark Goldberg did grapefruit, oatmeal, and bran muffins. Will Raymond liked two eggs up and crisp bacon. McKinnon took real coffee. The rest took decaf. They were good tippers and Emmet always fussed over them. He overheard, as he couldn't help doing, much of their talk—usually concerning company matters that meant little to him.

But this morning they were talking about someone he had known and admired—almost worshipped—for almost fifteen years, although she certainly had no inkling that he did. Claire Clemency-Graves!

"I just think we should have waited," Schlesser said. "She's undoubtedly very smart, very ambitious. It's not easy for a woman like that who thinks she's set for life to find out after her husband conks out that he was just about out of money. And to start a career when you're almost sixty—it's tough. But I get the feeling that what she does best is take clients and prospectives out to lunch. Nelly does most of the real work."

"That may be the best arrangement," said Raymond, sopping up egg yolk with a chunk of toast. "She's good at that social crap. What else could we have done? Put Holachek in charge? She couldn't give orders to the janitor. And can you imagine her taking anyone to lunch?"

"It's just the two of them. Why did anyone have to be in charge?" asked Schlesser.

"Listen, that records guidance service has paid for itself," said Goldberg. "And their business of helping speakers find audiences and vice versa was getting so popular. C.G. could never find Nelly when she needed her—we had to do something."

"She *said* she couldn't find her," Schlesser retorted. "But Nelly did *all* the guidance business by herself for a long time before we ever hired C.G. And did it very well."

"It is true that in a way, Holachek is better qualified," said McKinnon. "She has had some training in accounting and C.G. hasn't. But C.G. is certainly more worldly and sophisticated."

"Well, I'll just remind you all of one more thing,"

Schlesser insisted. "It's little Nelly Holachek who does all this speaker business. She started it before we hired C.G., who may take credit for running it, but it's Holachek who actually does run it. And that's a little deception I don't cotton to."

"We put C.G. in charge six months ago," said Raymond impatiently. "And it seems to work. So why do we keep talking about it. Give Nelly a raise, if you think we should, and let's get off the damn subject."

Emmet heard every word as he took his time refilling their cups. Did C.G. know they were talking about her position? How could they belittle her like that? He must let her know somehow. It wasn't just that he had been waiting on her all these years, starting way back when her husband, Reggie Clemency-Graves, was alive. No, it was much more. All he felt for her. Here was his chance to do something—however small—to show his loyalty. But how? Telephone her? Would she be upset if he did? Would she be annoyed?

He couldn't bear the thought. No, he'd better wait until the next time she came in. Meanwhile, he'd keep his eyes and ears open. If he could come up with anything better, he'd do it. And that Holachek woman—why, the time he had offered to speak at that seminar, she had not used him. He hadn't forgotten that. If she ever came up here for lunch—very unlikely—she could sit there all afternoon before he would so much as pour her a glass of water.

* * *

Nelly stopped at the office before heading for her meeting with Mac Britton. C.G., who usually didn't show up until after ten, was already there, puffing up a cloud of smoke with her cigarillo. As usual, she was wearing her two ropes of real, very large pearls, and plentiful mascara. "Oh, Nelly, dear, I've got something I want you to do for me," she said. "My brother's flying in from Montreal today. Why can't he ever give me a little notice before he comes? Anyway, that Ivan Talpano thing this afternoon in Pompano? Take my brother with you. Keep him busy until five or six. I'll tell him I need his judgment, that I don't trust yours. Forgive me, dear, but you know, you're not very sophisticated. I have appointments this afternoon I simply cannot cancel, and to which I cannot drag him. Pick him up at the airport. Wait. Let me get him back on the phone."

She dialed, staring blankly at Nelly until her brother answered. "Hello, Barton? It's Claire. I got your message. No, don't get a cab. Nelly will meet your plane . . . I can't. I'm tied up, but I want you to do something for me—with her. Attend a lecture by Ivan Talpano, the man who writes those self-help books. You know the one I mean? Nelly's going to talk to him afterward to see if we can use him as a speaker. His fee may be too high, and who knows if he's any good. You know how some of these famous authors get . . . No, I can't go. I'm sending Nelly, but I really don't trust her judgment, Bart." She looked at Nelly and then, dramatically, at the ceiling. "So go along, and let me know what you think tonight over dinner.

"What do you mean, I always have some dirty job for you when you visit? What's dirty about this? That's what brothers are for. Besides, you know very well that anything you do down here is infinitely more interesting than anything you have to do up there in that lodge. Watching the birds moult. Watching the snow fall. How exciting . . . Delta? 2:30? Nelly will be there. She'll drop you at the office afterward and I'll be here by then.

"Chat with Talpano at the little social after the lecture. See what you think. How he acts mixing with people. Then we can talk about whatever else you like. Yes, even that. See you tonight."

She hung up and turned to Nelly. "And now you're heading for your meeting with Britton? Give him my regards."

Nelly nodded, picked up her purse, and left. As soon as the door closed behind her, C.G. grabbed the phone and dialed Will Raymond's four-digit extension number. He answered. "It's me. C.G.," she said.

"Could you work it out?"

"Yes, just barely. My brother picks the worst times to visit. But I managed. My place at one."

* * *

In the car on the way north, Nelly's irritation was directed at herself as much as at C.G. Why had she let C.G. make her handle this meeting? C.G. was dumping everything on her lately. All C.G. could think of was that Woman of Our Time dinner she was trying to arrange, hoping she herself would be thus honored. She was too busy calling every mover in town to get them committed to the project. She knew how terrified Nelly was of elevators in tall buildings. Even lunch at the Sky Club shattered her. Ten floors, or maybe a couple more, she could handle, but those appalling rides of fifteen floors or more wiped her out.

Why couldn't Britton, Llewellen, & McVey have picked a nice low-rise building somewhere? But no, they had to have the twenty-eighth floor of the Temple Tower, north of Boca Raton. "Darn C.G.!" she grumbled to herself as she stepped into the elevator. "Darn Britton, Llewellen, & McVey." She clutched the handrail. The car started up. As usual, the first few floors were bearable. But after that, floor by floor, the frantic fear swelled inside her. She felt her knees melt as she passed the twelfth. Her heart was thumping; she was gasping for breath.

And then, a strange release! As she passed the twentieth floor, that familiar wave of premonition swept over her, masking her terror. Her sense of awareness heightened sharply once more and time slowed almost to a standstill. By the time she hit the twenty-eighth floor, Nelly could have sketched the inside of the car in detail, even to the spots on the carpet. Was something going to happen right now? But as the doors opened, the premonitions evaporated, and the anxiety over the elevator ride flooded back.

She managed to tell the receptionist who she was. That lady summoned a clerk who led Nelly down a hall to a richly paneled conference room. "Mr. Britton will be in shortly. Make yourself at home. Have some breakfast, if you like."

Nelly collapsed into a chair to catch her breath. Breakfast? She looked around the room. On an antique oak sideboard against the wall behind her, a small but elegant buffet had been set out—silver warmers of bacon, eggs, and grits. Trays of breads, Danish, individual jars of jam, and molded pats of butter. A silver coffee pot. She shuddered at the thought of eating anything just now. She poured herself a cup of coffee with trembling hands, then sat down and waited.

But when Mac Britton strode in minutes later, she stood and managed a faint smile.

He took her hand and shook it, looking at an index card in his hand. "Nelly Holachek? You were the assistant with Mrs. Clemency-Graves last week. The one who didn't stay for lunch." The penetrating blue eyes studied her for a moment.

Nelly nodded. He obviously wasn't quite sure if she was the same person he'd met. Why the pang of disappointment? She was invisible Nelly. What did she expect?

"Well, at least today you can eat something, if you like," he said, indicating the buffet. "We always provide a bite when we call meetings this early. Please help yourself."

He took nothing, moving to sit on the other side of the table where a pile of folders and a notepad and pen were laid out. Nelly said, "No, thank you. I've already had breakfast. This coffee is enough," and sat opposite him.

"Let's get right on this, then. I've got a very tight schedule today, and I'm sure you do, too. To be blunt, one of the reasons we chose your firm was because we heard that you give a few extras. Perhaps you could, for instance, come up with some good speakers for our employee seminars and meetings. Experts on health advice. On heart-healthy eating, breast cancer, and so on."

Nelly nodded. "Yes, we can do that."

"If you could find opportunities for some of *our* experts to give free lectures, too, that would be great. Maybe at the schools, yacht clubs, condos—on various legal topics people want to know more about.

Getting cheap legal help. Using the small claims court. When to fight a speeding ticket and when not to, when to sue."

Nelly nodded again and pulled a pad and pen from her purse. "Yes, we can help you there. I'll need a list of your speakers, their topics, and when they're available. And let me talk to the person who plans your in-house events, meetings, seminars, and such."

"It seems a good way to let the community know we want to be part of it. We are, of course, willing to pay fees to any speakers who expect them. And our people would be free."

Nelly scribbled that information on her pad.

He opened one of the folders and began explaining the kinds of records kept by individual employees, and by the accounting and bookkeeping staffers. While he spoke she took a long, careful look at him. Thin but nice-looking. A strong, muscled neck. Grey hair with a mind of its own, but also that subtle expression she had noticed Wednesday. Pain? Sorrow? A weariness, as though he bore a kind of suffering that only he understood. He was tanned. He moved easily. He looked fit.

An unlikely thought popped into her mind: What must it be like to be married to a man like him? Smooth, smart, considerate. She remembered how he'd tried to keep C.G. from chasing her away at their luncheon. What did it take to attract a man like

23

Mac Britton? She gasped inwardly in shock. Where did such an insane thought come from?

"Now, as to our individuals' work-related expenditures," he was saying, "I suspect we'll be much like any other law office. I'll call in Hugh Hanneman to go over all that with you." He began reading off facts as though she were a tape recorder. Was that a hint of impatience she heard again in his voice?

She interrupted. "Excuse me, Mr. Britton, but I'll be able to get all this figured out in a couple of days. If you're short on time today, don't worry—I'll talk to the people actually taking care of the records. I have to do that anyway. I don't want to cause you any extra work here, when you're so busy settling in. And we'll be glad to help in any way to get you involved in the community's affairs in a very short time."

He stood up, looking relieved. "Thank you for your time," he said stiffly. "Mr. Hanneman will be in in a minute." He shook his head. "What a complicated and specialized place this world has become." And he strode from the room.

Nelly was seething. Not at Britton, at herself. He had looked right through her, too. *Everyone* looked right through her. She was a nothing. Her mother and the girls were right. "Wake up, Mom," the twins would say. "Wear some make-up, for heaven's sake. Get some real clothes instead of those dustrags. Do you want to be a nebbish all your life?" No wonder

24

they preferred their grandmother Lauren's exciting life to their mother's dull, humiliating existence.

Driving back to the office, she blinked back tears. Yes, she *was* invisible. A doormat. Forgettable. No personality. No guts. But what on earth could she do about it?

She wasn't sure, but she knew that all those premonitions crackling through the air this week meant something. She knew, as surely as the sun would set this evening, that by this day's end, she would be doing *something* no one would ever have expected Nelly Holachek to do.

Reb Stepit looked at the handsome but almost sullen-looking young man sitting in the chair before his desk. "What Doc Hardy said, Mr. Britton, is that he wants us to ease you back into really using those arms and legs again. It looks like all your grafting healed up pretty good."

"Except my face," said Rocky Britton.

"Your face is healed."

"Yeah, perfect. I look like Dorian Gray."

"Like who? You mean the scars? Listen, scars fade. You can get a little sandpapering on the stubborn ones. Your body can do a lot of that for you. But you gotta give it a chance. Anytime you get heavy burns like yours, your body is stretched flat out just trying to heal and handle the grafts. Some

25

people check out from burns like yours, mister. Or their heart gives up a few weeks later. You been lucky."

"Oh, yeah. Lucky. Especially with my lungs."

"Well, Hardy says they don't know yet just how steep that part is. You may have some damage. Maybe not. Doing nothing for a whole year up in New York didn't help. That's why you want to get into top shape now. Give your body the best odds of being able to heal itself. Everything boils down to numbers, Mr. Britton."

"How do you know so much about this burn business, Mr. Stepit?"

"Call me Reb. Everybody does."

"Reb," his reluctant new client repeated. "I guess then you better call me Rocky, but you didn't answer me. How do you—"

"Because I've been working with Dr. Hardy and his burn patients for a long time. And Dr. Nizer's. And a few other guys with patients with other problems. Hardy was a client here. I work with a couple of sports doctors. You get to know a lot about healing. And when Hardy's son got burned, we worked out a plan to get him back as close to what he had been as we could. We did good, but not as good as we do now. We've learned a lot. We had a couple of people burned in Kuwait. They got not only burns, but all that smoke they breathed in, too. But if you ever saw Kip Hardy after that fire and saw him today, you'd know his dad and I have been doing a lotta stuff right."

"Sounds like *my* father. He can't stop interfering, either. He can't trust me to figure out how to take care of myself."

"Would you have come here if it hadn't been for your dad?"

Rocky Britton shook his head. "Florida, yes. Because they said the climate and the lower pollution is easier on your lungs. But here to this gym and you? Probably not."

In Monte Carlo, at the Hermitage, Lauren Brooks Durango Devalutsky Lassiter James dialed her daughter's number while her "friend," Leonard Tisher, watched impatiently. "Come on. Let's go get something to eat. If she's not there now, you'll try later." Lauren sighed a tiny sigh. That was Leonard. It was going to ruin this romance. She had a distinct distaste for taking orders from anyone and Len seemed hopelessly addicted to giving them.

She wasn't worried about finding a new friend. Lauren James never had that problem. She didn't begin to look her seventy-two years. It wasn't just the occasional nipping and tucking. It was also the healthy, diet-and-exercise regimen she had followed for decades, long before it became the thing to do. And weight-lifting. And sex, she firmly believed.

27

She had always, from the time she left Nelly's father, had a good sex partner—someone she really cared about. It kept the juices flowing. Anything that felt that good, her instincts told her, had to be good for you.

Her upper arms were quite as firm as they had been twenty-five years ago. She still caught approving glances in a strapless gown. She could still attract a man like Leonard.

"Why didn't you wear that blue thing I like?" he scolded. "I told you to."

"That's why I didn't," she muttered to herself. She put her finger to her lips. "Hush, Len. I can't hear. Just another ring or two."

"Put it down. You'll try again later," he ordered. "Leave that wrap up here. It's not that cold downstairs. We'll eat now. You tell the waitress the way I like my chicken."

"Len," she said sweetly, "didn't your mother ever teach you to say please?" She hung up. "She's probably still at work. I never get these time changes straight. That witch she works for is a slave driver. Of course, with Nelly's slave mentality, they're a perfect match. You're right; I'll try later." After dinner, she decided. All afternoon, she'd had a strong feeling that something was going on with Nelly. That was the only thing she and her mousy daughter seemed to have in common—besides their slender frames and melodic voices. They were both a little psychic.

She picked up her wrap and said firmly, "I *will* carry this down, darling."

This duet, she knew, must dissolve soon. Too bad. Len was still good in bed, which many men his age were not. He was generous. But he simply couldn't be trained. She had tried for two months while they had made three trips—Alaska, Argentina, and here. But he was a dog she couldn't housebreak. He could not stop bossing her. He constantly told her what to eat and wear—though he had little taste concerning either—and ordered her about.

Oh, well. Might as well enjoy the next couple of days. They'd be back in London Friday. She'd dump him then. And she'd be lucky tonight. She felt in her bones that she'd win a lot. Although with Len feeding her chips the way he did, she never really lost. She smiled at him, took his arm, and let him lead her from the room.

Three

Nelly and Barton deLys slipped into their second-row seats. "This is nothing you couldn't handle yourself, Nelly," he said. "So why did my sister insist I tag along? It doesn't add up. Unless," he chortled, "she has some heavy date this afternoon she doesn't want me to know about. Hmmm. That's an interesting thought."

Nelly grinned. She'd always felt at ease with Barton, from the first time they met almost a year ago. He saw past her timidity. In a kindly, fatherly way, he often assured her that she was very capable. And urged her to stand up to his sister. "She's always been a bit of a user," he confided to Nelly once. "I think we spoiled her. She was so much younger than the rest of us."

Nelly knew he was right. But what could she do about it?

"Before we get into this today, dear," he said, "I want to tell you the real reason I came down. It's that damned Woman of Our Time business. I think C.G.'s making a monumental mistake."

Nelly nodded. "Oh, so do I, Barton. But you know she never listens to me. She's already called so many people. She has a list of about 180 who are interested. And she's got a lot of them involved in a nominating luncheon. But what if she gets herself nominated and then they all find out the whole thing was her idea? And what has she done to earn that award? What community projects has she ever chaired? What committees for what causes has she run? Has she given big money to any cause?"

"Mercy, no. She's blown up the few times she's done anything at all. She underwrote the postage for some tea about ten years ago. She's been a hostess at several affairs where they've had thirty hostesses. The only real money she gives is all the membership dues, because she belongs to everything, but so do hundreds of other women. That doesn't get you any points. I'll try to talk to her again tonight," Barton sighed, "after we're through here."

He looked around the hall at the crowd of at least 400. "What a great position to be in. He's actually just pushing his own books here. He'll likely autograph and sell a bunch. Talk for half an hour, first. For which you know he's getting a hefty fee, his air fare, and his hotel. I'm in the wrong business."

Nelly hardly heard him. She was still churning inside over the meeting with Britton and the fact that

31

he barely remembered her. And she was resentful that C.G. had dumped this extra chore on her, assuming she had nothing better to do, when she'd much rather just go home and have a good cry.

After the first minute or two, however, Talpano's staccato shouts began to register. "You *can* change," he was saying. "*You* can change yourself. No one else can. You can be *whoever* or *whatever* you want to be. *You!*" Each word hit her like cold water in her face. She suddenly felt awake. Alert. She could almost hear the tingling in the air. Talpano's magic words jabbed at her. "All you have to do is define it. State it clearly. Figure out *how* you want to change. Exactly. Then map out a route. How to get from A to B. From what you are now to what you want to be. Then do it!" Nelly grabbed each word, squeezed it mentally, inspected it, and made it hers.

"Don't wait for something to happen," he said. "It rarely does unless you *make* it happen. Don't wait for someone else to promote you. Promote yourself. Don't expect anyone else to help you. They're too busy with their own problems. Help yourself. You *can* do it. *Anyone* can do it, if they *really* want to."

"He's not saying anything that hasn't been said a million times before," shrugged Barton. "By Nor-

32

man Vincent Peale, Dale Carnegie, and a dozen others. He just says it in more energetic language."

After his speech, after the deafening applause, as Talpano came down from the stage and began signing copies of his books, Nelly sat there staring at him, transfixed. People quickly lined up for the privilege of saying a few words to him close up, and to get their books autographed. "Funny, there are so many people who tell you things like that," she said to nobody in particular. "Why didn't I ever listen before?"

After Talpano signed his last book, he spotted them and started toward them. They met him halfway and all three leaned against the edge of the stage to talk. He was not as tall as he'd appeared from the stage. And close up, not as young. His curly hair was black enough, but hadn't it been touched up? And the face—a network of fine small wrinkles but no deep ones. Had it been lifted? No matter. He'd probably followed his own advice and looking young was what he chose to do.

"Your lecture was wonderful," breathed Nelly, almost speechless with awe.

"Of course, most people don't really catch on," he said. "They expect miracles. They try one little change and the first time they fail, they just lie back and give up."

Nelly noticed that even though she was the one who complimented him, it was Barton he answered.

As though she weren't there. She asked him, "How many books have you written?"

"About nine," he said, looking at Barton.

"And do you think you might be interested in speaking at condos and forums here? If we could book a bunch of them within a couple of days, for instance? And how much would that cost?" Nelly asked.

Again, he directed his answer to Barton. "I want to open new markets for my work. So if the groups are large enough, and you cover expenses, I would be flexible on my fees. Crowds would have to be 250 and up. And I have to book three or four groups a day. Crowds of 1,200 would be better, of course," he added with a confident chuckle.

Nelly quickly scribbled in her notebook. She asked him for his address and phone number in New York. He gave his card to Barton, who handed it to Nelly. The two men chatted for a few moments before heading into the lobby for the high tea that would wrap up the event.

There, Talpano sat behind a table and signed at least forty more books, which were being sold by a woman at another table. It took a while because most of the buyers wanted to chat. Many, to tell him how he had changed lives, to gush about how they adored his writing. She and Barton stood nearby, listening. "I feel like I just ate a whole bowl of frosting," said

Barton. "Think of listening to all that syrup over and over that way."

They passed on the tea and sandwiches and desserts. When the crowds thinned, they and Talpano's people all walked out to the parking lot together. Barton and Talpano first, chatting, and Talpano's secretary, body guard, and book seller behind, talking together. Nelly, angry to be walking alone, was in between. When Talpano and his people climbed into a waiting limo, she caught up with Barton and walked with him to her car.

Something inside her was ready to explode. As she pulled out of the drive, she started babbling—indignantly and not too coherently—to Barton. "He's the same as everyone else," she said. "He looks right through me. I ask him something and he answers *you*. Like I wasn't there. Am I invisible?"

Barton dodged her question. "I think he's going to be far too expensive for your purpose. And getting those big audiences together—what do you need that for?"

"But he's *right,* Barton," she cried. "The things he says. *You* have to make it happen. *I've* got to make it happen in mine. I've *got* to change," she howled, pounding her fist on the steering wheel. "I've *got* to stop being a nothing. Nobody listens to me. Nobody remembers me. Half the time nobody even *sees* me."

"Now, now, Nelly. Calm down, my dear. You know you *are* rather low-key," Barton said tactfully.

"No more, Barton. I'm going to change. I am! I've got to."

Barton spoke slowly, "Yes, in a way you should. You should look out for yourself. You should stand up to my sister. But if you haven't yet, Nelly, I wonder if you ever will. And *if* you do, will you be able to cope with the new you?"

"I should pretty myself up." Her mind was sprinting. "Make-up, hair. I should become interesting, like my mother. Oh, I admit it; she was right. All this time, and I wouldn't listen. Wouldn't hardly even talk to her. Assert myself. Why do I let people push me around?" She couldn't stop the tears now. "Well, just watch me," she cried. "Because I can't bear being a *nothing* anymore, Barton. My mother and my daughters are always telling me to wake up and live. They're right. I've *got* to do it. I've got to change. And I can. I know where to go for help. I'm in touch with more experts on make-up and clothes and fitness—I've been booking them into the condos and clubs for two years. I can do it. And I will!"

Her abrupt outburst frightened Barton deLys. Was something really serious wrong? An aneurysm? A nervous breakdown? When Nelly pulled up to the office entrance, he said, "Why don't you come up with me, Nelly. Maybe we should call a doctor."

She laughed hysterically. "No, no, don't worry. I'll

be on the phone with my mother right after I get home. She's been trying to reach me all day."

"How do you know that?"

"I just do."

He got out of the car and came around to Nelly's side. She rolled down her window. "Wait a bit before you do anything drastic, dear. Please. Maybe you're just having a bad day."

"I *always* have bad days, Bart. Now, I'm going to have some good ones. I'm taking over my life. It's time I did."

Four

Nelly ran inside, slamming the door behind her so hard the front wall shook. God, that felt good! Why had she never slammed it before? Only Albert had slammed doors in that house.

The TVs were off. Because he was gone. Monday was a bowling night. She dumped her purse on the couch and stomped her feet. And stomped them again. She groaned. And groaned again, even more loudly. That felt good, too, but stomping was better. "And from now on I'll stomp whenever I *damn* please," she said aloud.

In her bedroom, she turned on the light and studied her image in the dresser mirror. Actually, she had more to work with than some people, she told herself. Good features. Small straight nose, large green eyes, long neck. Lashes and brows that were pale against her fair skin, but they were there. A little pencil and eyeliner . . . Wait—she'd get an eyeliner tattoo like that doctor talked about at the Yacht Club that time!

She would leave no stone unturned and change anything and everything that needed changing. Her voice—she would stop talking so quietly so no one could hear her and start speaking in a normal tone. Her vocabulary—she would talk the way she thought, instead of stripping all the humor and color from her words before she spoke them. Her walk. Her attitude. Talpano said make a plan, how to get from A to B. That's what she would do—plot a highly organized strategy. Draw a new Nelly with as much detail as an artist could sketch. She grabbed a pad and pencil from her night table and began writing furiously. A list. Her strategy.

Get rid of Albert. That was first. She'd do that tonight.

And the rest?

Nails—manicure. Make-up—lessons and buy whatever's needed. Dance lessons—sign up. Reading—Emily Post, magazines like *Vanity Fair* and *Vogue* and *Cosmopolitan*. Figure—get that tummy-tuck operation, finally, and sign up for some workout lessons. Glasses—get contacts. Eyes—plastic surgery for wrinkles, plus eyeliner tattoos. Hair—get it styled and streaked. Clothes—get new ones. The twins would probably help her pick them, if she asked them. And slinky underwear, too, because she was going to change from the inside out. Speech—

she would speak her mind, speak up, make the funny comments she thought of instead of stifling them. She would learn how to be charming and gracious. She would get a tape recorder and listen to her own voice.

And speaking of tapes—she would buy one of those that tell you how you can take charge of your life. She wondered if Talpano had made one. No matter. Others had. Hadn't she seen an ad on the back of one of those trashy magazines Albert was always bringing home? At work—she would assert herself. No longer would she let C.G. or anyone else push her around. She was going to be a vivid, interesting person. No one would ever look right through her again.

And the house? She'd change the locks.

When she wrote "Change the locks," Nelly put her pen down. Better do that right away, if she could. She quickly grabbed the phone book and leafed though the yellow pages to the locksmiths. The first two didn't answer. What did she expect? It was almost seven, but Lock Lord, the nearest of the three, did. "Yeah, I can do it right now," said the owner. "On my way home."

"Just be sure it's a lock that's too strong to be forced in any way," said Nelly. "The front door, the back, the garage, and the patio. And four extra sets of keys."

"Gotcha. Be there in five minutes."

Might as well call the doctors now, too. Dr. Fendwell had just gotten home and quickly agreed to perform a tummy-tuck two days hence. Now Laker. She leafed through her book for his unlisted home number which she kept because she often received requests for him as a speaker. He was one of the county's top reconstruction aces. His wife, Sarah answered. "He's out in the garden, Mrs. Holachek," she said. "Tell me what it's about."

Two minutes later, Laker himself called back and Nelly explained what she wanted done. "In two days, Nelly? That's tight. But let me see what I can do and I'll get right back to you."

He dialed his secretary, Holly Breckenridge, and told her to fit Nelly in somehow. "Dr. Fendwell's doing her tummy at Miami Heart Institute the same day. We want her to come from him to us, if possible, and recuperate in our facility. Or I'll do hers at the Institute and then we'll bring her back. Call Fendwell now at home and see what you can work out. She'll be easy to work with. Good bones. Good skin. She's such a timid little thing, though, I wonder how she got up the courage to ask.

"Oh, and listen, she says she doesn't have much money. She needs a special rate. And deferred payment. She's given us a lot of patients through my lectures, Holly, so tell her we'll work with her on that. We may just eat the whole thing. Call Fendwell now, and then call her back and confirm it all."

* * *

The phone rang. Before answering, Nelly said "Hel-lo-oh?" slowly, melodically, the way her mother did. "It sounds cultivated but very feminine, too, dear. Please just try it," her mother would coax. "Say hello softly, with three syllables. 'Hel-lo-oh?' Pitch your voice a bit lower than usual, then slide up the scale on the last two syllables. 'Hel-lo-oh?' " And Nelly would sniff—as if her mother had just asked her to do something terribly dishonest—and refuse.

The phone rang again. She picked it up. "Hel-oh-oh?"

"Oh, dear, do I have a wrong number?" asked her mother's voice. "Is this 564-5—"

"Yes, it's the right number," Nelly said. "It's me, Lauren. Nelly."

"You didn't sound like you," said Lauren James.

"Good. I hope not. Did I sound more like you? I'm not the same me anymore."

"You're what? Not the same? What do you mean, Nelly? Are you ill?"

"No. I'm fine. Better than ever. But sit down, Lauren. I have something momentous to tell you."

"I'm already sitting. I *knew* something was happening. I've been getting these vibes. What on earth is it?"

"I'm changing. As of tonight. I'm not going to be invisible Nelly anymore. I've been invisible too long."

There was a pause at the other end of the line. "You're changing?"

"I'm going to divorce Albert. I'm kicking him out. Tonight. I was just going to call the lawyer. And I'm working on a whole plan, a strategy. I'm getting my hair styled, make-up lessons, eyeliner tattoos. I've been putting down everything I can think of to make myself into a different person. When and where and with whom. I'm going to be as glamorous and attractive and assertive as I can get. They'll notice me now! I'm getting my eyes done, my tummy fixed, dance lessons. And whatever else I think of. Any suggestions?"

"My God, I don't believe it!" exclaimed Lauren. "My little Anyella is finally crawling out of her shell? I *knew* something big was going to happen today!"

"I'm going to buy some very becoming clothes and launch a new me, just like you've always been pushing me to do."

"My child, I am absolutely stunned. And so happy. I have seen your potential going down the drain all these years. You have no idea what a knockout you can be if you really want to. You were such a darling child. I can't wait to see you. Are you going to get a new job and tell off that pretentious witch?"

"Sort of. I think I'm going to start my own company, placing speakers and experts. A kind of speakers' bureau. That'll show her. I do all the work; C.G.

43

takes all the credit. And they put *her* in charge of us six months ago? Let's see how she manages without me."

"I can't believe what I'm hearing, Nelly. I could cry for joy. What can I do to help? Need some money?"

"No. I don't like taking money from you all the time. Without Albert here spending so much on bowling and boozing, I should be able to get along on very little."

"What a coincidence. I'm just about to dump Len."

"But you're always dumping someone. I've never done it before. I guess there's a first dump for everyone. And listen, Lauren, I don't want you to think that just because I'm changing radically, I'm going to adopt anything *like* your lifestyle."

"I know, darling. You don't have to be like me. Just be yourself. All that you can be. After you come out of your cloister and live a little, my life might make a little more sense to you."

"We'll see."

"Well, I'm flying over as soon as I can. We're in Monte Carlo. I'll be back in London in a few days and I'll get tickets on the first flight I can to New York. I'll just stop at my apartment long enough to repack and then I'll be down. I might have to wait a few days to get the cheaper flights."

Nelly sighed. Her mother's pet economy was buying the least expensive air tickets, when she flew alone. Her finances were usually at sixes and sevens. She owned the house that Nelly and Albert had lived in for ten years, besides her Miami condo and her flat in London. And she had use of the apartment in Zurich for her lifetime. She received income from two trusts and an annuity, and from two or three properties acquired in divorce settlements.

But she didn't keep track of her finances very well. Often, she wasn't quite sure where her next Valentino was coming from. She was very generous to the twins, Emma and Jane, and tried to be generous to Nelly, who would accept only the use of the house, a small allowance, and a bit of help now and then when Albert was out of work, which was more and more often in recent years. But Nelly felt that if she disapproved of her mother's lifestyle, it somehow wasn't right to accept her money.

"Don't rush," Nelly said. "I'll have Minny help me if I need anything. I'll be very busy the next week or two."

"You know what I just thought of, darling? You should change your name, too. Say you're taking back your maiden name and instead take Devalutsky. You can say your mother's a countess."

"But you're not anymore."

"So what? I never use the title, but so many people who get divorced *do* keep using theirs. They like being called countess or whatever. It wasn't a very

45

grand title. In Poland anyone who owned more than a few acres had a title. But how many people know which titles are big time and which aren't?"

"But the name Devalutsky doesn't sound melodic enough," said Nelly. "If I'm going to change, I might as well pick a name with the right meter. A little Anglo, a little European. Wait a minute. How about if I Anglo Devalutsky up a little. Nelly Devin Lure."

"Why not Anyella? It's your real name, remember? And it's really so much prettier than Nelly."

"Anyella Devin Lure. Oh, Lauren, I think that's it! Anyella Devin Lure. 'Quoth the raven, nevermore.' Mary Tyler Moore. Yes, it has a musical sound and the right meter. Why didn't I ever like the name Anyella before, Mother? It's poetry."

On the other end of the line, Lauren gasped with delight. Nelly had just called her *Mother* for the first time in years. She was stunned with joy and a lightness she had not felt when talking to Nelly for more than thirty years. "At forty-nine, you're finally growing up, Anyella. Better late than never, darling. You're going to have such fun. You'll only be sorry you didn't wake up eons ago. You're going to need some cash, and I made a bundle here in Monte Carlo this week. I'm sending you half. But actually, darling, you shouldn't have to pay for any of this. You give those surgeons and experts enough business. Every time they talk at one of those condos, they pick up clients. They'll do freebies, I'm sure. Just ask. Meanwhile, as soon as I get my flights, I'll call you."

"You know, Lauren—I mean, Mother," said Nelly awkwardly, "we haven't very often seen eye to eye on much of anything. But this is one time, I—I really want to see you. So much. Let me know when."

The doorbell rang. It was the Lock Lord. Nelly showed him the doors and asked how much it would cost, then wrote the check. While he worked, she dialed the big-time divorce lawyer, Merve Morganthau, whose assistants and partners she had booked to speak at so many different organizations. In fact, one of those early bookings resulted in his taking the infamous Claymor divorce case and hitting the front pages with a seven million dollar settlement. She had planned to leave a message, but Morganthau often worked very late. He was still in his office.

"I want to divorce my husband, Mr. Morganthau. I won't change my mind," she told him. "But I want to change my name, too, to a form of my mother's name when she was a countess. Anyella Devin Lure. My first name is already Anyella. I just never used it before. Devin Lure is anglicized a bit. From Devalutsky, so people can spell it."

She gave Morganthau a quick, painful synopsis of her life with Albert. His chronic drunken state.

Mental abuse and threats. The fact that he didn't support her and hadn't for years.

"Irreconcilable differences," said Morganthau. "Enough for three divorces."

Then she dialed Minny, next door. "Minny, guess what? I'm liberated. I'm kicking Albert out, getting a divorce and making up a new me."

"Huh? You're doing what, Nelly? You feel all right?"

"I just called a lawyer. The big one—Merve Morganthau. I'm getting a divorce. I'm crawling out of a hole, Minny, and I'll never crawl back in."

"A hole, Nelly? You got a temperature or something?"

"No. I feel wonderful. Talk to you tomorrow."

Nelly headed for the storage closet and pulled out several large suitcases and cardboard boxes. Five minutes later, she heard a knock at the door and ran to open it. It was Minny, of course, in a robe, her curly mop flying every which way, her big brown eyes wide with worry. "I got Windy over," she said. "We were just, you know, getting busy when you called. You sound crazy. You OK?" She saw the boxes and suitcases, the fishing gear and bowling trophies. "Where you going?" she cried, alarmed.

"Not me. Albert. I'm kicking him out. Tonight. Here's a new set of keys. I had them changed so he can't get in here."

"Kicking him out, Nelly? What if he won't go? Jeeze, I've never seen you this way."

"Because I've never been this way before. It's time. Who on earth is Windy?"

"My new one. I met him at a singles night last week."

"I thought you were seeing someone named Buddy."

"No, that was two weeks ago. And Charlie all last week. Nothing is forever, is it?"

"Gosh, Minny, with all this AIDS and stuff going around, how can you jump in and out of bed like that?"

"I don't jump in and out. That's no fun. We stay a long time. I hate to say no in case it turns out to be the one I should have said yes to."

"But it's so dangerous, Minny."

"Not really. We do safe stuff sometimes. And some can't do it at all. How safe can you get?"

"Well, go back to what's-his-name. I'll talk to you tomorrow. All I'm doing tonight is kicking Albert out. So I've got a lot of stuff to pack here, and I'm getting sleepy." Minny looked alarmed, but she clutched her new keys and let Nelly lead her to the door. Windy was waiting.

It was after eleven when Nelly heard Albert's van pull into the drive. And a moment later, a loud thump when he stumbled into one of the boxes stacked on the porch. "What the hell is *this?*" he roared. She picked up the butcher knife she had put on the coffee table, and holding it in front of her, hurried to the door and threw it open. "Just stop right there, Albert," she cried in what she hoped was an intimidating snarl, flashing the knife in front of her. "You're *not* coming in."

He eyed the suitcases and boxes stupidly, and the knife in her hand. "What the hell are you talking about?"

"You're not coming in here," she said quickly. "There's all your stuff. I made a reservation for you for two nights at the Motel 6 on Route 84. I'm divorcing you. Mervin Morganthau is handling it."

Albert stopped at the door. "Oh, yeah? *Oh, yeah?* We'll see about that," he snorted, taking a tentative step toward her.

"Not another step," Nelly hissed, desperately jabbing the knife within an inch of his belly. "Morganthau will make legal mincemeat of you if you give me any tiny bit of trouble. You just load up your things and get out of here, or I'll—I'll cut open that beer barrel stomach so fast you won't know what h-h-happened. *Move!*"

Albert's mouth dropped open. He stepped back, drunk enough not to notice the trembling in her voice, but not so drunk he couldn't see that razor-sharp blade glinting in her hand. She could almost read his thoughts. He knew he was a little slow and foggy from his beer. His legs were not too steady. He could probably grab that knife in one swipe. But then again—what if he missed? What if she sliced through his hand, or thrust it deep into his gut? "OK," he said, hitching up his pants. "But I'll get a lawyer tomorrow, too, and we'll see who's divorcing who, you dumb bitch." Then he turned to pick up one of the boxes, and staggered back to his van with it.

Nelly closed the door, fastened it securely with the new lock. She stood there, knife in hand, shivering with fear, listening intently, as the stumbling Albert, grunting and grumbling angrily, dragged the suitcases and boxes from the porch and loaded them into his van. She heard him slam the doors, start the motor with a roar, and back out of the drive, spitting gravel and bumping the melaleuka tree again.

She slipped the knife back into the kitchen drawer, staggered back to pick up her pad, and carried it into the bedroom. Crawling onto her bed without removing the spread, she lay there and studied her long list. The toughest item, she decided, was the one that said, "Assert yourself with C.G."

But there was so much else to do. She should probably call the radio stations. Maybe some of the shows she had gotten guests for, and those whose stars she had arranged speaking dates for—or judging or emceeing dates at fundraisers—maybe some of them would now have *her* on their programs to discuss her new agency. She'd have to call Morganthau to incorporate it, too, and then line up more bookers and bookees.

Men? Sex? The most overrated activity in the world if her revolting experiences with Albert meant anything. But did they? It always sounded so different, so wonderful, in books and the movies. Despite her disgusting ordeals with Albert, was there still a kind of yearning deep inside her sometimes for something sweeter?

Marriage? Oh, no. Sex would have to be infinitely, gloriously better before she'd get trapped in any such straitjacket again.

She was exhausted. So fatigued she could hardly lift the pen to write in her notebook. But exhilarated, too. Light as air. She'd already taken care of four major items on that list. She *could* change! She *was* changing! This was what she felt coming on today. And last week. She kicked off her shoes, dropped her belt on the floor, and left it there. And without even taking off her clothes, she crawled under the covers. And slept like a baby.

Five

The phone rang. He grabbed it. "Yeah, Reb Stepit here."

"Reb, this is Nelly Holachek. Well, no, now it's Anyella Devin Lure. I'm changing back to my—my maiden name."

"Yeah, Nelly. Say what? You're changing your name?"

"Changing it back. You can still call me Nelly if you want to. Or Anyella. I'm finally going to use the name my mother gave me."

"Sheesh! At this hour of the morning? It's only seven o'clock, Nelly—uh—Anyella. What's the rest?"

"Devin Lure. Anyella Devin Lure."

"Yipes! A mouthful. Why you callin' so early. Who ya got?"

"No speaking date. Just me, Reb. I'm remaking myself—into the most glamorous femme fatale possible. Getting my hair highlighted and styled. My eyes done. New clothes. I want my body to look great. I can't afford you, but I need your advice."

53

"Heyyyy. Great news! And don't worry about affording, Nelly. Every time I talk somewhere I got thirty people calling for an appointment. Besides, you're already in shape, almost. You don't have thirty pounds to unpack first. All you got to do is learn to stand up straight and tighten up a little. And fix that little tummy."

"That's from an emergency caesarean twenty-seven years ago. I'm getting it taken care of surgically. Tomorrow. I should be ready to start with you in a week or ten days, don't you think?"

"Before that. Some gentle stuff before you even check out of the hospital. You know which one?"

"Miami Heart, or Dr. Laker's facility, I guess. I'll know for sure later this morning."

"Call me back and leave all the dope with Lizzie—the hospital, the doc. When you're scheduled, I'll talk to your doc and we'll work it all out. Consider it a done deal."

"Oh, thanks so much, Reb."

"But Nelly, what goosed you? I mean, all this time you've let a good bod go to waste."

"It's a long story, Reb. I should have done it a long time ago. I'll call back as soon as I get all the poop."

Reb scratched his head. Poop? She usually used words that made you yawn—like 'data' or 'relevant information.' Poop? She really *was* changing. This oughta be interesting to watch.

* * *

When Dora Lupe got Nelly's call at 9 a.m. she expected it would be about giving a talk and demonstration on the latest hairdressing techniques and styles, as usual. But not this time. "You mean you're finally going to let me do something with that ridiculous grandmother's bun of yours?" Dora chortled. "Oh, come in quick before you change your mind. Today. I have a cancellation at noon. The time is yours. We'll do a smart cut, streak it, tone up the highlights. You won't know yourself. We'll do a pedicure. A manicure. Tweeze your eyebrows. I've been dying to do this for years! . . . What? You've changed your name? You're not Nelly Holachek anymore? What then? . . . Anyella? What kind of a name is that? . . . Devin Lure? OK, but can I still call you Nelly for short?"

After she hung up, Dora waddled up to the front desk to put Nelly's name in her appointment book for the very first time. But even as she did, she shook her head. Hair color and a new style was one thing, but a woman needed a certain way about her, too. Energy. Confidence. Sexiness. *Something!* And poor, sweet, gentle Nelly Holachek, as far as she'd ever noticed, didn't have a trace.

Gwen Parker hung up and blinked. Nelly Holachek wanted to learn how to make up her face? It would be like teaching make-up to a nun. Not today's nuns, to be sure, but the ones she'd had in grade school back in Iowa. Gwen couldn't refuse. Hardly a month went by that she didn't get at least one call from Nelly asking her to talk about make-up at some club or meeting. She always picked up new clients. Sometimes six or eight. For a major ball, she and her girls might have twenty-five or more socialites to make up at $150 and up a crack. She scribbled Nelly's name in her appointment book. A few freebie lessons was the least she could do.

She tried to conjure up Nelly's face, to study it and think of some tricks she might try. But somehow she could only summon the blurriest image. That was unusual. It was rather automatic for Gwen to analyze the faces of people she met. Of course, most of the time, Gwen and Nelly dealt with each other by phone. She recalled that it was a pleasant face, but not exactly memorable. In a way, Nelly Holachek seemed almost invisible.

The office was next. Nelly dialed the phonemail number and her own extension and took her messages. One from Baron Viscante, from the Chamber of Commerce, trying to arrange a lunch with her. One from Adella Schranz of the Arts and Culture Guild wanting to know more about the Woman of

56

Our Time luncheon. One from Effie Homer at the Board of Education office. Wasn't she a friend of C.G.'s? She started to call Viscante back, then shook her head. No, there was one call she had to make first. No point in putting it off.

The phone was ringing when C.G. arrived at the office. "It's for you," said Georgia Peel. "It's Holachek. She's been calling every five minutes since 9:30."

"Why isn't she here? She's late," sniffed C.G.

"She wouldn't tell me. She only wants to talk to you. Says it's very important."

C.G. sighed dramatically and took the proffered receiver. "Yes, what is it, Nelly? Why aren't you here?" Her bored, put-upon expression quickly changed to one of shock and then anger. "Equal status with me? That's something decided by the partners here, Nelly . . . What? Because I've made them think I'm running things, when in reality you do all the work? Don't be absurd, Nelly," she sputtered. "If this is a joke, it's not funny. So please just get in here. You've got three new clients to see today . . . You what? My last chance? . . . You quit? You *are* out of your mind! . . . Run it by myself? Well, I certainly shall, my dear. Good-bye!" And she slammed the receiver into its cradle.

"Is something the matter?" asked Georgia nervously. When something was the matter, C.G. could be very temperamental.

"No, nothing. Absolutely nothing. I need a list of all of Nelly's appointments and so on for today. Tomorrow, too, come to think of it."

"Well, I don't know what they are," said Georgia. "She doesn't run her appointments by me. Don't *you* have a list?"

"Uh—I must have them somewhere," said C.G. Should she call Will Raymond and tell him what had happened? No. Nelly might think better of it and apologize. She'd better leave that door open. But would she have time to see Will tomorrow? She'd worry about that in the morning. Meanwhile, she'd show Nelly if she could handle this work without her or not. She was stunned. In a million years, who would ever guess that timid little Nelly had a side like this?

Daniella Raymond dialed her husband's number while she pedaled on her exercycle. Amazing how many things you could take care of while you were working out. She usually made calls, read the papers, or watched TV while on the bicycle. She watched TV while running on the treadmill or doing aerobics. She listened to her phone messages while she did stretching routines. Let those jealous types call her anorexic. Ha! They'd give their eyeteeth to be this thin. She was built like the designer Carolyne Roehm. Danny had seen her once at a fashion show and had spotted her at least three inches in height, but she'd match their willowy figures any day.

Will's secretary answered. "Judy, get my husband on the line. It's very important. I must talk to him."

A moment later Will Raymond's voice said, "What's so damned important, Dan? I'm late for a deposition."

"I just had the best idea, Will. You're always wanting me to head committees and run charity things because it's good publicity, right?"

"Yeah, yeah, but you know you like it, too," he countered.

"Let me finish, dear. That woman there who gets people speaking dates and interviews on radio and TV? Why don't you have her do that for me? Get me on radio programs and TV to talk about how the community needs volunteers. About what they do. About what a job it is to put on a major event. People would love to know about those balls and things—especially if they never go to any of them. And the announcers would always introduce me as your wife."

"Hmph," said Raymond, pondering her idea. Damned if she didn't come up with a good one sometimes. "Listen, Dan, I have no time now. But we'll talk. Sounds like an idea with possibilities."

"Then why don't you tell that lady today? Or

should I? I'll say it was your idea and you asked me to call."

"Oh, well—uh—" he stalled. He didn't much like the idea of Danny and C.G. getting chummy. Playing with fire. C.G. might let something slip. On the other hand, it's not like Danny didn't know he took a couple of extra classes sometimes. And the whole C.G. thing was fizzling anyway. She was a dud in bed. Talked big. Knew nothing. Last time, when he couldn't even get it up for her, she didn't have a clue of how to help. One of those who expected the guy to do everything. "Well, I don't know, Danny—"

"I do. Go to your deposition. What's her name again?"

"Claire Clemency-Graves, but everyone calls her C.G."

"When you're through, you call her, too, and back it up. I'll do a job and a half. And it will do you a lot of good."

After her husband hung up, Danny glanced over at her image in the floor-to-ceiling mirror. With her ultra-slim body, and the work she'd just had done to her jawline that made it smooth as a baby's bum, she'd look marvelous on TV. A door was opening to a whole new exciting world. As a regular on local TV she would probably meet all sorts of interesting people. Perhaps a thrilling new lover? Not to mention how it would enhance her position in the community as Will Raymond's wife and an activist. Let

Will move around if he must. Two could play at that game. She would call that Mrs. Clemency-Graves this morning.

Mac Britton pulled up in front of the gym. The door opened and his son, Rocky, came out, spotted the car, and hurried over to yank open the door and get into the front seat. "So how'd it go, son?" Mac asked, pulling out of the drive.

"Who knows? If that stupid jerk can do anything for me, I'll believe in miracles. He says he can."

"That's the word I got. He's incredible."

"Yeah, OK, so I'm trying it. But I'm never going to look like I did. And broads don't turn on to burn scars. Or a hacking cough."

"You don't have a hacking cough. And I don't notice you having any trouble connecting with women down here."

"The cough is probably just a matter of time," Rocky grumbled.

Britton started to answer, but didn't. This son of his had been such a disappointment. A playboy mentality. No commitment or deep interest in anything but women and goofing off. Just a constant chase after excitement and adventure. Racing cars. Motorcycles. Taking off for Kuwait with that fire-fighting crew, lying about his training and experience. Falling from a rig he really didn't know how to operate, and being burned so badly. His arms. His legs down to his ankles where his boots protected them and his feet. Trying to kill himself in the burn center in the military hospital in Haifa. What had happened to the eager little kid he'd taught to swim, taught to catch a fly ball, trekked all the museums with? Rocky had been more of a grown-up then, at only eight or ten, than he was now.

Yes, it was a terrible thing that had happened to him. But it was his own fault, and you had to keep going. Make the best of it. You can't curse fate forever. Would Rocky ever grow up?

But Britton said nothing. He dropped Rocky at his own apartment and headed back to the office. He had found that becoming absorbed in his work— tracking nuances and implications threading through involved and lengthy depositions—was the one way he could escape his sorrow and frustration over his only son. The young man simply couldn't quite grasp what it meant to be an adult.

Six

C.G. studied the bone-thin, ultra chic woman before her. This was all she needed: another impossible chore. Damn Nelly. Now *this* one wanted to guest on radio and TV, and C.G. hadn't the vaguest idea of how to get her there. That was Nelly's job.

She pulled a cigarillo from the box. "Oh, please," said Daniella Raymond delicately, shaking her head. C.G. dropped it as though it were poison ivy. "Well, I promise I'll look into it, Mrs. Raymond," she replied unctiously. "First, we'll have to see which broadcasters are interested."

"No, don't look into it. Just do it," Daniella replied, smiling sweetly. "Of course they'll be interested if you approach them the right way. You do have a little clout, you know, having been useful to them in the past. And you'll be useful to them in the future. Remind them gently of that fact." She smiled, again flashing the teeth that reputedly had cost Raymond fifty thousand dollars.

"Yes, of course."

"I've got a list here of possible topics. I'm sure I'll think of more. Just three or four spots and let's see how it goes."

"Well, actually, Nelly Holachek, who takes care of some of the detail work on this kind of thing for me, is off for a day or two. So it will be a few days before we—"

"But what difference should that make? You're in charge of the bookings, aren't you? That's what my husband said."

"Yes. Of course."

"Call and let me know what you get." She stood up, almost six feet tall in her heels and smiled. "Talk to you soon."

The minute she left the office, C.G. grabbed the cigarillo, lit it, and sucked on it eagerly. She fingered her pearls, those two ropes of huge freshwater beauties that Reggie had given her for their fifth anniversary. Her favorite jewels. Her worry beads.

Good Lord, what did she do now? And yesterday had been a disaster, too. The cryptic scribbles on Nelly's desk calendar told her nothing. She took on three appointments she could remember talking about, then had to cancel a luncheon with a new client and a mid-afternoon session with Will Raymond. She hadn't had any time at all to make Woman of Our Time calls.

Fourteen messages still waited to be answered this afternoon, all about people and bookings that Nelly had been handling. And when she had given in and called Nelly's home number—three times this morning—there'd been no answer. Then Schlesser came by and heard her explain to one client that she didn't know about a certain booking and that Nelly was out of the office for a few days.

"Nelly's not here?" he asked. "I didn't know that. Why not?"

"She took a couple of days off on short notice," said C.G. "I told her I'd cover for her."

"I hope everything is all right."

"Oh, I'm sure it is," she said blithely. When he left, she lit another cigarillo. She would give Nelly until tomorrow. If she didn't show up by then—surely she would—C.G. knew she'd better be prepared. She'd need a good story. Something that made her look like a heroine and Nelly, a villainess. Which, of course, she was.

If this rebellion wasn't squashed immediately, it would ruin the Woman of Our Time award and mess up her whole position here. She inhaled deeply, shaking her head and fingering her pearls as if trying to coax an answer from them. Where was Nelly right now?

The humming was familiar. But faint and faltering, as though the hummer might be drunk. What was that song? Ah, yes. She knew it. "Somewhere, over the rainbow, way up high . . ." Was it the nurse? This was Laker's clinic, wasn't it? Her lips stung. She struggled to open her heavy lids and ask if they could get started.

But she couldn't because—oh! Because it was *she* who was humming. She stopped and somehow pushed her heavy, heavy eyelids up just a crack. Was that Dr. Laker standing there? "How much longer before we begin?" she mumbled through lips heavy and frozen, as though from the dentist's novocaine.

"Actually, Nelly, we're almost through," he said. "Why did you stop humming? We've never had a patient hum during surgery before. But then, they don't often wake up this soon, either. Just relax, Nelly. You'll slip back to sleep now."

The light was so bright it hurt her eyes. She could make out the blurry nurse doing something to that bag. Was it over? "I was curious—about—all this—" Nelly's thick, sore lips could hardly form the words. "But—I think—I missed—most of it."

"We didn't do a peel," Dr. Laker said. His voice was fading, echoing from further and further away. "You really don't need one. Just a patch here and there, around your mouth. Use Retin-A and you'll look just fine . . ."

His voice petered out and she began floating, floating away into a cosy womb of silence . . .

"Nelly, you're spilling that potato down your front. Let me help you." She peered hard at the blurry form before her. Ah, Minny. Her eyes worked their way slowly downward to make out a tray in front of her, a half-eaten baked potato on the plate and potato bits spilled in her lap. In her hand, a large spoon full of potato. "Where's my fork?" she croaked.

"I took it away. You already jabbed yourself in the face with it twice. You've got a mark on your forehead. You can't find your own mouth, Nelly. Please, let me feed you."

"I can feed myself," she insisted, swinging the spoon up to her face, hitting her nose and spilling the potato.

"There, you've done it again. You haven't gotten one damn bite in your mouth yet, Nell. And you spilled your Farina all over you at breakfast, too. I missed my bowling league this morning and now I've got to get back to work. So just let me feed you and get it over with." Nelly closed her eyes. She felt the spoon at her mouth, opened up, took in the potato, chewed a bit and swallowed. Again. Again. And then she slipped back into that warm cocoon.

When Nelly woke, it was Minny's face she saw again. "Hi," she said. "Don't you ever go home? What day is it, Min?"

"Thursday. Oh, thank God you sound like you again. You've been a spook. You OK?"

"Of course I am. What did you think?"

"Well, for two days you've been in and out of it. You couldn't even put a spoon in your own mouth the first day. You kept hitting yourself and spilling everything. And you wouldn't let me help."

"The Valium, I think. I'm still buzzing. But they give you that stuff and locals instead of heavy anesthetic. Uhh! I'm still bombed. But it'll go away. How do I look?"

"Well, after the stitches are gone I'm sure you'll look great. But now? Kinda messy."

"I'm going to the bathroom."

"Here, let me help." Minny grabbed Nelly's arm and helped her to her feet. The room dipped.

"I'm still a little woozy. But I want to go home."

"Nelly—"

"Call the nurse, will you, Minny? Let's get out of here."

"I already talked to them. You can go today if you behave. But you have to come back in two days to get the stitches out."

At the bathroom door, Nelly paused, then stepped

in and faced herself in the mirror with a critical eye.

Yes, the wounds were still raw, the swelling distorted her features, and the patches of peel scabs were brownish. But the tattooed eyeliner looked great. Her eyes, even with the stitches, looked big and green and bright. She grinned at her image. "Minny, I did the right thing," she called through the door. "I look messy now. But my gosh, I think I'm going to look terrific!"

Seven

In the car on the way home, Minny tried to reason with her. "Listen, Nell, I think it's neat you got your eyes done, if you really wanted to. I've been thinking of it myself. I hate the way the mascara crawls up my wrinkles lately. The tummy? Sure. And I think it's about time you kicked Albert out. Maybe now you'll meet some guy who won't holler at you all the time. But quitting your job? You're not going to do anything else that's crazy, are you? I mean, jeeze, you're not thinking of bungee-jumping or getting a tattoo on your butt or anything nutsy like that, are you, Nelly?"

Nelly started to laugh, but it hurt. "No. And finding a romance isn't why I started all this, Minny. I'm revolutionizing my life. And myself. Romance is way overrated, anyway. Who needs it?"

Minny sighed. "Maybe I should change, too. I know. I'll go on a diet, lose ten pounds, and find myself a new man."

"That's not a revolution; that's a rut," Nelly said

with a grin. "You've been dieting ever since I met you. Always trying to lose ten pounds."

"And I've gained ten instead."

"And you're *always* finding a new man. I don't know why it's so easy for you when everyone else is complaining about the shortage of men over fifty. You need a revolving door on your bedroom."

Minny started to laugh, but then stared at Nelly and blinked. "You never used to make jokes before, Nell. You *have* changed. Anyway, those men never stay. Not more than a few nights."

"You may have to think up some new tactics, Min. Play harder to get. And I know you don't like to hear this, but with the AIDS problem, that's what you *must* do."

"Forget my sex life. What other changes are you thinking of?"

"I have a whole program. Pages long. A detailed day-by-day strategy, blocked out chore by chore. Wait until you see it. I've been working my way down my first list. I've already called the lawyer to incorporate the new company. I'm calling it '1000 Words.' As in 'A picture says a thousand words.' That way it implies that we have people who not only talk but who do things. Entertainers and such."

"It implies all that?" asked Minny incredulously.

"And I want you to do me a favor."

"Sure. Like what?"

"Call all the local newspapers and ask for the

community news editor and tell whoever answers that you heard that a local resident, Countess Anyella Devin Lure, is opening a speakers agency called 1000 Words, and you'd like to know more about it. If anyone calls back, take their number and say the person who asked isn't home but she'll call back. Do it from your phone, OK?" Minny looked confused, but agreed to make the calls.

When they arrived home, Nelly found seven phone messages from Albert on her machine. He had left a number. She dialed it immediately and a sober Albert answered, "Andrews Bowling Alley."

"What are you doing there?" she asked. "It's only six o'clock."

"I got a job. Day manager while the regular guy is on vacation. But it's only for two weeks."

"Then you'd better find another one, Albert. And from now on, you're not supposed to call me. You contact me through Morganthau."

"Now, listen, Nelly," he shouted into the phone. "This has gone far enough. You stop this crap right now or you're in big trouble!"

Nelly hung up.

"Albert's working at the bowling alley," she told Minny.

"Poor Albert," Minny sighed. "I know he's been a jerk, but this is hard for him, I'm sure, Nelly."

"He'll adjust. Oh, and listen, Min, do me another favor. Call my office right now and ask for me. Just leave a number—yours, not mine. I want to know if she's telling people I'm gone or not, because I need my notebooks of bookers and bookees and stuff for the agency. If she hasn't told them I'm gone, I might be able to just walk in there and pick it all up tonight."

"Tonight? With your eyes full of stitches? And those scabs?"

"I'll put on lots of make-up and wear dark glasses."

"You'll look like a spy," Minny argued. "They'll arrest you. What's your hurry? They're taking the stitches out Saturday."

"But at any moment, C.G. could suddenly realize that all the information she needs is right there, in and on my desk. I mean I *hope* it's still in and on my desk. She could have taken it already. But if you drive me there tonight and just wait for me while I go up and get my things—"

"I don't know, Nelly. You sure it won't look like a robbery? I don't want to end up in jail."

"It's OK, Minny. Trust me. But first make that call."

"Looks like I'm going to miss my league tonight, too. And we're right up there tied for first place. And I was going to go in early and practice a whole game of tenpins."

"I hate to ask you Minny, but—"

"I know. It's OK. I'll practice tenpins tomorrow."

"OK, now where do I park?" asked Minny, as she approached Nelly's office building.

"Right there in that little drive. Same place you do when we carpool." Minny turned into the little drive and parked near the entrance. "Leave the motor running," Nelly ordered.

"What if someone asks what I'm doing here?"

"Say you're making a delivery for the 1000 Words company."

"I feel like I'm driving a getaway car. You sure this is legal?"

Nelly got out of the car and grabbed the large, empty attache case from the back seat. "Of course I'm sure. If C.G.'s telling everyone the same thing she told you, that I'm off for a few days, that's probably what she's told the partners, too. *If* anyone's asked. And I can certainly go up there and pick up my own things."

"What if you run into her?"

"I'm not stealing anything. I have every right to pick up my personal belongings. But—ahh—keep the motor running anyway."

With the dark glasses on, she could hardly see what button to punch in the elevator. It was seven o'clock. C.G. should be gone—but what if she weren't?

On the eighth floor, the reception room was empty. But the doors to the other offices were open and the lights were on. She headed quickly down the hall to the office she and C.G. had shared. Oh, no! The light was on. Was she there? Nelly walked soundlessly past, holding her breath, and peeked in. One of the cleaning crew was just wiping her glass desk top. He smiled when he saw her and picked up his rags. "You workin' now? I'll vacuum later," he said, taking no notice of the dark glasses or the heavily-made-up peel spots. He slipped past her and into the next office.

Nelly set her case on her chair, opened it, and quickly stuffed in her Rolodex and date book. She dialed the code for her phone messages and listened to them, scribbling while she opened drawers and took out her extra glasses, her salt shaker, her files, and notebooks. She left the guidance book and folder. She tore the current page and next month's page from her desktop calendar and stuffed them into the case. And after taking down the last of her messages, she erased them all.

Back in the hall, she noticed lights burning in three other offices—one of them, Ben Schlesser's. She was tempted to go and talk to him, but Minny was waiting. And she didn't want him to see the raw evidence of the work on her face. She slipped back into her office and dialed his extension. "Hello, Ben? It's Nelly."

"Nelly, are you OK? C.G. said you had to take a couple of days off. What's going on?"

"It's more than that Ben. I—I'm leaving. I told C.G. that if she didn't explain to the partners that I do all the work and book everything, I was leaving. And she refused, so I quit. I'm starting my own speakers bureau."

"Oh, Nelly, no! Why didn't you come to me first?"

"I think you, at least, knew what was happening. But she's my boss, the one I have to report to. I'm not supposed to go over her head. But it's just as well. I was so upset. I've decided I don't want ever to be pushed around again. I'm changing, Ben. Altogether. I've gotten my hair styled and streaked. I'm wearing make-up and new clothes—I'm getting more tomorrow. I'm going to be a new person. And never again will I let anyone else push me around or take credit for work I do."

There was a long pause at the other end of the line. Then he said. "Well, I think you've taken a good step, Nelly. I have always realized that you were the worker, but I can't seem to make the others see that. I don't like losing you. But even if we do, I personally don't want to lose you as a friend. Can we have dinner one night this weekend or next week and talk about it? And if I can persuade them that *you* are the one who should have been put in charge, and the change is made, would you come back?"

"You won't be able to convince them until they see what a mess things are going to be. C.G. doesn't know how to do anything except give orders and go to lunch."

"Nelly, let me try. I'll call you in a day or two. We'll have dinner and I'll report whatever I can by then. Please?"

"I'm already incorporating my new company. I can't wait. I've got to make some money."

He sighed. "Well, maybe we'll be your first customer," he said. "I don't see how we can handle our service without you."

Nelly hung up. Ben didn't realize she was only a few rooms away. She picked up her case and quietly retraced her steps—down the hall, out the door, into the elevator.

Downstairs she threw the case into the back seat and jumped in front next to Minny. "OK, out of here!"

Minny tore out of the drive, burned rubber careening onto the street on two wheels, and gunned the engine heading west. Nelly grabbed her seatbelt and hung on, crying, "For heaven's sake, Min, why are you racing like that? We'll get a ticket. Slow down."

Minny eased up on the gas. "I thought someone was chasing you, the way you tore out of there. You get what you wanted?"

Nelly sighed a happy sigh. "I sure did. Not only

all the things from my desk. I also picked up an ally. But you know something, Min? I think Ben Schlesser's been on my side all along."

Eight

Nelly's face hurt just a little. The stitches were gone, the scabs had fallen off. The skin beneath them was still red and tender, but make-up would cover it. But it was her ear that hurt the most—from being pressed relentlessly to a telephone all day.

Minny's calls to the newspapers had gotten results and she was still contacting bookers and bookees from her notebooks, but she couldn't put this one off any longer—Mac Britton. She must call and explain why she wouldn't be taking care of his guidance program and apologize for wasting his time. When his office answered, she said, "I'd like to talk to Mr. Britton, please. I'm Nelly Holachek, from Raymond, Schlesser. And I—"

"Oh, I'm so glad you called," said the friendly voice. "This is Heather, Mr. Britton's secretary. I've been trying to reach you for days. He wants to talk to you about an idea he has. Oh, by the way, do you have any number where we can reach you when we can't get you at that office of yours? They always say you're not there."

Nelly gave Heather her home number. "But now—" she began.

"Let me see if I can put you through. Hang on."

After a long moment of silence, Britton came on the line. "Nelly Holachek?"

"Yes, Mr. Britton."

"I'm so glad Heather finally found you. Could I talk to you sometime tomorrow or the next day? I tried getting in touch with you via Mrs. Clemency-Graves, but she kept wanting to set up a lunch date and I don't think another lunch with her would be productive. I would much prefer to let my other people handle the social side of this. But I need an opinion on an idea. You're clearly the one to talk to about it."

"I—I—yes, I can do that. When do you want me?"

"Just a minute," he said and she could hear muffled voices and then his, saying, "How about tomorrow at one? I avoid going out to lunch as much as possible but we have little noshes here for anyone who can't get out, or doesn't want to. So have a bite here with me."

"Fine," said Nelly. "See you then."

She heard a knock at the front door and the turn of a key and Minny walked in. "So, how goes it?" asked Minny.

"I've been on the phone all morning lining up speakers and users. And guess what! I called Britton, Llewellen & McVey to tell them I wouldn't be handling their stuff, and I found out Britton has been trying to reach me for days. He wants to run something by me. Wait a minute. Why aren't you at work?"

"I was, all morning. But I kept getting a busy signal when I tried to call you and it made me nervous. Albert makes me nervous. I mean, I'm sorry for him but he's not going to take this sitting down, and you know how wild he can be. I thought I'd better check."

"What were you calling about?"

"This guy. Freddie. I really like him. I saw him all last week and he still wants to see me. He's taking me to a movie tonight. I thought maybe you might just stop over and borrow a cup of sugar around nine or so and see what you think of him."

"Give me a call when you get home from the movie."

Minny's huge brown eyes looked horrified. "Oh, no! I can't do that. I don't want it to look like I'm setting him up for an inspection. I want it to look accidental. Just come over."

"OK, if I remember."

Nelly worked on. An hour later during a fruit salad

break, she received a curious call. "Nelly Holachek? This is Daniella Raymond, Will's wife."

"Oh, hello, Mrs. Raymond. Yes, this is Nelly."

"Nelly, I've been trying to arrange something with C.G.'s help, and I'm getting nowhere fast. I was grumbling to Ben Schlesser about it this morning and he said Will should have told me to deal with you instead. That *you* are the one that really does all those bookings—speakers, radio interviews, and all that."

"Well, yes, I did."

"Then let me tell you what my husband and I thought would be a good idea." She quickly outlined her plan for making TV and radio appearances.

"It sounds wonderful," said Nelly. "A kind of liaison from activists to the rest of the community. But I guess you didn't know that I'm not really working for your husband's firm anymore. I guess C.G. hasn't told anyone yet."

Danny groaned. "But there's no one else who can handle it. Ben said that. Clearly C.G. can't."

"That's why I quit, Mrs. Raymond."

"You quit?"

"Yes, Mrs. Raymond."

"Oh, call me Danny. Everyone does."

"Danny, I started that service and handled it all by myself before C.G. ever came to work there. And I still do. Or I did until a few days ago. I laid out all the client programs, too. And they promoted her over me. I'm not very good at standing up for myself. C.G. just took over, but I did the real work. So I finally told her she couldn't keep taking credit for things I was doing or I'd quit. And I did. You're the only person I've told this to so far. Except Mr. Schlesser, who is not one of C.G.'s fans."

"But then how do I—"

"Oh, I'd be glad to do that for you this time, Mrs. Raymond. I mean Danny. I'm starting a little company that will do precisely that kind of thing—the bookings. And I'm sure I can get you on Channel 17 and some talk shows right away. When are you free?"

"Anytime during the next two weeks. I'll reschedule anything that's in the way."

"Give me a number where I can call you. I'll get back to you."

She dialed Channel 17's Faye Asher immediately and got the receptionist, Carol. "Hi, it's Nelly Holachek. Listen, tell Faye I have something that might be interesting to her or someone there." Then she briefly explained Daniella Raymond's idea. "She's a stunning woman and very articulate. Very qualified. She's been right in the middle of the social stream here for ages."

"Is she free next Wednesday? I think there's a space."

"Free as a bird. I'll give her your number and you can tell her what time and what to wear and so on."

"Good." Carol hesitated a moment and then added, "You know, you sound different, Nelly. So lively. Happy. Did you win the lottery or something? What's happening?"

"Oh, so much. I *am* different. I'm getting divorced, too. And I'm taking my maiden name back. Anyella Devin Lure."

"What a pretty name! Still Nelly for short?"

"Yes, but that's all that's the same. You won't know me when you see me. I'm opening a kind of speakers agency called 1000 Words. All kinds of speakers and experts and lecturers. And retired entertainers, magicians from the condos. Tell Faye I can get interesting guests, if she likes, and I can book her for money now, I think. If she has time for any extra work."

"What a great idea! Everyone you've sent us so far has been good. And I'm sure Faye would love to pick up a little extra change. Public TV doesn't exactly make you rich."

"I'll send her all the forms as soon as they're printed."

"And listen, Nelly. I think a couple of guys from some of the other stations might do something with this. A news item. An interview. Daryl Hardin always talks about the latest charitable fundraisers on his show. Or a couple of the people who do a lot of local coverage. Let Faye sniff around and we'll get back to you."

Next, Nelly dialed WTMI and got Danny on the list to cut a forty-second testimonial for the Philharmonic. She then called the producer of Buck Durango's outrageous morning show; Danny would be safe there. Buck was wild and woolly sometimes but always chivalrous toward pretty women—and half the county listened to him in the morning on their way to work.

She called Danny Raymond back. "I've got three to start with. But the symphony testimonial will be played over and over many times." She gave her the bookings.

"Well, Nelly Holachek—"

"Oh, excuse me, but I'm going by my maiden name now, Mrs. Raymond. I mean, Danny. It's Anyella Devin Lure."

"How melodic. It almost sounds familiar."

"Did you know my mother, perhaps? Countess Lauren Devalutsky or Devin Lure?"

"Why—er—no, I don't think so."

"Well, she has another name now, anyway. And I'm glad I could help you with these. If you have any more trouble, just call me and I'm sure I can get you some more."

"Wait. Don't you have a fee?"

"These are on the house, Danny."

After calling Ben Schlesser to confirm a dinner date for the next night, Nelly made endless calls to radio personalities and producers, broadcasters, talk-show hosts, hotels, condo associations, and charitable and cultural organizations until 5:30. Then she warmed a can of soup and started through her file of condo residents she had previously booked—clowns, two retired magicians, comedians, and country music singers. By seven she had filled several pages with names and data in each of two large new notebooks labeled "Bookers" and "Bookees."

She'd better get the sign-up forms done next. It wouldn't take long. Maybe if she helped Mac Britton book some of his people for free, he would return the favor by looking over her forms and telling her if she had made any glaring mistakes. She was so busy typing she hardly realized how late it was.

So when she heard a key poking at her front door, she assumed it was Minny and hurried to open it. "Oh, Minny, you won't believe how much I've—" She stopped mid-sentence.

It wasn't Minny. It was Albert standing there, the old key in his hand. A scowling Albert with the half-closed eyes that told her he was drunk.

"That key won't work, and you're not supposed to come here, Albert," she scolded. But just as she started to close the door, he lunged inside, all but knocking her over, grabbed her arm and twisted it behind her back until she yelped with pain. He kicked the door closed behind him and wrenched her arm again, so hard she screamed in agony. He grabbed her mouth and jaw with his big hand. "You shut up, Nelly, or I'll fix it so you'll never scream again. I'm gonna fix you good. I'm gonna knock that crummy shit right out of your head." He moved his hand slowly from her mouth, and pushed her into the living room. "No knife in your hand now, smart-ass," he snorted. "Let's see how tough you are now."

They saw the answerphone light flashing the minute they came in the door. The twins always took their messages first, even before unloading their luggage from the car or grabbing a diet drink from the fridge. Just good business. Besides, their grandmother Nana Lauren—she had taught them from infancy *never* to call her "Grandmother"—phoned them often from wherever she was—London, New York, Zurich. She often suggested real estate leads she had picked up in conversation, or even, occasionally, dumped an affluent customer into their laps. They talked to their mother once or twice a week—sometimes painful conversations, due to mutual disapproval of lifestyles. But they would usually call her office or let her get in touch with them so they didn't risk having their father answer the phone. Neither one would speak to him—a ten-year standoff.

And, of course, their various friends would leave messages, as they were so often out of town. Sometimes Nana took them for a jaunt, but it was their real estate business that kept them frantically busy. They had recently begun expanding into the Caribbean.

But just as Emma reached for the answerphone button, the phone rang. "Emma? Jane?" It was Nana's voice.

"It's Emma, Nana," she said, nodding at Jane who rushed to the guest bathroom phone and picked it up. "This is Jane, Nan. I'm on, too. We just got in from Ocean Reef and Nassau. What's up?"

"I've been trying to get hold of you girls all week. I called from Monte Carlo and then from London and now I'm in New York. I'm coming down. But I've been dying to tell you what's happened. You'll never believe it."

"What, Nana? What?" the twins cried together.

"Your mother has exploded. She's divorcing your father."

"She's *what?*" they cried.

"And she's changing, she says, from inside out, top to bottom. Hair. Make-up. Clothes. Personality. Really. She's got a whole detailed plan, soup to nuts—what she's doing and when and where, moment by moment. Desert Storm should have been as organized. She's quit her job and she's starting a booking agency. Please, get right up there and see her. Encourage and support her in every way."

"Yahoo!" cried Emma. "I don't believe it."

"We can sure help her buying clothes," said Jane. "We'll go up tomorrow, no matter what. We'll call tonight."

"That'll be—oh, wait a minute, girls. Oh, dear. I'm suddenly getting these vibes. Just like I did last week when all this was happening with your mother. I *knew* something was happening. Only these aren't good vibes. They're terrible."

"Nana, what's wrong?" cried Jane. When their grandmother got her vibes, *something* was bound to happen. She would be swept by a tidal wave of premonition. And she was always right.

"Emma, Jane, listen. Don't unpack. It's all going wrong. I don't know what. Something very bad, something terrible is going on. I've got this unbearable feeling. Get up there quickly!"

"Nana," wailed Jane. "Something's happening to Mom?"

"Yes, yes. Hurry up there. Right Now! Call 911 on the way."

Frantic with fear, the twins grabbed their purses, flew out of the apartment, jumped into Jane's car, and roared off toward I-95. Nana Lauren's vibes were always right on the mark. Their mother! Would they get there in time? When they crossed the county line into Broward, Emma dialed 911 and reported a break-in at their mother's address.

"Albert, owww!" Nelly whimpered with the pain. "Please stop. Albert, what you're doing is—illegal. You can't—ayah!" Another twist and another excruciating jolt.

"Stop talkin', or I'll get that knife out again and show you how to use it," Albert said thickly. "I'm doin' the talkin'. You're callin' that lawyer bastard right *now* and tellin' him it's all off. Then you're gonna make me some dinner. And then we're goin' to bed. And I'm gonna knock all this crazy stuff out of your goddam head!"

"There won't be anyone in Morganthau's office now."

"Try. Lawyers work late sometimes. If he's not there, leave a message sayin' the same thing."

"I can't remember the number," Nelly stalled.

"Well, I can. I talked to his office about twelve times last week." He tugged a slip of paper from his pocket with the number on it. "Now call!" he boomed, wrenching her arm again so hard he almost lifted her off the floor.

This couldn't be happening, she thought in terror. Oh, why had she opened the door? With her free hand, Nelly put the receiver beside the phone, dialed the number on the paper with shaking fingers, and picked up the phone again. Miraculously, Morganthau himself answered. But how to let him know something was wrong? "It's just the message machine, Albert," she said clearly. Surely the lawyer could hear her words.

Albert shouted back, "Then leave the message, stupid!"

She nodded and said into the phone, "Mr. Morganthau, this is Nelly Holachek. I've decided that I don't want a divorce. And—uh—so—would you please undo whatever we've done and just stop it all. Just stop it all. Thank you." And she hung up.

"Now, what is all this crap here," Albert demanded, pointing at the papers and notebooks cluttering the dining room table. His words were slurring. Oh God, please let him pass out, Nelly prayed. "You never brought that much work home before." With his free arm he swiped it all onto the floor.

"Albert, you're drunk. You know you really don't want to behave this way. You'll get in trouble."

"Yeah, who's going to tell them? You? After tonight you may not be in any condition to tell anyone anything, Nelly smartass."

His words hit her like chilling blows; she began to tremble uncontrollably. She had seen Albert this angry only twice before, and both times, he could have killed someone if he hadn't been stopped. There was that time when the twins were little and he had insisted she come along to one of his bowling leagues. And when a man from another team had made an admiring remark to Nelly, Albert, totally sloshed, had thrown him to the floor and beaten him viciously. It took four team members to drag him off.

Nelly had been terrified of her husband ever since. The other time, Albert wasn't even drunk. That was the night they woke up with a burglar prowling their room. The man had a gun, but Albert leapt at him, fought him for the gun while Nelly called the police, and finally overpowered him. By the time the police arrived he had beaten the man senseless.

He pushed her into the kitchen, still twisting her arm behind her. "I want steak."

"I'd make you steak, Albert," she said as docilely as she could, "but I don't have any."

"Well, find some!" he roared, kneeing her back and twisting her arm to make her scream loudly again.

Oh, God, the pain was making her dizzy. She felt disoriented. Unreal. But one corner of her mind was racing. She had to get free of him. If she could get him to let her go, she could make a run for the bedroom. She had to divert him. And she had to do it quickly or she was going to pass out from the pain. And what might he do then? "Albert, I can't cook while you have my arm all twisted like this," she whimpered.

He grunted assent, released her, and slumped onto a counter stool. He stared dully at her. "I'm watchin'. Don't try nothin'."

She opened the freezer and dug out a couple of frosty packages. No steak. But how would he know? She would pretend she was going to cook him some. She went to the cabinet nearest the hallway and pulled out a small pan, then went back to the other side and pulled out two plates, then back to the silverware drawer. Very deliberate moves, as if she were putting together a big meal. She tried not to look directly at him, but from the corner of her eye she could see him slumping. Please, God, let him pass out. Back to the cabinet nearest the hallway. She took out a large frying pan and a mixing bowl and set them on the counter, as though she had some particular meal in mind. And then suddenly she shot down the hallway so fast she was at the bedroom door before Albert registered her bolt for freedom.

Inside! Slam the door. Push the lock. Shove the dresser—unh—in front. Unh!

She dove for the phone and dialed 911, just as Albert reached the door, jiggled it, then threw himself against it. "This is Nelly Holachek, 3124 Cobblestone Lane, Plantation," she cried in a desperate staccato. "My estranged husband forced his way in and has been twisting my arm, threatening to—to take me apart. I ran away here to the bedroom but he's crashing the door down right *now!*" she sobbed in terror. "He's going to kill me!"

"You bitch!" Albert howled through the closed door, slamming against it again. And again.

Nelly dropped the phone. She had to get out of here! She tore at the window and had barely pushed out the screen when Albert came crashing into the room. She screamed. He lunged at her. She tried to scramble onto the bed, just as Minny and a man came running into the room behind him. The man carried a broom which he swung at Albert, who turned and caught it easily in one hand and broke it over his knee. Grunting, he swung back at the man, smashing him in the jaw as three policemen ran into the room. The man flew backward, crashing into the dresser. Albert turned back to Nelly, slammed her across the face, and grabbed her throat with both hands. Minny leapt at Albert's back, pounding on him. The three policemen closed in: one pulled Minny away; one yanked Albert's head backward; while the other tore at his hands to pull Nelly free. Three more policemen raced through the door and into the fray.

"Just stop right there!" hollered one. But Albert managed a swing at the stunned man leaning against the dresser, knocking him down before the police overcame him.

And Nelly, near the bed, slid downward against it in a faint.

She awakened on the sofa in the living room to a confusing, out-of-focus scene—people moving and talking. So many people. Was that Morganthau over there with one of the policemen? Where was Albert? But here was Minny, bending over her, crying and rubbing her hands, and a policeman patting her cheeks. "Oh, Nelly," Minny was babbling, "I was afraid he was going to kill you. When Freddy brought me home from the movie and I saw his car out there, I told him, 'We have to go in. She might be in trouble.' He made us call the police first. Then I heard you scream, but the door was locked, so I had to run back and get my keys. And we heard you hollering again. Oh, thank God we all got here in time."

"I was so frightened," whispered Nelly, shuddering. "He kept twisting my arm and hurting me."

Merv Morganthau came over and started to take her hand but then didn't. "You're OK now. I called 911, too, before heading over. I realized you were trying to tell me something and then I heard your husband's voice. I knew he'd somehow gotten in the house, and you were in deep shit. I told them what was happening and then broke every speed limit getting here myself."

"I dialed 911, too," said Nelly. "When I got away

and ran into the bedroom. I locked the door and pulled the dresser over and dialed while he was trying to push the door down. But then he came crashing through . . ."

A rap on the door and another policeman strode in and said to Nelly, "Two young women to see you. They say they're your daughters." And in marched Emma and Jane.

Their heads turned in unison as they took in the scene. The weeping Minny. The strange man with an icepack on his jaw. And there on the couch, white as a sheet, their mother. Jane wailed, "My gosh, Nana was right!" And the two of them ran to her and knelt to hug her gently.

"She told us to call 911 on the way up, that something terrible was happening," said Emma.

"So we did," said Jane. "And it was. Happening, I mean."

"Now it makes sense," said the policeman who brought the twins in. "We got a slew of 911 calls for this address within about ten minutes. We thought it must be a massacre."

Emma and Jane pulled back to inspect their mother. They saw the bruises on her arms and her swollen jaw and they cried together, "What the hell's been going on here?"

Nine

The twins and Minny dealt with two reporters waiting outside. They went with Nelly to Emergency at Plantation General, held her hand while the police questioned her, then returned and stayed up with her until after one. They let her ramble on, still half hysterical, about the terrible attack she had just survived. "Go home, Minny," Jane ordered. "You'll never be able to work tomorrow. Don't worry. We're staying over with Mom."

Despite her utter exhaustion, Nelly was still wound up like a top. She started telling them about her transformation and what finally pushed her into it, wincing every now and then or putting a hand to her bruised and swollen jaw.

"Mom, maybe we should wait and talk tomorrow. I can tell that's hurting you," said Emma.

"No. Whatever they gave me at the hospital—I'm OK. Just a little twinge sometimes. But I have to tell you—there's so much happening—" And she went on, spewing a torrent of words about her plans, her new agency, and what she had accomplished thus far. In disconnected detail she replayed everything that had transpired in the last two weeks along with her specific strategies to change herself even more in the weeks to come.

"Mom, I want you to know, it's working," said Emma. "We hardly recognize you. Even after this horrible business tonight, even with the welts and bruises, you look better, prettier, more alive than I can ever remember. Of course there's nothing like a little bruise on the jaw to add a smart touch—especially when you've just had surgery. But you should have told us. How's the tummy?"

"It healed so quickly. I only wore a little brace for a couple of days. I wanted that done a year after you were born and your father said no. But now, I make the decisions. I did it."

"You even *sound* different," chortled Jane. "We're tickled pink."

"And I think the agency will do very well," said Nelly. "I'm lining up so many people on both sides already. And I'm just getting started. I have a meeting scheduled with Mac Britton tomorrow—he heads that big law firm from New York that's opened up down here, and I think he might use the agency."

"You're not up to any business meetings tomorrow. Not after tonight," said Jane.

"Oh, but I *want* to," Nelly said, turning a little

pink. "It's not just that I hate to leave someone in the lurch. And it's not just that his company might use the new agency. It's that he was the one person who seemed to know I was there last week. Oh, he looked right through me a few times, too, but when C.G. dismissed me from the lunch at Down Under, that bothered him. He tried to get me to stay. And I think he's one person who sees right through her the way Ben Schlesser does. She's been trying to get him to go to lunch with her again and he's simply not buying it."

"Not buying it?" hooted Emma. "Mom, when did you ever use an expression like that? You really *have* changed!"

"I told you I have. I *think* in the same words and slang you do sometimes, you know, but I've always been so careful not to use them out loud. I edited everything I said. But no more. You just watch my dust now!"

"I love it," cried Jane. "Listen, we could give you lessons. Emma and I. On how to talk so people will listen. You have to talk their language. That's one of the things you learn in the real estate business. Talk *their* language, whatever it is. That flat, oh-so-gentle and grammatical speech of yours is—"

"Intimidating?"

"Not exactly."

"Boring?"

"That's closer. It's easy to tune out. So no one listens."

"True," said Emma. "But I don't think we should teach Mom. Nana should. She knows how to sound hip but elegant at the same time."

"Forget the lessons for now," said Jane. "Tell us more about this man, Britton."

"Well, I just get the feeling that he's kind—compassionate—fair. He was nice to me at our meeting. So even though he's on the twenty-eighth floor, and you know me and elevators, I'm going."

Jane and Emma exchanged glances. Was this newly emancipated mother of theirs getting her first post-emancipation crush?

"You toddle off to bed now, Mom," ordered Emma. "We've got nighties and stuff in the car—in our luggage. We didn't even stop to unload anything when we got Nana's message. We just flew."

Nelly nodded. "You two get some sleep, too. We'll talk more in the morning, and I'll give you your keys for the new locks."

The twins woke when they heard the newspaper thump against the door. Tiptoeing into the living room, they quietly eased the door open and snatched the paper inside. The two of them, with one mind, opened it on the kitchen counter. Right there on page one was exactly what they feared—a picture of their father and three policemen leading him from the house. The headline: "Plantation Man Attacks Estranged Wife." Below it was the story, which jumped to page ten, with quotes from Minny, her friend Freddy Hauptman, officer Gerald Trieman, and the twins, with Jane's words coming from Emma and Emma's from Jane.

They groaned in unison. "But we have to let her see it." Emma put the kettle on. Jane got out cups and a teapot.

"Oh, gosh, I hope she won't let this mess up her plans. Her new spirit," said Jane. "I wish Nana were here."

"Well, she said she will be in a few days or so," said Emma. "I think we'd better cancel Jamaica and spend Christmas with Mom. And Nana, if she's here. We can fly over tomorrow or the next day and take a quick look at that Farnum estate and the acreage and whatever else we can squeeze in without staying over. Maybe split up and check out twice as much."

"Twice as much what?" came Nelly's voice from behind them. She hugged them both. "It's so nice to wake up and find you here."

"Mom," they said together. "The paper—look."

Nelly stared at the picture, read the words beneath it, and turned to page 10 to finish the story. The twins held their breath. She closed the paper and shrugged. "Not a very flattering picture of your father. I'm just glad they didn't shoot me, with no make-up on. I never intend to go out in public without it again. I didn't know any reporters were there."

"You didn't know much of anything by the time everyone got here," Jane said.

"I know. I was—paralyzed with fear. I thought he was going to kill me."

"You're OK now, Mom?" asked Emma. "You can handle this?"

"Yes. I think so. That bastard will never get to me again."

"Mother!" cried the twins. "We never heard you call anyone a bastard before."

"Well, I probably should have, a time or two," said Nelly. "But I'm a late bloomer. My vocabulary has expanded incredibly the past week. Is he in jail? He should be."

"Yes, for now. And I don't think he can make his bail. I hope he rots in there forever."

"Now, Jane, don't be vindictive," said Emma. "Say forty or fifty years. That's enough."

"Let's not think of him," said Nelly. "Or of last night."

"I know what let's do, Mom," cried Jane. "Let's first have a big breakfast. After last night, we need a whopper. And then, if you're up to it, let's go shopping. For you. For some new clothes that suit the new you."

"What time does Lillie Rubin open up here? I think their pre-Christmas sale is this week," said Emma. "Mom, you sit. I'll do the grits and the eggs.

Jane, you do the toast and make some more tea. We have to get Mom back here in time for her heavy lunch date."

As soon as the manager, Evelyn Siegal, opened the doors, the three women who had been waiting outside marched in. The older one sat down, as the two younger ones began tearing through the sale racks. "This suit is your size, Mom. Here, this one, too. And this dress," called one of the pair, who were clearly twins. The other was pulling out size four skirts, blouses, and slacks. "The items with red stickers are half the sale price on the tag," said Siegal. "We know," said the one twin. "Half the clothes we own were red tag buys." Siegal put them in a dressing room.

In twenty minutes they had selected and paid for a black crepe pants suit for evening, a tailored day-time suit, a dress-and-jacket outfit, another dress, and several blouses, skirts, and slacks. And Siegal didn't even have to help with the try-ons. "We'll help her. She has a very sore arm," explained one of the twins. No alterations needed except for a couple of hems, and the older woman said she could do them herself. Siegal wrapped everything, and as quickly as they had come, they were gone.

They hit a shoe outlet in Hollywood next, and Fort Lauderdale's Swap Shop for bargain jewelry

103

and purses. "Rich-looking, classic stuff is your best bet, Mom," Jane giggled, when she saw her mother eyeing some shiny black stretch pants and lamé tops. "You're thin enough, you could get away with it, but I don't think you're quite ready for biker outfits yet."

Back at the house, they helped Nelly with her hair and make-up.

"Mom," said Jane, "you can't know how great you look. I always knew a gorgeous female was hiding in there somewhere. That streaking gives your hair such life. You're absolutely stunning."

"But how much have we spent?" said Nelly. "Nana just sent me some money but I'm going to need—"

"Consider this stuff your Christmas present," said Emma. "From Jane and me. It was all red tag stuff— half of the sale price. Not one of those slacks or shirts cost more than twenty dollars! That black suit was only ninety dollars, and it looks like nine hundred."

"Christmas isn't until next week."

"Be a good girl," giggled Jane, "and maybe Santa'll bring you some more. Emma and I are going up to Palm Beach tomorrow. We might have time for a quick stop at Designers R Less. They've always got some stuff on sale."

"No, girls, I can't let you—"

"You can't stop us. Not to worry, Mom We're just wrapping up a three-way trade including three huge houses in the Keys. We cleaned up, we can afford it. I can't wait 'til Nana sees you. She's so excited about all this, Mom. She's been waiting for you to break out ever since I can remember."

"And so have we," they exclaimed together.

"Well, don't think I've changed in *every* way," Nelly insisted. "I still don't really approve of all Nana's shenanigans. And I don't think the free and easy life—"

"Give yourself a month, Mom," said Emma. "Try it. You might like it. You might look at her a little differently by then."

Ten

So here she was in the Temple Tower lobby, dressed in the beige crepe dress-and-jacket outfit— the long sleeves hid her bruised arms—with a taupe bag and shoes. And the long rope of jade beads Lauren had brought her from the Orient years ago, which she had never worn. She caught her reflection in the lobby's mirrored walls. The make-up covered the bruises on her face and neck almost completely. My gosh, was it really her?

She faced the elevator, took a deep breath, stepped inside, and pressed the button for the twenty-eighth floor. As the door closed and the car began its long, fast climb, she tried to push down the fear that rose inside her and swelled with every floor. She began to gasp for breath. She gripped the rail with white knuckles and almost fell out of the car when it finally opened.

She blotted the sweat from her forehead with a

Kleenex. She breathed deeply until she felt her pulse slowing, then she approached the receptionist.

"Hello, I'm Nelly Holachek," she began.

"Oh, yes. Just take a seat there for a minute, Mrs. Holachek. Heather will be right out."

She barely seated herself before Mac Britton himself came through the double doors that led to the offices.

He looked at her, looked past her, and then looked back, obviously confused. He stepped closer, took off his glasses, wiped them, and put them back on. "Nelly Holachek?" he asked, tentatively.

She nodded and stood up. He stared at her a moment and cleared his throat, then looked down at the floor and up at her again. "Uh, excuse me for staring. You look so different. I wasn't sure it was you."

Nelly laughed. "Right now, that's the nicest thing you could say to me."

"Oh, I didn't mean—"

"I know," Nelly said. "It's all right. I do look different." Amazing. She felt very much in control. It was a new sensation. Her elevator panic had vanished.

"I came out because Heather's on a call," he said. "I didn't want to keep you waiting. Uh—we don't need a lot of room. Let's just use my office." He led her through the doors and past a cluster of cubicles through another set of double doors.

The back walls were all paneled with bookcases. The front walls were floor-to-ceiling windows looking out on a 180-degree sweep of the ocean and Boca Raton to the South. In the middle was his desk, facing the wondrous view, with a sofa, several stuffed chairs, a coffee table, and an oak game table and chairs to one side. A rap on the door interrupted her inspection, and Britton's secretary, Heather, poked her head in. "Good morning, Mrs. Holachek. Sorry I wasn't there to greet you. Oh, you're not—"

"No, it *is* Mrs. Holachek, Heather," said Britton. "I made the same mistake."

"Please don't give it a thought," said Nelly with what she hoped was a gracious smile. "I'm often confused with other people."

Heather smiled back, then stared, puzzled, at Nelly. "Mr. Britton, do you want me to bring both of you something to nibble on, or do you want to go help yourselves?"

Britton looked questioningly at Nelly and she shrugged. He said, "Bring us a little selection and put it on the game table, Heather. And coffee for us both. Make it decaf for me."

"Me, too, please," said Nelly.

"And no calls while we're busy here." He indicated a seat at the game table and pulled out the chair for her, then sat on the opposite side, staring at her frankly. His sad look was gone for the moment—or masked by open admiration and curiosity. Then he shook his head and pushed a copy of the morning's Sun-Sentinel toward her. "I assume you know that you made the front page this morning," he said.

"Yes, I saw it."

"I'm so sorry. A horrible experience. Are you sure you're up to this meeting?"

"I'm fine. A few aches and bruises. They'll go away."

"Well, I don't want to belabor the point, but I must say you do look like a different person from the one I met last week."

Nelly smiled. "I *am* a different person. It happened the day after I came here, when I asked my husband to leave," she said. "My daughters stayed with me last night and covered up the marks and bruises with make-up this morning. I'm wearing half a pound of pancake on my jaw. Just don't say anything terribly funny and make me laugh."

He grinned at that. "I'll be Bud Abbott," he said. He shook his head again. She not only looked different. The way she talked—she *sounded* different. The way she moved—she *was* different.

"I don't have to tell you how shocked I was when I saw the paper. Things like that don't happen to people you know, especially to such a gentle person. I'm so sorry," he said sympathetically. "It's like I've just seen someone I know get hit with a brick."

"Thank you," said Nelly, looking into those blue eyes, reading compassion in them. "I guess keeping busy and having other things to think about is the best medicine."

He smiled. "I agree. Well, then, let's get on with it. When we were talking about the extra service of yours—booking speakers and so on, at our meeting last week—it seemed a great idea. And we're ready to pursue it. But yesterday it occurred to me that we're overlooking something major. Instead of speaking on general interest legal topics, I thought it might be really useful to some of the businessmen down here if we talked about things like, say, the business climate in New York, what lawyers have to contend with there, what businesses have to cope with. How difficult the rules and regulations are to work with. How conditions affect the legal profession, investment, business in general. What's bad and what's good about New York's particular situation. What the trends are there, and what they may mean to business there and elsewhere. What to expect if one of your cases is tried in New York. Information that's interesting and that they might find very useful."

Heather brought in a tray with two plates, silver, napkins, a decanter of decaf and a platter full of salads, cold cuts and cheeses, and breads.

"All the comforts of home," said Britton as he grabbed a split hard roll, slapping some corned beef and a swipe of mustard on it. "Or the neighborhood deli. Don't be shy," he said. "Help yourself or this is for you."

Nelly laughed, winced at the pain, and groaned. Her jaw was still quite sore. "I told you not to be funny," she scolded, taking a plate and helping herself to some tuna salad.

"I could do some of those talks myself," he said. "And I've got two other men down here who were in key positions up there and who know enough about the inner workings of the city to be worth listening to. Well, what do you think"

"Mr. Britton—"

"Mac. We're very informal in this office. Well," he repeated. "What do you think?"

"Mac, it's a marvelous idea," she said enthusiastically. "Inside information business people want and can't usually get so easily. I think the response would be enormous from a certain audience."

"If we got a couple of subject outlines for you—"

"Businessmen here would come in droves. Lawyers. Entrepreneurs. Anyone contemplating opening a New York office. You'd quickly get to know the movers and shakers in town. You'd score a few points, so to speak. Holding an informal brunch might be a good way to wet your feet until you can find the right slots. You should do it soon, though. A lot of these meetings and seminars that would offer suitable audiences are booked way ahead."

"Good. We'll get something worked out."

"But let me tell you something first, Mr.—I mean, Mac. I don't know how to put this. But I have—quit my job at Raymond, Schlesser."

He looked up at her blankly. "Quit?"

"Yes. I could still handle this for you, and there's no one else at Raymond, Schlesser who can. But I'll certainly understand if you'd like to try that route first."

"I—I have to think about this," he said, obviously surprised. He began drumming his fingers impatiently the way he did at the lunch with C.G. "That certainly throws a new light on things. Am I being too inquisitive if I ask why you quit?"

"No. It's just because of that—the bookings. No one else does any of that, and I do virtually all of the customer guidance work, too. I work directly with the accountants and customers—I'm the link. But someone else was put in charge who does little but gets the salary boost, the title, the expense account. I asked her for equal status at least. I'm not going to get it, so I quit. I'm starting a speakers' agency to handle all such things. They won't be able to help you get those talks started. Not right away. They have no one to do it. You might consider using my agency. But if you feel you can't while you're using Raymond, Schlesser for your books, if it places you in an awkward position, I understand."

Britton scratched his head, sending the unruly grey hair in all directions. "Well, that's a twist. Certainly if you're the one who's doing this, you're the one we'll probably deal with ultimately. But for now—"

"Maybe you'd be more comfortable talking about it first with C.G. or one of the partners," she suggested.

"I think that might be a good idea. Just to keep everything on the up and up. Let's give them a call right now, and see what happens. He moved over to his desk and buzzed his secretary. "Heather, get me Mrs. Clemency-Graves at Raymond, Schlesser first. And probably one of the partners there, next."

They waited, eyeing each other expectantly, and a moment later the phone rang. "Yes, hello, C.G., Mac Britton . . . Same to you. Listen, I need to find out something about those bookings I talked to Mrs. Holachek about . . . no, I haven't time for lunch." He began drumming his fingers again. "No, I don't need a break . . . I don't see why we can't handle this over the phone. I want some specific information about such bookings—who would be interested in hearing a few of our men talk about . . . You what? . . . You've suspended that service until after New Year's? How interesting." He looked over at Nelly. "Oh, and listen, how do I get in touch with Mrs. Holachek? . . . She's still out? Well, you don't object if I use some other agency for now for the speaker business, do you? I wanted to get started right now . . . Good . . . Yes, thank you, and Merry Christmas to you, too."

He put the receiver down, looked over at Nelly, and without saying a word picked it up again. "Heather? You there? OK, get McKinnon or Raymond or Schlesser—any one of the partners over there." Again, he stared at Nelly and drummed his fingers for a few moments. And then, "Hello, Mr. Schlesser? Yeah, this is Mac Britton . . . Listen, I've been trying for a week now to get hold of Nelly Holachek or someone over there who can help me with bookings by and for our people here, and I've been put off again and again. And today, Mrs. Clemency-Graves said the service is suspended until after the holidays. Now I find out that Mrs. Holachek has quit and will be running a speakers' agency herself, offering similar services. I'm wondering if it will cause any problem if we hire her until your service gets straightened out . . . Good. Then that's what we'll do . . . Yes, as a matter-of-fact, she's right here . . . Sure, I'll put her on."

He handed the phone to Nelly "It's Ben, Nelly. I told Britton it's fine, that we've made a big mistake letting you get away. The whole business with C.G. is a mistake. Our guidance program has ground to a halt. I suspect that within a few weeks, we'll start letting you handle our booking service, too, or else drop it."

"That makes me feel better about it all then, Ben."

"And listen, Nelly. Instead of a quiet dinner with me tonight, I'd like you to come to the Chamber's Vaudeville Night. You know—to raise money for the children's charities. You got them most of their acts. And there will be a lot of people there who will be potential customers. Dress is casual and it starts at seven. Is that OK? Shall I pick you up at home or meet you at the office?"

"At the office will be fine. Oh, Ben, this is so kind of you."

"Not at all. We owe you, Nelly. We haven't treated you fairly at all. In one way, I'm really glad you've finally rebelled. We'll talk more about that tonight."

Nelly handed the phone back to Britton, who hung it up and said, "Well then, I guess we're on. A brunch sounds like a good place to start."

"Just pick a day, Mr. Brit—Mac, and an alternate in case it turns out to be tied up with something major. Tell me the time—and where."

"Here?" he suggested.

"That would be best because it's your home turf. Tell me how many people you can accommodate in your largest meeting room, or even your reception area if it's larger. The topic and who'll speak. For the first one, why not you? I'll get on it right away. Too bad I haven't ever heard you speak before. It would help when I'm inviting people, if I kind of knew your style."

He grinned. "Are you suggesting I should audition?"

She laughed, wincing at the pain again. "No, but I'll hear you at the brunch and take notes so I'll be able to tell people before the next one that you're absolutely marvelous."

"*If* I'm absolutely marvelous. Funny, this is the third time I've talked to you but the first time I've realized that you have a sense of humor. I always think anyone who laughs at anything I say has a sharp sense of humor."

"That's curious," said Nelly. "I've always thought the same thing about anyone who laughs at anything *I* say. Small world, isn't it?"

He chuckled and nodded. "At any rate, I'll get back to you later today or tomorrow at the latest with all those parameters" He took her hand and shook it. Only this time he gave it a squeeze, too. His grip she noted, was strong, and his hand was warm.

Just then the phone rang again, and Britton picked it up. "Hello, son," he said. The smile vanished, replaced by that sad look Nelly had seen at the lunch with C.G.

He listened intently a few moments, then said, "Rocky, wait a minute. Give him a chance. You waited over a year after the doctors said you should start this kind of program. You can't expect miracles overnight." He paused and shook his head. "Son, you don't look that bad. Those scars are fading. A little of that abrasion work they told us about and they'd be gone. Listen, I have someone in the office here and . . . What? It's gone already?" He sighed. "OK, I'll have Heather transfer some more money. And I'll meet you there. Just keep loose. It will all work out."

He looked desperately weary. To her surprise, Nelly felt an almost motherly urge to put her arms around him and comfort him. Was she out of her mind? She wasn't quite sure what to do. Maybe he needed to be alone. She stood up. "Well, thanks again," she said. "I'll talk to you later today or tomorrow and we can work out the brunch details," she added as she hurried from the room.

Eleven

"Well, at least we know she's still alive," said McKinnon. "And lucky to be, according to the morning paper. What a horror story. Who even guessed she was having problems like that? She's such a mouse; she never complained about anything."

"Yes, I would say that was Nelly's main fault. Too timid. Bright girl. Analytical. Efficient. Worked hard and did a good job. But so timid," said Schlesser.

"What are you getting at, Ben?" asked Will Raymond. "Why did you make us drop everything and race in here like it was some kind of emergency? It's not some hot gossip you gotta spill or burst."

"I called you all in here because I'm afraid we've lost one of our most productive employees. The people and organizations who count on her are left in the lurch, not to mention all the guidance visits that aren't being made. And the new clients who are *not* being set up. Many of them have come to us just because they've heard from others how helpful that guidance is. And suddenly, *no* guidance. Why isn't C.G. doing more of it? She just keeps stalling. The clients are asking what's going on, and we wouldn't even know *that* if it wasn't that Selma and Georgia and others have taken messages.

"*That's* what I'm getting at, Will," Ben went on. "We should call her in right now, ask her what the hell's going on, and take steps to cover the situation. Get Nelly back. Replace her. Do *something*. You can't provide a service your clients get to depend on and that *we* get to depend on, and then just suddenly yank the rug out."

"I say the same thing—call C.G. in right now," said Mark Goldberg. "Before we accuse anybody of anything, before we try to cure anything, let's find out why and how we're sick."

The partners nodded. Will Raymond looked pained beyond endurance but he buzzed his secretary. "Doris, send C.G. into the small conference room immediately, will you?"

Two minutes later there was a rap on the door and C.G. stepped in, closing the door after her. "You sent for me?" she asked with one of her broad, ever-so-charming smiles.

"Yes," said Ben. "Take a chair there, C.G." Raymond shot to his feet and pulled one out for her and she sat down. "We want to know for once and for all," Schlesser continued, "what's happened to Nelly Holachek, and why we haven't been told. Is she working for us anymore or is she not?"

C.G. hesitated, then sighed heavily. "Well, I guess I just can't cover for her anymore. And we can't wait any longer."

"Cover for her?" repeated Ben, wrinkling his brow.

"She walked out over a week ago; she was distraught. I tried to talk her out of it. I told her whatever was bothering her, go home and take it easy for a couple of days and come back. That I would cover for her. Who knew she had a husband like that? No wonder she just went berserk. But she just walked out. And took our files, so now I'm at a total loss with the bookings. Several people have called trying to reach her, who say they heard she's starting a speakers' agency and they want to know more about it. So I'm afraid we'll never get our files back. It's like I'm starting all over from scratch, trying to assemble lists of what we called the bookers and the bookees. She's left me in such an impossible mess."

"She took your files?" said McKinnon. "That's stealing. I can't believe shy little Nelly would take anything that didn't belong to her."

"Well, they were for our use, but she kept all that in *her* notebooks," said C.G. hastily. "That was part of the job that I pretty much let her take care of."

"She did originate the idea and handled it entirely from the beginning as a favor to people who dealt with us, not as an official service," Ben interrupted. "She wasn't ever paid anything extra for it. And I would hardly call her notebooks 'our files.' "

"Well, I guess she regarded them as hers," C.G. said lamely. "Anyway, she took them. And her Rolodex. I hated to get her in trouble. I hoped she'd come back. But now, I can't wait any longer. I need a replacement. In fact, I really need two people now—one to do Nelly's work, and one to help me set up new files."

"Well, no argument with that. You need the helpers, so hire them. That speakers' service has brought us many clients," said McKinnon. "So has our guidance program. No doubt that it's worth the investment."

"Yes, sir. I'll get right on it. Is that all?"

"Yes, that's it, C.G.," said Raymond.

After she left, Raymond said, "Well, is everybody happy now?"

"No," said Ben Schlesser. "You made a judgment based on one deposition. I would have liked to hear Nelly's side of this—I'm sure it would be quite different. You know, guys, it's too bad C.G. isn't a lawyer. She's incredibly slick. I can't imagine Nelly doing anything underhanded. And what about the guidance program? It's falling apart, too, since Nelly's gone. Why didn't we ask her about that?

Doesn't C.G. do anything but take people to lunch? And why didn't she come to us and tell us? I think the whole thing smells like Limburger cheese."

Goldberg nodded. "Ben's right. We may have made a premature judgment here, Will. What was the big hurry? I only hope we don't pay for it later."

"It's not final, necessarily," said McKinnon. "It got things moving again, hopefully. We can keep a closer watch on her and be ready to take further steps if necessary. Be glad we worked out a quick solution of any kind."

"Have we?" asked Ben. "I wonder."

In her office, a seething C.G. called her brother in Montreal. "I want you to know, Barty, that your nasty little friend Nelly Holachek is an absolute villainess."

"What are you talking about, Claire? What's the matter?"

"She walked out, taking her notebooks and Rolodex with her. Left me with everything and no idea how to start. And today, the partners called me on the carpet to find out what's happened to her. And to the booking service. Her drunken husband broke into her house last night and beat her and was caught. It was in all the papers. White trash! Well, I fixed her little red wagon with this bunch, let me tell you. But that woman has almost gotten me fired.

And now I'm going to have to work like a cane cutter to get things organized around here."

"But Sis, that's how Nelly was working before. Poor dear. Was she hurt badly? By her husband?"

"She has caused me more problems, and you take *her* side?" she hissed into the phone. "Well, I won't forget what she's done. I'll pay her back if it takes me forever. And I won't forget how loyal *you've* turned out to be either," she added, slamming the phone down.

Next, she rang Will Raymond's extension. "Is Mr. Raymond back in his office yet?" she asked his secretary, Doris.

Raymond took the phone. "I want to thank you for that wonderful show of support," she said.

"And I want to tell you, lady, you're lucky I didn't can you on the spot. It's pretty clear now that Holachek's been doing the work and you've been coasting and taking people to lunch. Either you get that office working in two weeks, or I'm telling Schlesser and Goldberg they're right. And you're out."

"Not before I tell a little story to your wife, Will."

"Go ahead, tart. Danny knows I like an extra course now and then. We've worked that out years ago. And if you want the whole town to know you sleep around, that's OK with me."

C.G. held out the receiver and stared at it, stunned, fingering her pearls like worry beads. Ben Schlesser rapped on her door a few minutes later and stepped in. "I just want you to know, C.G., that that was a supurb bit of ad libbing and toe-dancing you just did in there. You fooled everyone. But I know Nelly Holachek, and somehow, all this doesn't quite add up."

After he left, C.G. sat very still, clutching her pearls tightly.

No matter. Somehow, she would get it all worked out. She had a busy week or two ahead of her. Hiring two helpers. Organizing guidance and the speakers' program. Getting back to work on the Woman of Our Time dinner before it was too late. And somehow, she had to figure out a way to fix Nelly Holachek. She smiled grimly. She'd think of something.

The cocktail hour went by in a rush of introductions. Ben introduced her, at her request, as Anyella Devin Lure. "Nelly, this is Rod Hagwood, the paper's fashion editor, Jim Davis, the religion editor. Rod, Jim, this is Anyella Devin Lure, the woman who's got the new speakers' agency, 1000 Words." And two minutes later, "Nelly this is Gershon Trayle, the yacht builder. Tray, this is Anyella Devin Lure, the lady with the speakers' agency. She might book you to talk about the pluses and minuses of owning a yacht."

"No, I only talk about the pluses," grinned Trayle,

taking her hand and giving it a shake that was more like a caress. "How do you find a woman like this, Ben?" she said. "So smart and so gorgeous, too?" Nelly flashed him a smile she hoped was seductive. She was going to have to get the girls to give her a couple of lessons. Mentally she put that on her strategy list.

She met several other men, dozens of couples, and passed out more than twenty of her new cards. Two of the men acted almost smitten, standing around to talk with her and Ben for a time, pressing their cards on her. And suddenly, there was Daniella coming up to Ben and hugging him. She turned to Nelly and said, "I don't think I've met your friend, Ben."

"Anyella Devin Lure," said Ben.

Danny put her hand out and said, "Daniella Raymond." Then she stopped and stared at Nelly. "Devin Lure. You're Nelly. Anyella Devin Lure. You got my programs arranged." Nelly nodded. "Well, I had no idea you were such a femme fatale, Nelly. I mean Anyella."

"Takes one to know one," said Ben.

"I'm not really," Nelly said with a laugh "This is just the new me."

"New or old, don't change a thing," said Danny. "Listen, I want to thank you. I cut the symphony testimonial and they're already playing it and it sounds great. And I did Buck Durango's talk show.

It was a stitch. His producer called to ask me to come back in four weeks and talk about the symphony's social calendar."

"I knew you'd be good," said Nelly "I'm so glad it worked."

"But I'm not accepting this for free," said Danny, directing her remarks to Ben. "Here's this C.G. woman who's getting paid by you guys to take care of just this kind of thing, and she can't make the first call. And here's Nelly, no longer working for you, and she gets three bookings set up in fifteen minutes, and tells me it's on the house. If you don't send me an invoice, Nelly—Anyella—I'll just make a guess and write you a check."

"That's interesting," said Ben. "I think your husband is on the other side in this C.G. confrontation."

"Is he?" said Danny with a knowing sniff. "Well, don't worry. I'll straighten him out. I told Buck's producer to call you about the other booking, Nelly. I told them you were handling all my appearances— you and your agency." She flashed her seductive smile. "I feel like a movie star. Deal?"

Nelly grinned back. "Deal."

"I'm not staying for the show and dinner. Will's at the cocktail hour for the Byblos dinner at the library tonight, so I said I'd put in an appearance here for him. We're meeting at Burt and Jack's in an hour." She glanced at her diamond-encrusted watch. "Well, I guess I'd better buzz around here a bit. I only have about forty minutes left. See you, Ben. I'll call you, Anyella." And she slithered back into the crowd.

The vaudeville acts were presented on a stage in the dining room, between courses. Orrin Masters, the comedian. Abner DeLand, the magician. Singers, tap dancers, and a balancing act. Nelly had made the arrangements for three-fourths of them. Months ago. Four different Chamber officers came over to their table to thank her. Nelly remembered meeting three of them before but they didn't remember her. All were effusive in their thanks. And when Ben, after explaining that her name was now Anyella Devin Lure, pointed out that she had opened her own agency, all four urged her to join the Chamber. And asked for her card.

"You were a great hit during cocktails, too," Ben told her, after the third Chamber member left their table. "I don't know exactly what all you've done to yourself, Nelly, but you look fantastic. Every single guy you met tonight got that look in his eye. And some who aren't single, honey. I'm too old and I've been around too much not to know that look when I see it. You're knocking them dead. I'll bet you a nickel they all call within a few days."

"Oh, Ben, I—"

"No, listen to me. You have a lot of class, Nelly.

I always knew you had the brains, the character, the integrity. I always thought you were likeable, and pretty in your quiet way. But who knew there was an alluring woman hiding in there?"

"My mother always used to tell me I could be a cover girl," she said. "But I resisted all those years. Anything she suggested, I did the opposite. I let Albert grind me into the ground, just like my father used to grind my mother into the ground."

"How'd that ever happen? How'd you ever marry someone who could do that to you?" Ben asked, puzzled.

"My mother says I married my father. He was a gruff, strict, heavy-set man who drank too much. He sent me to parochial schools where I learned to respect and obey him no matter what he did. When my mother left, I stayed. I was very critical of her for leaving—that's how brainwashed I was. My mother moved on into a glamorous life, boyfriends, kind husbands, travel—always trying to get me to join her. She had custody but she wouldn't force me. And when I visited her I was really nasty. Disapproving."

"You were that brainwashed?"

"Yes. When I started dating—very little, actually—there was Albert, a younger version of my father. Bossy. Inconsiderate. I grew more and more insecure. Why was life so miserable when I was so devout, always trying to do the right thing. And there was my sinful mother, having the time of her life. Except that she missed me and almost mourned over me. But I didn't understand that, then.

"When my father died, I married Albert. My mother tried to stop me, but I couldn't see it was because she loved me. I took all those commandments so literally. It was a terrible marriage from the start. I had the girls. He was OK with them when they were little, but then he started treating them like he treated me. I was torn—always struggling to keep them out of his way. By the time they were about ten, he was drinking and losing jobs. They wanted to leave. He'd threaten them. By the time they were 13 or 14, they started spending a lot of time with my mother. Thank God.

"I encouraged it. I had to. When they were 16 they moved in with her. He grumbled but he didn't try to stop them. Maybe he was just glad not to have to pay their bills. I had to let them go. She could give them a better home life. Nice clothes. Everything. She was on her fourth husband then. And Albert was yelling at them all the time, coming in drunk and crashing on the living room floor. I had to get them away from that."

"Why didn't you leave with them? Did you still love him?"

"How could I love anyone like Albert? I felt obligated. My vows. I was a slave and he was the master. I was a possession he could push around. I thought it was sinful to rebel. He wanted everything perfect. He had me folding the dirty laundry before I put it in the hamper. I tried so hard to do everything his way."

"It must have just about wiped out your mother."

"Except that she knew she was at least saving the girls. I was so resistant to Lauren's advice by then. I didn't approve of her life. She was a free spirit before the idea was even invented. I shriveled more and more and just tried to keep out of Albert's way. He didn't work much. I supported us, with help from my mother. I couldn't have any friends except Minny. I became a spook. I did rebel enough to keep him away from me sexually these last few years. But that was all. I was still his servant, until I couldn't bear it anymore—and couldn't stand myself, the invisible Nelly. Doing all the work and letting others take the credit."

"You're a special person, Nelly. Not many people could do what you've done. Break free, finally, at your age. I've been watching you ever since you came to the firm. I'm a little old for you romantically, but I like you and I'd like to help you. Let me take you to a few of these things. Let me introduce you to some people. One of these dashing bachelors falling all over you tonight will probably sweep you off your feet. But if you don't care for any of them, you can always regard me as your ace in the hole."

Nelly was touched. "Ben, that's the nicest thing you could say to me."

"And meanwhile, I think you should be warned that C.G. is out to get you. I don't know how, but at the meeting with the partners today, she managed to make you look like the troublemaker, the one who walked out for no reason and took the files. Mark and I are in your corner, and McKinnon is halfway there. But Will is unbudgeable, defending her all the way for some reason."

"He hired her, remember? Maybe that's why."

"Maybe. She's going to hire two people to replace you."

"To do her work for her," said Nelly.

"I'm sure. But enough of that. We're supposed to be having fun here. Shall we dance?"

"I don't know if I remember how," said Nelly. "I haven't danced in more than twenty-five years."

"Don't worry. I'll push you around—gently, of course."

He was a good dancer. Nothing too fancy, but a strong leader and he moved with the beat. But Nelly didn't get to do one whole dance with him all night. Several of the men she had just met kept cutting in. And a couple she hadn't. A doctor named Angelo. A lawyer, Barney Jones. A yacht broker named Harold Schwand had her doing rock and roll. And Ben eased her into jitterbugging. By the evening's end she was glowing with delight.

"You're about to go up in smoke, Nelly," he said after they bid their tablemates good night and headed for the hotel entrance. "You look like a woman in love."

"I think I am," said Nelly. "With life. I never knew it could be such fun. This was a wonderful evening, Ben. Thank you so much."

"We'll do it again," he said. "It was a smashing evening for me, too. What man doesn't like to escort the belle of the ball? You were the most beautiful woman in the room, Anyella."

After he took her back to the office to get her car and watched her drive off into the night, Ben reflected on the evening. As much as he had always liked Nelly, he had never guessed all that woman had been hiding there behind that mousy facade. He had to be fifteen years older than she was. Damn. If only he were just five years younger, he thought, she'd never get away from him.

At home that night, as she had every night since her revolt, Nelly got out her plan and checklist. She did her exercises. She played her hypnosis tapes. First, the one that was supposed to give her self-confidence. Next, the one she had just found that was supposed to help her get past phobias—such as hers about riding elevators in very high buildings. She spent five minutes practicing certain expressions—her telephone "hell-oh-oh?" by now sounded wonderfully silky—exactly like her mother's. And her "I'm delighted to meet you," sounded like she really was. She listened to her calls and found that Faye Asher had gotten her a guest spot next week on two talk shows where the host wanted to know more about her new agency.

From her purse she dug the memo pad on which she had scribbled notes during the day about her makeover. One note said she should buy a couple of bathing suits, now that her tummy was flat again. And a strapless bra, just in case she ever needed one. And Gwen Parker had suggested she consider using Retin-A. Hadn't Dr. Laker said the same thing? She'd call him for a prescription. She read another couple of chapters of the Emily Post book and leafed through a few required-reading magazines. That's enough improvement, she told herself at midnight. You don't want to be perfect, Nelly. It's too intimidating.

Twelve

She was sitting in the waiting room in her leotard with a faded man's shirt thrown over it, when the door opened and in walked Mac Britton. "Well," he said, clearly startled, "I guess this was the last place I expected to run into you."

"Oh, dear, have I got my time wrong?" asked Nelly. "I thought I was supposed to be here at three. Are you waiting for Reb, too?"

"Not for a session," Britton assured her. "Just to pick up my son. If I tell him I'm picking him up, he's more likely to be here. He's missed a couple of times already."

Nelly nodded. "I guess some people simply aren't as devoted to fitness as others. I'm one of them. I'm just getting a few little routines from him to keep me moderately limber. My daughters are different. They have bodies like ballet dancers. They devote a lot of time to it. Is your son into body building?"

Britton shook his head. "I wish he were. He's into

girls and dangerous adventure. He was born with a great body. Never had to make any effort. Now he needs exercise for therapy, and it's hard to get him to see how important it is."

"For therapy?" Nelly repeated, puzzled.

"He was one of those who helped put out the last oilfield fires in Kuwait. He fell off a rig, got badly burned, and breathed in a lot of fumes before they could get to him and pull him out."

"Oh, good Lord, how awful! Is he all right? Did it all heal?"

"He has some scars. They've done a tremendous amount of grafting. The thing is, with burns that bad, the pain is so intense, they have to put you under to clean out dead tissue and change dressings. And anesthesia does things to you, too. Some people just lose their will to live. Rocky did. He got so fed up with it all, that for over a year after he was pretty much healed, he just refused to do anything. No therapy. No check-ups. Nothing. He wouldn't see a psychologist or psychiatrist to help him through it. He just holed up in the library in New York and read. Which was the only ray of sunshine in the whole gloomy story. Because Rocky used to brag that he got all the way through law school without ever cracking a book. At least now he reads. He can't read enough. He has six or eight books going at once."

Nelly shook her head. "They don't warn you when you're young and eager to have kids that it's a job that never ends. That it isn't always storybook easy. That the pain of parenthood can go on forever as well as the joy. Is he getting physical therapy now?"

Britton nodded. "I threatened to wash my hands of him altogether. He's thirty years old and he's never earned a living. Never quite decided what he wants to do in life—except be a playboy and search for adventure. He hired on an Amazon rainforest research team and loved it until he got a snake bite that damn near killed him. No training. He just crammed a couple of books down before he applied. He worked for a parachuting company where people pay to make a jump. And this Kuwait thing. He was no more qualified for that job—they wanted experts—than Betty Boop. He fudged on his application, and now look. So I brought him here. I threaten him—no more help from me unless he straightens up and flies right. But so far I don't think he's really changed direction. Just his address."

"I guess I've been luckier than I realized," said Nelly with a rueful smile. "For years my daughters wouldn't live with me because I wouldn't divorce their father. They wanted me to wake up and stop being a doormat. But I still had the idea that living with my mother was't good for them. My mother is a very free spirit. She's been married five times. But now that I'm divorcing my husband, now that I woke up, I realize that going to live with my mother was probably what saved them and let them grow up to be what they are today. They're wonderful. Independent. Gorgeous. Smart. Doing great in real estate. I don't know if they'll ever settle down and be housewives, but today, lots of women don't."

"Maybe we ought to introduce them—your girls and my son. Maybe they'd give Rocky a push in the right direction. He's not a bad kid. It's just that he's depressed, I think. And he's having a hard time getting through all this business of the scars."

Nelly looked at her watch. "Goodness, but Reb is running late. Maybe we should rap on the door?"

Britton nodded, got up, and instead of knocking, just opened the door into the gym. Through it, they saw Reb sitting at his desk, in the corner of the gym. He looked up. "Oh, Mr. Britton, are you here to pick up Rocky? Gee, I'm sorry. He didn't make it today. I didn't know you were out there."

And then he saw Nelly. "My gosh, is that you, Mrs. Holachek? You look great for someone who just had surgery. I didn't know you were here. Lizzie's off, and when she's not around you have to ring that little buzzer next to the door to let me know you're out there."

"Oh, boy," said Britton. "I had someone from the office drop me here. I was going to have Rocky take me back to pick up my car. I'm having the oil changed. Can I call a cab?"

"Sure, unless you want to wait until Mrs. Holachek is through and let her drop you. We'll only take about ten minutes or so."

"I'd be glad to give you a lift," said Nelly.

He nodded "I'll gladly accept. I'll wait out here." And Nelly walked past him into the gym.

The exercises were gentle, easy to follow. "I got a list here," Reb said, "and diagrams so you don't forget them. Now, here's the plan. You do the first five just four times each for four days, then increase one a day until you're doing ten. The last three, you start on the fifth day. Twice a day for three days, then increase one a day for three days. Then you come back here. And the other thing is walking. A mile every morning you can. Next time we'll give you a few more demanding moves to make . . ."

Mac stood up when they returned to the waiting room.

"This is very nice of you," he said to Nelly on the way out to her car. "I think the very least a stranded lawyer can do for a speakers' agent who gives him a lift is invite her to dinner. But it's only five. Kind of early. Not for me, though—I didn't have lunch."

"Neither did I," admitted Nelly.

"Well then, I think we should go somewhere and have a late lunch. A very late lunch."

"I'm not dressed for anything very fancy."

"Then we'll forget Le Dome," grinned Britton. "How about Shirttail Charlie's?"

She grinned back. "Perfect."

He helped her into her car. As she started the engine she took a quick peek at this man sitting next to her. That sad look he always seemed to have—right now she could hardly see a trace.

She took him to get his car, then followed him to the restaurant.

It was a delightful dinner. They were the very first customers, eating fresh tuna and sipping chablis as they watched the boats go by on the New River. "I'm not very big on boating," he admitted. "But I love to look down the waterways and see all the different boats docked. I watch them on the Intracoastal—especially the sailboats with those tall masts. There's something so timeless about it."

Nelly nodded. "Here, you see the bridge go up, a train go over, a yacht pull up and turn around. There's so much going on, all at its own pace. Never hurried. And it never stops. I like to watch it, too."

"Whatever your problems are, even the ones you can't seem to solve, you can forget them for a while," he said. "Man has been going down to the sea in ships, shipping goods, making a way of life on ships since he crawled out of caves. It puts problems into perspective."

Nelly was seeing a side of Mac Britton that he had only hinted at before. She had liked the other sides, but this one was more vulnerable, more sensitive. It was so pleasant to sit here watching the boats, letting their conversation meander, with all the gates open, all the guards down. Mac Britton, she decided, was a very special person.

When she arrived home, Nelly found a note taped to her front door. It said, "God will punish those who break their holy marriage vows. He is a stern God to those who break his laws. Repent before it's too late."

The street lamp lit the yard just enough so she could make out the trees and bushes. But if someone was crouching behind the sea grapes, how would she know? She peered up and down the dark street. The sheriff's deputy had told her to do that *always* before she got out of her car. It would be easy for someone to hide behind the bushes and trees in this dusky light, and step out and grab her. She felt the goosebumps rise, quickly fished her keys from her purse, let herself in, and locked the door behind her.

The reading lamp in the living room, the one on the timer, was lit, as it was supposed to be. She hurried through the rooms, switching on lights in every one.

It was empty. Of course, it was empty. What did she expect? Albert was in jail.

Her answerphone was blinking. She pressed the button and grabbed a tablet and pencil. The first message was from Ben Schlesser, asking her to call him at home if she got in after seven—he would be at the office until then. And three calls from people who had signed up for her agency, then changed their minds. One was more upsetting than the others. "Mrs. Holachek, I'm sorry, but as clients of Raymond, Schlesser we can hardly deal with a competing service. Please take our names off your list. People who will behave badly to one person, will behave badly to others."

Strange. Three such calls, right in a row.

Next, a call from Daryl Harding, the radio talk host. Could he do an in-person interview with her about her agency next week? And how did Friday sound?

And then, one more message—the last. No voice at first, just heavy breathing for about thirty seconds. And then a man's throaty voice saying, "God gave us his commandments to keep, not to break."

Nelly shrugged. Some religious nut who read the story in the paper, like the note. Albert was in jail. She was safe.

She got out her makeover strategy checklist and her tapes.

Thirteen

Nelly tried to get her chores out of the way before her mother and the girls got there. She made out the first deposit slip for the new company—a check for $300 from Danny Raymond, delivered by Danny herself. She had insisted that Nelly accept it. "If you're running a business, you have to charge. Don't worry, the firm will pay me back. I'll see to that," she said, tossing her glossy black mane for emphasis. And you're worth twice that. They pay that arrogant C.G. a good salary every week, and Ben's right—she can't do beans if you don't do it for her. And if you don't mind a word of advice, my dear, you should charge an initial sign-up fee. What agency doesn't? All that paperwork? You can't do that for nothing."

And the check for $400 from Britton Llewellen, also delivered by messenger this morning—"A deposit on costs for agency sign-up fees for seven speakers," and for arrangements for the holiday invitation-only brunch on the 28th at which Mac Britton would talk about business conditions in New York.

Sign-up fees? Apparently Danny Raymond was right—they were expected. No one she had signed up so far had been sent forms yet—they were just now being ordered. The thought of calling all of them back made her groan. No, she would add a paragraph to the invitation letter, requesting a small sum, say twenty dollars, or maybe thirty. She could raise it later if that was too low. And she would add a "payment enclosed" blank on the name-and-address form.

She ran to the store for groceries, to a stand on Sunrise for a tree, to the Swap Shop for some of the new button covers for presents for her mother and the girls, and made it back in time to take care of several phone messages by 10 a.m. She hurriedly dragged the Christmas decorations from the garage, freshened her make-up, put on earrings, and ran a comb through her gold-streaked hair.

As she put the kettle on for tea, she heard the car in the drive and ran to the door.

Lauren jumped out of her car and ran down the walk to wrap her arms around her daughter. "Anyella—my little girl. I can't believe it. You look so—so wonderful!" Her voice broke as she stood back and stared. Nelly pulled her inside, and the girls followed. "You can't stare at me out there like that,

Mother," Nelly laughed. "Like you were inspecting me for zits. What will the neighbors think?"

"See, Nana? What did we tell you? Not only a knockout but now she even cracks wise sometimes," said Jane.

Lauren kept studying her daughter's face, and looking her up and down. "I can't tell you how I get goosebumps every time you call me *Mother,*" she said. "And you look better than I had ever dreamed. I *knew* you could be a head turner. But Anyella— Nelly—you're a wonder!"

"Oh, Mother," Nelly cooed happily. "Come on. You'll have me blushing." And they all began talking at once.

"Did we tell you right, Nana?"

"I'm making tea—"

"Did you get a tree?"

"It's in the garage. You girls can decorate it—"

"Oh, Mom, just like the old days!"

"The girls told me about Albert, dear, and showed me the papers. The man's an animal!"

"How's the agency going, Mom? Is that all agency stuff on the table?"

"We need something to eat. We didn't even have breakfast. When we got Nana's call this morning we just packed an overnight case and headed for the airport, and then came straight here."

"I couldn't tell them what plane I'd be on," said Lauren. "They were all overbooked. You know

Christmas. And anyone I might have hitched a ride with had either gone down already, or was full, or leaving after Christmas. So I just packed a bag and went out to La Guardia at dawn on standby, and took the first seat I could get."

"We didn't even go to our aerobics class this morning, and you *know* we never miss," wailed Jane.

"Oh, my gosh," cried Nelly. "Aerobics. I forgot."

"What did you forget dear?" asked Lauren. "Aerobics? On Christmas Eve?"

"No, but there's a Christmas brunch at my guru's gym this morning and I said I'd be there for sure."

"Well, it's only ten," said Emma. "When did it start?"

"Ten."

"Is it very important? You could still get there—"

"It's just that someone was going to be there that—"

"Britton?" cried Emma and Jane together. "The man you thought was so nice?"

"Uhh—well—as a matter-of-fact, he might—"

"Then you're going," said Jane emphatically.

"Definitely," Emma chimed in as they winked at each other and slapped a high five.

"We'll go with you," said Lauren. "If you think it's OK. We're all starved. And what party wouldn't be better with four more gorgeous women on the guest list?"

Nelly grabbed the phone and dialed Stepit's gym.

"Hello, Reb? It's Anyella—Nelly Holachek. Listen, I'm on my way. My mother and my twin daughters just walked in."

"Bring them along," said Reb.

"Oh, they'd *love* to come." She nodded eagerly at her mother. "We'll see you in a few minutes." She turned to the girls. "Back into the car. The tree can wait. It's time for breakfast."

About thirty-five people were milling around the gym when they walked in—four slender, vivacious blondes of varying ages. And thirty-five heads turned. Reb hurried over. "Nelly! Merry Christmas. I'm glad you could come. Whatta quartet you make! How does anyone tell who's the daughter and who's the mother?"

"And who's the grandmother," laughed Lauren. "I'm Lauren James, Anyella's mother. I'm so glad to meet you. I've heard so many nice things about you."

"And these are my daughters, Emma and Jane Holachek," said Nelly. "Reb Stepit."

"Wow!" exclaimed Reb in frank admiration, shaking their hands in turn. "And I think you know this guy," he said to Nelly, pointing to the man striding over to them, Mac Britton. "He doesn't come here to work out, but his son does and Mac pays the bills, so I hadda invite him." He gave Britton a friendly slap on the arm.

"Mother, girls, this is Mac Britton. Mac, this is my mother, Lauren James, and these are my daughters, Emma and Jane."

The twins and Lauren looked him right in the eye in frank appraisal, Nelly noted, each with a kind of tentative smile. It certainly got Mac's attention. His face lit up. "Well, Nelly," he said, "I guess I should have expected it. Like mother, like daughters and vice versa. Beauty is obviously in your genes."

"You say the nicest things," Nelly shot back. And Lauren gave her an approving glance. "Did your son make it?"

"Not yet, but he's coming. He should be here any minute." And sure enough, the door opened and in stepped a young man whose face strongly resembled that of John Kennedy, Jr., the same kind of dark good looks. But he had to be Mac Britton's son. He had his father's very lean, T-square build, electric blue eyes, and a dark brown version of the unruly hair. But he was even taller, about six-feet-four. The expression on his face was unusual, almost haughty. He stood for a moment, letting his eyes slowly sweep the room. Nelly saw several of the younger women stare at him in numb adoration.

"Oh, here he is now," said Reb. "Let me say hello. The food's over there." He pointed to a buffet set up against the opposite wall, where a chef was making omelets to order. "Help yourselves. I gotta go talk to a few of these other people, too."

Jane and Emma looked at Britton. "That's your son?" asked Emma.

"What's he mad about?" asked Jane, but with an impish smile so Britton couldn't take offense."

"What isn't he mad about?" Britton replied with a sigh. "I think he's spotted you."

"You girls check him out," said Lauren. "I'm getting something to eat. That airline breakfast tasted like fried worms."

Rocky spotted his father and slowly strolled over, ignoring the other guests as though they simply weren't there. "Nelly, Rocky," said Britton when his son stood in front of them. "Rocky, this is Nelly Holachek, the lady you almost met here last night when you played hookey. She was the one who gave me a lift over to pick up my car."

"Mrs. Holachek," said Rocky, bowing his head slightly toward her. "Sorry I put you to all that bother."

"Girls, this is Rocky," said Nelly to the twins who were deep in a heated discussion beside her. "Rocky, Emma and Jane."

"Ah, twins," said Rocky. "One more beautiful than the other. Does that mean double the trouble or double the fun?"

"Wouldn't you like to know?" replied Emma, smiling sweetly.

148

"Yeah, I would," he said.

"Careful," said Jane. "Messing with one of us is playing with matches. Messing with two of us is playing with fire."

"Well, it just so happens I know a little something about playing with fire," grinned Rocky. "But I think I need to learn a lot more. The last time I tried it I damn near killed myself. Let's go talk about it over breakfast. I'm hungry as a bear."

"That's probably the one thing we all have in common," said Emma. "Where are the plates?" Rocky took both girls by the arm and steered them toward the buffet.

"A pretty girl can still get his attention," said Britton, watching his son's smooth approach. "I wish something else could." Nelly noticed that look in his eyes again. Clearly this son, and his seemingly total lack of direction, was breaking his father's heart. And it suddenly came to her with undeniable certainty that her own lack of fight, her total and timid acceptance until two weeks ago of whatever life had dealt her, had done the same to her mother all these years.

"You got the check?" Mac asked. "And my note?"

"Yes. Thank you."

"When you get everything organized, you can figure the total cost. But there's no reason to do things on credit until then. You'll be out of business before you get started. A down payment seemed in order."

"Thanks so much. It's all growing so much bigger than I had imagined," said Nelly. "So much faster. I guess I'm going to have to put everything on a computer. We'll probably charge a modest initial sign-up fee, maybe thirty dollars for the time being. We'll get a minimum of forty dollars per booking or 20 percent of the speaker's fee, whichever is higher. In the case of free speakers, I'm not sure yet. Most likely we'll do some freebies for charities, but not all. I'd go broke. I'm getting forms printed and I'll send them to you. I would have done this for nothing, though. I hated just leaving you in the lurch."

"Well, you should take a few days off during the holidays, while you can, after what you've been through. Your mother's spending Christmas with you?"

"And my daughters. The first time in many years. It feels so good that we're all back on the same wavelength again."

"But they don't seem any the worse for being with your mother. They're making a good living, they seem to be enjoying life, and they certainly still care for you. They seem to have their heads screwed on right. I only wish I could say the same for Rocky."

"Will he come to the breakfast when you speak?

That might awaken some interest in the business world."

"No chance. He avoids all such encounters like the plague. He looks on the world of business, law in particular, with contempt."

"Would you mind if I invited him?"

"Please do. But don't be disappointed if he turns you down. You'll be there, though, won't you?"

Nelly nodded. "I wouldn't miss it. I should be there to make sure everything works right, anyway."

She caught Reb Stepit's eye across the room as he beckoned. "Oops. Looks like Reb needs me," she said, excusing herself. Britton watched her go. It was amazing, he mused. He could hardly remember what she looked like the first two times he met her. He recalled only that she was sweet—and totally forgettable, like a piece of the furniture. But now—those expressive eyes, that slim, supple body, that long, slender neck, the surprisingly generous bosom for such a slim build. And that strong sense of empathy. They seemed to really get through to each other. He had already been invited to many social gatherings here in Florida by a dozen different women—and that pesty C.G. kept trying to get him out to lunch again. Since Moira left him, he had been attracting that kind of attention from women in New York, too, and running from it.

Such persistence left a bad taste in his mouth, but Nelly was different. She certainly hadn't been chasing him. He had found himself thinking of her several times in the past week. She was friendly but not forward. If he wanted to explore the possibilities, if there was any chasing to be done in this relationship, *he* was going to have to do it. Nelly, it would seem, didn't care to or simply didn't know how.

C.G. sighed with relief, glad to be finished with Allison Farmer's interview. She was far too well qualified, far too attractive. She had a degree in business and had minored in accounting. She was smart, pleasant to talk to, and understood exactly what was needed in the guidance program. She could probably run the bookings with one hand tied behind her. And she dressed beautifully.

No way. That's all she needed, competition like Allison Farmer right there in the same office. The accounting experience wasn't that critical—all the applicants had some. That was one of the requirements she specified to the agencies. But none of them had so many other attributes, too, which meant that *any* of them would be preferable to Farmer. She buzzed Georgia to send in the next applicant, the morning's last.

"C.G., this is Melissa Lendstone," said Georgia, escorting a small, fortyish, not particularly attractive woman into the office. Lendstone limped slightly, C.G. noticed. "Sit down, dear," she said, scanning the application. "Let me see, you're forty-two and you were working on a degree in accounting when you got married eighteen years ago. You haven't worked at it since. You're newly divorced and need to work. You've lived in Sunrise since you were four years old. OK. Now, do you understand what this job entails?"

"I think so," said Melissa Lendstone in a hushed little voice. "It's to help clients keep records and documentation and such. To help them save, sort, and cross-check everything so it's easy to handle at income tax time."

"Essentially, that's it. Or that's a big part of it," agreed C.G. "We play that by ear. We determine if there's anything special required for a given client's return and then we guide them accordingly. I also require intense loyalty. There are factions in all corporations and this one is no different."

A tiny wrinkle appeared on the applicant's smooth brow. "I understand," she said.

"There's another service we perform here. I'm hiring two people and probably both will have to help with this one at first. A former employee used to do it, so now our clients expect it. And the partners here want to keep them happy."

Melissa nodded again and waited for C.G. to continue.

"We act as a sort of booking agency for many of our clients," said C.G., launching into a description of Nelly's service. Lendstone was not fazed. She said, "Well, I've never done anything exactly like that before, but I would certainly do my best."

C.G. smiled. "Who could ask more than that?" She rose slowly from her desk. "Well, I have your resumé and the information we requested about salary requirements and so on. I think you would probably be able to handle the job. And you'll probably get it, but I do have a few interviews to finish up. I'll call you sometime this afternoon or perhaps not until tomorrow. Can you find your way out?"

Melissa Lendstone stood up. "Thank you very much," she said uncertainly, backing out of the office.

When she closed the door behind her, C.G. wanted to let out a triumphant hoot. She was perfect. Timid, not very pretty, mousy and uncertain, just like Nelly had been. She had the training, the motivation, she was local. The limp didn't keep her from doing anything, but it might make it a little more difficult for her to find another job. No competition at all. Perfect! She dialed Georgia. "Send in the next one, will you?"

At a quarter to twelve, she finished the last interview. She had just a few minutes before she had to leave for the Sky Club and her lunch with Boz Richter, the head of the huge Marlborough Condo Association in West Fort Lauderdale. She had met him before—a big, husky, good-natured fellow of about sixty or so. There was no real reason to have lunch with him, but she'd think of something to discuss. She had read his wife's obituary exactly one month ago, and one had to move quickly. Those widows would swarm all over him and someone would snap him up.

But she had time for a phone call or two. She pulled out the little book in which she had put all the numbers she intended to call about Nelly. She dialed the first one without a checkmark in front of it, the Anderson School of Country Dance.

"Mr. Anderson? This is Mrs. Clemency-Graves at Raymond, Schlesser, McKinnon, and Goldberg."

"Ah, yes, Mrs. Graves. What can I do for you?"

"It's about your bookings."

"Oh, yes. You've got something for us?"

"Well, not just now, but we will, of course. I just wanted to be sure that Mrs. Holachek hadn't done anything. I don't know how to put this, Mr. Anderson—"

"Mrs. Holacheck? She's the lady who books us."

"Yes. Only now, she has taken all the names of people we used to do this for free, and is charging them money to do it. And in some cases she is taking their money ahead of time and then not—no, I don't want to tell any of those stories. They're too upsetting. But we do want you to be warned, in case she approaches you. She does *not* represent this firm anymore, and we deplore her taking advantage of our clients. Please remember, if you deal with her, it's at your own risk. I wish I could tell you more."

"Well, I'll be! And she always seemed so nice on the phone. We've never met her, but—"

"I don't want to tell you any stories, but I just don't want it to happen to you—in case she calls you."

"I sure thank you for warning me, Mrs. Graves. And don't you worry, now that we know. We weren't born yesterday. And any booking you get for our dancers, we'll be glad to take it."

C.G. hung up. Another one that wouldn't use Nelly. Why didn't she feel better about it? Why did she feel instead as though she had done something dreadful? Shameful? Four or five such calls a day, maybe twenty or twenty-five a week, being careful to imply, not to state any thing, would really affect Nelly's agency. If she could make them. But somehow, she wasn't sure she had the stomach for it.

Not today, anyway. She would make calls about the Woman of Our Time luncheon instead. Every organization officer she had talked to thus far, from the Red Cross, Miami City Ballet, and the Heart Association, was interested. She had planted a seed in each of their minds that might grow to a sponsorship. "I heard that you would be taking part in the new Woman of Our Time award luncheon," she had said to each. "Who told me that? Sorry, I just can't remember. It was at a luncheon last week, I believe. Someone said she had heard that you were going to undertake it. I just wanted you to know I would help in any way I can. It's a wonderful idea."

Little by little the word would get around. The luncheon would fly—she was sure about that now. And they would certainly appreciate her more here, when she was named Woman of Our Time.

Humming happily, she turned her answerphone on and grabbed her purse. She would freshen up her make-up at the Sky Club. She didn't want to be late.

Yes, it had been a good morning. And now, perhaps this Boz character might turn out to be interesting. And, hopefully, interested in her. You had to keep trying. Life was so much better with someone to care for you and look after you—and for you to care for and look after. Alone, you were so vulnerable. Life was a scramble—sometimes it hardly seemed worth the effort. The shortage of men was so frustrating, but maybe she'd be lucky today.

Emmet spotted her while he was taking the order at table 17. Her table, number 12, wasn't in his station today. But there she was. Wearing her pearls. Nemo, one of the other waiters, once said that if Claire Clemency-Graves was ever in a horrendous accident that destroyed her teeth and they had to identify the body, they could do it by those pearls. Emmet thought they looked magnificent—he thought everything about Claire Clemency-Graves was magnificent: her splendid carriage; the grand way she waved those graceful, long-fingered hands when she talked; that deep contralto voice mulling over menu choices. She had been his fantasy for fifteen years—and his friend, in a way. She had often reported his exemplary service to the current manager—they came and went. She had no idea that Emmet was more than just a waiter there. Neither had the manager. But several times, in the years when her husband Reggie was alive and they had entertained at the Sky Club frequently, she had slipped him an extra ten or twenty when she felt her husband's tip was inadequate. Since Reggie had passed away, she hadn't come in as often. Until she began working for Raymond, Schlesser, that is. Now she was here once a week or so entertaining clients.

Somehow, he had to report to her what he'd heard. But was that man with her a friend or foe? It wasn't anyone from Raymond, Schlesser that he knew of. He'd better play it cool. Should he write her a note? No. Evidence could backfire. The partners might somehow see it and object. Oh, but here she was coming this way, toward the ladies' room.

Good. He stood right there in the hallway and as she approached, he said quietly, "Mrs. Clemency-Graves, I have something I think I should tell you."

She stopped, digested those few words, and pulled

him into the alcove that the rest rooms opened onto. "What is it, Emmet?"

"I overheard the partners talking about you last week," he said. "At their Monday breakfast here. About you and Mrs. Holachek, and I thought I should tell you."

"I appreciate that, Emmet. What were they saying?"

Emmet looked up and down the hall and then whispered, "Schlesser was saying they shouldn't have put you over Mrs. Holachek and that she does all the work, and you just go out to lunch a lot. Raymond was defending you. He got kind of hot and said, 'Well, it's done now and its working and why do we keep talking about it? Leave it be.' "

C.G. pondered his words. Nothing new, but it underlined what she previously thought. Schlesser was the enemy. Raymond, for reasons of his own, was her ally for now, unless she went to his wife. The others were neutral. She pulled her card and a ten dollar bill from her bag and put them in his hand. "Emmet, I can't thank you enough. You're a good friend. If you hear anything more, please call me." She squeezed his arm and entered the ladies' room.

Emmet stood there a moment, savoring a sensual thrill from the spot on his arm where she had just touched him. How dare Nelly Holachek cause trouble for her? Holachek was the woman who hadn't selected him to speak about fancy restaurant desserts at that seminar that time. And who knew more about them? She had lunched here with C.G. once or twice, he was pretty sure, but for the life of him he couldn't remember exactly what she looked like.

Oh, how he wished there was something he could do to help C.G. He couldn't think of a thing, off-hand. Except to keep his ears and eyes open and report anything he heard that could be of interest. Immediately. And if Holachek ever came in for lunch at his station, he'd give her the worst possible service. No, he took too much pride in his work and the Sky Club standards to do that. He'd have to figure out something else.

Fourteen

"It's beginning to feel a lot like Christmas," Nelly sang along with the kitchen radio. She slid the cookie pans into the oven and set the timer. The twins couldn't imagine a Christmas at home without her Magic Bars.

"Every Chistmas away, that's what we missed the most," said Emma. They and Lauren had put up the tree and decorated it, and were now doing the yard. The phone rang.

"Doesn't it ever stop?" grumbled Nelly, reaching for it. "How did people live before telephones were invented?" It was Ben Schlesser.

"I hope I'm not calling too late, Nelly," he said. "Two things. One, I have something for you that I want to deliver today; then a technician will come in the day after Christmas or whenever it's convenient and install it and tell you what you need to know to use it. But it's the same kind you've used at the office so I don't think you'll have any problems."

"For me? Ben, I never thought you—I don't know what to say."

"Don't say anything. And the other thing—did your family get there?"

"Yes. They put up the tree and I made cookies and we're humming carols. We haven't had a Christmas together in five years."

"Well, let me just run this by you. I wanted to be sure you didn't spend Christmas alone. But if you were planning to, I was going to take you out to dinner. Now, you may have already been cooking up a storm. Or you may have plans to go out. But if not, I would like to invite all of you to dinner. I made a reservation at Burt and Jack's, just in case."

"Oh, Ben, I can't let you—"

"Yes, you can. It would be my pleasure, Nelly. But I don't want to intrude if you'd rather be alone with your family."

"Wait a minute," she said laughing. "Let me take a vote."

She hurried outside where Jane was up on a ladder fastening one end of a string of lights to the orchid tree, while Emma held the rest of the string ready and Lauren directed.

"Listen, Mother, girls. One of my bosses at work, the one who's on my side and who took me out last night—he's inviting us all to dinner tonight at Burt and Jack's. But he'll understand if we want to be together alone. Isn't that nice of him?"

162

"Burt and Jack's is my favorite restaurant here," said Lauren.

"I'd ask him to come here, but I was just going to order pizza. I wasn't planning to cook that turkey until tomorrow."

"And he's your friend?" asked Lauren. "Well, I think that's damned nice of him. He really must like you. I vote for him and Burt and Jack's."

"I always vote with Nana," said Jane. "She might cut our allowance if I didn't."

"I always vote for Burt and Jack's," giggled Emma.

"And he says he's bringing me something. I never thought of getting anything for him."

"Now, wasn't that nice of him," said Lauren. "Don't keep him waiting on the phone. Ask how soon we should be dressed."

While they were changing, Nelly received two more calls. One from Boz Richter, the condo association president whose wife, she heard, had died suddenly a month ago. "Mrs. Holachek, I had lunch today with Mrs. Clemency-Graves—your former boss, I guess. And I don't know if I'm butting into something I should butt out of, but I wonder if you and I could have lunch or dinner one day next week. Anyplace convenient for you."

"You don't want to just talk on the phone, Mr. Richter?"

"No, I think I want to do this in person. You're not working there anymore?"

"No. I'm starting a speakers' agency and I'm pretty much doing that out of my home for now."

"Where's that? We can meet somewhere nearby."

"I'm in Plantation, but I'm downtown a lot. How about the L&N on Federal Highway?"

"I know the one you mean. What day and what time?"

She had no sooner hung up when Mac Britton called. "Nelly, I'm almost embarrassed to do this at the last minute, but my son insisted. We were just planning to have Christmas dinner by ourselves. We're having it catered here in my apartment at two, tomorrow. But he says I must call and invite you and your daughters and your mother to join us. I think he's really taken with your twins, and he thinks your mother is something else. Her candor intrigues him. So let me repeat the invitation. This dinner will be ten times as pleasant for us if you four can be there. When Rocky and I are alone, we just endure a truce. I don't have much patience with him anymore. And he doesn't have much with me. You wouldn't have to dress up. We won't. And we've already called the caterer and they can do it easily. I know it's a lot to ask, but—"

"No, not at all. It would rescue me from having to thaw and cook that darn turkey tomorrow," said Nelly. "Wait a minute until I ask the others."

She called Lauren from the guest room and led her into the girls' room. "Another vote, another invitation. For tomorrow—the four of us. A catered Christmas dinner with Mac Britton and his son in Mac's apartment, which I think is a grand oceanfront place way north of here. At two. Casual dress."

"Oh, isn't this exciting?" said Lauren. "Your mother has barely crawled out of her cocoon and she already has two suitors."

"Three," Nelly corrected her with a smug grin. "That other call was from Boz Richter—to ask me to lunch or dinner."

"Well, tell Mr. Britton we'd be delighted," said Lauren. "We'll be there with bells on. Right, girls?"

The twins nodded and said, "Right!"

When Ben arrived, his Mercedes was followed into the driveway by a small truck. Nelly threw open the door, ran out, and cried, "Merry Christmas! Come in. You found it all right?"

Ben beckoned to the truck's driver, who hopped out and unloaded a wheeled wagon on which he then stacked several boxes of varying sizes, then followed Ben and Nelly inside.

"Ben, this is my mother, Lauren James. And these are my daughters, Emma and Jane. Ladies, this is Ben Schlesser, as in Raymond, Schlesser, McKinnon, and Goldberg."

"Happy Chanukah," said Jane with a grin. "See our pretty Chanukah bush?"

Lauren took Ben's hand and shook it. "I'm so glad to meet you. Any friend of my daughter's is a friend of mine."

"Ditto," chorused Jane and Emma.

The driver deposited the boxes in the dining room and began opening them. "Sorry, no pretty wrapping," said Ben. "I don't know where you'll want to put all this, but you can decide that later. Is it OK to unpack it all right here?"

Nelly nodded. "Yes, fine. Wherever you think. I'm dying of curiosity. What is it?"

"A computer—IBM compatible. The same kind you've used in the office for the guidance files, so you'll know how to use it. It has the software, a printer, keyboard, monitor, two boxes of printout paper, ribbons, disks, instruction manuals—the works."

Nelly was aghast. "Ben, I can't let you do this."

"Oh, yes, you can. I have to do it, Nelly, to live with myself. We've treated you so badly. And that woman is diabolical, but I can't seem to quite convince the others. It's Will. For some reason he's on her side. I can't think why."

"He hired her and did the promotion. Maybe he hates to admit he made a bad choice."

"Well, whatever the reason, the results have been shameful. And sooner or later we'll have to face it." He handed her a card. "This is the computer service to call. He'll come out and show you whatever you need to know and how to connect it all. I haven't the foggiest idea how or I'd do it now. It's all arranged and taken care of—all you have to do is call."

"I don't know what to say," gasped Nelly.

"Try *thank you,*" said Lauren. "I still have to tell you everything, Nelly."

"Oh, Mr. Schlesser," blurted Jane. "That's the nicest thing you could do. Mom has been absolutely buried in paper."

"OK. Enough said," said Ben. "Let's go to dinner. Can we all fit in my car?"

"Sure, and we can sing carols on the way," said Emma. "Isn't this a perfectly beautiful Christmas Eve?"

Fifteen

They opened their presents before breakfast Christmas morning. Lauren gave Nelly and the twins gift certificates from Saks and Neiman's. The twins gave their grandmother two antique pepper grinders for her collection, and their mother a tailored suit, a washable silk pant suit, and a long black beaded gown. Nelly gave them each four sets of striking button covers and written IOUs for a future present that read, "Once my agency takes off and I have some money I will buy you something splendid."

"You've already given us the best present we could imagine," said Lauren. The girls nodded, and Emma went to turn the air conditioning on full blast and then lit a fire in the fireplace.

"There's one thing more I want from you three," Nelly said. "I know there are still a few expressions that I use that are rather stilted. Out of place. I need you to tell me better ways of saying the same thing.

And if you hear me say something awkwardly, please, tell me a better way to put it."

"We'll do it," said Jane. "No problem."

"And also, I notice that when you're introduced to someone, you all manage to grab their attention in no uncertain terms. I need you to teach me how to do the same thing."

"That's easy. You look right into their eyes," said Lauren. "Keep your eyes glued on theirs like they're the most fascinating person you've met all week."

"You don't try to say much. You let them talk and listen to what they say. Hang on every word. And have a very friendly expression in your eyes," added Jane.

"Soft," said Emma. "Or kind. Sexy. Knowing. Anything but blah. And a hint of a smile. Sexy and friendly all at once."

"Come to the hallway mirror," ordered Lauren. "Now pretend you're just meeting me. Introduce us, Jane."

"Mrs. Devin Lure, I'd like you to meet a friend of mine, Sally Gotrocks. Sally, this is Anyella Devin Lure."

Nelly took her mother's hand and said, "I'm very glad to—"

"Try *delighted,*" said Lauren.

"Mrs. Gotrocks, I'm delighted to meet you—"

"More accent on *delighted,*" her mother interrupted. "So it sounds like you really mean it. 'I'm *delighted* to meet you.'"

Nelly nodded and took her mother's hand again. "Mrs. Gotrocks, I'm so *delighted* to meet you." She looked at her mother with as pleasant a half-smile as she could summon.

"That's it!" cried Jane.

"By George, I think she's got it," cried Emma.

"Now, if it's *Mister* Gotrocks, it's a little different," said Lauren. "You can say the same thing, but you want to be a little seductive. Tilt your head back just a bit and close your eyelids a fraction of an inch. Try it."

Nelly took her mother's hand and lifted her head back and half-closed her eyes.

"No, Mom," said Emma, shaking her head. "Not that much. You look like you're stoned."

Nelly tried it again. "Mr. Gotrocks, I'm *delighted* to meet you." Then she added, "I've heard so much about you from the twins."

Her three teachers let out a whoop. "You're skipping ahead to the next lesson," giggled Jane.

After an hour of working on introductions and thank-yous, the twins called time out. "You're doing great, Mom, but people can only absorb so much at a time."

"But I have so much to learn," wailed Nelly.

"Not really. You're an A-student. You already know most of it by instinct," said Emma. "Because you've picked up a lot just from being around three of the most charming people in the state."

"But one other thing, daughter," said Lauren,

"you want to stand up as straight as you can, always. You used to seem to shrink up, somehow. I don't see you doing it now at all, but I think you could stand just a bit straighter." She gave Nelly a light rap on the back and Nelly jerked upright. "That's it. There's always something regal about people who stand tall and proud."

"OK, enough for now, Nana," said Jane. "School's out. Time to figure out what incredibly smart outfits we're going to wear to the Brittons' dinner. Mom, I think that washable silk pantsuit. He'll go absolutely ape. And let's wrap up a package of the Magic Bars."

"I'll do it," said Emma. "The way to a man's heart is through passion—for homemade cookies as well as sex."

They found the Glades Terrace easily enough. But when they told the man at the desk who they were visiting, he directed them to the elevator to the penthouse. "The penthouse?" repeated Nelly, dismayed.

"Too late to change your mind now, Mom," said Emma.

The twins held her hands in the elevator on the way up. "Maybe I'll just get off and go back downstairs and let you three go up for dinner," she groaned at the fifteenth floor.

"Pretend you're somewhere else, Mom," said Jane.

"Relax, we're almost there," soothed Emma as her mother squeezed her hand until it hurt, then gasped, as if she was desperate for oxygen. Britton's oversized front door was just opposite the elevator and he was waiting there for them when the twins and Lauren helped Nelly stagger off.

"Good Lord, what's the matter?" he cried, reaching to help her through the door.

"Oh, that's just how Mom handles elevator rides in really tall buildings," explained Jane. "She collapses with fear."

"Or gets hysterical," added Emma.

"Or both," added Lauren. "She'll be all right in a minute if she can sit down." Britton nodded and eased Nelly into a chair.

She caught her breath, and reached into her purse for a hankie to blot her face. "I'm so sorry. It's just that I'm so afraid of elevators. Sometimes it's not so bad."

"But at your job—" began Britton . . .

"She's OK if it's only ten or twelve floors," explained Emma. "It's skyscrapers that get to her."

"My office," he said. "You managed that."

"No, I really didn't. But each time, I had a few minutes to settle down. I'm fine after a minute or two, and I'm determined to get over it. Sometimes lately, I don't even want to kill myself." They all laughed at that but Britton looked a trifle impatient, Nelly thought. It was probably hard for him to understand. A person who is used to being in control has a hard time comprehending such a weakness.

Jane handed him the tin of cookies. "Hope you like these. Mom always has to make a double batch because Emma and I can eat a whole pan of Magic Bars at one sitting."

"Magic Bars!" cried Mac. "I haven't seen those in years. I used to be addicted to them."

Jane turned to look out the windows. "Wow, whatta view! It's better than yours, Nana."

The apartment wrapped around two sides of the Glades Terrace's north wing, affording a 270-degree sweep, even broader than the panorama from Britton's office. "I told them to find me something with more than just the ocean view. Unless you're on a cut, or an entrance channel, at night there's nothing to see."

"True," agreed Lauren. "My first apartment on the beach, I made that mistake. But my place now has two views. One west to the city and one east to the ocean. But it's not like this. Then again, I'm not there more than two or three months a year. I spend more time in New York and London."

"Speaking of magnificent views, where is the handsome hunk?" asked Emma. "Or did we scare him away when we said we'd come?"

Britton laughed. "He doesn't scare easily. He ran

173

out to get some packages to put under the tree. He decorated it this morning."

Lauren inspected his handiwork. "I think he needed the girls to help him," she chortled and Britton laughed with her. The star on top tilted at a rakish angle. The tinsel hung in clusters on some parts, while others were virtually bare. The lights, too, were strung heavily on one branch, skimpily on another. Some twinkled on and off, some glowed steadily. One string was totally out. "Don't say anything," said Britton. "It was his first try."

A uniformed waiter rolled in a cart, loaded with a punch bowl of eggnog and various bottles of imbibables. "If you don't see what you like, just ask," Mac said.

As the twins accepted cups of eggnog, the front door burst open and Rocky strode in, toting three bulging shopping bags. "Hi, gang," he said with a grin. "Sorry I'm late. I had to get a few things for under the tree." Humming "Jingle Bells," he dumped the bags in front of the tree, arranged the packages under it, and handed the empty bags to the waiter.

"Dad, the tapes," he said. Britton quickly hopped up and switched on the stereo. The soft sounds of "Hark the Herald Angels Sing" filled the room. Emma and Jane exchanged puzzled glances. This was the condescending, bored fellow they'd met at Stepit's gym? "And the candles," said Rocky, pulling a pack of matches from a desk drawer and lighting those on the mantel and buffet along with two tall, thick ones on the coffee table. His father quickly turned the lights off.

Rocky called out, "Hohoho," picked four silver-wrapped boxes from under the tree, and handed them to Lauren, the twins, and Nelly. "This is all Rocky's doing," said Britton. "I have no idea what he's up to." The four women eagerly unwrapped their packages.

"I thought we needed a touch of Santa," said Rocky. "It's not easy to get in the Christmas mood when you're surrounded by beaches and palm trees and no snow."

Emma got her box open first. "What a beautiful mirror," she cried. It was oval shaped, with an ornately sculpted sterling silver back. Jane and Lauren and Nelly in turn pulled similar mirrors from their packages.

"They're Turkish. The Turks hang them with the mirror to the wall and the silver side out," Rocky explained. "But those faces were made for looking into mirrors."

"Why, thank you, Rocky. How very sweet of you," said Lauren. She turned to Britton. "We may just adopt this kid of yours."

The waiter came out again to check for refills and nodded at Britton, who stood up and said, "We may as well go in and sit down. They tell me dinner is ready." Father and son each escorted two ladies into the dining room, a large paneled chamber off the living room, with bookcases lining an entire wall and a broad, screened-in terrace adjacent. "We decided to do it indoors," said Rocky. "Too humid outside."

Over lump crabmeat cocktails they watched a string of sailboats heading out to sea. "Doesn't that look like fun, sailing in a group that way," said Jane.

"My last husband, Edgar James, was really into boating," said Lauren. "We belonged to four yacht clubs, and he was always sailing off to Bimini or Ocean Reef. The twins were with us then. They went on a few of those real sailing expeditions where everybody works his tail off. But the girls and I really preferred power boats with a captain that runs it all for you. A sailboat can be so hard on your nails."

"But we sort of know what to do," said Emma. "We went on a few sailboats with Edgar, too. You couldn't live in the same house with him for five years without learning more about boats than anyone really needs to know. Even at home he called the upstairs the upper deck, the roof terrace was topside, and the bathrooms were heads."

"We get asked to go sailing all the time," said Emma, "because people think we can carry our weight. But we have no time. We've been racing flat out expanding our real estate business. We have a few people we can count on now, but we still work like beavers. If you want to be top-notch, you can't let anything get in the way."

"Could you take off long enough for an outing day after tomorrow?" asked Rocky. "The Sea Rats Yacht Club is running a—"

"The Sea Rats Yacht Club?" repeated his father. "Where the hell is that? You're pulling my fin. I've never heard of it."

"They don't have a real clubhouse. But between them, their members belong to every yacht club in South Florida. They have meetings in members' homes or boats, and they do outings and rendezvous at member's clubs. They're dead serious about sailing. The wives and kids take second place. I was invited out with them once before, but I couldn't make it that time."

"Oh, yes, I remember them," said Lauren. "Edgar sailed with them to Ocean Reef a couple of times."

"Ordinarily, we'd probably have to say no," said Emma. "But things might ease up this week because of the holidays. What do you think, Jane? Could we play hookey?"

"That's the day of your brunch and lecture," Nelly said to Britton. He nodded. She thought Mac looked just a trifle uneasy, but Rocky was wired. This cool, condescending young man-about-town was friendly, eager to please, and soooo charming. She couldn't quite figure him out. But here in the dining room with all that sunlight pouring in from the terrace

177

windows, she could see clearly the facial scars Britton had told her about. And a patch of scar tissue on his left hand.

Oh, well, she shrugged mentally as the waiter passed a huge silver platter of sliced turkey, sweet potatos, and cornbread stuffing. She might as well enjoy the meal. What could taste better on Christmas than turkey and cornbread stuffing?

When they started to leave at four, Rocky pulled out a Trivial Pursuit game and talked them into staying another hour. He pressed them to stay even longer, but Jane explained that they had to go. "We have a number of things to help Mom with. We're hooking up her new computer, and she needs it by tomorrow," she said smoothly, stretching the truth in several directions.

Britton, on the other hand, seemed almost relieved. "Thanks for the cookies," he said. "And thanks for joining us. I'm riding down in the elevator with you."

"Oh, no," cried Nelly. "I'll be fine. Going down might be better than going up. And the more people in the car, the more jitttery I get." That was a bit of fudging, too. The truth was she didn't want Mac Britton to see her come unglued on the ride down. He seemed, at this point, to like her. It was a good feeling, and she didn't want to lose it.

He shook hands with each of them at the door, Nelly last. "Well, see you at the brunch," he said. "It's all set?"

"Right. Not forty people, though. It was up to sixty when I last counted, and it could be more by tomorrow. We didn't get the usual number of regrets. Everyone wants to come and bring someone. Your office is taking care of the food. No point in trying another caterer when the one you have does so well. And thanks for everything today, Mac." The elevator doors opened. He watched her turn resolutely, take a deep breath, and step bravely inside—like Lady Jane Gray walking toward her beheading.

Back at the house, they found another note taped to the door. "A marriage vow is a pledge to God. Those who break their pledge will invoke His wrath. Beware the wrath of God."

"What kind of fanatic writes notes like that?" asked Emma. "Did you call the police?"

"Yes," said Nelly, turning the key in the lock. "They came to get the first one and said that it's probably because of the thing in the paper when your father broke in here. The piece said we were estranged. The sheriff's office said it's probably a cult that's been leaving messages like that in the area lately, all to people who had been in the paper for one reason or another right before they got the note—the articles always mentioned they were divorced or separated. A couple of them were mothers with illegitimate kids or unmarried women living with boyfriends. The police didn't seem too concerned—all they've had so far is notes."

"So far?" repeated Lauren. "I don't like it. Didn't they tell you to take any precautions?"

"The same things they said before. Be very careful getting out of the car and going into the house to be sure there's no one around. But Albert's in jail. Who else would do anything?"

"Any one of thousands of nuts who do unspeakable things to people all the time, Mom," said Emma. "Wake up. They're out there."

"And any nut who read that article figures you're living alone now," said Jane.

"I'm getting rid of this house," said Lauren. "Get a condo for you instead, with security."

"Mother, you've done enough for me. Let me make some money from this agency and I'll buy an apartment myself."

"No, we can't wait," said Lauren.

"Or *we* could get one for you," said Jane and Emma in unison.

"But an apartment won't have a real fireplace, most likely," said Nelly. "Brrr! It's freezing in here. We forgot to turn the air conditioner down before we left."

"Good excuse for another fire," said Jane. She

and Emma busied themselves arranging more logs and tinder and paper in the fireplace, then lit it. Nelly put on a tape of carols and the four of them plopped down on the carpet in front of the flames and hummed along.

"You know what I think?" asked Nelly. "I think you girls might be able to help me a little with this agency business. You meet everyone in Miami, and I'll need a little help getting automated. Minny will help me, but it's just getting so big so fast. I think it'll make a lot of money and I'd like you to learn something about it. It'll be yours someday, and it would be nice to work together on something, even if you could only spare a couple of hours a week."

The girls looked at each other meaningfully, as they often did, talking in their own verbal shorthand, reading each other's minds.

"Hm?" said Emma. "If you think—"

"Right," nodded Jane. "And the time. But we have—"

"Right. So long as one of us—. We won't waste time on—"

"Just the big stuff. And we have—"

They both turned to Nelly as Emma said, "Good idea, Mom. We'll work it out."

"One of us will be up here one day next week," said Jane. "We'll help you computerize everything. When we get back tonight, we'll check our schedules, and make a list of people you can probably use."

Emma got up and put more wood on the fire. The tape was playing "Little Drummer Boy." Lauren drummed lightly in time on the coffee table with a pencil. They hummed along, staring at the crackling orange flames and feeling close.

"It's like we've turned the clock back twenty-five years," sighed Lauren, contentedly. "It's so wonderful seeing you become the person you really are, Nelly. And being together like this, just the four of us, is the sweetest part of all."

Sixteen

Yesterday's, her favorite restaurant, was packed, but C.G. always got a good table. She and Reggie had been regulars here, too. She especially loved it this time of year when it was swathed in twinkling Christmas lights. But during this dinner with her brother she was for too agitated to enjoy the decorations, much less the food.

"I don't know why you bothered to come down if all you're going to do is scold and preach," she said indignantly, dabbing at her eyes with her hankie. "Whose side are you on?"

"You know I'm on yours, but not blindly so," said Barton. "I don't want to see you do something you'll feel guilty about for the rest of your life, Claire. Nelly Holachek has done nothing to you, absolutely nothing. You've used her shamelessly. Of course she rebelled. Who wouldn't?"

He cut into his steak with angry jabs. "And this Woman of Our Time farce is preposterous. Sooner or later, a few of these people you're talking into this thing will put two and two together and figure out that the whole idea was by you, and *for* you. I can't think why having a big name in this city has suddenly become so important to you."

"I'll be a more valuable employee. Everything I do will be noticed. I'll be at the top of the totem pole instead of near the bottom. I despise it at the bottom, Bart. And that's where I've been since Reggie died. I need to be someone on my own."

Barton deLys looked at his sister sadly. "Well, when you decide you've become someone on your own, I hope you find it's worth the price you've paid."

"I think you've said quite enough, dear brother," she snapped angrily, looking down at the barely touched slab of beef on her plate. "You've managed to ruin this Christmas dinner. I'm so upset I can't swallow. I'd like to go home. And the next time you come down, if you can't change your tune, please don't bother to call."

Nelly tiptoed around the house the next morning, trying not to awaken her mother. But Lauren never slept that soundly—she was up by eight. They sat in the kitchen talking for a time, neither in a hurry to start the day. In fact, both were still in their robes when the doorbell rang at 8:30.

When Nelly started for the door, her mother

stopped her. "Ask who it is first, dear. Like the Sheriff's man told you."

From behind the locked door Nelly called, "Who is it?"

She was shocked to hear a man's voice. "Barton, Nelly. Barton deLys."

She quickly opened the door. "Barton! Goodness, I didn't even know you were in town. Come in," she cried, pulling him inside. "Oh, this is my mother, Lauren James."

"So glad to meet you," said Barton.

"And I'm so delighted to meet *you*," said Lauren, looking right into his eyes and smiling a tentative half-smile. "You'll be kind enough to forgive our formal dress, I trust?"

"You look upset," said Nelly. "Is anything wrong? Your sister?"

"She's fine. No, she's not OK. She's practically deranged. That's what I've come to see you about. I know it's ridiculously early but I'm flying back this morning, and I *had* to talk to you."

"Why don't we all go into the kitchen?" suggested Lauren. "We'll have a cup of tea while you discuss whatever it is that's upsetting you."

"That would be kind of you," said Barton. "And I must say I'm so happy to meet Nelly's mother. I've heard so much about you."

"No, that's supposed to be my line," said Lauren.

"A family joke," explained Nelly quickly.

185

"And your daughter is one of my favorite people," Barton added.

"Isn't that a coincidence," said Lauren warmly. "Mine, too. You're clearly a man of taste." While he and Nelly sat down at the kitchen table, she began preparing tea and toast.

Barton took a deep breath and began. "Nelly, my sister is holding it against you that you quit. I have explained to her until I'm blue in the face that she provoked it, that she had been taking advantage of you, bullying you, taking credit for your work—and that you had every right to quit. But she feels you left her in the lurch. I've explained over and over that if she had been helping at all with the bookings and guidance, she wouldn't have found herself up the creek, as it were.

"Everything in your office has just ground to a halt. I mean everything. Hardly anybody has been getting any guidance visits. Nobody's been able to arrange any bookings. I knew she was letting you carry more of the workload, but even I didn't realize how lopsided it was. She's had to hire two people to replace you, to try to set up some sort of booking service and get the guidance rolling again. And even that may not work."

"But that's not my fault, Bart," said Nelly gently. "Except that maybe I should have given her a few more days' notice instead of an ultimatum. But I didn't, and it's done now."

"I know, my dear, I know. I'm just telling you so you'll understand how frustrated and angry she is."

"The bottom line," said Lauren, putting the toast, cups, and teapot on the table, "is, what is this anger and frustration leading her to do? If you'll forgive me for butting in, is she going to punish Nelly? Get back at her?" She poured their tea, set a plate with two pieces of warm buttered toast on it in front of Barton, and pushed the sugar and jam toward him.

"I'm afraid so. And I'm talking to a deaf person when I try to reason with her. Deaf and indignant."

"But what would she do?" asked Lauren.

"I don't know. I can't think of much that she *could* do, except badmouth you. She may do that. I've never seen her so vindictive. She's been a different person since Reggie died. She might have looked down her nose at some people before, but she would never have really hurt anyone. I think she might try to give you some grief with your new agency if she can figure out a way."

"I wonder if that's why those three people called the day before Christmas to change their minds about signing up. They'd heard something about us. I'll bet it was C.G."

"I really don't know for sure, but I wouldn't be surprised. I'm wondering if there isn't something we can do to persuade her to just forget the whole thing."

Nelly took a thoughtful sip of her tea, and then

shook her head. "I can't think of anything. She was absolutely furious with me on the phone when I quit and it doesn't sound like she's changed her mind."

Lauren had been observing Barton deLys carefully during this exchange. He had the weathered skin of an outdoorsman, the grooming of an English aristocrat, the hooded eyes of a Frenchman. He had had an almost fatherly attitude toward her daughter when he arrived, but now he stared frankly at Nelly with a puzzled expression. "Nelly, dear, you *have* changed. You're so different."

"I told you I was going to, Barton. And I did. My hair, and I had my eyes done—."

"There's more to it than your appearance, although I certainly do see the difference."

"I know. It's the way I think, the way I talk."

Barton nodded. "Yes, the way you talk. You seem so much more confident, outgoing. Your voice is so—so—melodic. But how could you change so quickly?"

"I just say what's on my mind now, Bart. Before I used to think in color and talk in black and white. I was so afraid I'd offend someone, afraid to disagree. No more. It was so easy. When I can't come up with exactly how to say something, I just try to imagine how my mother would put it."

Barton nodded eagerly. "Yes, I see it. I hear it. I'm in awe." He turned toward Lauren and confided, "She told me she was going to do all this—an about-face, changing everything—the last time I was down. But who would have expected she really meant it? Or so *much* of a change. It's incredible."

Lauren beamed. "It was all there before, Mr. deLys. Nelly was a bright, bubbly, adorable child. But she was squelched unmercifully by her father, and then by her husband. All she's really done now is set her real self free."

"If my sister sees you, she might be even angrier, though," he said. "That you've come out of this so well. Oh, and there's one other thing that's really upsetting me. I want to run it by you again—that Woman of Our Time business. I've talked myself blue in the face about that, too, but she's plunging ahead anyway."

Nelly sighed. "I couldn't get her to listen either. When C.G. sets her mind on something, she's a locomotive—not easy to stop."

"That's probably true only if you're too particular about what means you use to stop her," suggested Lauren. "Excuse me for adding my two cents, darlings, but I feel I should. I've been aware of your sister's manipulations for some time now, Mr. deLys, and although you seem to be a wonderfully kind and sympathetic person yourself, just like my daughter here, your sister, if I may be frank, behaves like a vulture. I think there are times when ladies and gentlemen such as yourselves have to stop being so nice and try thinking like the enemy. If you want to control your sister, you have to think like her. If she doesn't understand reason, consider threats or bribes, as parents have been doing since time immemorial. They're two of the most effective means known to man for adjusting someone's behavior.

"Tell me," she said, looking up into Barton deLys's eyes with an innocent expression, "have you ever considered blackmail?"

Barton and Lauren had just left—Lauren found out he had cabbed over and insisted on driving him to the airport—when Ben Schlesser called. "How's the computer working?"

"Just fine, I think, but I haven't really tried it yet. We just got up a little while ago. Mother's driving a friend to the airport. You received the invitation to Mac Britton's brunch?"

"Yes. I'll be there. So will McKinnon, I think, and maybe Will. I hope so. I want him to see what you can do with no help from C.G. We should turn all our requests over to you, if we can just convince Will that's the way to go."

"Maybe when he sees how we handled this, he'll be more willing. You'll enjoy it."

"Are you going to be there? I think you should show up for as many events as you can while you're getting started. You'll meet a lot of people and they'll think of you in terms of bookings."

"Yes, I'll be there. Mac Britton thought the same thing."

"Will you be free for dinner? We can go anywhere nearby. I want to talk to you about a couple of things."

"Let me see," said Nelly, grabbing her appointment book. "Oh, dear, no. I have an appointment with a condo group's president."

"Then what's today look like? Find forty minutes somewhere."

"Oh, dear. I'm taking my mother back to Miami at two. I won't be back until—"

"Let's do that, then," said Ben. "I'll pick you up at two, we'll take her home, and then I'll bring you back up. That'll give us time to talk and I can still keep an appointment at four. And don't forget to bring your appointment book."

"Oh, that's so nice of you, Ben. We'll be ready by two."

After she hung up, Nelly remembered that she was supposed to call Morganthau. He wasn't in but his secretary gave her a long message. "Mr. Morganthau has been in touch with your husband's lawyer. He says your husband has been a model prisoner. Remorseful. Couldn't remember what he'd done, couldn't believe it when they told him. They had a psychiatrist talk to him and the guy says your husband is depressed and guilt-ridden—and determined to quit drinking. Wants to join A.A. Morganthau thinks they'll let him out. It's iffy. But Morganthau is against it. He's afraid he'll just get drunk again and try something worse. He's going to fight it. You can leave a message or he'll get hold of you tomorrow."

Nelly said, "Just a minute," and repeated the secretary's words to her mother.

Lauren frowned. "Jerk though he is, I'd certainly be in favor of him getting rehabilitated if it weren't so dangerous for you. Once is enough."

Nelly took her hand off the phone. "If I have any input on this at all," she said, "I'd like to talk it over with Morganthau. I'd hate to get in the way of Albert stopping his drinking. If he can. But I'm afraid—terrified—of him. I don't want to do anything that could delay the divorce. Maybe I should visit with him and talk to him. I think I could tell if he really means it."

"Except that he may mean it and still not be able to resist if they let him out," said Lauren. "You don't want to risk any more from him." Nelly repeated her mother's words into the phone.

"Got it," said the secretary. "I'll tell Mr. Morganthau what you said, and he'll call you. Personally, Mrs. Holachek, I don't think you should ever give a bastard like that a second chance. Even if he means what he says now, once he got out, he might not be able to resist drinking. And then what? I shouldn't be butting in, but I had an alcoholic husband. I know what I'm talking about. You don't want to take any chances. He might do worse next time. I'd lock him up and throw away the key."

Nelly sighed. "Nothing is easy, is it? Well, tell your boss that my friend Minny offered to talk to Albert for me if that would help. But Morganthau would have to be there—I don't want to put her in any danger. If he thinks I should talk to Albert, I'll do it, but only if he's there, too."

When Ben picked them up, he helped them into the back seat and handed Nelly a list. "Take a look at all this stuff I'm invited to the next few weeks. We routinely buy two tickets to these things, so I can take you to any of them you'd like and you needn't feel the least bit obligated. Or if your mother is up, we can always get another ticket. Of course, then you would be deep in my debt," he added, chuckling wickedly.

Nelly dug out her date book and pored over Ben's list, checking off several events. Two were black tie affairs. "Oh, I'll get to wear the gown the girls got for me."

"Or borrow something from me. It would fit," offered Lauren.

They pulled into the Harbour House at 2:40. "You don't have to come up," said Lauren. "One of the parking boys will bring my cases. Go, so Ben isn't late for his appointment. You never know how much traffic there'll be. "Ben, thank you so much. And thanks for giving Anyella so much support."

On the way back, Nelly sat up in front and Ben spoke of weightier matters.

"Nelly, I have so many things to talk about I don't know where to start. I guess C.G. is a good place. She realizes now that if she doesn't get things humming again pretty fast, she's in deep trouble. Even with her two new helpers, I'm not sure she can manage. I'm going to have a talk with her and explain that we do *not* want you maligned to our clients, that you could sue her. But I'm sure any hope of you coming back at this point is microscopic."

"I'm not even considering it. I just want to get my own agency humming. I'm getting some help from the girls."

"Good. You know, I hope we'll ultimately drop our booking altogether. Use your agency and divert it all to you. That makes sense. Just let C.G. run the guidance, *if* she can."

Nelly nodded.

"OK," Ben continued. "Next on the agenda—the business of your husband. I think you should move into a place with good security. Why do you need a whole house to take care of? You're dealing with an alcoholic. Let's face it, he's pushed by urges beyond reason. The only safe place for you, really safe, is somewhere beyond his reach. Behind a gatehouse he can't get past."

"My mother talked about selling the house and getting me a condo. It belongs to her."

"Good. Let her. I like your mother, Nelly. She's a smart woman. One thing more—I want you to know I'm your friend. Even more so now that I see the new Nelly," he added with a grin. "You look wonderful. You've taken charge. But you're still the sweet person underneath that you've always been. If there's ever any problem you need help with, I want you to call and run it by me. Will you do that?"

"Oh, Ben, how can I cause you so much, trouble—?"

"I wouldn't think of it as trouble. I would think of it as looking after someone I care about."

Nelly didn't know what to say to that. Did he mean—? She finally answered, saying, "I really appreciate that, Ben."

"And just one more thing. Perhaps I shouldn't interfere in matters like this, but I feel I should say something. Your daughters, and Mac Britton's son, Rocky."

"Yes, he seems quite smitten. He made his father ask us for Christmas dinner and wants them to go on some kind of boat thing with him. He can be very persuasive. But I don't think even Mac considers him exactly a pillar of society."

"He's trouble, Nelly, with a capital 'T'. Nothing but a playboy, into one scrape after another. He's put Mac through a wringer. Never made a living. Mac bails him out when he gets into jams. I don't know Mac Britton that well, but I know someone in New York who knows the family well. Mac's wife Moira was a plastic surgery freak, always getting something fixed or tucked. Into designer clothes and society. Spent more time on her appearance than on the kid. No wonder he turned out nuts. They tell me Britton's kid has damn near killed himself a couple of times."

"Mac told me a little bit about Rocky's Kuwait thing," said Nelly. "But Ben, my daughters, by their own choice, have been living with my mother since they were fifteen. They didn't want any part of their father and if I wouldn't leave him, they wouldn't live with us anymore. They're grown-ups. They love me, but they have minds of their own. I can't tell them what to do or who to see. Then again, they're pretty level-headed."

"You all seem to talk to each other easily enough."

"Yes. It's so good to be this close again, but I haven't tried giving them any advice in a long time. Lately, they give it to me."

"I think you'd better try on this one, Nelly."

"Maybe you're right. I'd better have a little chat. They're coming up tonight because of that boating thing with him tomorrow, but they won't get in until late."

"If I were you, I wouldn't let them so much as go paddling in a puddle with that kid, even if I had to lock them up to keep them from it. Yes, he's charming. Good-looking. But why would he be any more sensible in a boat than he is on dry land?"

"You're right, Ben. I'll talk to them. Or try."

Back at the office, Nelly finished going through the mail. Four more invitations. Three from men she thought she'd met at that Chamber of Commerce event. Baron Viscante was hosting a dinner. So was Barney Jones, the lawyer. A dermatologist named Edward d'Angelo wondered if she was free Thursday night but didn't say for what. And who was this Erhardt person? A party aboard his yacht? She took the calls. Faye had come through with a radio interview on WPKY. She should call to confirm the date. Erhardt's secretary, asking about the yacht party. A call from Dr. Laker. She needed to schedule a follow-up appointment, to be sure everything had healed properly. Healed properly? Nelly laughed to herself. She couldn't even find a scar.

* * *

Rocky Britton and Evan Gumbel stood in front of the club docks peering up, up, up to the top of the *Buttbuster III*'s mast. "What a beauty," said Rocky. "She's like no other boat I've ever seen."

"She's a perfect racer. Not one damn thing on her weighs two ounces more than it has to. Open head. Canvas pipe berths."

"A little rebel, all right," said Rocky. "But I never met a boat yet that I couldn't tame. We'll pick off that cup without taking a deep breath."

"I'll just settle for getting to Freeport and back. I've been having work done all week. The engine catches. Between the listing and the radio crapping out, I was going crazy, but I think it's OK now. You sure your friends will be able to go?"

"Yeah. They're looking forward to it."

"And they're good hands?"

"Practically pirates. Been sailing since they could crawl. We'll be here at nine tomorrow morning."

"I guess the only thing that can stop us then would be if I have to go to that hearing."

"Listen, said Rocky. "Most likely you'll be able to go. But if not, hell, we'll sail the race for you if you want. It'd be a shame to miss her first trophy."

"Yeah, but this baby is a handful. And I don't know if you ever sailed an ultralight before, but they take a firm hand."

"Don't worry, Evan. We'll make it fly. And these twins, they can't bear to lose. If the hearing gets in the way, too bad. But we'll bring you home a cup anyway."

"Maybe you could. Arby will be with you. This girl I told you about. No romance, but I take her to dinner now and then and I sail with her a lot. She doesn't weigh anything but she's a better sailor than most guys I know. Well, come on. Let's give her a quick run. I'll show you everything. You don't want to be totally unfamiliar with her tomorrow. I'll take her out of the entrance channel and back in and explain what I'm doing and why."

Rocky chuckled to himself. Perfect. Gumbel would explain, and Rocky, with his photographic memory, would absorb every word and movement like an imprint on his brain. And tomorrow morning he would glide out of that same channel as though he'd been doing it for years. Of course, he had stretched the facts like rubber bands. He didn't know a Briny-28 Ultralight from a rowboat. He had only sailed a few times before, but it would all come back.

And this was a chance at an adventure he couldn't resist. He could see himself passing up the other seven boats in the race as though they were standing still. What a fantasy trip! He could feel the adrenaline pumping just thinking about it. He'd be lucky if he slept two hours tonight.

Nelly heard the girls come in at ten as she was

going over her strategy checklists before climbing into bed. She had forgotten her walk this morning. And she had forgotten to go to Blockbusters to look for more of those confidence-building tapes.

They marched right into her bedroom. "Mom, we're playing hookey tomorrow," said Jane. "Isn't this fun?"

"And don't believe anyone who says it's OK to goof off during the holidays because business is slow. 'Taint true. We've had a million calls this week, but we couldn't resist this. We've never sailed in a race before."

"I wanted to talk to you about that, girls," began Nelly. "Ben thought I should. He says Rocky Britton is not a good person to tangle with. He's always getting himself nearly killed in some harebrained stunt or other. Here he was getting over some Amazon fever and as soon as he was barely OK, he had to try bungee jumping. You don't want to let him get you into something dangerous like that."

"Don't worry, Mom," said Jane. "We already know he's a schmuck. Gorgeous and hunky, and the scars just make him look interesting. But he's a racing freak, an adventure freak. This'll be fun, though. And we never have to see him again if we don't want to."

"You know about Kuwait."

"Well, gee, that was almost understandable. How else was he going to get there and see it for himself?

He's cute and fun, and he's a gentleman, Mom. He won't try anything crazy with us. And if he does, Jane and I will cut him to ribbons. We both just had our nails done," she said, swiping her ultra-long talons through the air, "so that's a very real threat."

"After the race, we'll introduce him to a bunch of dishy young bimbos," said Emma, "and we'll probably never hear from him again."

Nelly tried another tack. "He's never worked. He just lives off his father."

"Oh, pooh on that, Mother. Over here that's a crime. In England there are hordes of respectable young men doing essentially the same thing. Waiting for a title or lands or whatever."

"But this isn't England. And he does those nutty tricks—"

"Well, hopefully that Kuwait business has sobered him up. He certainly didn't sound like the daring young man on the flying trapeze on Christmas Day. Go to sleep, Mom. It's Evan Gumbel's boat and he's well-known as a top-notch sailor. No, Emma and I haven't sailed all that much in years, but it's like swimming. It all comes back the minute you hit the water."

Seventeen

The girls showed up promptly at nine with coolers of beer, Diet Coke, sandwiches, cookies, pretzels, bagels, apples, and candy bars. Rocky met them at the parking lot entrance. "Over that way," he waved, directing them toward a space at the docks nearest the *Buttbuster III*, where Evan Gumbel waited.

"My God!" he cried after Rocky introduced them. "I never expected to have one Miss America shoo-in sailing with us, much less two." The girls smiled sweetly and began unloading the trunk. "How does anyone tell you two apart?" he asked as he and Rocky hoisted up the coolers to carry them on board.

The twins grabbed the other bags of edibles. "I have longer eyelashes and more freckles," said Jane in a confidential tone. "And Emma's waist is a half-inch smaller."

"Oh, Jeeze!" he groaned. "And we're supposed to concentrate on sailing?" He scanned the skies, frowning at the grey patches to the south and east, then led them inside the cabin to stash the food and drinks away. "It's like the powers that be don't want us to race today. First, Arby can't make it—this friend I sail with sometimes," he explained to the twins. "She's half dolphin. But she had to go to Tampa for a funeral."

"Some people pick the worst times to die," said Rocky.

"And the forecast is iffy," Gumbel continued. "The weather can't make up its mind. I wouldn't be surprised if Hayes calls it off. We may end up sailing up and down the Intracoastal."

"Now, now, think positive," said Jane.

"But you'll be able to go if it's on?" Rocky asked.

"That's not sure either. My secretary will call as soon as she hears. Within twenty minutes, or we're off to the starting line."

"The Lauderdale Sea Buoy?" asked Emma.

"Right." After they stowed the food and drinks, he gave the twins his quick VIP tour. "It's the new Briny-28 Ultralight," he said proudly. "Only 2600 pounds. This keel is just 1200 pounds of lead—bolted on. Open head, 15/16ths rig with a Cuddy cabin. So light she damn near flies. Feels like a hydrofoil. Actually, I don't know this little canoe like the back of my hand yet," he said. "And I don't 100 percent trust any boat until I know every rib, bone, and freckle. I've only had her a month or so, and she's been in the boatyard half that time. But she's neat."

"Looks like she'll be fun to sail," said Jane, thinking a compliment seemed in order. She and Emma actually preferred boats with all the amenities to these stripped-down, spartan racers. An open head?

"They didn't take all the challenge and fun out of a Briny, like they do on so many of these tubs. They aren't automatic shift cars. They won't sail for you. You make 'em go. Most of the Sea Rats' boats are like that, one way or the other. We're the kind of people who like to buck the sea and win."

He showed them the surprisingly small engine, hanging off the stern. "That saves weight, too." He pulled the cord to start it up. It wheezed asthmatically at first, then smoothed into a loud, even drone. He nodded to Rocky. "We're fine."

But just then the portable phone in his back pocket rang. He yanked it out and flipped it open. "Yeah, it's me . . . They did? Oh, shit! Well, can we . . . OK, gotcha. Tell them I'll be there." He turned to Rocky. "Well, buddy, I guess it's all yours, if you're sure you want it. Just the three of you—it'll be a grind. I wouldn't let most people try. Don't push yourselves. Don't do anything dangerous. Any problems, forget the whole thing. But if you still want to, OK. Go get me a trophy."

Rocky grinned broadly. The twins could see elation light his eyes—and a look of eagerness. He slapped Gumbel on the arm and said, "It's already yours." He looked down at his watch.

204

Gumbel looked at his, too. "Yeah. About time to head out. I'll help you off, here." He scrambled from the boat, untied the lines, and flipped them aboard. Jane quickly coiled them and stored them below. Evan Gumbel stood there smiling as Rocky—reading from memory the exact moves Evan had made the day before—guided *Buttbuster III* out into the Intracoastal, and headed it south toward the Port Everglades entrance channel.

"*Buttbuster III?*" asked Jane, watching his apparent skill at the tiller. "Whatever happened to the others? Did he sell them?"

"I don't know the whole story," said Rocky, his eyes glued to the waters ahead. "I only met Evan a few weeks ago. But we've gone out together about five times since. He's a great guy. Kind of daring, though. He's raced in cigarettes, too. Supposedly one of his boats capsized and sank on the way to the Caymans once. But Stepit told me he heard Evan and a fishing boat crashed head-on once, during a monster storm. They both sank but it was so stormy out that other boats collided, too, and no one was blamed. Everybody else I talked to said he's a damned nautical genius."

"Maybe it's just as well he couldn't go with us," said Jane uneasily. "He might expect real perfection from his crew, and Emma and I have never sailed an ultralight before."

"That makes three of us. Heck, I was never on

the damn thing 'til yesterday," said Rocky. "All I know is how to run the engine. I can get us out the Entrance Channel to the Fort Lauderdale Buoy. Piece of cake. But you two are going to sail it."

Jane and Emma laughed uproariously. Rocky was very funny. Of course, he was just kidding. But you almost believed him.

"There's one boat in the race whose owner isn't a Sea Rat," said Rocky. "Evan told me, but I'm not sure which one it is." They turned into the entrance channel. "He says they let other clubs compete in their races sometimes. Everyone wants to win a Sea Rat trophy but hardly anyone but a Sea Rat ever does. They're a gutsy bunch. He says they're the best damned sailors you could find anywhere. They belong to every major yacht club on the East Coast and the Keys. And many others. But no clubhouse. He says they make their own rules. And *none* of them likes to lose."

He glanced up at the grey patches to the west. Were they a little darker? "Doesn't look too great up there," he murmured, pointing. "But it's a long way off. We'll likely hit Freeport before that hits us. Now which one of you wants to run the show out here? We gotta name one person to take the helm and her word is law."

"You're not taking it?" asked Emma in disbelief.

"I told you—I'm an amateur. Which one?"

"Very funny," Emma said. "But if you insist—

OK, I'll try it. Only if I screw it up, you have to take over." But even as she laughed, she wondered why Rocky was reworking this joke about being an amateur. He was an expert, like he'd said when he invited them on this adventure. If not, what were they doing out here with him in a race in a strange boat?

They put up their sails in the port harbor. Emmy started calling out orders. "Raise the genoa. The mainsail." She cut the engine and worked the breeze from the southeast, and brought *Buttbuster III* out toward the Fort Lauderdale Buoy.

The Rambler, a J-35 from the Lighthouse Point Club, and *The Cutup*, a Tartan-35 from William's Island, were at the buoy ahead of them. And Hayes in the committee boat, a forty-foot Ocean, called *The Guardian*. The other four boats competing approached one by one during the next twenty minutes, two from the Lauderdale Yacht Club, another from Coral Ridge, and one more from Lighthouse Point. They bobbed in the water, jockeying for good starting positions. Hayes, the official starter, would start them right at ten, they knew. The minutes ticked by. Then exactly at 9:50, Hayes lifted his gun in the air and fired one shot.

The seven boats tacked closer to the start, the invisible line stretching between the buoy and Hayes's boat. At 9:55, Hayes raised the gun and fired the second shot.

Emma backed off a little, trying to judge the breeze and the distance. They mustn't cross over the line before ten—that she knew—but just be approaching it at the right moment. At a few seconds before ten, Hayes lifted his gun again. And at exactly ten, he fired the third shot. The boats began moving forward, pushing for the lead.

Emma looked at Rocky. He grinned back. "You're on your own."

"OK, trim the jib, Rocky," she ordered. "Jane, trim the main in. Let's go."

The Cutup eased out in front at first. Then *Barry's Bimbo* from William's Island slowly pulled ahead of her. Within half an hour the seven boats were spread out over a broad patch of ocean.

Next stop, Freeport.

Nelly pulled into the Temple Tower parking garage, driving up and around, up and around, all the way to the fifth floor before she found a space. She hopped the parking elevator back down to the second-floor meeting room, where Britton had kindly agreed to run the brunch instead of in his office reception area so she wouldn't have to endure that ride to the twenty-eighth floor.

She was early. It wouldn't start until 11:30. But

that was the only way to be certain everything would work—to get there early enough to catch any mistakes before the crowds came. Britton arrived and came over to her as she was talking to the caterer. "Please make sure the decaf coffeepot is clearly marked," she was saying. "A ribbon on the pot handle is not enough. A little sign saying 'decaf' is better. Too many people don't dare drink regular coffee for medical reasons and they need to be 100 percent sure which is which. And would you please pull that buffet table out from the wall, at least three or four feet, so guests can go down both sides? Then it will only take half as long to feed them, as time is very important for these people."

Britton nodded his approval. "One other thing, Nelly. I'll be taking questions at the end. That can go on forever. If I give you a look, come up and take the mike and say something like, 'We know you all have to get back to your offices. Sorry, but no more questions,' and thank them for coming."

"Me? But I'm not—I don't know—" she sputtered.

"You don't have to make a speech. Just those few words. A friendly explanation. And you and I will leave, right then. Out the door and disappear. OK?"

Nelly nodded reluctantly.

"Well," he said, "I guess our kids have left on their sailing adventure by now. I only hope they

209

don't run into bumpy seas. The sky looked a little threatening this morning."

Nelly nodded again. She felt uneasy. She wished this day was over. She wished Lauren's last husband, Edgar James, hadn't insisted on trying to interest the girls in sailing. Not that he had been all that successful. They sailed with him several times and then were caught up in other interests. And she wished Mac Britton's thrill-seeking son had just stayed in New York and the girls had never met him.

By 11:15, guests were pouring through the meeting room doors in such numbers that the caterers quickly set up more chairs. Ben was the first of the partners to arrive and hurried right over. "I tell you, when you break out, you really break out. I had four calls last night from men who met you or saw you at the Chamber thing, and they all wanted to meet you again. Gershon Trayle has been an absolute pest. Baron Viscante, too. A matchmaker, they think I am. I told them I'd introduce them again, but if I'm making any shittocs, they'll be for me."

"A shittoc?" repeated Nelly.

"It's Jewish: it means a match," he explained with a grin. "As in matchmaker. Well, could you do anything about the race?"

Nelly shook her head. "No. I talked to them. Seriously. But they went anyway. I'm very uneasy about it."

"Maybe it'll be postponed. The weather doesn't

210

look too great, gloomier by the minute. Everything will be fine, I'm sure. But telling the girls all about his escapades wouldn't hurt." He moved away to talk with some of the new arrivals.

Will Raymond and Jack McKinnon came over after chatting briefly with Britton. "Morning, Nelly," said McKinnon. "My gosh, you look wonderful. Britton said it was you. I wasn't sure we were talking about the same Nelly Holachek."

"It's Anyella Devin Lure now," said Nelly, smiling demurely and looking into McKinnon's eyes. "I've taken back my maiden name."

"Well, I don't blame you, my dear. After what that bastard pulled—we just couldn't believe what we read in that newspaper."

Raymond was not quite as friendly. He stared at her frankly for a moment. "Are you sure you're the same woman who worked for us?" he growled. "What the hell happened to you? Someone wave a magic wand? And now you've put this little shindig together for *our* client." But Nelly was not about to accept a scolding—that was one of her new tactics. She smiled back warmly, looking up into Raymond's eyes as she had McKinnon's. There had to be some reason he was so down on her. She hadn't a clue. But she would use every chance she got to try to change that. She said in a gracious tone, "Yes, Mr. Raymond, I did. I'm *so* glad you could come. I'm being asked to do a lot of different things for my

211

clients—we share Britton and several others—and they all seem pleased. Certainly, if you ever need me to make arrangements for any of your clients, just call me. I'll gladly do it." She handed both men her new cards.

Raymond grunted and shoved the card in his pocket, but McKinnon smiled back. "We'll probably end up doing that sooner than you think, Nelly. Sure looks like you got the cream out for this one."

"We thought we'd have about forty, but nobody refused and some called to ask if they could bring another partner or someone. By last night we expected sixty and the count this morning is over eighty."

Just then Ben returned with two men in tow. "Nelly, this is Burt Hampton from Hampton, Barnett, and Devon, the law firm. And this is Elliott Schward, the yacht builder, and they'd both like to know a little more about your agency, and about you."

She fished two more cards from her purse. "Why don't we trade cards?" she asked. "And I'll send you a folder that tells all about us, and some application forms."

"I'd like to have lunch with you one day next week," said Hampton, who had the muscular look of a boxer.

"You took the words right out of my mouth, Burt," said Schward. He was shorter, with a tiny paunch and laugh wrinkles.

"I think if you call me, it would be better because then I could look at my appointment book," said Nelly. "I'd hate to make plans now and then have to cancel."

"Meanwhile, we can buy you brunch," said Schward with a chuckle as the two men escorted her to the buffet.

Nelly only caught about half of Britton's speech— enough to know he was articulate, informed, and very interesting. "The city has many problems, many bonuses. Some you know about. Some you may not. They all have an impact on anyone doing business there. Did you know there are more than one million people on welfare in New York City? Did you know that the Manhattan-Brooklyn Williamsburg Bridge's maintenance and repair was showering the surrounding community with deadly dust loaded with lead?"

The guests listened with eyes glued. But halfway through his talk, Nelly excused herself to Burt Hampton and Elliott Schward and slipped out to call the Coral Ridge Yacht Club and find out if Evan Gumbel's boat had left for the Sea Rats' race.

"What race?" asked the receptionist.

"Well, did Mr. Gumbel's boat go out this morning?"

"It sure did. Oh, I know what you mean—that

group he belongs to. But I know Mr. Gumbel wasn't on board. I saw him leave here twenty minutes ago. Mr. Gunderson told me Mr. Gumbel wasn't happy to let his new boat sail the race without him, but he had no choice."

Nelly returned to the meeting room, where Britton was answering questions and twenty hands were waving at once trying to catch his attention. She saw McKinnon nudge Raymond and heard him say, "She did it all right. And this guy knows everything you want to know about New York. I think we picked the wrong horse, Will." And she heard Ben, on the other side of Raymond, add emphatically, "No kidding! What the hell have I been telling you all this time?"

She watched with a mounting uneasiness she was unable to explain. It couldn't have anything to do with the brunch. It was clearly a huge success. Mac Britton was as articulate answering questions as he was with a prepared speech. Four company heads had asked him if he could come and talk to their people and he had said each time: "Check with Mrs. Devin Lure; she makes those arrangements for us."

Several of the guests had approached her about the roster of speakers she had on tap, or offering themselves or other experts from their companies for booking.

But the sky outside, she noticed, was not very bright for this hour of the morning. Was that what was making her so uncomfortable? Then Mac caught her eye, and deliberately blinked. Twice. She quickly made her way up to the podium and as he finished answering the last question, he handed her the mike. "Mr. Britton, I know, would like to answer all of your questions," she said slowly and clearly. "But he is aware that you all have to hurry back to your offices. So we'll wrap it up now. We hope you enjoyed this morning and we thank you so much for coming." She attached the mike to its stand and she and Mac headed for the door, shaking hands with people right and left on the way.

But before they got there, the darkening skies outside flashed with the blinding blaze of one lightning strike after another and boomed with thunder that seemed to shake the very walls.

"Oh my god, and they're out there in this?" cried Nelly.

"No, probably not," he said in a deliberately cheerful voice. But his jaw was clenched and his eyes looked grim. "They're way out to sea by now. It's 12:30 and they started at ten. And this came from the west. It may not move much further. Or it may move south or north and skip them altogether. You know how the rain is down here. And maybe they didn't even go."

"I'm afraid they did. I called Coral Ridge. The boat left, only the owner didn't go with them."

"Didn't go with them?" Mac repeated indignantly. "Well then, who the hell's running the show? Are your girls good sailors?"

"Of course not. They only did it on and off for a while because their step-grandfather was pushing. They probably know enough to crew pretty well, but your son is the expert."

He didn't answer, but his face was grim.

"Isn't he?" Nelly asked with a sinking feeling. "He told them he was."

They reached the door and he opened it, and the two of them ducked out onto the mezzanine and over to a cluster of chairs. Instead of sitting, he began pacing up and down while she stood deathly still, watching him. And waiting for his answer.

He stopped, closed his eyes, and bent his head, as though facing her was too painful. But then he managed to look up at her and said with a groan of despair, "My goddam son used to get seasick in the bathtub! He can't even swim. He's gone out in other peoples' boats just often enough to be able to tell forward from aft and port from starboard, but he can fake anything. He can turn on a motor and steer. He's a quick study, so he may know a lot more about sailing than I'm aware of. But I doubt it. That's not his way. His way is to skim the top, to learn enough to be able to fool the experts into letting him take

216

part. Oh, Christ, Nelly, don't tell me that's what he said to your daughters."

She stared at him, open-mouthed, slowly bobbing her head up and down. "My God, Mac," she whispered, "What do we do now? How can we find out if they're all right?"

"Now, don't panic. Most likely the storm won't even touch them. And if it does, those boats are made to handle a lot of rain. It's nothing to them. They can sail through a hurricane—just bobbing around like corks 'til it's over. And this *isn't* a hurricane. Just a little storm. They're surrounded by the other boats and some of the best sailors you could find anywhere, so there's no reason to worry. They're probably safer than if they were driving I-95. Nothing's going to happen to them."

"No, nothing," Nelly repeated softly. "Of course, you're right." But he could hear the tremor in her voice.

"What's your schedule like for the rest of today?"

"I'm supposed to work at home on agency stuff this afternoon. And I've got a dinner appointment at 5:30. I'll get out of it."

"No. Do your regular work. Go to your dinner. I'll get Heather to call the Coast Guard and the Port and find out if they have any info. To keep track of them. Where is your dinner thing?"

"At that L&N fish place on Federal Highway."

"How soon will you be through?"

"By about 6:30, I should think."

"Good. I'll meet you back here about then. No, that's silly. Why should you have to make a whole extra trip up here? Just call me when you're through, and by then I hope I'll know everything there is to know, whether there's even any reason for concern. So we can put our minds at rest. Or if there's something we want to do, like calling them, we can do that."

Eighteen

Sailing the Briny was a lot different than using the engine, but there was a good breeze blowing in the right direction, from the southeast. The girls managed, by moving fast and working frantically, to keep abreast of the other boats most of the time. Rocky jumped at Emma's orders and worked with Jane, but he almost seemed unable to grasp some of what Emma shouted at him. When she called out, "Ease the traveler down a bit," he grinned at her blankly. Dummy, she scolded mentally. This amateur pose isn't funny anymore. "On that track in front of you," she fumed, "Let the slide go down to leeward a bit." He looked confused, so she had Jane do it. Didn't he hear well?

When she hollered, "Both of you keep your weight on the weather rail," it was the same thing—she might have been talking Chinese. Still, it took a couple of hours at sea before the truth finally sank in.

Rocky wasn't doing that to be amusing, and it

wasn't her orders that were strange. It was *him*. He had no idea what she meant! No matter how skilled he had seemed when he brought *Buttbuster* through the entrance channel, the fact remained that all his talk about being able to handle any boat was bullshit. When he said this morning that he was an amateur, *that* was probably the God's own truth. She was furious when it finally dawned on her.

And she didn't like the way *Buttbuster* was reacting now, either. Was she crazy or was it listing a bit? She noticed it more after the skies began to darken. Great. All they needed. Back to the west, patches of grey had blurred into one bigger, darker patch. A storm for sure. But was it moving this way? Maybe. Edgar would have known at one glance, but she'd have to look back a few times minutes apart to be sure. All they needed now was a storm, with three of them instead of five to keep this featherweight skimming. And one didn't know a storm jib from his left elbow.

"Rocky, get us a sandwich and a Coke, will you?" she ordered. He jumped to do as she asked. He was willing at least, but how had he dared lure them into this by telling them he was a hot-shot boater? Well, when they got into Freeport tonight, she and Jane were taking a plane home. It would serve him right. Didn't he realize a stunt like this could be damned dangerous?

"Take the tiller while I visit the head," she ordered

Jane. The *open* head. Yuck. But she couldn't put it off. If that storm did hit, she'd better be ready.

By 4:30 Emma had been peering back at the grey mass to the west for an hour as it grew bigger and bigger and moved closer and closer like a dark, expanding scrim hiding the heavens. The skies to the south were darkening, too. Another storm? Were they about to get pounded by a double-header? The wind was gusting, whipping the seas into a tumbling froth and smacking the sails into proud, taut arcs.

"We're going to catch hell in a few minutes, guys," she cried. "I think we ought to change down to the jib." With Jane's help, Rocky managed that one. The skies grew even darker as they watched and the winds whipped furiously. Emma struggled to keep the Briny on course.

A smatter of rain quickly blew up into a torrent. But when the lightning flashes in the west drew nearer and the boat began bobbing so erratically it was hard to stand, Emma hollered over the noise, "I think we're in over our heads, gang. I guess you've finally met the boat that's your match, Rocky. I don't think we're good enough to sail this thing through the tantrum that's about to hit us. And we're listing again. We'd better forget the race and use the engine. We don't want to lose the others."

Rocky and Jane nodded in agreement as the lightweight craft bounced from one wave to another, all but flinging them off the deck. After three tries, Rocky got the engine started—coughing, spitting, and whining perversely before settling into a steady loud churning through the chop. He and Jane lowered the sails. The winds were whipping more strongly and the boat bounced and lurched sickeningly. "Now I don't know what to do," Emma called to Jane. "Try to keep up with the bunch under power? Or just turn back?"

"With this storm bearing down?" cried Jane over the engine. "We can't turn back. We'll head right into the worst of it. And if we get bounced around, God only knows what direction we'll be sailing in. I think we'd better try and stay with the bunch. I hope there's enough gas. There's a dial there, somewhere. Rocky, do you know how to use that radio?"

Rocky inspected the expensive VHF, turned the dials, bent close to the speaker, and frowned. He fiddled for another five minutes and then said, "I don't think it's working. All I get is static." Jane took a turn. "Me, too, Sis," she yelled, to be heard above the noise. It turns on. A lot of racket, but that's all."

"Great," Emma cried back. "We're batting zero." Frustrated, she turned to Rocky and snapped, "You know something, mister? I don't think it was so cute of you to fool us about your boating skills. I think it was a fucking crime. You've got us out here in the goddam middle of the ocean, in the middle of a storm, with no radio. And none of us quite knows what the hell we're doing."

"Oh, come on," he retorted, grabbing the rail as a wave slapped the boat halfway over. "Live a little. This is an adventure."

The storm behind them, with its rain and lightning, was sweeping down as the storm from the south raced to challenge it. Their outer edges crashed, grappled, and raged. And the Briny was suddenly in the middle of the fight. Lightning zigzagged over the rolling black seas a few hundred feet away. The waves leapt up and slammed the boat like a tennis ball, sending it bouncing, skidding, dipping—then slammed it again, bouncing and skidding in the opposite direction. If they got through this, vowed Emma, fighting as she'd never in her life fought a tiller, she'd never set foot on another sailboat as long as she lived!

Nelly worked at her computer the rest of the afternoon, trying to concentrate. She could see how much easier it would be once all their new bookers and bookees were in the automated files. You wanted a comedian? The computer searched for comedians. You wanted a clown? An expert on nail care? Let the computer do the looking. Better than your fingers through the yellow pages. Britton's secretary, Heather, called three different times—but there wasn't much news. The boats were out there and on course. One storm was west of them, with another to the south. At five o'clock, she turned off the computer and freshened her make-up. Time to leave for the L&N.

Boz Richter guessed immediately that something was wrong. That pale, almost white face, the frantic eyes. But surely this pretty lady couldn't be the troublemaker Mrs. Clemency-Graves had hinted at. She had certainly never sounded that way when he had talked to her on the phone. He hated to tattle, but then again, there were rare times when tattling was the only honorable thing to do. Was this one of them? That's what he had to find out.

"Just soup for me, please," Nelly said as he studied the menu.

"That's not enough for a meal," he said.

"No. I'm sorry, but I really couldn't handle anything more."

"Listen, Mrs. Holachek. I asked for this meeting for one reason—I wanted to meet you in person. I know, I've talked to you on the phone a dozen times and you've gotten us speakers and always really good ones. And you've given some of our owners, who are retired entertainers, or are pretty good amateurs, a chance to entertain around town and they've loved it. Entertainers don't like to retire. I always wanted to thank you personally."

"Well, you're very welcome," said Nelly.

"But then I also heard you were going to start your own agency to do bookings like that."

"Yes, I have. It's called 1000 Words. Didn't you get a brochure ? I'm sure we sent one to you."

"Well, yes, I did. But I also got a call from the company you used to work for, Raymond, Schlesser. A lady named C.G. Clemency-Graves called and insisted I come to lunch. She told me about your agency—she wasn't too happy about it. I thought I'd like to give you equal time and see what it's all about."

"That's very nice of you, Mr. Richter. I have a whole lot of material for you to read. A brochure, application forms, and the rest. I'm doing the same thing I was doing there. I started that service. It was never an official part of my work. I did it on my own, and spent a lot of time on it."

"Yes. I've never dealt with anyone but you."

"But I felt that my boss there, the lady who called you, was given all the credit when she never did one booking and wouldn't know how to start." She told him about her rebellion. "So if you want to wait a while and try to get the same service from Raymond, Schlesser, I can understand that. They do your books and it might seem awkward. But then when you find they really can't handle bookings and you want to come to 1000 Words, we'll be glad to have you. Some of their clients are already using us. Including Raymond's wife, Daniella."

"Mrs. Raymond? Well, I'll be. Well, after hearing all this, we're ready to sign with you. I can tell— you're too nice a lady to be up to anything shady."

Nelly smiled and nodded thanks.

Boz Richter stared at her a moment and then blurted, "I guess it's none of my business, Mrs. Holachek, but you seem terribly upset. Is there something wrong? Is there anything I can do?"

"I'm sorry, Mr. Richter. I almost didn't come to this meeting. My daughters are out in a sailboat race to Freeport and this nasty storm is headed their way. I'd give anything to know what's going on out there and if they're all right. I'm sure they are," she said as if trying to convince herself, "but I just have this anxious feeling. Their radio doesn't answer. The boat's owner couldn't go. And the man in charge can't really handle a boat."

"Is the Coast Guard looking?"

"I don't know. The father of the young man who is out with them is checking on all that now. He says everything is OK so far. Is there something else I could be doing?"

"I'd want to find out if there's really any trouble— a storm here may not even get close to them. That's often how it works. But if there is a problem, if they're lost or anything, I'll get my friends who have planes to go out and try to find them. It's a pilots' club I belong to—we do that all the time. But you don't want to go off half-cocked. There's probably no problem. Wait and see what we can find out first."

The waitress brought Nelly's soup and Richter's fish. "How'd they get in a race with someone who can't handle a boat?"

"I think this young man wings it a lot—is that the term I want? And gets away with it. He wanted to spend some time with my twin girls. They're—very pretty, and he's a bit of a playboy."

"Yeah, but that ocean is nothing to fool with," said Richter. "Boating can be a lot of fun, but it's dangerous if you don't know what you're doing."

"Yes," said Nelly, poking her spoon in her soup to push a chunk of potato around.

Richter wolfed down his fish and then said, "Well, I think we'll use your service, Mrs. Holachek, like I said. Now I'm going to try and get all my ham pals on this. Give me the details and I'll let you know anything they find out. You gonna be home? Give me the number. And if there's any trouble, I'll get some planes out for you."

"Oh, that would be wonderful," said Nelly, ready to cry. "I don't know how to thank you."

"After this is all over, maybe you'd come to a condo outing with me. We do theater parties, ballet. I'm not a big ballet fan, but my wife used to love it." He sighed. Nelly could hear the loneliness. "I got twenty women at the condo wanting to go with me, but I'm not getting mixed up with anyone who lives right there. I won't open that can of worms."

Nelly looked up and saw him for the first time. Nice face. Kind. Grey hair thinning on top. Glasses down on his nose. A big man. He looked like an unpretentious, practical kind of person. "Thank you," she said, and then added, on impulse, "Going to one of your events would be very nice. But right now, of course, I have this situation on my mind."

"I'll tell you what, Mrs. Holachek, or can I call you Nelly? I'll get a couple of ham friends on this right away. You call me as soon as you know something and I'll call you as soon as I hear anything. If you need planes, we'll fly over every damn inch of that water out there. If your kids are lost, we'll find them. But most likely you're going to hear there's no problem at all." He signaled for the check, paid it, and escorted Nelly to her car. She hadn't touched a drop of her soup.

Nelly called Mac the minute she got home. "He's been waiting for your call, Mrs. Holachek," said Heather, recognizing Nelly's voice. "I'll put him right on."

"Are you at home, Nelly?" he asked.

"Yes. I just got back."

"I'm afraid the storm did move east. They're probably fighting it right now, and it's a doozy. Two for one. One was moving in from the south, too, and they collided in the wrong spot. I'll keep you posted. If we don't get some firm good news by another hour or so, I'll come over there so we both get whatever news there is at the same time. If we do it here or at my place, you've got an elevator ride and I don't think you need that right now. Stay loose. Most likely everything is fine, but I don't much like the sound of that storm."

"I don't either," said Nelly. "But listen, Mac. Some good news. The man I had the early dinner with, Boz Richter? He belongs to this pilots' club and can get private planes out to search if needed. All these ham radio operators are his friends. He's getting them on it right now. He says they pick up everything and they're wonderful in emergencies."

"Wow! That's a lucky break. Let me know whatever you learn and I'll get back to you as soon as I hear anything at all."

In Miami, Lauren paced up and down in her living room. She had tried Nelly three times and no answer. Something was wrong. She could feel it. Was it the twins?

Maybe it was just because she was supposed to go out with Alfonso Lord again this evening, and she didn't want to go. One date and she knew he was not for her. Well, she would call Len, who was making a bit of a nuisance of himself. He didn't like to take no for an answer, either. She would explain again, slowly and patiently, why they were not really suited to each other. And then she would try Nelly once more. If she didn't reach her, and if she still felt this way, she would simply get in her car, drive up, and see for herself.

When Mac called back at 8:30, his voice was tight as a drum. "Nelly, the news is not too good. Both storms did hit at once. The boats were blown off course. The seas are so bad they can't see anything down there. They're in radio contact with five of the boats. Not ours. Call your friend with the planes and hams and tell him. I'm coming over."

"Oh, yes. Please," she said. "Oh, Lord, what do we do now?"

"Pray," he said grimly.

She hung up and called Boz Richter and repeated Mac's words. "He's coming over here so we can get information at the same time."

"I'll call my friend Roger LeNou and get him to help us. He's got a pretty decent portable ham shack. I'm coming over there, too, if that's OK. We'll set up a kind of headquarters. Tell your Mr. Britton to bring a portable phone and anyone else the same thing. So no one will tie up your line." She gave him the address.

The phone rang again and it was Ben Schlesser. "Hear anything more?"

"Oh, Ben!" she cried, pouring out a babble of what she had just learned. "The boats are separated. They're way off course. The storm is terrible. Mac Britton is coming here. And a ham radio operator and a man from a pilots' club. The members will go out looking."

"I'll be right over, too."

"The man who's getting the pilots and hams on it said to bring your portable phone. They'll want to keep mine open."

"I'll bring two," he said. "And I'll order in some food and coffee."

Nelly then called her mother, who immediately said, "Nelly, what's wrong? I *know* something's wrong. I've been trying to reach you since this morning. I'm getting you a portable phone. I hate having to wait hours to find out what's happening, when I *know* something's not good. What is it?"

"Oh, Mother, I was at this brunch I put together for Mac Britton and—well, I was tied up all day. It's the girls and Mac's son—they're out in a boat race to Freeport and there's a storm raging. Their radio seems to be broken. They're lost."

"Oh my God!" cried Lauren. "I knew it! I knew it was something terrible. I'll be up as quickly as I can, darling. Don't you worry. We'll find them."

Nelly called Mac back. "I talked to my mother.

She's frantic. She's coming up, too. Oh, Mac, I can't stand it. Our kids—"

"Nelly, don't do that. We'll find them. They'll be OK. I promise you." The phone felt heavy in his hand. He hung it up slowly, very deliberately, praying he hadn't just made a promise he wouldn't be able to keep.

Nineteen

The engine revved up when the prop lifted out of the water, then choked and sputtered when it plunged in again, as the Briny bounced around like a cork—tipping, straightening, tipping, straightening—lurching wildly in ever-widening swings.

"I hope you're a good swimmer, Rocky," warned Jane. "We may all hit the water any minute. Let's load up our pockets with candy and stuff." As they struggled to do that, during a reverberating roll of thunder, the engine killed for good. It took them a few moments to realize it was gone. The rain was flushing down in sheets—only when the lightning flashed could they barely make out one of the other boats.

"I can't swim at all," cried Rocky, suddenly doubling over and vomiting on the deck.

"It figures," shouted Jane. "Get your lifejackets on, gang." The girls tugged their jackets on and Jane helped Rocky into his while Emma struggled with the tiller. They stuffed food packets into their pockets with cans of diet soda. Jane put one in Rocky's, too, as he lie groaning on the deck, clinging to a stay, retching and trying to get up as the waves crashed over him. Jane bent over and yelled into his ear. "Listen, Rocky. This is salt water and you've got a jacket on, so you're not going to drown no matter what happens. Don't panic when we hit the water. Just let the jacket hold you up. Keep your head out of the water. If anything stays afloat, we'll get you onto it. Some part of this boat might, it's so light. Don't fight us in the water. You hear me? Don't fight us if we're trying to help you. Just do what you're told and we'll be fine. You fight us in the water and we'll leave you behind. Can you hear me?"

He groaned and managed a feeble nod.

"Get that chart and see what you can figure out, Jane," shouted Emma as another huge wave swamped them.

"You know I can't read those things," Jane screamed back. "I'll take the tiller. You do the chart. I don't think we're too far from Freeport." She took the wheel while Emma pulled out a drawer, squinting to make out the names of the charts stuffed inside. She tugged one from the bunch and tried to read it.

"I'm not sure exactly where we are," Emma said, "but I think you're right. In all this bumping and turning, I think the stream is probably pushing us north. Looks like there's a little island or sandspit there above the West End." She folded the chart and tucked it down the front of her shirt.

The boat felt like it was shaking apart. They were careening even more wildly now, almost tipping over again and again. Suddenly, with a deafening crack, the mast split free from the boat and crashed into the water, dragging behind them for a few minutes in a grotesque rock and roll before it tore loose and was sucked beneath the angry water. The boat tossed and tumbled in a grotesque dance in ever-widening swings—until the big one.

Just as Jane dove to catch Rocky, who began sliding down the deck, *Buttbuster III* swung over so far it was suspended, teetering on its edge for a moment, then dumping the three of them in the angry seas. They thrashed around frantically, trying to get clear of the tipping boat. On the next swing, the keel bolts sheered off with a screech and the keel broke free and disappeared. The all-but-weightless shell, like a twenty-eight foot white frisbee, bobbed to the surface and danced around atop the swells, just out of reach.

"Jane!" called Emma. "Where are you?"

"Here," her sister cried. "The shell! Catch the shell!"

"Rocky," cried Emma. Nothing. No response. "Rocky," she cried again. And again, nothing.

Then something banged Jane in the head. She stroked with one arm like a rudder to turn in the water. The shell! Through the rain she could see it glide obligingly toward her again and dip. She lunged for the edge, caught it, swung up, and flopped inside.

Oh, God, what a break! How she craved just to lie there, gasping, until she could get enough air into her lungs again. But the flopping shell was rolling her about like a rag doll. "Emma," she yelled into the storm. "Emma, where are you? Swim toward my voice. The shell. I'm in the shell." As it turned and dipped, she peered out into the dark rain.

"Here," came Emma's faint voice. "Over here!" But how to get to her? There was no way to steer. Nothing to do but wait until the shell's erratic bobbing swiped near them. Then she could try to hang over the side maybe, and help them catch the edge and climb on. Emma could swim toward her, but could Rocky?

With the lightning diminishing, she couldn't see. Was that Emma over there? In the quick light of one small, distant flash, she saw her! Was that Rocky behind her? The shell took a dip toward Emma. She wasn't sure, but it looked like Emma was towing Rocky and his head was bobbing as though he had passed out.

The shell bobbed toward them. Jane kept yelling, "Emma! Emma!" to guide her. Emma stroked toward Jane's voice but then the shell bobbed off to the left, out of reach. Emma turned and started swimming toward it again, Rocky still in tow. Again it bobbed off to one side. Jane kept calling. Emma kept swimming. It took fifteen frightening minutes with Emma changing directions again and again before it came crashing directly toward her and she flung her free arm at it and caught hold of the edge so Jane could grab her and hold on. Jane then clutched at and caught the edge of Rocky's jacket and held it tightly as Emma hoisted herself aboard. Barely catching her breath, she crept to the edge where Jane was hanging onto Rocky by his jacket. She grabbed the other side. On the next dip, the two of them yanked him forward, his arms over the edge of the shell. And on the next big push from the sea, they managed to hoist him halfway over. One more big dip and they dragged him aboard, tugging at his legs and feet until he rolled down into the shell bottom.

The two of them slid down on top of him, and they all three lay in a tangle, catching their breath, flopping this way and that as the shell skipped over the waves.

"I think it's easing," said Emma. "And isn't the wind coming from the southwest now? Or am I totally messed up? Rocky OK?"

"He's breathing. Let's let him sleep. Jesus, what a ride."

Emma panted in agreement. "For someone who gets seasick, this must have been sheer hell." They lay there, rolling, panting, letting their utter fatigue take over at last.

"Look, what's that?" Jane asked as they passed what seemed to be a blinking light.

On the next dip Emma saw it, too. "Oh, thank God," she said. "I'll bet that's the Memory Rock lighted buoy. Which would mean this is the Little Bahama Sound. I just saw it on that chart." She felt inside her jacket. The chart was gone.

"So where are we then?"

"I don't remember exactly, but north of West End, I think. This could be the Gulf Stream we're floating in. It's right around here somewhere."

"Well, at least the storm is petering out, it looks like." She was right. As quickly as the two storms had come upon them, they were passing. To the east, together, as if having once joined, they would not be put asunder. The tumbling eased. The stormy seas were calming noticeably. The rain was still pelting, but not like a raging waterfall anymore.

They floated along, twisting and turning, slipping further and further away from the storm's anger. The night was ticking by. Rocky's intermittent groans became mumbles. It sounded like he was saying, "I can't swim. I can't swim," over and over.

"I'm sure the Coast Guard is already looking for us," said Emma. "And the Bahamas Rescue. You

238

know for sure the other boats reported anything they could. So I think while it's relatively calm here, we ought to sleep. We can't see anything much anyway, and right now there isn't a thing we can do."

Twenty

Lauren answered the door. "Holachek?" asked the man who stood there in front of a carrier loaded with boxes.

Lauren nodded.

"Hugh's Catering. Where do you want all this?" She led him past the hubbub into the dining room, where two other deliveries of food had been deposited earlier. He looked at the array of edibles and laughed. "Boy, you really needed more of this, didn't you?" He unloaded the top boxes and opened them to reveal platters of fruit, cold cuts, breads, and salad—and then closed them again. He opened disposable servers full of butter pats, condiments, sweeteners, salt and pepper packets, and such, and then resealed them. "Want me to put these in a fridge somewhere?" he asked. "You got a lot out here already."

Lauren shook her head. "I think it's full."

"Jeesh, it's a shame to let it all spoil. Wait. I got some ice and a couple foam coolers out in the truck.

240

We use them for deliveries sometimes. You could return them when we pick up the coffeemakers. I got two coffeemakers to bring in, too."

Lauren followed him back to the door and held it open for him. It would automatically close and lock otherwise—Nelly had gotten the right kind of locks this time. He returned with his little cart loaded with two oversized coolers, and balanced on top, two coffeemakers with cords wrapped around them. No one in the living room even looked up as it rolled by.

"But who's going to eat all this food and drink all that coffee?" Lauren groaned as he lifted the coffeemakers onto the buffet, next to two that were already there. She had called Hugh's from her car phone on the way up, and both Ben Schlesser and Mac Britton, busy in the living room on portable phones, had also apparently called caterers before they arrived. "These are ready to go, but you've already got coffee and decaf, so we won't plug them in yet," said the deliveryman. "When those pots run low, plug these in. Takes about ten, fifteen minutes. Hey, they're our coffeemakers, too."

"Yes. Another Hugh's truck delivered some of this stuff a couple of hours ago. I guess we all had the same idea—that no one was going to be able to think of food today. What we didn't realize was that nobody was going to want to eat, either."

"I'll just put these coolers in your kitchen. Through that door? They've got all the ice I had left in the bottom. You might want to have someone pick up another couple of bags later. You got enough food here for the tenth army. Coffee, too."

After he carried the coolers into the kitchen and stored most of his delivery inside them, he handed Lauren an invoice to initial and she handed him ten dollars and let him out the back door. "What's going on here?" he asked on the way out. "Everyone looks uptight."

"Our children," said Lauren, her voice breaking. "They're—lost at sea. But we'll find them. We know that."

He looked down at the pretty older woman in the doorway, so small and distraught, and he managed a hearty smile. "Of course you will. They got that stuff down to a science. You can't even hide out there if you want to anymore."

She forced an equally hearty smile and said, "You're absolutely right," and slowly closed the door.

Nelly hung up. Mac and Ben both looked at her expectantly. "No, it was only Minny, from next door. She just got in. She'll be right over." The phone rang again, as it had been ringing all afternoon. This time it was Merve Morganthau. "He's going to get out, Nelly. A.A., counseling, a job. Some clunk who used to work for your husband when he had his repairs company—someone he bowls with—has offered him work on the condition that he's on the wagon."

"Oh, dear. Oh, no!"

"Now, with this boating thing, I guess he's been weeping in his cell. Says they're his kids, too. He wants to help. He wants to have a meeting with you and whoever else you say. Today or tomorrow."

Nelly groaned. "Will he be out by then? Not today, Merve. I just can't. Tell them we don't know much of anything yet, except that the boat probably went down. They can't find it anywhere. The Bahamas Air and Sea Rescue is on it now and the Coast Guard. And a number of private planes. Maybe my mother or my neighbor Minny would see him. I just can't."

"What about in a few days, in my office, with me there?"

"Oh, I don't know. If we have to, I guess. If it won't delay the divorce. Ask me tomorrow. Not today, please. By tomorrow, everything will probably be all right anyway."

"I'll make it in my office if we can't get out of it, Nelly. I'll try to arrange a three-way call instead. But we'll see. Don't be upset about it. Nothing can happen. And nothing's going to delay your divorce. You'll have that paper in your hands in another three weeks or so."

The front doorbell rang. Everyone looked up and froze for a second as Lauren ran to answer it. There

243

stood Minny. Everyone took a breath and returned to whatever they had been doing. "I didn't use my key," she whispered. "All those cars out front. We don't want everyone to know I have one, right? Oh, Nana, I don't believe it. Lost? Not those kids. They'd find a way home if they got dumped on an iceberg. That Bermuda Triangle is attacking the wrong pair."

"Of course it is," agreed Lauren. "But until they're found, it'll be a madhouse here."

"I been working a couple of hours a night for Nelly on the agency stuff," Minny said. "She doesn't want me to quit my Quick-Shop job until I can retire. It's coming right up, and she wants to be sure this thing is going to fly. I guess I'll just take care of that stuff now unless you got something else I can help with?"

"Nothing I can think of right now, dear. But do take some food home later. Three of us had things brought in and, of course, everyone is so upset they can't eat a bite."

Nelly came over. "Morganthau called, Minny. Albert wants to talk to me. He's joined A.A. and he's probably getting out. He wants to know about the girls."

"Poor Albert. He probably feels terrible. I mean, he should, but can you imagine how down he is? Listen, Nelly, if you need me to talk to him for you, I'll do it. I already saw him at the bowling alley. He was so lost. He's not the same Albert. I could keep him informed. Would that help?"

Lauren squeezed Minny's hand. "That would be wonderful, except that we don't want you in any danger, Minny."

"I don't think he's dangerous anymore. Let me try."

"You're sure you don't want a bite?" asked Lauren.

"I'll eat as soon as Freddy gets here. He's going to help me with the agency stuff. He sounds very good on a phone. Too bad he doesn't like to bowl. He likes tennis and he *hates* bowling alleys. He won't even come with me to my leagues. Too bad. Otherwise he's so nice. Well, maybe I'll just have a slice of pizza to keep me going until he gets here." She gave Nelly a long, tight hug. "Don't be upset, Nell. Those kids of yours can handle anything."

"Of course. I know you're right," Nelly said. "Minny, let me introduce you to everyone." She took her over to Ben. "Minny, this is Ben Schlesser, one of my former bosses and my good friend." Ben put his phone aside for a moment to give Minny's hand a squeeze.

"And over here," she said, leading Minny toward a man in headphones who was listening to some kind of radio equipment set up on the secretary. "This is Boz Richter's friend, Roger LeNou. This is a ham radio he's set up here so we're right on top

245

of it all—getting news faster than it happens, almost. The hams are so good about helping when someone's in trouble. And this is Boz. He's got members of a pilots' club he belongs to out there flying around and searching."

Nelly introduced her to a man Boz had brought over to talk to Nelly and interpret the Coast Guard messages and other reports, then to the man from Merve Morganthau's office. She then introduced Evan Gumbel, explaining that it was his boat that Rocky and the girls were lost in. Then they moved on to another member of the Sea Rats named Ed Sparrows. At that point Boz beckoned and she hurried over. "Roger just found out something. Get Britton." She caught Mac's eye and he joined her. "We didn't get this from the Coast Guard yet, but one of our guys picked up the Bahamas Rescue radios. I hate to tell you this, but they don't see that boat anywhere. They think it's gone down." Nelly gasped and clapped her hands over her mouth. "They're probably floating around there somewhere or someone's picked them up. We don't have any word yet, but at least the storm is beginning to ease up in the area where they were last seen. That's what Roger got." He moved about the room, telling the others the grim news.

In a daze, Nelly took Minny by the hand to finish introducing her and turned back to Mac, who hadn't moved. He was just standing there, staring at the floor.

"Minny, this is Mac Britton," Nelly said in a voice so limp it was almost a whisper. "Mac, this is my friend and neighbor, Minny. Minny, it's Mac's son Rocky that the twins went out with."

"Well, don't be so worried, Mr. Britton," said Minny, flashing a cheery smile. "Your son is in good hands. The best. Jane and Emma could tame a tornado. They always know the right thing to do. They're probably sitting on a beautiful island out there somewhere right now, sipping rum-and-Coke and playing backgammon."

Mac looked at Minny like she was deranged. Nelly looked toward her mother expectantly, but Lauren, for once, couldn't think of anything to say. Ben Schlesser broke the awkward silence, nodding at Minny. "From your mouth to God's ears, honey."

The rain eased off, the clouds blew away, the seas let up, and the stars came out. The sky was a twinkling dome of awesome beauty. But the three exhausted passengers in the shell slept, oblivious to the spectacle overhead and to the gentle twirling of their craft. It had become their cradle, lulling and comforting them in their slumber. Rocky coughed and sniffled. No one heard. Jane and Emma moaned in their sleep. No one heard. Time eased on, and the shell glided this way and that, drawn, despite all the twists and turns, to where the Gulf Stream was carrying it: closer and closer to the one island Emma had seen on the charts—a nameless, treeless, all-but-nude sandspit above Freeport.

Mac left at midnight. He asked Nelly to take a short walk with him first. She told her mother they would head toward the cul-de-sac so Lauren could find them if they heard anything.

"Nothing's going to happen this late, most likely," he said, closing the door behind them. They walked slowly out to the street and turned toward the cul-de-sac.

"Nelly, I can't tell you how sorry I am. I wish I could turn back the clock. I would have steered clear of you rather than bring you into all this."

"You haven't done anything to me—and there may not even be any trouble. It's not knowing that's so hard. They're probably OK."

"God, I hope so, but my son has a nose for trouble. Rocky is bright, personable, articulate. A quick learner. He could do anything, but he always has the same excuse. There's one more experience he has to have first. He sees nothing wrong in stretching the truth a little about his qualifications, if it's something he really wants to do. Like the oil rig job. He doesn't seem to realize he's risking other peoples' lives, too. I should have looked into this. I'd have put my foot down."

"Well, maybe this will be the turning point. After they come back." Mac stopped and looked down at her. In the glow of the streetlight she could see that his face was a picture of agony. "Mac, you mustn't think of the dark side. We'll face whatever we have to face, *if* we have to face it. But we have to be positive now." Her voice broke. "Because I just can't bear the idea of anything happening to them."

Mac pulled her into his arms and hugged her tightly, his hand cupping her head against his neck. He stroked her hair. Nelly felt the tears welling. "Oh, Mac," she sobbed. And he took her face in his hands and lifted it so she had to look right up at him. "Nelly. Dear Nelly, I wouldn't have put you through this. You're the last person I would ever want to hurt." He bent and kissed her hungrily. She stood on tiptoe to feel more of his kiss, to reach up to kiss him back. He hugged her tightly again, pulling her close; she felt sheltered by every part of him. They clung to each other under the streetlamp, saying nothing, sharing unspoken compassion—and fear. A current of silent comfort flowed between them. Finally, he let her go, took her trembling hand in his, and walked her slowly back toward the house.

"I want you to turn in now, Nelly. I don't care if those people have to stay to take messages or whatever. You go to bed. Let your mother run things. I'll be back first thing in the morning, and together we'll handle whatever we have to handle."

Nelly nodded. His voice was heavy with defeat. Did he really think they wouldn't be saved? No, she wouldn't allow such thoughts. Because when she did, she felt a welling of unbearable pain.

Back in the house, she leaned against the door listening to Mac's car pull away. Had he really kissed her out there? Did she imagine it? Albert had never kissed her like that. And how could either of them even think of a kiss when their children might just be bodies, floating somewhere out in that vast ocean?

Ben came over and led her back into the living room. He eased her into a chair and began rubbing her hands. "Nelly? Nelly? Are you all right?" Her mother rushed over. And Minny.

"Nelly, I think it's time we got you to bed," said Lauren. Ben nodded, scooped her up from the chair, and carried her, following Lauren and Minny, to her bedroom. He laid her ever so gently on her bed, kissed her forehead, patted her cheeks awkwardly, and turned to slip out of the room.

"Everything's going to be fine tomorrow, Nelly. Please don't look so white. Please don't cry," pleaded Minny as Lauren tugged off her shoes and skirt and jacket and pulled up the covers.

"Oh, but I didn't—"

"You'll brush your teeth in the morning," said Lauren.

"I'm not crying," said Nelly. "It's just that my

eyes are making tears." Minny took a handful of Kleenex and wiped Nelly's wet cheeks, and then her own. At the door, Lauren turned out the lights. Nelly slipped downward into a blessed limbo of numbness. And slept.

Twenty-one

Emma woke up, started to thrash her arms, and then remembered where she was. As the shell dipped gently she saw the first fingers of pink light grip the sky in the east. The rain had stopped. The air was cool—fresh and light on her skin. Next to her, Jane opened her eyes. She, too, started to lurch, saw Emma, and realized where they were. "I'm starving. And thirsty," she whispered.

Emma nodded. They patted their pockets and pulled out a Snickers bar and a packet of cookies and split them. "Look. the can of soda—it's still here," whispered Jane.

"We better wait until Rocky wakes up and the three of us share it," Emma whispered back. "Mine's gone. I hope he's still got his."

"Hope I still have what?" mumbled Rocky, opening one eye and quickly closing it. "Oh, Christ, it's for real. I was hoping it was just a bad dream." He snuffled and coughed.

"Eat a candy bar or some cookies, Rocky," said Jane. "We just did. It's the can of soda. Have you still got yours?"

He felt his pockets. "I think so." He pulled one slightly bent can from his jacket pocket and put it back.

"Well, that makes two and that's it. We'll share one."

"Why don't we wait as long as we can?" Rocky suggested. "Once they're gone, they're gone. And we don't know how long—"

"Right," Emma nodded. Groaning, the three of them sat up. "Well, I'm sure they'll find us any minute. As soon as the planes come looking." She peered upward. No movement in the dusky sky yet, not even a bird. "The thing to do is kill time as painlessly as possible until then."

Rocky shook his head. "No. Nothing gained by trying to hurry time," he said. "It won't budge. And this is a unique experience. We should live every moment of it. Savor it. Most people will never know what it's like to have an adventure like this."

"Lucky them," said Emma. "Because fortunately, most people don't have a wacko friend to lead them into this *unique experience.*"

"One who thinks that danger and thrills are what life is all about," added Jane. "To heck with accomplishing something. To heck with developing your talents. So what if you scare your parents shitless? So what if someday you kill yourself and God only knows who else? Thrills and danger are worth it. Wowee!"

Rocky was silent for a moment. "Yeah, you're right." He sighed heavily. "I really did it this time, didn't I? Shit! Sometimes I see why my dad goes nuts. Am I ever going to get my act together? Will I ever do anything that matters to anyone but me?"

"Good question," said Jane sternly. "Why haven't you?"

"I always meant to. I got my law degree and never worked a day at it. There were so many things I wanted to try first. Places to go. I saw my dad work, work, work. Never go anywhere or do anything that didn't have to do with his cases. He made a fortune, but he's missed so much. I wanted to do a few things first. I didn't have to work yet. Ever since I was twenty-one I've gotten a little income from a trust my mother made him set up for me when I was just a kid, and Dad's been picking up the rest."

Emma sniffed. "Didn't you ever want to make your mother and father proud of you?"

"My dad, maybe. My mother? Couldn't care less. Looks are all that mattered. Were my teeth getting straightened OK? She's had more plastic surgery than any ten people you know. Anything I tried to talk to her about, she'd interrupt to ask how I thought her forehead looked after her last tuck—or should she get her eyes done again. But my dad? He cares. Too much."

"Well, we just don't think the way you do," said Jane. "Nana would give us anything we want. We have little trusts, too, from her, but we've never spent a dollar from them. We let them accumulate. And we've paid her back every cent she spent sending us to college. It was so good of her to do that. My father couldn't and wouldn't have if he could. He always had enough money for his hooch, bowling, and fishing trips. But not for us for school. He worked less and less and my mother worked more and more. We made up our minds when we were twelve years old that we'd never get trapped like Mom. We'd run our own lives, and let in whoever we really wanted. We've known what we wanted and we've never let anything get in the way—and we haven't missed all that much."

"Well, if we get out of this—" Rocky began.

"*When,* not if, Rocky," said Emma. "Mother and Nana would make them drain the whole damned ocean before they'd give up. They'll find us. We just have to make the soda and cookies last—and keep our minds on pleasant things so we don't jump overboard."

"Maybe killing time wouldn't be such a bad idea at that," said Rocky. But I forgot the fishing poles. And the chess set."

"We could play backgammon," said Jane. "But we forgot to bring the board, too."

255

"And charades aren't easy when the floor is rocking. How about Twenty Questions?"

"Sure, if you want to," said Jane. "But you'll probably lose."

"We'll see about that," Rocky snorted. "I used to be pretty good."

"Like you are at sailing?" asked Emma slyly. "After your performance yesterday, you're lucky we didn't leave you for shark food."

"And getting seasick! So gauche!" added Jane. "This is the last cruise I go on with him, Emma. I hate it when people get seasick."

"Very funny," said Emma. "But back to Twenty Questions. You're first."

"No, ladies first," said Rocky.

"Why not? OK. It's animal," said Emma.

"Human being?" asked Jane? Emma nodded.

"Historical figure?"

"No."

Rocky's turn. First he sneezed and then he asked, "Male?"

"No," said Emma.

"Marilyn Monroe!" cried Jane.

"Right," whooped Emma.

"Now wait a minute. How did you figure that?" cried Rocky. "There weren't enough questions yet. It could have been anyone."

"That's why Jane and I hardly ever play that game. We can read each other's minds."

MORE PASSION AND ADVENTURE AWAIT... YOUR TRIP TO A BIG ADVENTUROUS WORLD BEGINS WHEN YOU ACCEPT YOUR FIRST 4 NOVELS ABSOLUTELY *FREE* (AN $18.00 VALUE)

Accept your Free gift and start to experience more of the passion and adventure you like in a historical romance novel. Each Zebra novel is filled with proud men, spirited women and tempestuous love that you'll remember long after you turn the last page.

Zebra Historical Romances are the finest novels of their kind. They are written by authors who really know how to weave tales of romance and adventure in the historical settings you love. You'll feel like you've actually gone back in time with the thrilling stories that each Zebra novel offers.

GET YOUR FREE GIFT WITH THE START OF YOUR HOME SUBSCRIPTION

Our readers tell us that these books sell out very fast in book stores and often they miss the newest titles. So Zebra has made arrangements for you to receive the four newest novels published each month.

You'll be guaranteed that you'll never miss a title, and home delivery is so convenient. And to show you just how easy it is to get Zebra Historical Romances, we'll send you your first 4 books absolutely FREE! Our gift to you just for trying our home subscription service.

BIG SAVINGS AND FREE HOME DELIVERY

Each month, you'll receive the four newest titles as soon as they are published. You'll probably receive them even before the bookstores do. What's more, you may preview these exciting novels free for 10 days. If you like them as much as we think you will, just pay the low preferred subscriber's price of just $3.75 each. *You'll save $3.00 each month off the publisher's price.* AND, your savings are even greater because there are never any shipping, handling or other hidden charges—FREE Home Delivery. Of course you can return any shipment within 10 days for full credit, no questions asked. There is no minimum number of books you must buy.

GET
FOUR
FREE
BOOKS
(AN $18.00 VALUE)

ZEBRA HOME SUBSCRIPTION
SERVICE, INC.
120 BRIGHTON ROAD
P.O. Box 5214
CLIFTON, NEW JERSEY 07015-5214

AFFIX
STAMP
HERE

"OK, I bet you can't read mine," Rocky said. "It's animal."

"Human?" asked Jane.

Rocky said, "Yes." And then sneezed again and broke into a paroxysm of coughing.

"Was that a clue?" asked Emma. "Then I've got it. The inventor of tuberculosis." The girls roared and Rocky threw up his hands.

"Maybe we should try to sleep again," said Emma. "Or we might just want to keep an eye out for that island, that sandspit. I think it's around here somewhere."

Could it be an optical illusion? Or maybe some kind of cloud formation on the horizon. Please God, no. Jane had seen Rocky and Emma, in their sleep, cuddle together unknowingly. They were curled up like two lovers. She wouldn't wake them unless she was certain. She watched as the blurry, cloud-like image hardened into something more solid. A mass of seaweed? The island? Finally she whispered, "Emma, wake up. Look over there."

Emma sat up. "Huh? What? Look where?"

"There. Way out. What do you see?"

Emma pulled herself up to the rim of the shell and her eyes opened wide. "My God, is that an island? The one on the chart? It's not just a clump of seaweed, is it?" They stared at the mass. "I think it might be the one I saw. But whatever it is—I don't care if it's Pitcairn—I think we should land there if we can."

"Of course, we should land there," said Jane dryly. "If we stay in this tub and let the stream keep pulling us along we'll end up in Greenland. We'll land all right. But how?"

"Why we just—" she stopped. "My gosh, that's right. We haven't got a rudder or a paddle or anything. And this damn shell is too big for us to swim it in." She looked over the rim again. "It looks like we're headed right toward it, but what if we miss? I guess we'll just have to abandon ship and swim," said Emma. "As soon as we get close enough, if it looks like we're not going to beach there. I can't think of anything else. Can you?"

"But Rocky can't swim."

"Heck, if it's like it is right here, he can probably walk ashore. Look down."

Jane, hanging over the edge, did as she was told. "My gosh, this *is* shallow!"

"Right. There are shallows all around here, but I don't know what it'll be like there. But we may have no problem."

"What if there are no shallows when we get nearer?"

"We have no choice. If the shell doesn't head in, Rocky has to hit the water. His jacket will keep him afloat and we'll just steer him. Yo, Rocky," she reached over and shook him. "Wake up, mate," she ordered. "Look, Rocky, land ho!"

It was barely seven when Lauren called Barton deLys in Montreal. "Nothing new since last night, but now it's daylight and the planes will be out and they'll surely find them."

"When this is over and the twins are back safely," he said, "I want you to come up here to the lodge and just unwind for a few days. You're going to need it."

"Life never lets up on us, does it, Bart? I'm frantic about my granddaughters and my daughter. You're frantic about your sister. Mac Britton's frantic about his son."

"If I don't hear anything from you by noon, I'm coming down."

"You'll hear from me. If we were going to hear terrible news, I think I'd somehow know. I don't have any of those desperate vibes this morning—the ones I always get before a catastrophe."

It looked like they would pass a little to the west of it. And indeed they would have if it weren't for the sandbars—and the fact that there were so many shallow patches on that side, at least, of the spit. The shell seemed to lodge on one twice, then moved away.

"Rock it!" ordered Emma each time, and when they all crawled to one side, that was enough to tip the shell so it slid off into the water again. Emma hung on near the edge. As the shell seemed headed to pass the almost-barren spit far to one side, she ordered, "Abandon ship, kids. On that side, so we can try to push the shell in. It might be shallow enough here."

Rocky, terror etched on his face, jumped in, then found himself sitting upright, his head and chest out of the water. He stood up, leaped into the air and crowed, "It's shallow! I can stand up!"

Emma and Jane tried to grab the shell, but without the weight of the three bodies, it bobbed off like a feather toward the north. "Should we go after it?" Rocky asked.

"No way," said Emma firmly. "Let's get onto that island." They began walking toward it until the bottom dropped away, then Rocky floated and the girls swam, taking turns pulling him along toward the nearly-barren spit ahead. It looked, at the moment, like the most beautiful patch of land on the planet.

"My gosh," said Emma as they hit bottom again in the shallows just out from the beach. "Will you look at all that mess?" The edges of the long island were cluttered with washed-up debris—plastic pop bottles and crates, boards, pieces of rope and sail, rags and clothing, parts of chairs, fishing gear. Even a plastic shell similar to theirs, only much smaller and broken at one end.

Emma was indignant. "That's all junk people throw overboard from their boats. Don't they care what they're doing to the environment? They're mucking up the whole ocean!"

"This one time, we can be thankful that mess landed here," said Rocky. "Some of it might just save our lives." They moved slowly through the shallows closer in, and finally up onto the beach.

Then, suddenly, Rocky took over. "I know we'd like to just collapse," he said, sniffling and clearing his throat. "But we can't. Not until we salvage everything we might need from all that junk on the shore before the waves wash away something important. Or we could have another rainstorm and it all disappears. We want that shell, rope, bottles. Driftwood for a fire. If you find anything with rainwater in it, for God's sake, don't tip it. I think it's time we drank that can of soda." He dug it from his pocket, popped it open, and passed it to Jane. "Ladies first."

Jane drank what she hoped was about a third of the can. Emma was next, then Rocky finished it. "I'll go this way, you girls go that way," he said. "Bring back anything you think we might be able to use." They dumped their lifejackets and started down the beach, Rocky in one direction, the girls in the other. There were a few patches of scrub, but no woods or shade. "Now I understand the difference between a lush tropical island and a sandspit," said Emma. "You could bake to death on this one."

There was a lot of debris, some just at the shore-line, some washed up twenty feet or more from the water's edge. They began carrying armloads of empty plastic bottles and containers, swatches of rope, and pieces of driftwood back up to where their lifejackets lay. Ten minutes later they heard Rocky let out a whoop. They ran toward the other end of the spit and found him standing next to a pair of deep stainless steel sinks that had washed ashore and become wedged between driftood and a battered, peeling cabinet. The sinks were full of water!

"Go get the soda can," he told Emma. "It's rain-water. We're all going to drink our fill." Emma ran, panting, back to where they had landed and grabbed the soda can, but she simply couldn't run back. She walked, with a pain in her side, gasping for breath, as fast as she could in the sand.

"You first; you found it," said Emma. Rocky filled a can and drank it down in long gulps. He passed the can to Emma, who did the same, and then to Jane. Then Rocky filled the can and drank again and so did the girls. Jane walked down the beach until she found a bottle, brought it back, and filled it.

"I don't think we're going to be here for too long,"

said Rocky. "But still, we don't want to waste this. Did you collect a lot of those plastic bottles yet?"

"Dozens."

"Then we'll use the can to fill a couple of the bottles. And we should somehow hack off the tops of some of the other bottles and wedge them in the sand to catch more rainwater. Just in case."

While Jane went to get more bottles, Emma and Rocky continued collecting. By now the sun was up and they were getting hot. And very tired.

They had amassed a great assortment of junk. When Jane finished bottling the water, she carried the full bottles to their little settlement and put them into holes she dug in the sand to hold them upright.

Then she hurried down the beach to help Emma, who had found the small shell and loaded it with more bottles, rope, driftwood, and the remains of several tee shirts, sails, towels, and even parts of blankets. The two of them tugged it back to their collection.

They found Rocky twirling a smoking stick in a depression in a piece of driftwood. Nearby, he had dug a pit in the sand and filled it with small pieces of driftwood and a couple of scraps of paper. "It takes forever but you can make a fire this way. When I was a Boy Scout you did it for a badge. I'm cheating a little—I found these papers in a box down the beach. It'll light easier than with little sticks." He looked approvingly at the shell behind them. "Oh, great. And I found a pole—we'll have a little shelter here as soon as I get the fire going."

"We can do it," said Jane. She and Emma tied the pole to the beat-up shell, then stuck the other end of the pole into the sand to raise a crude slanted roof. By that time, Rocky's fire was burning. They dug candy bars from their pockets. "Time for din-din," said Jane. "And a rest."

"Save the wrappers," said Rocky, shivering as he spoke. "Isn't this neat? All the comforts of home. I mean, if you don't mind the mosquitoes." He slapped himself on the arm.

Emma came over and felt his forehead. "I think that sniffle and cough are more than a sniffle and cough, Rocky," she said. "You've got a nice little fever there. You better get under the shelter and wrap all those rags around you and rest."

"And I think we all have a little lesson to learn from this," said Jane. "That adventure is not the be-all and end-all in life."

"Yeah, as my father keeps telling me," Rocky said. "Like he keeps saying a few scars do not make you Elephant Man."

"You can hardly see those scars," snorted Emma. "You have to look for them. And what difference do they make, anyway? Look at Noriega. Absolutely lumpy face. His face makes yours look like a baby's bottom. And remember Richard Burton—he was pock-marked, every inch. It never stopped him from

264

winning Liz Taylor. Scars make a man's face more interesting, just like wrinkles do. But neither one does that for a woman. It's not really fair."

"Well, anyway, you're right—I do feel kind of rotten," he admitted. "I think I'll try to rest. But don't let the fire go out, and I think we should gather up some of that green stuff and put it on to make smoke. Anyone find any rubber tires? We want to burn them if a plane goes over. Easier to see."

"I think I saw a bicycle tire down there somewhere," said Jane. "I'll go find it."

"And keep an eye on the sky. They'll be looking for us; you know that." He grabbed some rags, crawled under the shelter, burrowed into the sand, and wrapped the rags around himself. He coughed again and groaned, but he was soon fast asleep.

The girls hiked a short way down the beach to find the tire, urinate, and wash themselves in the shallows. On the way back, Emma said, "Well, he's better at playing Robinson Crusoe than he is at playing Columbus. He's right. One of us ought to stay awake in case a rescue plane comes over."

"You nap first, I'll watch," said Jane. "And I think I'll put some shreds of this tire on the fire now. They'd notice the smoke from further off if it was black."

"I hope they come soon," said Emma. "Boy, do I need a bath. All that salt water drying on my skin— I feel like a pretzel."

Twenty-two

The acrid smell of burning rubber filled his nose. More than tickling, it was badgering and tormenting him—dragging him from his exhausted stupor. And that noise. How could he sleep with that rowdy screeching and laughing out there? What was so damned funny? He forced his eyes open, peered out of the shelter, and realized where he was. Emma and Jane were leaping and kicking in front of the fire, hooting uproariously. Didn't they smell that burning rubber sending up black smoke spirals behind them? "Rocky-Jockey, wake up," they ordered, as he pulled himself upright and sat blinking stupidly into the painfully bright sunshine. "We're OK. We found it!"

"Found what?" He struggled to take a deep breath. It just didn't want to go down. His chest felt tight. It hurt.

"The Fountain of Youth," cried Emma, crawling into the shelter to give him a fierce hug, then crawling out again to do a kind of Indian dance in the

266

sand. "The land over the rainbow," she chortled. "The Loch Ness Monster. The pirate's treasure. We found it all, right out here in the middle of nowhere!"

Rocky groped for the bottle of water, drank, coughed, sneezed, and drank again. "Drink it all," urged Emma. "We'll go get more. And help is on the way!"

He stared out at them, twirling and stomping, and at the thick smoke rising behind them. He still didn't get it. Pushing his rags aside, he crawled out of the shelter. The girls pointed to the sky. He looked up and saw the first plane. "Oh my God! Look!"

"It's a bird. It's a plane. It's *superman!*" cried Jane. "We're saved! That's what we found."

The plane dropped low and dipped its wings as the three of them waved frantically.

And then he saw a second plane. And a third.

Four planes were circling, two of them so low they could see the pilots waving. Rocky grabbed an old towel from under the shelter and swished it back and forth above his head.

After several minutes, two of the planes flew off. But a speck in the sky to the west grew into another one that dipped its wings. "I think they're calling in other planes to take turns marking where we are until someone gets here to pick us up," said Jane. "A Coast Guard cutter or a yacht in the area or something. Maybe even a helicopter."

"I'll wait for a yacht, thank you" said Emma. "I

am *not* climbing up a flimsy ladder into the sky to board a helicopter."

She spotted the boat first. Another speck—but on the horizon—that grew larger and larger. It dropped anchor almost a mile out and lowered a motor boat that came skimming toward them at top speed. But halfway in, it stopped, too. "It can't get all the way, cried Emma. "Too shallow. Get on your jackets, gang. We'll go out to meet it."

They scrambled into their lifejackets again. Jane kicked sand on the fire, and with Rocky in the middle, the three of them waded out into the sea toward their rescue.

Fifteen minutes later they were on board a sleek ninety-footer, laughing, crying, hugging the two crew members and the owners. "Give him some aspirin quickly, please, if you have any," pleaded Emma, pointing to Rocky. "Or any cold pills—and a good belt of whiskey. And can he flop in a bed somewhere? I think he has pneumonia." Rocky tried to say something. His mouth moved but nothing came out. His legs began to tremble and he reached for the rail, but the crew members caught him and half-dragged, half-carried him off.

"And could you let our mother and our Nana know we're OK?" both girls asked at once. "Please?"

The tears began welling. "They must be worried sick."

Every chair was taken. Every surface seemed to have a cup of coffee and a portable phone on it—or a plate of food. Roger LeNou was there again with his portable ham shack set up on the secretary. Boz Richter wasn't there—he was out flying the skies near Freeport, searching with his pals. But he had sent another friend, Chad McNulty, to coordinate this unofficial search for him. Nelly and Lauren had been up since six, Ben had arrived back at seven, and Mac, a few minutes later.

Will Raymond had sent a caterer with more food—scrambled eggs, bacon, Danish—and more coffeemakers plus his secretary, Doris. She helped Lauren and the two staffers set out the breakfast in the dining room, then stayed to help serve and wash cups and plates afterward. Before she left, she brought in folding chairs from the garage, stacked hand towels in the bathrooms, and ran a load of laundry.

McKinnon and Goldberg had both stopped by. One of Lauren's new suitors, Donald Brandt of Brandt publishing, had arrived at 9:30 and stayed over an hour.

To Nelly, the morning was dragging by painfully and slowly. LeNou announced every scrap of news as fast as it came in, but it was mostly empty. Data about where they were searching and what they had and hadn't found, what the seas were like. None of it was very encouraging—except that the other boats were all accounted for by nine. They had been blown far and wide. Four had made it into Freeport during the night, damaged, but under their own power. One had limped in at 8:30 this morning, barely afloat, with major damage. One crew member, Debby Gibbs, had been tossed off the Gibbs boat and had miraculously clung to a rope for almost ten minutes in rough seas before her husband and brothers realized she was missing and managed to haul her back on board.

All boats accounted for. Except *Buttbuster III*.

Nelly talked to everyone. To LeNou at his radio, to Chad McNulty about the pilots' club and what Boz Richter and his friends were finding out. If she kept talking, she didn't have to think.

At nine the Sheriff's office called about the messages on the door and said they were sending someone over. Minny came in but Nelly insisted she go on to work. "I promise I'll get hold of Albert today, Nelly, and catch him up on everything. Then maybe you won't have to see him." Calls came in every few minutes for the agency, as though nothing so frightening and draining were happening. She took numbers and called back on Ben's extra portable, trying to keep her voice even.

Mac slumped on a folding chair in the middle of it all, the picture of defeat. Every time he looked at Nelly, Ben observed, his face seemed to cloud with despair. At one point, Mac caught Nelly's hand as she came over to report the latest from the Bahamas Air and Sea Rescue people, and said something to her. Then he got up and followed her out the front door.

It was drizzling a little, as they headed up the street toward the dead end again. "Can't talk in there," he said. She nodded.

"I'm responsible for all this, Nelly," he said. "No, don't say anything. You and your girls couldn't know about Rocky, but I did. I knew that if there was a way to con the people in the space program into thinking he was qualified, he'd have been walking on the moon. I'm not saying this so you'll tell me I'm not responsible and then I can feel better. Because I am. I never should have let them go."

"How could you have stopped them?" asked Nelly with a sigh.

"I don't know. But somehow. I have never felt so helpless and ineffective in my life, never wanted so much to help. There is something fine about you, Nelly. I could see it even those first two times, when you were such a timid, quiet little thing. But when that C.G. started pushing you around, just dismissing you at that lunch, that really got my hackles up. I told myself to butt out, but I didn't want to. I felt

271

like defending you." They reached the cul-de-sac and stopped, turning toward each other.

"And at our first meeting at my office. I was so swamped that day. I'd just had a very frustrating talk with Rocky about the workout classes with Stepit. And I was irritated that I'd had to go over all this endlessly with C.G. and was then having to go over it with you. Not at you, but at her that she was wasting my time. She wanted to socialize with me, whether I wanted to or not."

"You don't have to explain, Mac. If you noticed me at all, I'm flattered. Nobody used to notice me. I've just become a different person, now. I was not only invisible before, I was easy to push around. So people did. It was my own fault."

"But even then, there was something about you," he said. "And the next time I saw you, you had suddenly bloomed into this lovely creature, very much in charge, but still very sweet. I have been so wrapped up in personal problems the past couple of years, I haven't had any desire to get involved with anyone. Until you.

"But you're the kind of woman that only good things should happen to, and I've brought you only the worst. I can't seem to do a fucking thing to help you. I've wanted so much just to hold you and kiss you. But I just haven't got the right."

"You're here," said Nelly. "That's all anyone can do right now. Unless you're a pilot. Or a radio ham."

"Your friend, Ben, your former boss—are you—uh—have you—?"

"No," said Nelly. "Ben was always friendly when I worked for them, but now he's my champion. He feels so badly about the business with C.G. and that he couldn't get the other partners to see it until just lately, that he can't do enough for me. He feels the company owes me."

"Then no romance?"

"Yes and no. I'm more than fond of him. He jokes that if I don't find anyone else, he'll be my ace in the hole. And he has said that if only he were five years younger—. But that's just meant to be like a compliment, I think. Nothing serious. He knows me from my years of being pushed around and invisible and scared of my shadow. He thinks he needs to give me lots of compliments and encouragement, now."

"I think he might mean a lot more than that, Nelly. I don't blame him. I'm glad there's someone you can count on. And I'm sorry you can't count on me, too."

Nelly saw the anguish in his eyes. Such sad longing. He didn't try to kiss her this time. He just squeezed her hand and held it tightly as they headed back to her house. But out front, before she unlocked the door, she turned to him and stood on tiptoe and kissed him. He started to wrap his arms around her, then stopped. But he kissed her back. Nelly had never kissed anyone as she kissed him, trying to caress his lips with hers, to taste his mouth as he had tasted hers before, trying to tell him how she felt. The empathy between them was even stronger than before. It was like they could talk without words, with a kiss. They looked at each other for a long moment. And then Nelly unlocked the door.

Ben watched them come in. He had never seen such sad, hopeless expressions on any two faces before. He had thought that perhaps this was the man for Nelly, but now he wasn't sure. Britton looked utterly whipped. Nelly deserved a fighter. Then again, how would he look if his son was lost at sea? Maybe worse.

At 10:30, the caterers emptied their warmers full of breakfast foods into paper cartons, put them in the kitchen, packed up their equipment, and left. Lauren and Nelly ran another load of dishes, dug out Nelly's warming trays, and made new pots of coffee and decaf. They pulled out several trays of food left from the night before, then stacked clean plates, silver, and cups and saucers. Breakfast was over, and it would soon be time for lunch. It was good to have something to do. Minny came in on her lunch break, emptied the dishwasher, and slipped out again.

Just as the first few people began strolling into

the dining room for a bite—Gumbel and Chad McNulty and Ben among them—Roger LeNou let out a whoop and hollered, "Yippee! Hot damn! Gang? They got 'em. They're A-OK! They found them. On some goddamn sandbar above Freeport!"

Ben grabbed Lauren and gave her a hug, then ran to grab Nelly and gave her a hug. He turned to Mac, and said, "Oh, what the hell, why not?" and gave him a hug, too. The whole crowd started cheering and hugging and crying. Lauren grabbed a phone to call Bart. "They're found. They're OK, thank God! I'll talk to you later." She took Ben's arm and began to dance with him. Then she stopped, picked up a glass, and clinked a spoon against it until she got everyone's attention. "I don't know who's got anything planned for New Year's Eve and who hasn't," she announced, "but you're all invited here that night for all the food, drinks, music, and dancing you can stand. Ten o'clock. Just let us know if you and your spouses or whatevers can come. All your ham friends are invited, Roger, and all those wonderful pilots. And all their better halves, of course. Doris and her husband. The partners and you, Ben. Minny."

Nelly, dazed with happiness, went to the phone to call Morganthau so he could pass the news on to Albert. Then she hurried over to Mac. "You and

Rocky will come to Mother's party, too, won't you?" she asked. "Please?"

"You're a glutton for punishment," he said. "But, yes," he said. "If you want us, we'll be there."

Twenty-three

"Mom, will you look at this paper?" groaned Jane and Emma together. Nelly stopped stirring the oatmeal, turned it on low, and grabbed the *Sun-Sentinel* which Jane pushed before her nose. "Lost and Found," screamed the headline. "Sailboat Sinks In Storm off Freeport—Survivors Found," announced the subhead. And there was a picture of the three of them getting off the yacht in Freeport before being flown back to Florida.

Nelly scanned the story. "But it says nothing about the fact that he can't sail," she said indignantly. "He sounds like a hero."

"Well, it's not their fault. We didn't tell them. How could we? There were so many people throwing questions at us and taking pictures. He was so sick and half out of it, all snuffy and coughing and weak like that," said Jane.

"Listen, Mom, how could we tattle on him?" asked Emma. "Were we supposed to announce,

277

'Hey, everybody, we just want you to know it was all this jerk's fault. He doesn't know how to sail worth ten cents.' Were we supposed to say that in front of God and everybody? Besides, when you know the whole story, he *was* a hero. A lot of it was just bad luck. We'd probably have made it if it wasn't for the storm. And even Evan Gumbel isn't mad at him. I mean, did you read that part where they interviewed him by phone? He just felt bad because he wasn't out there fighting the storm with us."

"I wondered about that. While he was here, he didn't even hint that Rocky had done anything so terrible. I guess no one told him. I don't think Boz told all his friends anything much, either, except that you were lost."

"And something else," Jane added. "He did what he could. He lied, yes. But on the boat he followed every order Emma gave him, unless he didn't understand. He got seasick. He practically got pneumonia, but he kept on trying. Once we got on that sandspit, he just took over and told us all the right things to do. With his know-how, we could have survived there forever."

"But it was *his* fault you were there in the first place!"

"Oh, Mom, things in the paper are so permanent—whether they're true or not. A piece that's down on someone puts a shadow on them for the rest of their lives. Someone can always haul out that article and show it to someone and people believe anything they see in print."

"I don't care," said Nelly stubbornly. "When someone darn near kills my daughters, I'm not very forgiving. And I certainly don't like to see him made out to be a hero."

"Then why did you tell Mac to bring him here for New Year's, Mom?" asked Jane.

"I don't know," replied Nelly. "I really don't know."

On the fourth floor at the Reef Memorial Hospital, Nurse Mary McMann saw the two attractive young women headed down the hall toward 407, caught up with them, and stopped them. "Who is it you want to see?" she asked.

"Oh, er—Rocky Britton," said one, looking uneasy. "The man whose boat went down in the Bermuda Triangle. He's in 407."

"Yes. Will you give me your names, please? You'll have to take a seat in the guests' waiting room, if you can find one. Visiting hours haven't started yet and there are already several people waiting who arrived before you. Your names?"

"Well—uhh—he might not remember us, but we met him at—"

"Please, your names," said Nurse McMann, pulling a little pad and pencil from her pocket and leading them to the waiting room, in which there was standing room only. It had been going on ever since McMann came on duty this morning. Endless calls. Women who apparently didn't even know him, try-ing to get into his room.

And what he needed was rest. McMann headed back to the nursing station and said to Nurse Andrea Stone, "Two more. I've never seen anything like it."

"Well, Dr. Clyde just fixed it. No visitors, no calls, except family and a short list he can give us. Don't give his room number to anyone. It's disrupting the whole damn floor," she grumbled. "We've got more important things to do than police this man's room, take his calls, and deal with his horny fan club."

"What does he need them all for, anyway?" asked McMann. "I mean, heck, there are at least half a dozen of us unattached nurses here who look as good as those dames."

"Oh, who'd want him?" retorted Andrea, who was just a shade over five feet tall. "Try to dance with a guy that tall and either you're smothering with your face buried in his jacket, or you've got a crick in your neck from looking up all the time."

For Rocky Britton, mused Mary McMann, it might be worth it.

Barton deLys arrived at Nelly's for Lauren's party at the same time as two men he figured had to be

Rocky and Mac Britton. In his rearview mirror he watched Mac drop Rocky off—it had to be him—how many young, handsome, six-foot-four guests could there be tonight? Then Mac drove off to find a parking space down the block. Barton stayed in his car, watching Britton walk heavily toward the house, then climbed out and followed him in.

Don't even talk to that young man, he told himself. How could he have done such a thing with so little regard for the girls' safety? When he passed through the living room, there was Rocky sitting on the couch, talking to another man Barton didn't recognize. He wanted to step over and say, "Hi, there, expert," and a lot more. But this was not the time or the place. Barton deLys often restrained himself from things he wanted very much to say and do. He would have loved to punch Rocky's teeth in, too. But he never gave in to such impulses. For better or worse, Barton had always been a gentleman, and he had found, over the years, that sometimes restraint was the most effective tactic of all.

Rocky was holding court in the living room like some kind of hero. He had been in the hospital since the rescue, but he had insisted on attending this party. Because he had responded so well to two days of rest and medication, Dr. Clyde had consented. "You go at 10:30 and you're out of there at 12:30.

That's enough. No dancing, no carousing. Just sit on your butt."

When Evan Gumbel arrived he made a beeline for Rocky, even before seeking out his hostesses to say hello. "Jeeze, Rock, I tried to visit you at the hospital, or at least call," he said, "but they said no calls, no visitors. I was afraid you were a lot worse off than the papers said. You OK?"

"Yeah. I had a bad cold or pneumonia or something but it's almost gone already."

"So I called your father's office and left a message—he called me back and said he thought you'd be here."

"Yeah, I got the message," Rocky said. He paused, trying to figure out just how to say something about how sorry he was about Gumbel's boat, but Evan interrupted him.

"Listen, I'm so sorry about the boat," said Evan. "Damn, that was just plain stupid. I *knew* I'd been having trouble. I never should have let you guys risk that kind of disaster. I don't know why I didn't say, 'Hey, we'll catch the next one, and let you take her up and down the Intra.'"

Rocky was stunned. Evan wasn't furious with him? He had half-expected some kind of scene. He wouldn't have blamed him. The new and beloved Briny was destroyed. "Evan, the insurance—"

"All taken care of. We got a tape of the interview at the dock in Freeport, and all that. Damn lucky you were able to catch the shell. Damn lucky you ran into the spit."

"*Damn* lucky," agreed Rocky. "And the twins were good sailors. On the spit they were female Daniel Boones. Anything you asked, they did it. I was feeling pretty rotten by then. I was asleep when they spotted the first planes but they got that tire on the fire and the black smoke pouring. Those planes couldn't miss us. We looked like Mount Vesuvius."

"That was some picture in the paper this morning," said Gumbel. "The one of you three getting off in Freeport. I know the Rajevskys, the people that owned the yacht. I talked to them that night, from Freeport. They told me you felt lousy."

"That's putting it mildly. I hardly remember walking off that damn boat. What that picture didn't show was they were practically holding me up."

"And you know what else, Rock? I found out they had more women calling the Bahamas Rescue and the Coast Guard and the port here, trying to get in touch with you. The hospital was swamped. Women who saw that picture and read that story, wanting to invite you out on their boats. To their clubs. Anything. They all wanted to meet you. I saw it the few nights we hung out together. You draw women like a magnet. That's one thing I'm looking forward to in this friendship, Buddy. It may be hard on my

283

boats, but I'm probably going to meet more gorgeous women than I'll know what to do with."

"We'll think of something," laughed Rocky.

Daniella Raymond had seen the picture, too, and when Will had mentioned being invited to the party at Nelly Holachek's, even though they were committed to the Loftkisses, she insisted they go to Loftkisses' party, which started at nine, *first,* and then to Nelly's.

When they arrived, Will, of course, cornered Mac, and the two of them headed out to a quieter corner of the Florida room to talk. Danny zeroed in on Rocky, who was chatting with Rob Mundelein. "I'm Will Raymond's wife, Daniella," she said.

"You don't have anything to drink. Can I get you something?" asked Mundelein.

"Oh, that's so nice of you," she said. "I would love a Diet Coke." When he shot over to the bar to get her one, she took his place next to Rocky. "OK if I park here for a minute?" she said, turning her head slightly so that long black hair slid over the side of her face. "I've heard a lot about you, Rocky. You've done everything but spaceships."

Rocky studied the sexy, smart-looking woman before him. As she stared boldly back, he took in the small waist, the good legs displayed to the thigh in one of those new short, clingy beaded dresses that were at least as revealing as a bathing suit. She was maybe ten or so years older than he, but looking good.

He smiled. "Yeah, I guess that's next," he said. "What else did you hear about?"

"Let's see. Kuwait. The Amazon. The Antarctic The bungee jumping. Shooting the rapids. The car racing. Have I forgotten anything?"

Rocky laughed. "I guess you don't forget much."

"You're so right, darling," she purred "Listen, I've been doing some radio interviews lately. I'm not sure if you're quite the topic they're looking for, although I'm sure the audience would love it. Why don't we have a little talk sometime and you can fill me in. I might even take notes. Some things are worth exploring."

Rocky gave her a half-smile and shrugged. This skinny smartass was a lot of woman, and she didn't care who knew it. And she was coming on with him! What the hell, why not? Sometimes these older ones were the horniest broads around, and you didn't have to teach them a thing—they already knew all there was to know. "Yes, I'd really like to do that, Mrs. Raymond," he said. "You tell me when and where."

"Just call me Danny," she said. "Everyone does. Where? Let's see. Well, there's a great buffet at the Cypress Creek Westin."

"Yeah, I've heard of that. Always wanted to try it."

"How about Wednesday? Will you be—er—strong enough, by then?"

"Count on it. What time?"

Danny smiled. Will was always out on Wednesday night. His night out with the guys playing cards, he said. And maybe sometimes he did, indeed, play cards. But that made it Danny's night out, too. With the girls. Sometimes. "About six? That would give us plenty of time." He nodded.

"Oh, and Rocky," she said as she stood up, "We don't have to tell the whole world about this—until we see if it'll work for the radio interview or not. Is that all right with you?"

"That's just perfect with me, Danny," he said. "Just perfect. And in case one of us needs to change the time or anything, let's trade numbers." He pulled out a card and handed it to her. She wrote a number on a slip of paper and gave it to him. They smiled. Danny could see he knew what she was up to, and that he didn't mind a bit. He was ready to fly.

Evan Gumbel strolled out to the Florida room where a magician was performing tricks for a fascinated audience. In the yard, a guitar-player with a synthesizer sounded like a whole combo, and couples were dancing around the pool.

The twins stood next to their mother and grandmother, shaking hands and greeting guests in a kind of receiving line. Evan stepped up behind Boz Richter, one of the many people he'd met while the search was on. He was the one who got his pilot friends out there looking and the next morning flew out himself and actually was in one of the three planes that first sighted the smoke rising over that sandspit.

Standing behind Richter, he heard him say, "I'll tell you, Nelly, these are two of the prettiest fish I ever caught down Freeport way."

"I'll never be able to thank you enough, Boz," said Nelly.

"That goes for all of us," said Jane. "We might still be out there swatting mosquitoes and chewing minnows if it weren't for you and your friends."

"Nah! They were all working their way there. They just weren't overlooking any possibilities on the way. They're the best damn bunch of searchers. We just got there first because I had a hunch. And because I was trying to talk your mother into going out with me sometime. I figured if I found you first, she'd have to say yes."

Nelly smiled. "You have to admire a man who simply won't take no for an answer," she said, taking Boz's hand and letting him give her a friendly kiss on the cheek.

"Gee, I'm glad to hear that," said Evan. "I won't take no for an answer either."

"Oh, Evan, hello," said Emma. "Mom, Nana, you met Evan the other day, I think. He's the man whose boat we sank. And it was the friskiest, lightest, most beautiful boat you've ever seen."

"It didn't sail—it danced across the water," added Jane. *"Requiescat in pace."*

"And Mom told us how you were here all through the search," said Emma. "That was so dear of you."

"Hell, I was just trying to get my boat back," he grinned. "Of course, I was gonna be pleased as punch if they saved you, too."

Everyone laughed at that, but Emma looked mournful for a moment. "Such a shame. It was brand new. You didn't even have all the bugs out of it yet. And you were so proud of it."

"It was insured. And a couple of those bugs were what helped sink it," said Evan. "The best experts in the world can't do anything if they hit the wrong storm in the wrong boat."

"Oh, Evan, we're not experts," said Jane. "We've done a little sailing, sure. But we were nuts to go out with a storm threatening, in the first place."

"Well, it's all water under the bridge, now," he said. "Or over the Briny's shell. And I'm sorry as hell you had to have a hair-raising experience like that, and put your mother and grandmother through such a scare."

"That's very kind of you," said Lauren. "But please just call me Lauren. And if you ever want to see either of my granddaughters again, never, *never* call me a grandmother. I consider that the G-word.

Obscene. I'm Nana. Or Lauren. Those are your choices."

Evan laughed and gave her a hug. "I'll call you anything if you'll just put in a good word for me with Lady Jane, here."

Jane's mouth dropped open. "Wait a minute, Evan. You know you can't tell us apart."

"I can so. You told me how. You've got longer eyelashes and more freckles. I can see that—at least four or five more. And Emma's waist is smaller by half an inch."

"OK. You've got my approval," laughed Emma. "You can take Jane out. Only nothing nautical. Neither one of us is going to set foot on a boat for a long, long while."

Ben wandered in about then and grabbed Nelly out of the line. "Come on, miss. Before Mac gets hold of you and I don't get another chance. I bribed the musician—he's going to play a hora." As the strains of "Hava Nagila" broke forth, Ben and Nelly swung around, first hooking one arm, then the other. A small group gathered around them and began dancing in a circle—the hora, Greek dancing, Turkish dancing, whatever similar ring dance they knew. "Actually, this is a little like square dancing, too," said Nelly as she and Ben ducked back into the ring and another couple took over in the center.

* * *

Mac Britton, Will Raymond, and Mark Goldberg, sitting at a table in the yard, watched the dancing. "Yeah, we'll probably just do all our booking stuff through Nelly, now," said Mark.

"What else can we do?" asked Raymond. "If we don't use her, we have to start all over. The woman we thought was running it before, actually can't get out of her own way. We may have to let her go. She can't seem to get much of anything working since Nelly left."

"I can see why Nelly left," said Mac frankly, "if she was doing all that work and the other woman got the credit and more pay."

"Yeah. We goofed there. But it's best to move slowly in these things," said Raymond. "We'll give C.G. a little more time to straighten out the guidance. If she can't, she can't. But you hate to fire someone that's been there two years, even a total loser."

"Well, if you want an outside opinion on Nelly," said Mac, "we're finding her very efficient, very thorough. And she can get people for anything. That magician tonight—she books him often for condo parties, she told me. And the man doing the pencil sketches in the living room? And this one-man band? When her mother decided to do this party, it was too late to get anyone. All the musicians were booked long ago for New Year's, but she called all her condo folks and found this guy whose party had just been cancelled. These people are loyal to her, too, and now they'll get paid, all the time. Her agency's bound to do well."

"I think we're having another meeting next week," said Raymond, "to decide what we're going to do. I'd like to give C.G. a chance. On the other hand, I don't like to let that guidance service drop to nothing."

Barton and Lauren danced out on the pool patio. So did Ben and Lauren. Evan danced with both twins and so did Jack McKinnon. "It's like dancing with a huge, friendly bear," they told Nelly later. The ham operators and pilots and their wives danced up a storm to any kind of music. Rocky didn't dance— and neither did his father. Mac sat talking business with the partners, chatting with the hams and pilots, and thanking them over and over. He hardly talked to Nelly at all.

At twelve o'clock they watched the countdown on TV and everyone hugged or kissed somebody. Nelly managed to be close to the table where Mac was sitting, but it wasn't he who grabbed her on the stroke of midnight for a kiss. It was Ben, who by now had had a few drinks. "Happy New Year, you wonderful creature," he said, kissing her hard on the mouth and quickly releasing her. And as she stared at him, surprised, Mac got up and gave her a disappointingly quick hug and a peck on the cheek.

They toasted with champagne and watched the city fireworks, and soon, the first guests began to depart. Nelly went out to talk to Rocky—the girls hadn't paid any attention to him all night. She was there when his father came to get him. "I'm going for the car, son. Come outside in a couple of minutes."

"I'll walk you to your car," said Nelly boldly, following him out the door. Mac walked in silence. She was humming "Send in the clowns . . ."

"You have a sweet voice," he said.

Champagne always makes me want to sing. Are you upset with me about anything?"

"Oh, God, no. I'm just trying not to make any more trouble for you. I felt we had to go through with this charade tonight, though I'm not sure why. My son damn near kills your daughters, and he's treated like a hero."

"The other night you kissed me," said Nelly. "That wasn't trouble. That was the nicest kiss I've ever had. No one ever kissed me that way before. I got to hate it when Albert would kiss me. But if you don't ever want to kiss me again, I don't want to lose you as a friend because of something our children got into together."

Mac looked down at her for a long moment, then

shook his head. "I don't guess that will happen, Nelly," he said, "although it might be the best thing for you if it did. I just wasn't sure if you'd ever want me to kiss you again, so I didn't try in front of all those people." With a sigh that was almost a groan, he very slowly and deliberately took her in his arms. Tenderly his lips found hers, and gave her a kiss so gentle and sweet that when he let her go, she ached for more. He opened the car door and helped her in, and they drove the block and a half back to the house.

He turned to her. "If the doctor says Rocky's OK, I'm giving him an ultimatum. No more money. Get a job, do something. This could have been the most horrible tragedy. I've got to try this tough love business. Nothing else has worked. I can't risk having him ever pull a stunt like that again." He got out of the car and went around to let her out. "At this point, I don't know if being friends with you is doing you much of a favor." He walked with her to the door and went inside to get his son.

Twenty-four

He was a different man. He looked beaten. Good
Lord, had she done that to him? He was fifteen
pounds thinner. No stubble; he was clean shaven.
And he wore a clean tee shirt with his usual khaki
duck pants and brown cardigan sweater. He was already there, sitting next to Morganthau, when the
receptionist led her into the room. He said, "Hello,
Nelly," and his voice wasn't curt or snarling. It was
hoarse, low, almost supplicating.

"Hello, Albert."

He stared at her, pulled his glasses from his pocket,
put them on, and stared some more. "Minny was
right. You sure look different. You got through this OK,"
he said. "You look like someone goin' to a party. All
prettied up. You don't even look like *you,* anymore."

"I hope not," Nelly answered coolly.

"I'm glad the girls are OK. They *are* OK, aren't
they? The paper said so. They won't talk to me."

"Yes. They were knocked around during the

storm. Bruises, sore muscles, and bug bites. They each lost about five pounds and it's never easy for them to gain weight back. But the newspaper said that they're successful realtors. Did you see that? And so they've had more new business than they can handle ever since."

"It mentioned you and some agency—"

"My new 1000 Words agency for speakers and all that. We've had a hundred extra calls, too, if we've had one."

"So for you three it wasn't so bad. But for me—I was so worried. At least Minny would tell me what was goin' on. But I never felt so helpless. Nothin' I could do. Nothin'."

"Well, I couldn't do anything, either. It was a nightmare."

"But you got someone to fly over and find them."

"The Bahamas Air and Sea Rescue would have found them, too. But it was good to know we were trying everything we could."

Morganthau interrupted. "Mr. Holachek, why don't you tell Mrs. Devin Lure your proposal?"

"My proposal? Oh, yeah. But can't I talk to her alone?"

"No," Morganthau said. "Sorry. But I won't say another word."

Albert shrugged and turned toward Nelly. "See, Nell, I was thinkin' that we could maybe forget this whole business. Just go back together. I'm gonna be workin' startin' Monday. I'm rentin' a little apartment. No drinkin'. I've joined A.A. I would try to be more—more understandin'. And, uh, kinder. I'd try to look after myself, so you wouldn't have to do everything for me."

Nelly looked at the miserable man before her. But her mind's eye saw the monster swinging at her again—felt his hands on her throat. She shook her head to chase away the image. "No, Albert. No. I can't—there's no way I could ever go back. I'm a different person. And I'll never forget that night. I only wish I could."

"But with your help—"

"I'm sorry, Albert, but I can't help you. No one can help you. You have to do this by yourself. You don't know how to take care of yourself. You'll have to learn. And if I'm there, you never will."

"I could try. I'm changin', too. You're not the only one. I talked to the doctors and shrinks. I'm gonna work. No drinkin'.."

She shook her head again. "I hope you stick with it. I hope you become a new person, too, Albert. But we're a thing of my past. I couldn't go back if I had to. It would be putting myself in jail. A butterfly can't go back into its cocoon. I can't help you.".

Albert clamped his jaw. "That's a lot of fancy words, Nelly, but when you take all that away, what's left is this. We been married a long time and you bitch, but you came out a lot better than me. Look at you. Look at me. And you don't give a shit. You're just goin' to let me struggle and not do a thing to help."

She sighed. "That's pretty much right, Albert. You think *you're* the one who got shortchanged in this marriage? That's remarkable."

"Well, I guess I don't blame you." His tone was heavy. "You look like one of those glamorous broads in the fancy magazines, now, instead of the Nelly I been married to all these years. I'm not fancy enough for you anymore. But if you think that because you dumped me I'm goin' to jump in a sewer and drink myself to death and do crazy things so you can have me locked up, think again. You're dead wrong, Miss Nelly."

He stood up and glared at her. "You just wait and see. I'm gonna start my own company again. I'm gonna do just fine. I've had about enough of this meetin'," he said to Morganthau "I know a set-up when I see one. Just get me out of here."

She was supposed to meet one of the girls up at Designers 'R' Less in Palm Beach at one o'clock. Sure enough, when she parked, there was Jane's car with Jane in it, waiting three spaces down.

"Before we go in the store, Jane," Nelly said, "tell me about Rocky. You and Emma aren't seeing him anymore, are you? I mean, we had to invite them to the New Year's Eve party, but I just—"

"Good grief, Mom, we're not that dumb. You were right. Your friend, Ben, was right. He *is* trouble. He's so screwed. Would you believe he called yesterday and asked us to have lunch with him? We told him we didn't have time. New Year's Day or not, we were swamped with appointments. So he stops in the office."

"To try to take you to lunch?"

"No, to tell us he's reforming. He's taking a real estate course and he's going to get his license and with his legal background he might be a good broker. We told him, 'Yeah, sure.' I'll believe it when I see it, Mom. And that's just what we told him. Bottom line: He lied to us. He risked not only his life, but ours—not to mention Evan's boat. We don't need that kind of friend, we told him."

"How'd he take that?"

"Actually, he kind of surprised us. He said he agreed, that we were right. His father was fed up with him and he was fed up with himself. And he was turning over a new leaf. We said, we'll wait and see. It may be true, and it may be just another tack he's trying."

"I'm so relieved to hear you say that," said Nelly. "He seems to be so good at charming people. He fooled Evan. He fooled you two."

"On the other hand," said Jane, "he did everything he could to help once we got in trouble. He was brave—and so organized when we hit the island. He just took over, sick as he was, and set us up for survival. We could have lasted for weeks if we'd had to. We don't want to get too involved with him, but we hope he makes it."

Inside the store, Jane gave her mother a briefing. "We don't have a lot of time," she said briskly. "You just go through the racks and pick stuff to try on and I'll tell you which ones we would agree on and which not. And why not."

"OK," said Nelly. "But I just got those new things at Christmas. And I've been wearing them to death."

"Which means you need lots more. Mom, have you been doing your required reading?"

"*Vogue* and *Bazaar* and such? Darling, no matter how liberated I become I will never dress so outlandishly."

"You're not supposed to dress like the women on those pages, Mom. For one thing, they're all seven feet tall, with no chest. But you're supposed to get a feeling from them. Those outfits are designed for shock value. But they should talk to you—give you coded messages. That's why we also sent you *W* and *Vanity Fair* and *Town and Country*. Don't just read them, Mom. Study the women in the pictures. Their outfits are much more realistic, yet usually very smart. Figure out your look. You need a lot more clothes."

"I don't want to devote that much of my time and energy to it," said Nelly stubbornly.

"But it's important. Now that you're going out and being asked out you need things to wear. You're going to those events with Ben Schlesser and that Mr. Richter. And maybe Mac Britton. And you represent your agency now, too. First impressions are important. A picture says 1000 words. Remember? The first impression you give isn't from what you say, it's how you look."

Nelly skipped through the racks of cocktail outfits, suits, and dresses suitable for evening. "Remember, don't say 'I'll take it' about *anything,* warned Jane. "You dicker here. It's all discount priced and you can get them lower sometimes. And always ask for alterations included. It can't hurt to ask." Nelly picked some fifteen outfits to try on before Jane steered her to a sale rack of beaded dresses and another of evening gowns.

In the dressing room, she slipped on a Carolyne Roehm creation that had caught her eye—a green brocade, three-piece evening suit with jeweled buttons. "I like it," she said. "The color's great. But that tag says $599!"

"Don't worry about that. We'll dicker it down. It doesn't need a bit of altering. And I think Carolyne

Roehms are going to be collector pieces in no time, now that she gave up her line.

She tried a Scaasi with a plunging neckline. "I can't bare my chest like that!" she protested, starting to unzip the back.

"Wait, Mom. Come out here to the three-way mirror."

In the three-way mirror, Nelly could not believe how good she looked. She followed her daughter back into the dressing room, where Jane mouthed the words, "I'll get the price down. Don't act like you like it."

After zipping in and out of maybe twenty dresses, suits, and gowns, and selecting many for possible purchase, Nelly let Jane deal with the manager on prices. "How much?" Jane asked about the low-cut gown.

"It's $800 but I'll give it to you for six."

"No, that's a little rich for our blood," said Jane. "Just as well. My mother would never take it out of the closet. She doesn't like to show her chest."

"Well listen, I can go to $450 but that's about it."

"Nah," said Jane. "What's the price on that blue one?"

The manager shrugged, went to talk to the owner and came back with a final offer of $375. "No charge for alterations and you pay the taxes?" asked Jane. He sighed and nodded.

* * *

They walked out with four outfits from the $69 supersteal sale rack, two gowns—the Scaasi and the Roehm evening suit—and five other outifts. Plus a beaded jacket that would make a nice evening suit with some black crepe pants.

How much do you have left of Nana's check?" asked Jane.

"About $1,400."

"OK, charge it all. Emma and I will take care of the rest."

"No. I've got money coming in now. You've seen how the agency is going."

"We don't want you to pay yourself a salary or expenses until you have about $10,000 in the bank," said Jane. "Then you can take a salary from back when you started. Consider it a loan, if you like. It's only another $200 or so. Now listen to me. Saturday we're going back to the shoe outlet. And an evening bag or two. And now let's try Braman's for some shirts and pants."

They carried out the clothing that needed no alterations and put them in Nelly's car. The others would be shipped. "Follow me, Mom," ordered Jane. "If you lose me, get off I-95 at Sheridan and drive into the Shell station on the west side."

At 3:30 they were pulling off I-95 at Sheridan Road and heading east to a group of stores, one of which housed Braman's. After an hour of combing through mountains of rejects, irregulars, and damaged clothing, much of it perfectly wearable, Nelly had spent another ninety dollars and had added four pairs of slacks, several cute shirts and tops, a silk blouse, and two jackets to her collection.

Jane helped her carry it all to the car. "OK, Mom. Mission accomplished. Gotta go. Oh, I almost forgot. Nana asked us to go ahead and sell the house, or roll it over into a condo. We might be able to make a trade. The only thing she insisted on is security, so we'll be bringing prospective customers to look. We'll call you to look at any condo that might be a good possibliity."

Nelly's last stop was another make-up lesson with Gwen Parker at her studio at 6:30. "Well, I think the eye job was successful," Parker said, inspecting Nelly's eyelids. "You healed beautifully. And the eyeliner tattoos are great. You've been doing the little facials I gave you. I can tell."

"And I've been wearing the make-up the way you showed me," Nelly said. "The Ultima, the hint of rouge, and I've been getting looks from people I don't know. I've been introduced to dozens of men and asked for dates. I get a call or two or even more every day from someone I've been introduced to at one or another of these events. They're asking me out. Can you believe it? I think it's all working magnificently."

"Well, you had good raw material," said Gwen. "Better than I realized. Now. Today let's talk about evening make-up. You can be more dramatic at night. You can look more glamorous, more vivid. For evening, you can outline with a lip pencil a shade darker than your lipstick. You can wear eyelashes. They look great as long as they're not too long or full for your eyes."

Nelly listened while Parker went on about the lashes. "Like your mascara and eyeliner, they should never be black. Brown or taupe, with your coloring." She opened a package and showed Nelly how to snip off the ends. "Those are too long for you. Always shorten them a bit, about one eighth of their length." Nelly watched and listened. Gwen had her glue on the lashes herself so she'd be sure she could do it. And then, under Gwen's direction, she applied a ravishing evening eye make-up.

After the lesson, still wearing her new evening make-up, Nelly headed home. She had agreed to attend a St. Patrick's Day committee social with Ben. She had to bring in all the new clothes from the car and dress—she'd just about make it in time. The first thing she did after letting herself in was check the mail. Another invitation from this Erhardt guy?

There were several agency messages on the answering machine. One from Richard Merton. Now where had she met him? He wanted to take her to dinner. Calls from Gershon Trayle and that Dr. d'Angelo, also asking her to dinner. No time to answer them. She had to dress. Thank goodness, it wouldn't be a late night. She had too much to do tomorrow, including interviews with a couple of women for a job with the agency. But for now, she couldn't wait to see if Ben noticed her new make-up.

Twenty-five

Emmet made a point of hovering attentively during the partners' Monday breakfast, as he had for the last couple of Mondays. He would love to overhear something so important, so critical, that C.G. would be grateful to him forever. And how grateful? Maybe grateful enough to hug him, like she did that time when he found out it was her birthday and brought over a cupcake with a candle on it after her lunch. Maybe even enough to want to get to know him a little better. Enough to invite him to her apartment for a cup of coffee and a chat? Or even—? No—unthinkable. But the pulse in his neck throbbed at the very idea.

"Well, I think the whole thing's gone on too long and we should stop all this and take some action," said McKinnon. Ben breathed a great sigh of relief. At least *he* wasn't the one who was going to initiate it, as he had been fully prepared to do that morning "Listen, Will," McKinnon argued, "none of us bats

1000 when it comes to hiring. I mean, we *all* thought she had a lot of class when she came here. She *does* have class. We *all* thought she'd be good dealing with customers, too. And the guidance. When she started doing lunches all the time, we picked up the checks gladly. It saved us from having to do it, and we all thought it was probably good customer relations, whatever that means. Nobody's blaming you, Will, but you're the only holdout. And I'm damned if I see why."

"Unless you had your hand in the cookie jar again," suggested Mark Goldberg.

"Now, just wait a minute here, Mark," said Raymond huffily. "I don't ask you about your extracurricular activities and I'll thank you not to ask about mine." He looked up, saw Emmet looking at him strangely, and said, "Bring us some more decaf here, Emmet." But the pot on his warmer was empty, so Emmet had to hurry off to make more, thus missing Mark's retort.

"I had a feeling there was something more to it, you old dog," chortled Mark, slapping Will on the back. "But that does make it stickier, if we want to get rid of her."

"I'll say," agreed Ben.

"Listen, it didn't amount to a hill of beans," said Will. "Nothing happened when I hired her, but I kept getting the feeling she'd be available. And she was."

"Did she take those damn pearls off?" asked

McKinnon with a chuckle. Then he turned sober. "Anyway, what happens if we let her go?"

"Let her go?" repeated Ben. "Last time we discussed this we were going to keep her forever. Now we're letting her go? We should think this through carefully before doing anything—especially in the light of this new information."

"Well, the fact is, she isn't accomplishing a hell of a lot," said McKinnon. "She's still best at lunches. The thing is, do we have enough of them to keep her busy? Her new girl—Melissa—looks like another Nelly, but she's doing a heck of a job getting the guidance working smoothly again. And the other new one is trying to put together the booking stuff, but to start all that from scratch is a huge job. I think we should forget it and just turn all that stuff over to Nelly."

Ben nodded. "I'd vote for that." Will nodded, too, just as Emmet came back with the decaf. "I'm sorry. I had to make a new pot," he explained, frustrated at having to leave. What had he missed?

"OK, so we're going to turn the booking stuff over to Nelly," said McKinnon. "I think this Melissa can handle the guidance. Normally I'd say, OK, let C.G. handle the social end. But I really don't like the very deliberate deception she perpetrated, making it look like she was doing the work Nelly was actually doing. And *not* telling us when Nelly quit and why. Letting it all go to hell. And now, it looks like she's been going after Nelly's agency vindictively, even bad-mouthing her."

"I talked to her about that," said Ben. "I warned her in no uncertain terms. Nothing like that can come out of this office."

"Why don't I talk to her?" Will said with a grimace. "I got us into this."

"Tell her you think she'd be happier somewhere else and she can stay until she finds something," said Mark. "I think that's being pretty decent, all things considered. But don't say a word yet, until we're sure this Melissa is as good as she seems."

"Give her a few bucks," said Ben. "Termination pay. What's a few bucks?"

"How old is she? Hey, there's an out. Tell her we're trying for a younger image. That's the answer. But then there's no reason *you* have to handle it, Will. If you want me to, I'll do it."

Again, Will looked up and saw Emmet staring at him. "Give that man another cup of coffee," he told the waiter. "He's my goddam hero. Thanks, Ben. I could just wash my hands of the whole thing. But we'll talk. Maybe it's something I shouldn't duck."

Emmet was furious. How could they talk that way about C.G.? Thanks to this troublemaking Nelly Holachek. Those stories in the paper about her dumping her husband, and him trying to beat her? Well, maybe she provoked it. Leaving him after all those years? And her children getting lost at sea? You could tell from the story, they didn't live with her. When your own kids can't stand to live with you, you must be pretty bad. And now, because of this same person, they were firing C.G.? How dare they? It was so unfair. And what was that 'hand in the cookie jar' remark? C.G. would never do that. Not that it would be anyone's business if she did. Her husband was dead. She was single.

The minute Raymond signed the check and Emmet turned it in, he raced to the phone and called the number she had given him. "Mrs. Clemency-Graves," he said breathlessly, "this is Emmet. I've got some things I must tell you."

"Go ahead, Emmet. I appreciate this. There's no one in my office just now."

"No, I don't want to say them over the phone. I think you are the most admirable, beautiful person, and I just could hardly listen to that partners' breakfast this morning. It made me ill."

"Well, shall I meet you somewhere?" she suggested.

"Yes, let's do that. I get off at four."

C.G. thought about it. She didn't particularly want to be seen in public with Emmet. "Listen, dear, why don't you swing by my apartment? I'll get home about 5:30. Just tell the guard at the gate that you're there to see me and they'll ring."

He could hardly believe his ears. "Oh, that would be perfect," he said. "About a quarter to six?"

"Fine. Now let me tell you my address and how to get there . . ."

Minny sat in the booth and stirred her coffee. She felt uneasy. For two reasons. First, because Freddie had told her to butt out of this, not to meet with Albert. And second, what if Albert exploded again and attacked her? Not that she had ever thought of him doing anything like that before. He'd always been a jerk and a drunk, but not crazy.

But when he suddenly stood before her, and then slid into the booth and sat opposite her, she wasn't uneasy any more. She was more concerned. He looked like one of those street people. Lost. Confused. Jaw slack, eyes drooping like he was only halfway tuned in. "You look like you lost five more pounds, Albert. You eating?"

He grunted and picked up the menu and squinted as if reading it were a chore. "I been workin' my tail off. Twelve hours a day. Only bowlin' twice a week. Sometimes I been just too tired to eat."

"But why do such dumb stuff? I mean, it's good you're turning over a new leaf and working and not drinking, but why so much?"

"I don't know. Partly it's easier to keep from buying a six-pack if I'm keepin' that busy. Partly 'cause it costs money to start up your own business, and I'm doin' it as fast as I can. I'm workin' all the jobs I can get. I got ads in the *Sunshine Flyer* and the *Neighbors' News,* and I'm gettin' jobs. Paintin', insulatin', settin' tiles—makin' twice as much from that stuff as from workin' for Paddy."

The waitress came over—the chubby one, Amy, who had been working at Lester's ever since Minny had first eaten there. "You guys ready or you need to meditate some more?"

"I'll take the hamburger steak, kind of pink," said Minny. "With mashed potatoes. I haven't had them in weeks. Freddie won't let me. He says I'll never get thin if I keep eating potatoes."

"I'll take the same, and coffee now, and we'll both have extra sides of mashed potaoes and gravy," said Albert. When Amy hurried off he said, "Who's he to tell you what you can eat?"

"You used to tell Nelly what to eat."

"Well, that was different. She never ate enough. So damn skinny. What guy likes a bag of bones?"

"Freddie didn't want me to meet with you. And after what you did that night, I suppose he's right. But I figure if you're really trying to change, you should have your chance. Even Nelly thinks so. It's just she doesn't want to see you right there in her face."

"Neither do the twins."

"Well, hell, Albert, do you blame them?"

Amy brought bread, butter, and the oversized cups of coffee Lester's was famous for. Albert added cream and sugar and stirred his. "OK, so I had a problem. I'm an alcoholic. I'll always be an alcoholic. I'll always have to take one day at a time. But I'm doin' it. And they're my kids. I'm their father. When I thought of them out there drownin' or somethin', and not knowin'—I wanted to go out and drown with 'em."

"Big help, Albert. That would've solved everything. Anyway, they're OK. I think the guy who owned the boat—his name is Evan Gumbel—is interested in Jane. They got a few bruises from being bumped around in that shell-thing. And sunburn. But they're fine, and they're making money hand over fist with their real estate office. Freddie says they're getting to be big hitters down here."

"You gettin' serious with this Freddie?"

Amy brought their hamburger steaks and mashed potatoes and placed them on the table, and both Minny and Albert dug in. "I thought so. But now, I don't know. He can't stand bowling alleys and he won't go with me, so I go to my leagues alone. That's OK. But even if I want to practice a line or two, I gotta go alone. He wants me to quit." She took a large, comforting bite of her potatoes.

"Well, anyone who doesn't like bowlin', he's gotta be missing a few marbles. What's Nelly think of him?"

"I don't know. She's so wrapped up in her business. And all kinds of men want to take her out, now. The girls and Lauren are up a lot. We don't get much chance to talk. And she's different."

"Boy, I'll say. I maybe wasn't the perfect husband, but I'm changin' and all. But at that meetin', she didn't wanna hear about nothin'. She's not giving me a chance, like she doesn't believe I can do it. I'll show her. She's not the only one who can change."

"She can't forget that night, Albert. And who could blame her? You hit her. You hit Freddie."

"Well, he shoulda minded his own business. Hell, I don't remember it at all. Just a few little parts. But listen, could we do this again? I'm not going to get drunk and go crazy. I just wanna know what's goin' on. After the league next week?"

Minny thought about it for a moment, then nodded. "And would you tell the twins what I'm doin'?" he asked. "When I get goin' in business again, maybe they won't be so pissed at me."

Minny nodded again.

"And if you ever want to shoot a few practice lines and this guy won't go with you, I'd go, if I'm not workin' that day."

Minnie finished her last bite of potatoes and looked up at Albert. Was he so lonely he would come along with her to practice? "OK," she said noncommittally. "But when you wanna talk to me about what's going on, or about going bowling, call me at work, not at the house. Freddie wouldn't understand."

"Sounds like a jerk."

"Look who's talking, Albert. After what you did? You're lucky they didn't keep you in jail and throw away the key. You gotta promise never to do anything like that again."

"Not while anyone's lookin', anyhow." He dug a toothpick from his pocket—Albert always kept them handy because of his terrible teeth.

"Now, let's figure out dessert," said Minny. "I'd better not, but you look like you could use the calories."

Rocky tried to call the twins' office again Monday morning, early. But the secretary answered and said that neither one could come to the phone.

He thought of the way they had acted at the party. Cool. Not angry. But not like friends, either.

Then he remembered Danny—Daniella Raymond. The tall, thin witch with the milky skin and the black hair and the sexy eyes. Wait. He had her card somewhere.

He looked in the large ash tray on his desk where he threw change and cards when he came in, and whatever else had accumulated in his pockets. And there it was. She answered on the first ring. "Good morning. This is Rocky Britton. We met at the New Year's Party at Nelly Holachek's."

"And we're meeting Wednesday," said Danny. "That's still on?"

"Oh, sure thing," he said quickly. "But I was wondering—I know it's an imposition—but I was wondering if you had a few minutes sometime today or tomorrow to let me talk to you about something else. I need some advice and I thought maybe you—"

"Well, I've got a pretty full day, Rocky, but I'd love to help if I can. Listen, I can squeeze in fifteen or twenty minutes. Why don't you meet me at the deli next to Publix on the 17th Street Causeway? Now, I can either meet you there at three, or, let me see . . . or I can meet you there in twenty minutes."

"I'll be there in twenty minutes. Thanks a lot."

He whistled as he pulled on a pair of slacks and a shirt and some loafers. Now let's see. What kind of problem could he dream up to ask her advice about? He'd come up with something. He never had any trouble with that. He felt a twinge of misgiving. Yeah, he was reformed. But for this kind of situation, maybe a little fudging was still OK. Hell, he wanted to get laid. And Daniella Raymond? Her, too. He read it in her eyes. It was all just a game.

Nelly toiled away at the computer. Taking calls, making calls, filing new customers into the system, making out mail deposit slips for the dozens of checks pouring in, sending off payments to the printer. She had a date with Boz tonight. A theater outing at the Performing Arts Center—a Miami City Ballet production—with a late supper afterward in the New River Room. "You can either come up here and ride down in the buses with the condo crowd, or I'll pick you up there in my car," he had said.

"I could meet you in the theater, if you like," Nelly offered.

"No, I better pick you up. If I bus down with the crowd, I'll have five women trying to sit in my lap before we get there. There's a few in this place that drive every single guy nuts."

Nelly laughed. "See you here, then."

"About 7:30?"

"Fine."

She was still working on the mail when she heard a car pull in the drive. It was Allison Fisher arriving for her job interview. Her resumé from the agency had sounded pretty good. Nelly hurried to the door to let her in.

"You know, I just found out that you used to work for Raymond, Schlesser, McKinnon, and Goldberg," said Allison after Nelly had settled them in the kitchen with tea and cookies.

"Yes, 'til a few weeks ago. It wasn't a pleasant

parting, although I'm on good terms with all the partners now, and I'll probably be doing some work for them."

"I think I was interviewed by your old boss," said Allison. "Mrs. Clemency-Graves?"

"Oh, dear. Yes, that's her," said Nelly.

"The job I was interviewed for involved working on what they called their client guidance system—and to help set up a new booking system. Essentially, I gathered it was to replace you."

Nelly scanned Allison's brief resumé again. "And by the looks of this, she ought to have hired you, but she probably wouldn't. You're more qualified than C.G. and me put together. Too much competition."

"Well, for whatever reason," laughed Allison, "she didn't hire me."

"I don't do guidance work anymore, but I have a booking agency," explained Nelly. "Brand new. Swamped with customers. Bookers and bookees, we call them. I'm about to go under for the third time. My daughters are trying to help a little—they've set up my computer programs. They live on Miami Beach so they're lining up lots of Dade clients. And my next door neighbor puts in a couple of hours a night. But I need someone here full time to do everything. Send out checks and bills. Set up files. And of course, match bookers and bookees. Pretty soon I think we're going to need a couple more people."

"You list retired and amateur entertainers as well as speakers?" Allison asked.

"Yes. And some of them are really great. Part of your job would be going to some of these affairs we're booked into and checking out how well the newer bookees do, until I get someone to take care of all of that. We don't want to handle anyone who's not good."

"Sounds like a fun kind of job."

"It is, I think. The lady next door I was telling you about? Working two hours a night? As soon as she gets another three months in at her job at the Quick Shop, so she's eligible for her pension, she's quitting and coming to us about half-time. She has no grasp of accounting or computer files or anything like that. She'll be an Indian, not a chief, but she's diligent, thorough. We'll need you both. We've just started this agency and we've already got 300 bookees and we've booked 50 things—just this week!"

Allison nodded as Nelly went on. "Starting pay would be nine dollars per hour, and you'd start tomorrow, at nine, and I guess we'd call you the manager."

"You mean you're offering it to me?" asked Allison.

"Yes. What do you think?"

"I think you just hired yourself a new manager."

* * *

Rocky got there before Danny and ordered coffee. It was one of those places where you stood at a counter, called your order to one of the chefs, picked it up, and carried it to a table yourself. You dug your own beverages from the coolers and poured your own coffee. He poured himself a cup and sat down. She hurried in two minutes later, wearing tight jeans and a clingy shirt, open at the neck and knotted in front. She spotted him, got herself a Diet Coke from a cooler, and slid into the chair opposite him.

"I would have gotten that for you," he said. "A woman like you should be waited on hand and foot."

"My, aren't you wise for your age?" she said, giving him a sexy grin. "Now what's the problem."

"It's the twins. Nelly Holachek's daughters. You met them at the New Year's party."

"Stunners. Young yet, but stunners."

"I always like a woman who's a little older, myself," said Rocky. "I like that song about when the woman with a touch of sin walks in. She's the one who knows what it's all about."

Danny gave a throaty chuckle. "Do you, now? You're sounding smarter by the moment. And what about those twins?"

"Well, you know. After surviving that boat incident together, now I kind of get the feeling they're a little pissed with me. Like I should have prevented it or something. And I don't know how to explain to them that the boat was faulty. Hell, it listed, then the engine went, and the radio didn't work. Then the whole damn hull sheared off. I did make one *big* mistake, though. I should never have let us go when, at the last minute, neither Evan Gumbel nor his girl-friend could come. But I hated to disappoint them, and once we did go, I broke my ass trying to make it work."

"Surely, they know that—"

"Or maybe they were too worried about their fin-gernails to realize what was happening," said Rocky, repainting the scenario to suit his need at the moment.

"Well, *that* I can understand," said Danny. "I don't do sailboats myself. I can think of much better ways to find adventure. I prefer power yachts. My husband isn't into boating at all, but then we're that way about a lot of things. We have very different interests sometimes."

"So what do you think I should do about these girls? Apologize? Send them flowers?"

"I think you probably know exactly what to do, Rocky. With them or any other female. I don't think you have any problem figuring that out at all." She chuckled again, looking at him with one eyebrow raised halfway up her forehead.

Rocky leered back at her. She was sharp as hell. He could tell she could read his mind. "You know, I'm glad I met you at that party. I really like you a lot."

"I know," she said, tossing her head provocatively. "And know what? I think I kind of like you, too, even if you *are* rather outrageous." She looked at her watch. "Sorry, darling. I'm out of time. I have a luncheon that I'm co-chairing today at Pier 66. I have to be there. Early. And I can't exactly go dressed like this." She stood up and started fishing in her purse.

"I've got the coffee," he said. "Get out of here before someone grabs you. Maybe me. See you on Wednesday."

"I can't wait. We'll have more time then," she promised. Grinning to himself, Rocky watched her leave as he dug into his pocket for money. It looked like Wednesday was going to be a very good day. If Emma wouldn't talk to him, screw her. He just found someone who would.

Mac Britton pored over the forms and agreements Nelly had sent him at his request. When your son damn near kills someone's two daughters, the least you can do is offer her a little free legal advice. He should ask her to come in and go over everything with him, and he could suggest changes. But that meant she'd have to take an elevator ride. No, they'd go over the papers at her place. He buzzed Heather. "Call and see if Mrs. Holachek has any time late this afternoon or this evening," he said. "Tell her I'd

322

like to come over or meet her someplace where we can go over her forms. We can get a bite to eat somewhere if she'd like." Despite the strong attraction, he had decided to see as little of Nelly as possible until he got Rocky straightened out. It was the only fair thing to do. So many men seemed attracted to her now. Hopefully, they wouldn't bring her as much trouble as he had. Then why was he arranging to see her today? This, he reasoned, didn't count. After all, he couldn't really do it on the phone.

Emmet told the guard that Mrs. Clemency-Graves, in 1070, was expecting him. "Yes, sir. She called down. Park in the first lot on the left there, sir, and take the elevator right across from it to the tenth floor and turn right."

Nice building, he thought as the elevator climbed. Right on the ocean. Not way out west like he was. Well, she deserved it. She knew how to live—how to dress. A class lady in every way.

She was standing in the doorway at 1070, looking regal in a black crepe jacket and skirt, a black-and-cream print blouse, and her pearls. She stepped back to let him enter, and led him over to a small table set with a pitcher of a clear beverage and a plate of what his friend Mildred called "snackies."

"This is so good of you, Emmet," she said effusively, squeezing his arm. He felt his pulse charge immediately and took a deep breath. He had planned to be so careful when he talked to her, but up close, like this, his pent-up emotions overwhelmed his caution. He knew he was going to simply dive in and spill his guts to her.

"Well, to me, you've always been one of the most wonderful women I've ever met," he said. "You have more class in your little finger than all those partners at Raymond, Schlesser put together. And I couldn't stand this today. I had to tell you. I'd do anything to help you. I'd run Nelly Holachek out of the state if I knew how."

"You had to tell me what, Emmet? So I'd be warned about what? Here, let me pour you a martini," she said, filling to the brim a goblet that would hold more than two normal drinks, handing it to him, and filling another for herself. "I don't normally drink much," she said. "But when you called, I decided we might need a little help with this."

"Me, neither," said Emmet. "But maybe this will make it easier." They each took a long, thirsty swallow. He blinked, coughed, and gasped for breath. Then he took another sip, and began.

"It was like this, C.G.," he said. "Is it OK to call you that? You've told me to a couple of times, but at the Sky Club I just feel I shouldn't."

"No, it's fine here with just the two of us. Please do."

He took another swallow and began relating word

for word, as best he could remember, the partners' conversation of that morning. As he talked, she kept shaking her head in dismay. And sipping. Halfway through, she poured what was left in the pitcher into their glasses. "Go on, Emmet," she said in a pained voice. "I'll mix up some more of these, if I can remember how." She brought the pitcher over to the adjacent bar, threw more gin, vermouth, cubes of ice, and strips of lemon peel into the shaker, shook it, and poured the results into the pitcher. Back at the table she topped off their glasses.

Emmet, his heart aching for her, groping for the words to soften his tale, finished it. "I mean, they're planning to get rid of you," he said indignantly, taking another comforting swallow from his glass. "How dare they! You're the only bit of class they have. Holachek is just a little nebbish. No shtyle. No polish. No wonder she could only find a husband who would shlug her!" What was happening to his voice? His tongue was tripping. He reached for C.G.'s hand, took it in his, and stroked it.

She finished her glass and poured them both more. "I think, actually, I've been half expecting this," she said. "I can't run it all by myself. That woman left me in the lurch. I don't know much about the actual guidance. I just orchestrated and set up appointments. Nelly was the one who went to their offices. And I certainly have no skills as an agent. Now I hear she's starting up with Ben Schlesser, so he's always defending her. The partners went to her New Year's Eye party and I wasn't even invited."

"I didn't like the way they hinted that maybe you and Mr. Raymond—"

"That was insufferable!"

"Not that it wouldn't be your right to—uh—find a little comfort. Your hushband's gone. And everyone needs shome affection. But he'sh not good enough for you. The idea makes me shick. You should have shomeone who truly adoresh you." A pulse was throbbing violently in his neck. Could she see it? "Like—like me."

He took another long, anguished swallow, and looked at her adoringly.

C.G. stared at him, reading so clearly the love and longing in his eyes. She was amazed. And yes, pleased. To be absolutely bathed in a gaze as melting as a caress, was so soothing—so wonderful. Her anguish at his news was somehow slipping away. "I think you really *do* care about me, Emmet," she said. "To come over like this and tell me everything. How many friends would do that?"

"Well, you know how I've alwaysh felt about you. And your hushband, too, of course, back when he was with ush." Impulsively, he reached over and touched her face. He felt a flow of peace. Of pleasure.

So did C.G. She slipped her hand over his on her cheek and pressed. His touch was warm and caring.

She didn't want it to stop. Nobody had looked at her like that in such a long time. Certainly not Will Raymond, nor the few other sexual partners she had had since Reggie died. Not even Reggie, actually.

"Oh, Emmet. Dear Emmet. I'm going to cry." He stood up quickly and came around to pat her on the shoulder, but she stood at the same moment, too, and he found himself with his arms around her, and her arms creeping around him. They kissed. Emmet could not believe this was happening. He was kissing his adored Claire Clemency-Graves! He kissed her again. He wanted to swallow her up.

"Oh, dear. I'm so sorry," she said. "I shouldn't—"

"I'm not," he said boldly. "I've always dreamed of this. I never thought—I mean, I would have given my eyeteeth to be—I mean—. Oh, C.G., can I kish you, again?"

She stared at him, her eyes wide with wonder. She nodded. And he kissed her again, their arms still wrapped tightly.

And somehow, still clinging to each other, they staggered into her bedroom. Emmet remembered later how they fumbled at each other's clothes, trying to tear them off quickly. How she pulled the pins from her hair and it came tumbling down, so thick and silky. How he groped under the coverlet for that soft white flesh, and drew her close. But he didn't remember much more after that. It was just a long and beautiful blur of ecstasy.

Until the middle of the night, when he woke with a crunching headache, sat up, and realized where he was. And incredibly, there was C.G. nestled beside him, snoring faintly.

He watched her in the light from the open door. He would never again be content with someone as dull and common as Mildred. It was the difference between making love to a peasant and to a queen. And then she stirred, and moaned. And slowly sat up and stared at him. "I think you'd better go, Emmet," she whispered. "I don't know what happened. But would you—would you call me in the morning? Please?"

Twenty-six

"This is only the second time I've ever been here," said Nelly. "But I know it's one of the hottest spots. The top people in town entertain their best customers here, even though it's not easy to find. I see it on their expense records. And the partners at Raymond, Schlesser, too. They all say there's no place quite like it." They were sitting at a window table at Burt and Jack's in Port Everglades, captivated by the panorama of boats gliding past, heading in and out of the port channel at dusk, their lights twinkling. A tug. A tanker. A cruise ship. A sailboat. A huge yacht. "I know what the in-spots are, but I've never been to most of them."

"You'll soon know them personally, every in-spot in three counties, the way your social life is taking off," said Mac. "From what I've seen, every single guy over fifty that meets you wants to take you out."

"It's a big change for me, Mac. Albert never took me anywhere, except sometimes to his bowling alley.

My mother took me out all she could but first my father, and then Albert, didn't like me to see her very much. I'm afraid most of this socializing now, though, has to do with the business. And I feel I should attend a couple of things with Boz Richter, if he asks me. Look what he did for me. For us. And he's a good person. But I can't spend all my time going out. I need to hire someone who can do a lot of that agency socializing. It has to be done. People expect it. We need someone like C.G."

"You mean you don't like partying constantly like a college kid?" grinned Mac.

"I never did that as a college kid. I was keeping house for my father, and working and going to school. And dating Albert once in a while. We didn't go anyplace fancy. To a movie or a diner. Or he'd take me to a park and have me toss baseballs at him and he'd hit them and I'd run and retrieve them. I was a slave even then. I wasn't one of those pretty Betty Coeds. I was a mousy little bookworm, very intimidated by my father."

"I almost can't imagine that, seeing you today," said Mac.

"This is Anyella, the new me." She laughed. "But to the old Nelly, this is a different world. Although I must admit that my mother and daughters are quite at home in it and the new me is rather enjoying it. It's just a matter of time priorities. Keeping up with the nuts and bolts of this agency has me spinning."

"Spinning becomes you," he said, handing her a few papers to inspect. "Well, I've looked over your forms. And I've made some computer printouts at my office of some clauses and phrases I think you should insert, and where. We keep all that stuff on file. Don't get any of these printed until you check the changes. The sooner you get everything back to me, the sooner I can check it again and you can get it to your printer."

"What kind of changes?" asked Nelly.

"Mostly things to protect yourself and the agency. You have to do that, today. It's a tough, litigation-happy world out there. And you have to cover yourself money-wise, too. To be sure you get paid."

The waitress brought them the plump Australian lobster tails that the restaurant was known for and that Mac had insisted she try. As Nelly ate, she kept peeking over at Mac's face. Even though he seemed to be enjoying her company, she sensed that the sadness was not far from the surface. Finally she blurted, "Mac, I know it's none of my business, but you seem so down. Whatever it is, would talking about it help?"

He shook his head. "I'm sorry it shows. You know what it is. Same thing. This whole business of Rocky and the girls and that boat. You know I've decided to get tough with him, but it's not easy. I keep think-ing there must be another way to get through to him, to make him see what he's doing without practically threatening to disown him. I've even tried to talk him into seeing a shrink. At least he seems to be out of the deep gloom he was in about the scars—I think your girls had something to do with that. I've decided to wait until I'm sure he's OK after that cold or pneumonia or whatever it was, and then let him have it. Until I get this problem with Rocky worked out, how can I get involved in anything else? No matter how much I want to."

Nelly nodded. "I think I understand," she said. He was telling her not to expect too much of this relationship. He liked her but he couldn't cope with an emotional attachment just now. Or was he just trying to let her down easily? To tell her that despite his getting carried away for a moment or two, he didn't much want to carry things any further? Whichever it was, there was something she felt she must say, even if it irritated or insulted him.

"Meanwhile," she said, "did you ever think that you're an enabler? You're enabling him to stay on that same path, exactly the way I enabled Albert. Not intentionally, but we're still guilty."

"You may be right," he sighed. "I've been told that before."

The old Nelly, she realized, would have been heartbroken at his words, if she could ever have gotten to this point in the first place. She would have disappeared into the woodwork, making as little fuss as possible. But Anyella would *not* be sad or hurt. She would just be lively good company and make this a delightful evening whether he wanted it or not. He might walk away from her, but she would darn well make him regret it if he did.

"Enough. No more of these depressing thoughts," she ordered. "The situation with Rocky will still be there when you get home tonight. But while you're here, take a break. Come on, let's dance."

"But that's rock they're playing," said Mac, reluctantly.

"So? What do you have against rock? I like it," she said with a naughty smirk. "Come on. A gentleman always obliges a lady."

They stepped out onto the tiny floor and began moving to the music. "Smile, droopy," she ordered. "It only hurts for a minute." And she bounced around the floor in a fair imitation of the rock and roll dancing she'd seen on TV. "Shake your booty on this one, Mac. You can do a minuet later."

He followed her stiffly to the floor. "Come on. Loosen up," she urged. "Don't worry. They probably never raid this place."

Five minutes of clowning on the floor and she had him laughing and clowning with her. And then the combo segued into a ballad she loved, "Memories." As he pulled her to him for a slow dance, Nelly boldly pushed closer and nestled her head in his neck. They moved in a kind of trance, mentally and physically. It was so easy to follow when your bodies were glued together this way. The next piece was a rhumba, and Mac knew how. Grinning, he led her through the fancy turns and twirls. Good, she thought, it's working. She was making him forget his problems, enjoy himself, and enjoy her. She could have danced all night.

Just as they pulled into Nelly's drive, they saw the man in the car lights—a spare figure at the door. He ran off and was gone before Mac could get the door open. "Stay in here," he ordered. "Lock the doors." He ran around the side of her house where the man had fled, and was back a few moments later. "Not a soul back there. No one on the next street, either. Maybe it was a neighbor delivering something. Let's go look. Get your key out, first."

He helped her from the car and led her by the hand to her door, where they found a note tacked. He took it down. Nelly let them in and switched on the lights, and they inspected the note.

"Oh dear, another one of those wacky cult warnings." She read the crudely printed words: "Repent. Return to God's laws. God embraces the repentant sinner. God punishes the unrepentant sinner, with the vengeance of the just."

"Friendly little note," said Mac.

"The Sheriff's department told us some religious nuts have been doing this to a lot of people. So far, that's all they've done—put up notes."

"You don't want to be the first target when they try something worse, Nelly," said Mac. "Could your husband have anything to do with this?"

"I doubt it, but I'll call the sheriff's office again. Otherwise, it was such a lovely evening."

"Yes, it was. You have me so confused, Nelly. I'm not sure what I should do about you."

"One of my mother's husbands had been in the Navy before they met. He taught her all kinds of Navy rules and expressions. Two about when you're in doubt. One was 'When in doubt, punt.' "

"Probably very sensible advice. What was the other?"

Nelly giggled. "It was, 'When in doubt, run in circles, scream and shout.' I think you should kiss me good night and then go home and get a good night's sleep and forget the whole business. Listen, Mac, you're not the only one who's confused. I'm not so sure if I should get involved with anyone, either. I mean deeply involved. I kind of want to, but I've had almost thirty years of a lousy marriage. I—I never had the kind of sex life you read about. Is there such a thing? My husband was rough, demanding. He'd hurt me. My daughters once told me that sex can be the greatest thing since Coca-Cola. But you can't prove it by me.

"The old Nelly just accepted whatever Albert dished out. But the new Anyella is almost afraid to try, for fear she'll find out it's all just more fairy

335

tales. And yet she wonders if it could be better, maybe even beautiful, with the right person. The new me is so curious. I've never ever been kissed before, the way you kissed me the other night. It made me wonder how long this has been going on. I want more, but I've got so much to learn. I need a patient teacher. And I'm not sure how to pick him."

When Mac put his key in the lock, he knew his son was inside again because the door was already unlocked. Rocky was always careless about locks. He didn't much like the little studio apartment his father had found for him when he came down, but he was unwilling to spend any of his own money for something better. Instead, a few nights a week he bunked at his father's penthouse, and he received his mail and messages there. He also sometimes spent a night or two with a woman, although his amorous pursuits had diminished considerably since Kuwait. All in all, he spent little time at his own place.

When Mac came in, the TV was blaring. No time like the present, he thought. He went over and switched the set off. "Hey, what's that for?" cried Rocky. "I'm watching Jay Leno!"

"I want to talk to you—serious stuff," said Mac.

Rocky scowled. His father started pacing up and down. "From now on, no more money from me," Mac said slowly in a tight, deliberate voice. "You want any more, earn it. From now on, I'm not accepting your mail or calls and you will no longer use this phone to make long distance calls. You can't bunk here overnight unless you're specifically invited. You're on your own."

Rocky's face drained to a chalky white. He stood up abruptly. "But Dad, I've just—"

"You heard me. You pay your rent at the Snail or they'll kick you out. If you won't want to make anything of your life, if you want to continue flirting with danger and endangering others, that's your choice. I don't approve, but I can't stop you. I hope you'll get a job. I hope you'll do anything that makes sense. I'll be eager to hear what you do and how your life goes. But I am not going to support you anymore, in any way. I am not going to keep putting my own life on hold because I'm wiped out by yours."

"Dad, I—was going to tell you—I've been thinking that I—"

"I'd appreciate it if you'd gather up your things and take them with you tonight. Now. I don't want you to stay tonight. If you straighten up and fly right, in any damn direction you choose, I'll be delighted and maybe we'll change all this. I don't care if you become a mailman, or a bank president. I just want to see you doing something a little bit productive. That's what life is all about."

"But Dad, that's what I was waiting to talk to you about. I—"

"I don't want words. I want action, Rocky," said Mac wearily. "Get your things together and get out."

"Dad, I can't believe you won't even listen to me," said Rocky. "You're right. I'd better go!" He picked up his mail, strode out, so distraught he didn't even close the door behind him.

Mac closed and locked it. Tomorrow morning he would have the locks changed. He would tell the gatekeeper and the desk not to let his son in. And he would have all of Rocky's things in the guest bedroom packed up and delivered to the Snail.

Funny. Rocky hadn't looked angry as much as shell-shocked. Hurt. But he wasn't going to fall for that. He wasn't going to relent. This time he meant it.

Nelly spent the whole morning showing Allison everything she could think of about the agency files, booking procedures, sign-up applications, and the computer files and programs. And then she remembered to call the Sheriff's office about the note. "I don't know what to make of it," she told Deputy Greensong, who was handling the case. "And I don't think my husband Albert has anything to do with it. But then again, I never thought he'd try to choke me, either. Last night, about eleven, and just as we pulled into the driveway, we saw someone at the door. A man, kind of thin, medium height. That's all we saw. The second we caught him in the headlights he was gone. The note was on the door. My friend quickly ran around the back of the house, but he didn't find anything or anybody. I'm sure you're right. It's some religious freak. But it's making me very uneasy."

Greensong assured her he'd be over to get the note and look around.

She called Merve Morganthau next to tell him about the notes and the man at the door. "One thing—a skinny, medium-height man certainly couldn't have been Albert," he said.

"Could he have someone doing it for him?"

"I don't get the impression he's that creative. Bashing heads is more his kind of thing."

"I wish this were all over. How much longer will the divorce take now—until I have it in my hand?"

"I'd say about two weeks."

After hanging up with Morganthau, Nelly called her mother, who was in Montreal, staying at Barton deLys's lodge. "Hello, darling," said Lauren in an absolutely lilting voice. "I'm having the most marvelous time, Nelly. We're snowed in and huge fires are burning in the fireplaces. They're made of stone, and one of them is high enough to stand in! We ate a kind of scrambled eggs with maple syrup in them. Sounds disgusting; tastes marvelous. And Bart has such interesting friends."

"You're not bored?"

"You couldn't be. He has TV, every kind of game you've ever heard of, a library that takes up three rooms, and the most delightful guests. We've gone tromping in the snow. Yesterday we made snowmen. I may never come home."

"Has he heard anything more from C.G.?"

"Not really. He calls every day and she won't talk to him. But finally today she said she couldn't talk then, but she'd call him tonight. He said she sounded different, so maybe she's ready to make up. We're trying to think of some way she can gracefully drop this Woman of Our Time thing without looking like a jackass. The nominating luncheon is coming up— she's not directly involved with that. A committee is running it. Have you heard about it?"

"Yes, Mother. I've been invited. We're supplying some entertainment, so I may go. I keep saying that what I need now is someone exactly like C.G. to do all that social stuff for me. She'd be perfect."

For C.G. the day went like any other—none of the partners spoke to her. But every time the phone rang, or she heard footsteps approaching her office, she cringed, half-expecting this was it.

They probably wanted Melissa to learn the ropes before they made their move. She already knew more about keeping books and bookkeeping guidance than C.G. ever would.

At noon, Emmet called her. She was so relieved. His voice was balm to her nerves—he was her balancing pole. All right, so he was a waiter. But how wonderful it felt to have someone 100 percent on her side. And last night in bed with him, as much as she could remember, had been utterly lovely. He was in charge. But he was loving. Tender, but passionate. "Mrs. Clemency-Graves?" he said.

"Why aren't you calling me C.G." she asked coyly.

"Because I didn't know if anyone might be listening there," he said. "You know what I'd really love to call you is Claire. It's so beautiful. Saints and outstanding women have had that name. Look at Clare Booth Luce. You're a Claire if anyone is."

"Permission granted," she said, pleased.

"Is anything happening?"

"No. It's maddening. I keep expecting someone to say something and no one has. It's business as usual, but I'm a nervous wreck."

"Oh, this is so unfair. What can I do to make you feel better?"

"You're wonderfully supportive, Emmet. I've never known anyone quite so supportive. Maybe if you would just talk to me—"

"Tonight?"

"Yes."

"At your place?"

"Oh, yes."

"I don't get through work until nine."

"That would be fine. Just knowing you're coming will help. Will you have had dinner or should I save you a little something?"

"No, I'm not going to make any work for you, Claire. I'll eat here first. I'll be there by 9:30."

"Just enter the same way."

"Yes."

"Oh, Emmet, this is so dear of you."

"You needn't have anything for me to drink, Claire," he said, enjoying the feel of that name on his tongue. "I'm not a very good drinker."

"I'm not either. When I have a drink I can hardly remember what happens next. And some things—well—"

"I know," he said, breathing heavily. "Some things you want to remember."

"You get the room," ordered Danny, slipping some bills in his hand. "Two keys. Then come back here and we'll finish dinner." He quickly headed out of the dining room to do her bidding. He had known this would happen, from the first moment he saw that body leaning toward him at that party. He couldn't wait to get her upstairs. She'd melt the damn mattress. She had that look.

"Is that for one or two, sir?" asked the clerk.

"For two, said Rocky. "My wife is parking the car." He got out his card and put Danny's bills in his pocket. Checking out, he'd use the cash but for now they needed a charge plate.

"Two keys, please," he requested with no explanation.

"Yes, sir," said the clerk, nodding to another clerk who disappeared behind a door for a minute and returned with a second key. Rocky headed back to the dining room.

She seemed to be enjoying her shrimp and stone crabs but he noticed she ate nothing else. No bread and butter. Nothing with a dressing on it. He wolfed down a few ribs and some pasta and then said. "I don't think I want any more of this."

She shrugged. "Give me one of the keys," she said. He passed one to her. "You go up first. I'll take care of this."

"No, I'll get it," said Rocky, reaching for his wallet.

"Do what I say, darling, and everything will work smoothly. No glitches. You go upstairs now to 707. I'll come up in ten or fifteen minutes. I'm going to have a cup of coffee. That way you'll have time to clean up or whatever you might want to do."

Rocky nodded. "Yes, sir! Whatever you say, sir. My aim tonight is to please."

"I'm so glad." She dismissed him with the flick of a hand. Rocky got up and headed for the restaurant entrance, the elevators, and their room.

It was a decent room. He pulled some condoms from his pocket and tossed them on the nightstand. He'd have time for a shower.

Afterward, he donned one of the robes in the bathroom, turned on the TV, and waited.

When he finally heard her key in the lock and she walked in, he came over to reach for her. "One minute, darling," she whispered, ducking into the bathroom. She came out a minute later in a sheer, short black wisp of a nightgown, a tiny pair of silver slippers, and nothing else. She had done something to her hair. It was a black halo of curls with tendrils hanging down in her face, sexy as hell. Her eyes, glittering, locked on his. They radiated heat. She walked slowly, deliberately, toward him, pulled open his robe and put her arms and one leg around him, rubbing her body sensually against him, opening her mouth to suck on his chin and then almost swallowing his lips in a wet, lascivious kiss.

He hoisted her by the buttocks and carried her—

one leg still wrapped around him—to the bed where he laid her and threw his robe aside. She grabbed at him and stroked him, pushing her sheer nightgown up spreading her slender legs apart, staring up at him hungrily. He knelt beside the bed, bending over to work on her chest and neck with an expert tongue. She reached for his penis again, the same moment he licked his finger to probe that black mound. "Oh, God, now, now," she cried, and he clambered on top of her and in her. She was hot, tight. He felt her starting to come within a few short thrusts, and it was only with the most determined restraint that he let her peak first. Then he allowed himself to go crazy inside her, prolonging her orgasm, making her wail at the intensity of her pleasure. He lifted her up to press into her until she cried out, "Ayahhhh!" and clung to him, wrapping her legs around him and squeezing him tightly as he pushed through the downside of his own orgasm, as though she wanted to pull all of him inside her.

Spent, panting for breath, she dropped down. He lifted himself to let her roll to his side, and collapsed next to her.

After they wallowed for a time in the happy languor enveloping them, he said quietly, "I put the condoms on the nightstand."

"Mine are in my purse," she said.

"Now you tell me. Oh, well, next time."

"Can we?" she asked. "I mean, tonight?"

"We can fuck the whole damned night away," he said. "If you want to. Just give me a few minutes to nap and catch my breath.

"The TV's still on. Want it off?"

"No," he mumbled, turning away from her and quickly slipping off to sleep.

She drowsed beside him. She couldn't quite sleep when the TV was on. But she certainly hadn't heard it at all a few minutes ago. She listened to his even breathing in the semi-dark. He was out for more than fifteen minutes. She didn't realize he had awakened until she felt those long, warm fingers on her breast.

She smiled. This time, she knew, would be something else, too. He would feel he had to prove he could still do more, that he could satisfy her like nobody else. These young men, the ones who liked older women, seemed to feel they had to show they were more than a match, sexually. She had known it would be good. From the minute she met him at that party.

She feigned sleep, letting him touch and kiss her so gently here and there, until she couldn't help responding. Couldn't help writhing to his touch, sighing and moaning as the tension mounted. Stroking his tight, muscular arms, tasting that tight young chest, pinching those tight little buns, soaking up the sensations she was so marvelously addicted to. And when she felt him hard inside her again, she knew she had found a winner.

At eleven she slipped from the bed and into the bathroom, cleaned up, tucked the miniscule nightie and slippers back in her large purse, and put her clothes back on, arranging her hair more sedately and using a purse-sized spray. When she came out, Rocky was asleep. She woke him. "Rocky, darling, I have to go. I have to get home before Will. It's been a fantastic night."

"Mmmm," he mumbled, half-asleep. "When can we do it again?"

"I'll call you."

"Better let me call you first, and give you my other number. I won't be at my dad's. We've had a little disagreement."

"Whatever you say," replied Danny. She bent over to give him a kiss on the mouth that was more like a bite, grabbed her purse, put her key on the dresser, and let herself out. In the hallway she reapplied her lipstick and checked herself in a wall mirror. Yes, her eyes, to someone who knew her intimately, would reveal what she had been up to. But Will never noticed things like that anymore. When he wanted her, he pounced on her and got it over with. But only once or twice a month at the most. Will was rapidly winding down. It was sad. They had once had such great times in bed together. No one would ever be for her quite what Will had been. She boarded the elevator.

In 707, Rocky considered getting up and heading home. But what for? He might as well stay the night. This room was a darn sight more comfortable than his lousy digs at the Snail. He dug deeper under the blanket and went back to sleep.

Twenty-seven

Barton shook his head in amazement. After refusing to talk to him since Christmas, C.G. had not only called him, but here she was babbling confidentially like a teenager to her most trusted friend. "Wait, Sis. Slow down. This is too much to take in so quickly. You say you're going to be fired? How do you know?"

"Because a dear, dear friend of mine overheard the partners talking in the Sky Club," she said, relating what Emmet had told her, editing out the part about a hand in the cookie jar. "So it's only a matter of time. I have to find something else. And what am I good at? Talking to people."

"Why not take some training in something that you might like doing? They have aptitude tests to help you decide."

"At my age? I don't want to be a hairdresser or a dental technician, Barton."

"Well, you could be a restaurant hostess. A concierge. Go to work for that new convention center."

"A restaurant hostess—it might come to that. That brings me to the other part of my news."

"Yes. You say you've met someone you like?"

"Very supportive. Very loyal. Very perceptive. The only thing is, he works as a waiter."

"Oh, Sis, what's wrong with that, if you like each other? You let this status business run your life."

"Not altogether. I've decided I don't want to lose Emmet. We're toying with the idea of getting him into some related work, but, you know, with a little more—"

"A little more status."

"Well, yes."

"Such as?"

"He could make elegant desserts for top eateries in town. And deliver them. He already does that for a couple of places. I could help promote them—by running a little social evening, desserts and coffee, for a group of owners of top restaurants."

"Sounds very good. But now tell me, what's happening with that Woman of Our Time business? Have you dropped that?"

"Oh, no. Of course not. It's all going as planned. The luncheon for the nominations is coming up and I'm invited. I'll let my new assistant, Melissa, nominate me. I'll tell her what to say. And I'll have to get someone else to second it with a little speech."

"But when they realize you're the one who started all this—"

"They'll just be glad I did. Four or five different charities are sponsoring the nominating luncheon and they will each make a little something, even from that."

Barton sighed. "There's one more thing, Sis. Have you made your peace with Nelly yet?"

"Absolutely not. How can you even ask after hearing what's happening to me because of her?"

"Not because of her, C.G. I hate to say this, Sis, but it's all your own fault and no one else's. You weren't doing the job you were getting paid for. You were doing only the part you liked."

"The only part I knew how to do. But I needed the job. What was I to do?"

"And now, Nelly's become a rising star in that world you prize so. She's a very kind lady. She would be understanding if you ever went to her and apologized and made your peace. She might be able to get your friend some business for his bakery."

"Do you think so?" Then she said, "I don't know if I should apologize. I'll talk to Emmet about it. But I do know, brother dear, that I owe you one. Getting to know Emmet better after all these years, and seeing how good it is to have a strong and loyal friend to count on, it's made me realize I have a strong and loyal brother to count on, too. Even if he doesn't always see things the same way I do. I—I'm sorry I was so angry with you. I know you meant well."

"You realize now that I care about you?"

"Yes, you always have."

"Then please, Sis, think about what I said about Nelly. If I were her brother, instead of yours, think how I might react."

"I'll try, Barton. I promise I'll try."

After hanging up, he turned to Lauren and shook his head. "She sounds completely different. Was it my imagination? Softer. Almost like she'd turned the clock back five years. Or fallen in love. I think I'm going to have to fly down again in the next week or two and take a look at this Emmet. Nobody can be as nice as she thinks he is. He could be a con man, for all I know. I don't trust her judgment at this point. Or maybe she just sounds that way because of the job. I suppose knowing that you're going to be fired any minute is enough to shake up anyone. It's not like she has a good reserve. She's got her apartment, that old Mercedes, her jewelry, and a small annuity. Enough to live on, but not in the style she's used to."

"You know something funny, Bart," said Lauren thoughtfully, "when I talked to Nelly this morning, she told me she's hired a manager. And Minny works part time. But she said what she really needs now is someone like C.G. to do the social end. To go to these seminars and meetings and see if the speakers are good enough, and to determine who might want to book them. And to go to the bookers' events to see who they might use. To attend fundraisers to give the agency a high profile. She's being invited constantly now to all sorts of things. She can't get to them all."

"Hmmm," Barton murmured. The same idea was hatching in his mind as was hatching in Lauren's. "If only there were some way to get the two of them together again," he said.

"Now, Barton," she said, breaking into a grin. "Don't make it all sound so hopeless. There's *always* a way to do anything you really want to. You make a plan. You just have to poke around a bit sometimes before you get it all figured out."

Mac pulled into the drive at six-thirty. Nelly called out, "Who's there?" as she had been instructed to do by the Sheriff's deputy. She let him in, led him into the kitchen, and poured him a cup of tea. "OK, now what is this all about?" she asked, digging out some homemade peanut butter cookies. She hadn't baked much in years but now that the girls were back and forth so often, she had to keep a stock of cookies on hand.

"You won't believe what just dropped in your lap," said Mac, taking a bite. "Damn, these are good. Anyway, Perry Wales, you know, from the TV show *Clues?* He's a friend of mine. Two of his wives were women my wife introduced him to. We belonged to a couple of the same clubs in New York. We saw each other a lot up there. He called and said he's coming down next week to do some shows from the Fontainebleau. I told him about you and he gave the info to the guy who books guests and you're going to be invited to be one. That's why I came over. I didn't want to tell you such great news on the phone."

"Me? On TV?" Nelly wailed. "I'd die of stage fright."

"No, you won't. You handled that little speech at the mike last week just fine. And those radio interviews. The coverage for your agency would be the kind money can't buy. You'll make a great guest. Pretty, smart, articulate. The kind of person they love."

Clues, Nelly knew, was the quiz show *everyone* watched on Friday nights. Two teams of three each viewed a short skit packed with clues and then tried to answer sets of three questions. It could be a whodunnit, or any other brief scene. The teams had thirty seconds to decide on their answers, but if they were wrong, it was the other team's turn. The skits were usually inane, and so were many of the questions, but the answers and guesses were often hysterically funny. The show had in unbudgeable high rating.

"I've never been on TV before," said Nelly.

"It's not nearly as intimidating as an elevator

ride," he assured her. "And the exposure wouldn't be just local. So many companies from all over the country do conventions and seminars down here, and they all need speakers and entertainers. Things to keep the wives busy, too, besides the corporate sessions. They'd use your agency."

"I've only seen that program a few times. Albert watched mostly sports. Some news. Never a quiz show. Since he's gone, I hardly turn the TV on. No time."

"I think we might have a couple of tapes somewhere," said Mac. "I'll look for them. You'll do it?"

"If you think I can."

"That sounds like the old Nelly you told me about. I thought I was talking to Anyella."

Nelly blinked at that. "You're right!" she answered in a deliberately animated voice. "Sometimes I relapse a little. What I meant to say was, I'd be *delighted* to do it. I can't wait. I can't thank you enough for thinking of me. It sounds like a lot of fun. We'll send out a little notice to tell all our clients to watch. When will I be on?"

"One day next week—I'll know for sure in a day or two. And I think I can get tickets for your mother and the girls." He finished his tea. "I won't stay. I know you've got more to do than you can handle. And we've got that date in Deltona next week, too."

Nelly nodded. It was a forum on business conditions countrywide, with about ten speakers, twenty

355

to thirty minutes each—a long, intense day of brain-picking. Her agency had supplied five of the experts and Mac was one of them.

She walked him to the door. He stopped for a moment. "Rocky's on his own," he said. "I finally did it. We'll see what happens. That's all I can do. Meanwhile, the real reason I came by with this news instead of telling you by phone is because on the phone I can't do this." He swept Nelly into his arms for a long, hungry kiss. "I hope one day you'll know all the good things making love can be, Nelly," he said. And he was gone.

Twenty minutes later, Boz pulled into the drive. "Coming this late is cutting it a little fine, but then we can skip all those introductions in the lobby before the ballet," he said.

Boz was a perfect date. Attentive, considerate. He tried to buy her a drink during intermission but they never quite got to the bar. The seats around them were filled with his condo neighbors and at least fifteen women blocked their way up the aisle, wanting to be introduced. And to size her up, Nelly realized. Most were saccharin-sweet, but not really friendly. Each one told her some little anecdote about Boz that even Nelly, with her limited experience, could tell was designed to appeal to him—and still let Nelly know that they knew him better and were his friends, too.

Even Boz noticed it. On the way home, he said, "Maybe this wasn't such a good idea, attending one of our condo outings. I didn't realize they'd be so tough."

"It's OK. I can take it," she said.

"But why should you have to? I know two guys at our place that not only don't ever mess with any of our single women, but they never come to *any* condo event. I'm beginning to understand why. Next time, why don't we just go to a movie? The two of us."

"That would be fine," Nelly replied.

At her door, Boz seemed uncomfortable, as though he didn't quite know what was expected of him. Nelly felt sorry for him. She stood on tiptoe and kissed him lightly on the cheek. But then he quickly took her face in his hands and kissed her on the mouth. A kiss surprisingly sweet—tentative, but sweet. "You're a nice lady, Nelly," he said. "I could tell right away. I'll call you tomorrow and we can pick a day for that movie, OK?"

He watched Nelly let herself in before he pulled out of the drive. Inside, she leaned against the door, confused. Here she was so turned on by Mac's kisses that she could remember every minisecond of each one. And when Ben had kissed her on New Year's Eve, it had been so good. A straightforward kiss. Warm. Loving.

And now Boz.

Wonderful kisses from all three. And she had felt warm and loving right back, each time! She had wanted more. Oh, how much she had wanted more! With each one, she had wanted to feel them closer. Good God! Was Albert the only man in the world who didn't know how to kiss a woman? No wonder she had been so turned off all those years.

But now, how could she react to all three of them this way? Granted there was more of an electric charge and emotional pull toward Mac, who seemed equally attracted to her. But he also seemed very determined to control that attraction.

But she felt a strong current from all three. If Mac weren't around, she would probably be very happy to get serious about Ben. If Mac and Ben weren't in the picture, she would have been delighted to have Boz's attention. Goodness, was she more like her mother than she knew?

All Nelly knew now was that she wanted more. She *craved* more. She had to find out if it was still that good if you went further, when you actually made love. Was that part still as dreadful as it had been with Albert? Or were the movies right, after all? She couldn't imagine Mac or Ben or Boz being anything but wonderful to be close to and intimate with.

But one thing she was sure of. Now that she had come this far, now that she had awakened something inside her, pretty soon her curiosity and her feelings and this new hunger were going to get the better of her. Pretty soon, with somebody or other, she was going to find out what it was all about.

Would it be Mac who would teach her? Or Ben? Boz?

"You're dropping it, Min," Albert said. He had watched her roll a line after their respective leagues wound up. "You smack all the action off it. You gotta roll it. Get down further to the floor when you let it go. If you can't bend down that far, you gotta work at loosening up if you really wanna pick up your average."

"I guess I do," she said, packing her ball and shoes into her bag.

"Come on, let's grab a hamburger or something."

"I don't know. First I got something to ask you."

"So? What you gotta ask?"

"Why have you been putting those damn holy notes on Nelly's door?"

"What holy notes? What're you talkin' about?

"Those holy notes someone's tacked on her door. Saying God's gonna get her."

"I don't know, but for Christ's sake, I never even heard about them. Come on. We'll get a sandwich while you tell me about it."

"Something fast. I gotta get home."

"Freddie's waiting?"

She ignored the question. They climbed on the stools at the restaurant counter. "I'll take tuna salad and a Coke," she told the waitress.

"Give me the same thing. And some potato salad or something," said Albert. "Now, what's this about notes?"

Minny told him what she knew. "So the Sheriff's office knows and they're watching. And they don't think it's anything serious. I was afraid it was you."

"Yeah, thanks a lot," he grunted. "At night you say?"

"Yeah."

"I gotta think about this," said Albert, taking half of his sandwich in one bite. "Maybe I can't see Nelly, but I'm damned if I like the idea of some nut hanging stuff on my house."

"It's not your house anymore."

"So what? It was my house a long time, and it's still my wife's house. We're not divorced yet. What else is going on?"

Minny told him what she could about the agency, the new manager, and how wonderful Nelly looked—prettier all the time. Albert walked her to her car. When she unlocked it and climbed in, he actually closed the door for her. He looked so sad. Minny found herself rolling down her window to say, "Thanks for the bowling advice, Albert. And thanks for the sandwich."

"Nah, it's nothing," he said. "Thanks for keeping

me posted, Min. Be careful driving home." He pulled a toothpick from his pocket and headed for his own car, walking very slowly, as if it took a great effort.

Rocky couldn't believe how easy the course was. Not for his classmates, who were grumbling and complaining. But with his legal background and his photographic mind, it was a snap. One week of intensive concentration, non-stop classes, exams, and more exams. Hell, they barely gave you time to take a pee. But he found it so fascinating, on the second day he signed up for several follow-up courses—and arranged to audit a few related seminars on topics he wanted basic knowlege of—title searching, surveying, restrictions, pollution, and ecology trends. He studied local codes in various communities. He ordered back copies or machine copies of past Sunday classifieds of the *Sun-Sentinel* and the *Miami Herald* to read after his long days of classes.

He passed his salesman's exam with such flying colors that he didn't have to wait to find out. The teacher called and congratulated him. His next course, on commercial real estate, began the same way, and as happens with star students, he found himself deluged with work offers from more than a dozen major real estate companies. He'd probably give Broward Top Realty the nod.

After he passed the main course, he decided to

call Danielle Raymond. No matter how sexy Danny was, it was Emma he would really like to see. But Emma, at this point, was clearly not eager to see him. And he wanted to get laid. By now, he figured, Danny would be panting for another round, too.

He was wrong.

"No, I won't meet you at the Westin," she said, "but I'd like to talk to you for a few minutes. Only not at the deli. I don't want to be overheard. How about meeting me at the Coley Hammock around four o'clock today?"

"Can you make it any later? I can't get there until five-thirty at the earliest." He had a class until five.

"Five-thirty, then, if you can manage that."

"Yeah, I guess I can."

At the Hammock, she was sitting on a bench down by the New River. He hurried over and tried to kiss her, but she pulled back and leaned away. "Are you out of your mind? A dozen people I know might see you do that."

"Why didn't we meet at your house then?" said Rocky. "You could say I'm a repair man and whisk me in to fix some furniture in your bedroom."

She stared at him, eyes flashing. "Or why not just come up to my place on a Wednesday night?" she suggested. "Would you like that? Getting it off when we know my husband might get home any minute, and you'd have to hide in my bathroom until he went to bed and I could sneak you out the door?"

"Hey, I'm game if you are," said Rocky, missing the sarcasm in her voice. "This Wednesday? We'll have a ball. What time?"

Danny shook her head at him sadly. "Never, Rocky. I'm afraid we've had our one and only meeting. And we haven't had that. If you ever mention it to me, I won't know what you're talking about. Got that? It never happened."

Rocky stared at her, puzzled. What the hell was this? "You mean, you don't want to see me? You want me to fade out? I don't get it. We had fireworks last week. You want more. I want more."

"And if you were just a little discreet and responsible we would have had more," she said. "But I can't take a chance with you, Rocky. You're nuts. Ben and Nelly are right."

"What do you mean?" he snapped. "Right about what? What the fuck are you talking about?"

"I discussed with Nelly the possibility of talking about your adventures on one of the shows she's booked me on. She told me the whole story about you and the girls in that race. The boat sinking. Some hero. Lying to get into the race, risking their lives, just for a thrill. She told me Ben said you lied to get to Kuwait, how you're hooked on adventure. Addicted.

"So I called Ben, and he told me more. You're

363

crazy, Rocky. And no job? No career? You're more than crazy. You're an irresponsible child. You're trouble. You can just get up and dust yourself off after one of these crazy escapades and go after your next big thrill. But I have my life and my future in this town. I can't be caught in a scandal. I'm not perfect, but at least I'm discreet and so is my husband. And if push ever comes to shove, we're a team. We care about each other. I'm not risking making him or me a laughingstock just because you get your jollies from danger and close calls. So don't ever contact me again. Ever. There's nothing to discuss."

She stood up, tossed the black mane defiantly, and strode purposefully across the Hammock to her car.

Rocky sank onto the bench, stunned. What was he supposed to do? Run after her, yelling, "But I *will* have a job. I'm training for it now!"

He felt like he'd been kicked in the face. She was right. His father was right. The twins were right. He was a fucking, thrill-seeking nut. He thought he'd reformed, but here he was ready to take the same chances for a sex thrill as he had on the high seas. He was totally screwed up.

He put his head in his hands. There was no Thrill-seekers Anonymous to join that he knew of. He'd talked to shrinks before. A waste of time. In Kuwait, he'd picked up some scars. This time, it could easily have been his life and two others. He sighed heavily and lifted his lanky form from the bench. Maybe it was hopeless, trying to control this crazy need of his always to be skirting the very edge. One thing for sure. If he didn't do something about it himself, nobody could do it for him. Maybe he had to find some other source of excitement. Maybe this real estate business? Maybe, like a drinker, he had to do it one day at a time.

First day: today. He'd go back to the Snail and get busy again with his books.

Albert brought his friend Paddy along so he'd have a witness if he needed one. After all this time without booze, he felt different. Stronger. More energetic. He was even bowling better. He was working ten to twelve hours a day, more some days, and no matter how tired he got at night, he felt ready to go the next morning. He wouldn't miss an A.A. meeting for anything. And no matter how he longed for just one small beer, especially when he was bowling, he'd cut off his oysters before he'd take one.

He felt righteous tonight. He'd show Nelly what she'd dumped. He'd show everyone he wasn't the gorilla they made him out to be. He'd protect her now even if she was treating him like shit. Even if, in a week or two, she wouldn't be his wife anymore.

This was the fifth night he'd tried this. He was supposed to let her alone. Well, he was. He hadn't called. Hadn't stopped and knocked on the door.

Nothing. He just drove around the block a few times each night, parking on the cul-de-sac for an hour or more, and watching the house from there. He didn't know if Nelly was home or not any of those nights. She kept a light on in the living room anyway, nowadays. The first night, he had been parked in the cul-de-sac when she had come home, but she hadn't known he was there.

He drove down the street toward the house. So they thought they'd put notes on her door, did they? Well, he'd show 'em.

He passed by the house slowly. Nothing and nobody moving. He didn't pay any attention to the extra cars in Minny's driveway. They had been there all five nights, but Minnie always had a friend over. Probably that Freddie. That wouldn't last. She wasn't the tennis type. He passed Minny's house, headed for the cul-de-sac, turned the car around and parked, as he had done the other nights.

"See anything?" whispered Paddy as Albert stared back the way they had come.

"Christ, I think I do!" Albert whispered back. At the other end of the street, a block past Nelly's, a car with its lights out pulled onto a swale and stopped.

Albert peered down the street. He could make out a man emerging from the car. He whispered to Paddy, "Stay here. Bet that's him. I'm going to pound that son of a bitch right into the cement."

He crawled from the car, and bending low to be hidden by the bushes, he cut into a backyard. A few minutes later, he reappeared, creeping around Nelly's house toward her front walk, still half hidden by the sea grapes, just as the man from the car reached the door and tacked a piece of white paper on it.

Albert came barreling out of the bushes, hunched over like a football tackle. He let out a bloodcurdling "YAAAAAHHGGG!" and hurled himself at the stranger, just as one of the extra cars in Minny's driveway turned on its engine and beamed its bright lights right on the door, catching Albert as he landed on top of the stranger, knocking him to the ground and grabbing his arms up behind his back as he had Nelly's. He kneed the man in the back so his face thumped into the concrete walk.

"Just hold it right there," cried Officer Brendan Duffy, charging from the car in Minny's driveway, gun in one hand, phone in the other. "OK, I think we got 'em," he said into the phone. "Get us some help over here, quick."

And to Albert and the stranger he barked, "The two of you just stand there, hands in the air, NOW!"

Albert gave the man's arms another wrench that made him scream in pain and stood up, raising his own hands. The stranger just lie there.

"You, the guy standing, leave him alone. Where the hell did *you* come from, and who the hell are you?" asked Duffy. "Don't move, just talk. Fast."

"I came to catch this bastard who's been putting threatening holy notes on my house," said Albert. "It ain't my house anymore but that's still my wife he's scaring and I caught him. I'm Albert Holachek. He was just putting up another one."

"I saw that," said Duffy. "But where did *you* come from?"

"My friend is parked in my van down on the cul-de-sac. I ran through the backyards. I been watchin' for a few nights. I saw this creep get out of a car down there. And now while you're talking to me it's probably gone."

"Not far. I saw it, too," said Duffy. "I called in. It's probably been stopped already."

The man on the cement tried to stand up, but couldn't. He settled for a sitting position, leaning against the wall. "I can't raise my arms. They hurt," he said hoarsely.

"Then just keep them perfectly still," barked Duffy. Two more police cars, lights flashing, barreled onto the street down at the corner, pulled up to the house and over onto the swale. Three policemen leapt out and ran over to Duffy. "I think the big guy just caught this sign-hanger," he said. "Did they get the car?"

"Two blocks from the corner," said Officer Jamison, who went over to put handcuffs on the man sitting on the walkway.

"My friend's right down there in my van in front

of the two-story house. It's the only two-story house over there," said Albert. One of the policemen hiked down to get Paddy. Just then Minny's door flew open and Minny and Freddie ran out. "What's going on here?" she cried.

"We got the man who's been doing the signs, looks like," said Duffy. "Thanks for letting us use your driveway. We figured if we sat there long enough in an unmarked car, we'd catch him."

"And I caught him, Minny," said Albert. "It's that religious bugger, over there. He's the one who's been puttin' signs on the door. I told you it wasn't me. Tell Nelly that. Everyone's thinkin' it's me and I never did anythin' *that* dumb in my life."

"You two come down to the station," said Duffy to Albert and Paddy. The other officers helped the cultist into a police car. "You guys follow that car and we'll follow you," he said. He wasn't quite sure how to handle this. Albert Holachek was the guy who pasted his wife and got put in jail a few weeks ago. And tonight he nails this religious nut who had been putting those threatening signs on all those houses, scaring the shit out of people. So tonight he was a hero. Go figure.

"Do you need us?" asked Minny.

"I don't think so," said Duffy.

"Maybe we'd better go along so we can find out what happens and tell Nelly—Mrs. Holachek," she said.

"Nah, don't worry. I'll call you from the station and tell you. That OK?"

"Oh, thanks," said Minny. "I've got better things to do than spend time in police stations. 'Night, Albert. See you at bowling." Albert could hear her arguing loudly with Freddie as they headed back to her house.

"Whaddya mean you'll see him bowling?" snapped Freddie. "I thought you were going to quit? Those alleys are terrible places."

"How would you know? You won't even go look at one. They're much nicer now. And they don't call them alleys. They're 'centers' now."

"But with tennis you get real exercise. Bowling's no exercise. You probably wouldn't have a weight problem if you took up tennis."

"No, I'd have all your skin cancers instead," Minny shot back. "I don't want to hear another word about my weight! That's not—" And her front door slammed angrily behind them.

Twenty-eight

When Ben called to set the time to pick her up for the Vanities Ball, she told him about the capture the night before. "The police said they're not really even a cult—just a handful of religious freaks who decided that instead of complaining about the wicked world they live in, they should do something about it," said Nelly. "Notes and calls are all they apparently planned to do. They weren't going to start handing out God's punishment themselves."

"Well, they won't now, at any rate," said Ben.

"They said they would stop, of course. The funny thing is though, this man who did it—Andrew Merritt was his name—he admitted making that one phone call, but he swore this was the first note he'd put on my door. But it was the fourth or fifth I've found, and they're all on the same paper, same printing, same wording. He can't explain it and he and the man who drove the car admitted the other houses they've put notes on and how many, but they both absolutely insisted this was his first at my house. Isn't that strange?"

"Well, they probably don't keep great books," replied Ben, chuckling. "They need Raymond, Schlesser's guidance. Curious they're so insistent about it, though. What are the police doing with them?"

"I think it pretty much amounts to scold, warn, and watch. I think the fact that they didn't threaten you helps. There was a blurb in the paper about it this morning. It just said that a suspect had been picked up at a home in Plantation. And what the notes said. But no names, thank goodness. And no address."

Mark Goldberg and Jack McKinnon wandered into Ben's office just as he hung up. "That was Nelly," he told them. "You know on top of everything else, some religious nut has been pasting threatening notes on her door. 'God will get you for breaking his commandments.' Stuff like that. They caught the nut last night. And know *who* caught him? Get this! It was her husband, Albert!"

Ben repeated the rest of the story, and the three men shook their heads, then quickly moved on to the day's business and comparing schedules for the next week. Goldberg headed for Will Raymond's office and told him the latest on Nelly, too. McKinnon headed for C.G. and Melissa's office—he was keeping a fairly close eye on that operation, stopping in two or three times a day—and there he retold the story again.

As soon as McKinnon left the office and Melissa departed for a guidance visit, C.G. called Emmet. "Emmet, dear, I'm glad I caught you before you left for work. Guess what? McKinnon came in with more news about Nelly. Ever since it was in the paper when her husband tried to beat her that night, she's been getting threatening notes from some religious fanatics. 'God will punish you. Repent and change your ways,' or messages like that. And last night, of all people, Nelly's husband Albert, the one who tried to beat her up? *He* caught the man who was putting up the notes. Caught him in the act, with a police car right in the next driveway! I tell you, that woman leads a life I don't envy. I almost feel sorry for her."

There was a big pause at the other end of the line. "Emmet? Are you still there?"

"Yes, dear. I'm listening. Uh—did he say anything else?"

"No. Except that the man they caught said this is the first note he has ever put on her door, but the police say she's gotten several. And they have the notes to prove it."

"Well, isn't that curious?" said Emmet. "Maybe the others were sent by someone who wanted to— well—punish her for some reason."

"But what a despicable thing to do," said C.G. indignantly. "To anyone. To frighten them to death like that."

"But maybe to some people it wouldn't be so frightening. Just irritating."

"I don't know to whom. It's despicable."

"Yes, despicable," said Emmet, quickly. "And did you find out what time your brother's coming in, Claire?"

"About six. You'll still be working, so I'll pick him up at the airport. Just come over whenever you're through. Don't rush yourself. Is that all right?"

"Fine."

"And my brother will be staying the night, dear, so I—we—"

"I understand, Claire. I know I can't be with you every night, no matter how much I want to. I'm grateful for every minute we can be together. I never thought we ever would. I'll be there later."

Did he sound just a little bit upset or uneasy, wondered C.G. Because he would be meeting Bart? Yes, that was probably the reason. What else could it be?

Rocky called Jane and Emma at their office, but this time he didn't ask to speak to them. He left his name and his number and a rather lengthy message. "Passed my real estate salesman course with one of highest grades ever recorded. Took or audited or am still taking several courses on related topics. Getting to be a goshdarn expert. Have several job offers. 'Druther work for you. How about a trial week? I really am settling down. No adventures. No thrill-chasing anymore. Promise to do well, without conning customers."

Emma saw the note ten minutes later, but Jane didn't get back to read it until noon. Over lunch they argued over what to do. "Charming he is," said Emma. "Customers would love him."

"Until he lied to them a time or two, to sell them something they shouldn't buy," said Jane. "We don't want him to be misleading our clients and ruining our good name, Em."

"But he said he wouldn't."

"That may be the first lie," said Jane. "He says whatever he thinks you want to hear. Or whatever's useful. We know that already. Why do we need it? I know we sort of felt close while we were out on that ocean and on that sandspit, but it was his fault we were out there. Sure, I know this is the new Rocky. He's changed. Yeah, yeah. But people don't really change, Emma."

"Sometimes they do. Mom did. And I think Rocky might. I think we should give him one more chance."

Jane threw up her hands. "Oh, all right. But only if we tell him: no lies, no conning people. A week's trial and that's it."

"Deal," said Emma. "Should I call him or will you?"

"You," said Jane. "I'm not even going to *talk* to him until I see him produce. And if he can't, he goes overboard."

"He'll produce," said Emma. "I bet he'll surprise us both."

Ben came to pick Nelly up at seven. She was wearing the low-cut gown she had first objected to at Designers 'R' Less. She looked ravishing, thought Ben. Like a very sexy angel. "I don't know, Nelly," he said as he helped her into his car. "When I see you looking like this, I think maybe I better forget how much older I am and just steal you to the altar before your head gets turned by all this attention. I have to think about that. Any comment?"

"Oh, Ben," she said, looking into his eyes the way her mother had taught her, "you say the loveliest things."

Barton couldn't get over his sister. Gentler, more reachable. She was more like the C.G. of five years ago, before Reggie died. They talked for over an hour before Emmet arrived. He told her about Nelly's mother being his guest for five days last

376

week. "She's a fascinating woman. We had a delightful time."

"Nelly's mother? Life takes curious twists and turns, doesn't it?" C.G. said, fingering her pearls. "Are you serious about her?"

"I don't know exactly what you mean by that. Do I have a crush on her? Yes, I guess I do. She's well-traveled, well-read, very funny, independent, interesting. And very down to earth. I think the competition may be formidable, as it's getting to be for Nelly. That rather discourages a fellow, if he wants a committment. And I've gotten along by myself for so many years now—I don't know. I just know I'm enjoying her company and our telephone chats.

"We've been putting our heads together and we've come up with some interesting ideas. One's about healing this breach between you and Nelly. And on solving the problem of you and your job. Oh, yes, Lauren and I could solve the problems of the whole world if they'd only listen to us."

"What kind of ideas?" asked C.G. tentatively.

"Well, for instance, Nelly needs someone to handle the social side of her business. Someone to go and meet with and check out the speakers and entertainers. A company representative with class. And you need a job like that. I mean, we both felt that the opening Nelly needs to fill is perfectly tailored for you."

C.G. digested that. "The problem is that you're not speaking," said Barton. "And that by now, your bad-mouthing has gotten back to Nelly. We're not quite sure how to get around that—or if you even want to. But I think that in this case, the ball is decidedly in your court."

"But I—I—" C.G. sputtered.

"I think you have to look at things from Nelly's perspective, for a change," he advised in a very gentle tone. "Really put yourself in her shoes and imagine how she felt. Maybe once you understand that, you can find some way to make up with her."

"I'll—I'll think about what you've told me," said C.G. "I'll talk it over with Emmet. He says I don't need to work, but then I'd be partly dependent on him. And I feel that I really *want* to work, to know for sure that I can take care of myself."

When Emmet arrived at 8:30, Barton chatted with him in as friendly a tone as he could manage, observing him carefully and weighing every remark and gesture. The man clearly adored his sister. Instead of assuming they would go out for a bite, C.G. brought out a huge Cuban sandwich, slaw, and potato salad, plus a tray of seafood on toothpicks with cocktail sauce—all obviously picked up on the way home. She had never done that for him before.

Emmet seemed a bit intimidated, but Barton's

gentle probing turned up a number of interesting facts. The man had once owned a popular restaurant in Chicago—The Courier, one of many destroyed by arson many years ago. He owned a restaurant supply outlet in Miami, his modest house in Plantation, plus an identical house next door which he rented. He had stayed with the Sky Club for years because he owned 15 percent of it, a fact that most of his co-workers were not aware of. He also made more money working there twenty or thirty hours a week than he could at any two other waiter jobs. It kept his hand in, and it gave the other owners significant input that enabled them to keep the service and menu first-rate. But for all this, his manner was unassuming, almost subservient. He seemed an unlikely type for his proud, sometimes haughty, sister to be attracted to.

Barton was surprised to find himself rather liking Emmet. He was determined to reserve judgment for as long as possible. But Claire had softened and blossomed under this new blanket of affection, delighting in Emmet's adoring glances. My God, I'll bet they're already going to bed, he suddenly realized. When Emmet prepared to leave, Barton shook his hand and tactfully retired to the guestroom. Emmet and C.G. ducked into the kitchen and kissed passionately. "Oh, my darling," he whispered, "how I wish you could come home with me tonight."

"So do I. Tomorrow," she promised.

379

"But I have something terrible to confess to you," he said in an anguished tone. "You may never want to come with me again."

"What is it Emmet, darling?" she asked, puzzled.

"It has to do with Nelly Holachek."

"Well, I've heard enough about her tonight from my brother. And I have to tell you about what he said, too. We'll talk about it all tomorrow, darling. Whatever it is, it can't be as important as our friendship," she said firmly.

"Our love," he corrected her, giving her one last, lingering good night kiss.

As he headed for the elevator, Emmet could think of just one thing. Tomorrow, he must call Mildred and explain that he wouldn't be seeing her anymore. After three years. Not that he had ever felt that close to her—they had been a sexual convenience for each other. Since he and Claire had melded so wondrously, he had been putting Mildred off when she called. But that wasn't fair. Not when there was no way he could ever want to touch her or bed her again.

Nelly loved Coley Hammock, this tiny patch of a park on the New River, a peaceful and quiet place to think. And now at midnight, with the moonlight outlining the majestic banyan trees in silver, it was a setting for dreams. They sat on a bench, an unlikely couple. Paunchy Ben in his tux, slim and supple Anyella in her revealing black gown. "You were the belle of the ball tonight, as I knew you would be, Nelly," he said. "Damn, I don't know what to do about you. I thought I just owed you a little kindness at first because of the way we treated you, the way we let C.G. treat you. And then I realized that I wanted to be your friend, aside from that. For real. And help you the way real friends help each other. So I've been trying to do that."

"And you have been the best friend anyone could want, Ben," said Nelly. He put his arm around her, pulled her head onto his shoulder, and stroked her cheek.

"But now," he said, "I think I want to be more than a friend. I want to hold you and love you and make you happy." He brushed his lips across her forehead and sighed. "But I don't know if it's fair to try and tie you up with an old fart like me. I'm almost fifteen years older than you, Nell. The body doesn't always do what I tell it to. I'm not all that active in the business anymore. I'd been thinking of retiring in a couple of years. Now, I find myself not wanting to retire. I think of conquering new worlds—and bringing home trophies to place at your feet."

Nelly reached up to hug him back. "That's the loveliest thing anyone's ever said to me," she whispered into his ear.

He stood up and pulled her to him and kissed her

long and hard, his large hands clasping her bare shoulders, then her back to pull her closer. When they broke apart, he said, "Oh, Nelly, there's so much woman in you. Come on, before I make love to you right here in Coley Hammock—I'm taking you home."

At the house, he came in with her. When he closed the door behind them, she found herself trembling. "Are you afraid?" he asked. "I wouldn't do anything you don't want me to."

"I've never had anyone but Albert, Ben. It was awful. He was rough. I'm not sure if—"

"You're not sure if it would be any better with me?"

Nelly stared back mutely.

"Relax, honey," he said. "I don't want to upset you. I just want to hold you. To show you that holding and touching each other is one of the nicest things two people can ever do together. Lie down on the couch here."

He knelt at her side and began touching the bare skin of her shoulders and chest in long, light, slow strokes. He bent to kiss the swell of one breast above the low neckline, and then the other, then began licking the same sensitive places. She was rigid and uneasy at first. But at his touch—his wonderful touch—she felt herself easing, melting. Savoring the sensations. He was kissing her everywhere—her arms, her neck, her ears, her chest—murmuring her name, squeezing her nipples lightly through her dress, just enough so she wanted more. And more.

She was wallowing in a tangled swarm of bewildering, beautiful feelings—some too sweet to bear without a moan. She began squirming, arching upward for more.

He reached down and caressed her hip bones through her gown, reached under its skirt to touch her ankles, her calves.

"Oh, Ben," she whimpered, reaching for him, trying to pull him up to kiss her mouth. And then with a cry, he crawled on top of her, his mouth found hers, and began devouring her. She could feel him pressing hard against her pelvis. She strained up toward him, but there were all those clothes in the way. He reached under her backside and pressed her to him and with a cry of release, he came, shuddering, and shuddering again and again. And then groaning, "Nelly, Nelly, Nelly," into her neck.

But he was still dressed. She held him close, murmuring, stroking his back, feeling a rush of affection and a sweet ache to do more. If only they had taken their clothes off . . . she still didn't know what it would be like with him inside her. But she knew it would be lovely. "I'm so sorry!" he whispered in her ear. "I thought I could stop, baby. Christ, forgive me."

But she clung to him even more tightly, and wrapped her free leg around his as he tried to get up. "Oh, Ben, don't go. Don't be sorry. I love how it feels with you on top of me. It was so wonderful, I wanted you there."

"Oh, Nelly, it wasn't fair to you. I could—let me—. No. Oh, hell. I'm just getting out of here. In the morning, if you're not mad at me, let me know. And—if you want to then, we'll finish the story. And it'll be all yours."

"Ben, please—I—"

"Let me go clean up and get out of here, darling," he said, "before I go ahead and do things I'm not sure you know if you really want me to do." He got up and ducked into the guest bathroom.

Nelly sat up on the sofa, her arms around her shoulders, replaying the moments just past. Oh, how she hungered to relive them. The girls were right. Sex could be beautiful. Making love could be wondrous. She could tell, now. She had been enduring Albert's grabbing and fumbling and shoving when there were men out there who knew how to make you feel like this?

Ben emerged from the bathroom, gave her only a quick sterile peck on the cheek, and said, "I'm leaving. I swear I never meant to go that far or that fast—I just couldn't stop. We're still not in so far you can't get out, honey. Talk to me tomorrow."

And he was gone.

Twenty-nine

Nelly got up at seven and raced around picking up, shoving papers in cabinets, giving a quick wipe to everything in the kitchen that wasn't already gleaming. Seven different appointments to show the house today! Jane and Emma were coming up for lunch with Evan Gumbel, aboard the yacht of a friend of his. They would bring Lauren and Barton, who was in town, with them, and they'd all go look at a couple of condos that seemed to fit Nelly and Lauren's needs. Plus, she had four new bookees to talk to before her dance lesson. And tomorrow, the TV show. And the next day, that business seminar where Britton was speaking. Her life was getting so busy she could hardly remember what day it was.

She called Ben at eight. "Nelly! I was afraid you might never want to talk to me again."

"Ben, don't be silly. You're my dear, close friend. And last night, you didn't do anything wrong."

"I did more than I meant to—for myself, I mean."

"But I was practically begging you to show me what it's all about. Now I know more about—about how glorious it can be."

"And have you thought about what I said?"

"Yes, but I need a little more time to think about it. I don't know what to say yet. I have a crunching couple of days. You and I have a Nova Forum breakfast, and a Women in Business luncheon coming up. And that Canopy Ball. Don't worry. You won't get rid of me so quickly."

"Well, you're safe at the breakfast and the luncheon. I never give sex lessons in public restaurants— they get so mad when you break the dishes."

Nelly laughed. "And here I thought you felt fatherly toward me."

"I do, my dear. That, too. Who was it that said, 'Vice is nice, but incest is best?' We'll go whichever way you feel comfortable, Nelly. One thing I think I should ask you—when will your divorce be granted? Do you know?"

"Another ten days or so, I think. He's not making any trouble. There's no property to divide up. This house is my mother's."

"I know you'll be relieved when that's finished, Nell. You'll feel freer to do what you choose. I'm thinking of you. I'll talk to you tomorrow. Keep me posted."

If you were here right now, Ben, she thought, I know exactly which way we'd go. I'd have you back on that couch in two minutes. But first, dear Ben, I have to get all these feelings sorted out.

The first prospective buyer arrived at nine, just after Allison. "Don't tell them anything," Jane had warned. "Let the salesman do all that unless he asks you a question or he says something wrong. Just smile and go about your business."

But Nelly was having a hard time concentrating on her work. She kept looking over to that sofa, remembering the night before. Had she been too abrupt with Ben on the phone this morning? But she couldn't have affairs with him and Boz and Mac all at once. She'd feel like a prostitute. Wouldn't she?

And what about all those other men who were calling? She had finally agreed to dates with three of them—Trayle, d'Angelo, and Viscante, starting two weeks from today. What if one of them seemed infinitely more interesting? The old Nelly would never have expected even one of them to be attracted to her. The new Anyella accepted all the attention. She found herself looking at men speculatively, wondering what it would be like to have them touch her. She had no frame of reference. She was hungry for foods she had never really tasted. She wanted, craved, to taste them all.

* * *

At ten the second broker and prospective buyers arrived. Nelly heard them drive up and went to the door. There stood Rocky! "Good morning, Mrs. Holachek," he said, giving her a big wink. "I'm helping the girls out this week." He turned and explained to his clients, "This lady's daughters own Emjay Realty. So of course we're handling this sale." He took them through and Nelly listened. "The reason I'm showing you this one, even though you're used to two-story homes, is so you can see that you can still have privacy in another part of the house without having to climb stairs. See? All the bedrooms are off the hall in that wing, or over here. And because this is hurricane country, be aware that these low-to-the-ground, compact styles don't catch the winds. They survive better."

She heard the man say to his wife, "You know, honey, it *is* kind of nice to have it all on one floor. There's still plenty of yard."

"Northern-style houses don't always have Florida rooms, one of the best things about Florida living," Rocky added. He led them to the main bedroom wing, but in a few minutes he came back into the living room alone. "They want to tromp around the yard by themselves—I think they want to talk. I betcha they make a bid."

"I didn't know you were going to be—"

"My father told me to get a job or get lost, and the twins told me pretty much the same thing. So I took those courses you have to take to be a real estate salesman and I aced them. And lo and behold, I found something I really like to do! I'm going to learn this business inside out and sideways and then take the broker's exam."

The couple came back into the house through the patio doors. They were smiling. "I knew you'd like that yard," said Rocky. "Plantation is like that. Big yards. More like being in the country than many communities. Lots of big old banyans and native trees and plants that grew here before the landscapers took over. Well, I guess we've got a couple more to look at."

As they started for the door, the wife turned to look back at the kitchen. "And all the appliances go with it?"

"Everything but the freezer in the garage," replied Rocky. He caught Nelly's eye and winked broadly again as he followed his clients out the door.

The girls and Bart and Lauren arrived after the fifth showing. They all went out on the patio to get out of Allison's hair. "Girls," said Nelly. "I think Rocky may have sold the house. They wanted a two-story, Northern-suburb type of place, like they're used to, but he showed them why this kind of house is better."

"We just got the word by the car phone on the

way up," said Emma. "They're putting in a bid for just $1,000 less than we listed it. Which is about $3000 more than we thought we'd get. Not only that, but he got a bid yesterday on a place in North Miami that's been on the market for a year. Not high, but decent. I think they'll take it. He's working for us three days and I think he's sold two houses."

"Amazing," said Nelly. "Wonderful."

"I told you, Jane," Emma went on. "If he did that well in his courses and took all that extra stuff—and he's still taking other courses and reading booklets from every seminar or convention you ever heard of, plus all the trade journals—he's going to know more than anyone in the business."

"Yeah, too bad he wasn't that thorough when he learned about boating," sniffed Jane. "And you know what else? He's still chummy with Evan Gumbel. But I still don't think Evan realizes what a job Rocky pulled on him. I like Evan. I'm tempted to tell him. Somebody will, sooner or later, and then what'll happen to that friendship?"

"Maybe he'll tell Evan himself," said Emma, so defensively that Nelly's heart sank. Good God, don't let her be falling for Rocky, she prayed. Anyone but Rocky.

Barton and Lauren were giggling up a storm at the other side of the table. "What's all that about?" asked Jane.

"It's the list of apartments you girls are planning

to show your mother and me today," said Lauren. "They're so slinky. One of them is on the tenth floor of a building on the beach."

"Oh, that's much too fancy for me," said Nelly.

"Too bad, darling," said Lauren. "I don't have to sell the house. We could trade it—just roll it over for an apartment that's worth about what the house is selling for. That one on the tenth floor—the lady said she might want a house in Plantation."

Barton suddenly grabbed the listings and looked at one very closely. "But the truly amazing coincidence," he said, "is that the person with the apartment who's considering a house in Plantation just happens to be my sister!"

The dance lesson was a disaster. "The jitterbug, I can see," said Nelly to her teacher, Marston Tannor. "It's really fun. And the rhumba is OK. The fox-trot is so basic. But why the cha-cha? I hate the damn thing. I don't like any dance where you have to keep counting. And where I'm on the wrong foot every other step."

"But look, Mrs. Devin Lure—"

"No, Mr. Tannor, you look. Teach me the merengue, the samba. Fine. I'd even learn to tango. You hardly see anyone doing it anymore but it's an elegant step. But forget the cha-cha. It looks like a dance lesson. To me it's contrived. I will try anything

391

else you suggest but I absolutely refuse to do the cha-cha."

"Even if I advise you to learn it?"

"Yes, I still refuse. So flunk me." Nelly could hardly believe the words coming out of her mouth. She was actually standing up to someone, and it wasn't all that difficult. She felt drunk with power. Damn it, she wasn't going to do anything she didn't darn well want to. Nobody was going to push her around again. Not even her dance instructor.

In the Temple Tower, Mac Britton paced up and down in front of his desk. How did he get himself into this? Reb Stepit's idea. When Mac had called to find out how much he owed, Reb had asked casually how Mrs. Holachek was, and Mac had gotten kind of embarrassed and confused. Then Reb had said. "Got a case on her, huh?"

Mac had started to deny it, tripped on his words, then finally admitted, "Well, in a way. But right now, with all the trouble with my son, I'm not so sure I should even think of anything like that. Rocky pulled that boat number, risking Nelly's girls' lives."

"Is she mad at you about that?"

"No, but she should be. I never should have let that happen. And meanwhile, every guy over fifty in the whole damn county seems to have discovered her. Every place you go, five men ask to be introduced. They ask her to dance. They ask her for dates."

"Yeah, sometimes all that competition just isn't worth the effort. But listen, Mac, let me fix you up with a gal who can get your mind off her. Best cure for a rotten romance is a new one."

Mac had refused five times but Reb kept insisting. "I'm not taking 'no' for an answer. This girl will knock your socks off." So now here he was facing dinner with Reb and his girlfriend, Angel, and this Joanie Jackson who owned an upscale florist shop.

No way, really, to get out of it.

If he was going to spend time with any woman right now, he wanted it to be Nelly. Maybe Rocky was straightening out. And she didn't seem to hold the boating incident against him as much as he did against himself. Of course there were other men interested in her, too. Even if she favored him, maybe when they got to know each other better, a lot better—it could turn out that they wouldn't really mesh anyway. But he didn't believe it for a minute.

C.G. inspected the little house with intense interest. It was certainly small. A large kitchen, though, plus a living-dining room, two small bedrooms, a den, two small baths. And ample closets. It was impeccably neat, and decently, if not beautifully, furnished. In fact, several of the larger, heavier pieces of furniture were lovely, solidly made antiques. That side bar. The oak table and chairs. The secretary. There were few luxury touches—no bar, no track lighting, no pool—but the kitchen was large and modern and equipped with three ovens and two microwaves. A forty-inch TV dominated the living room, and the den was paneled. Why had Emmet insisted they come here this afternoon, instead of to her place, which was twice as spacious? "I wanted you to see how I live, Claire. Not very glamorous, but comfortable. I have always been careful of money. My wife and I lived simply. And since she died, I haven't changed. But you're accustomed to something nicer—like your apartment."

"I may not be able to afford it much longer."

"No, you'll be able to afford it. You shouldn't have to change your lifestyle. I'll help you if you need help, but for now, I have something to confess. Let's sit down." He led her into the kitchen and pulled out two stools at the counter. "I don't keep liquor in the house. I usually have some wine, though, in case a friend stops by." He pulled a full bottle of chablis from his refrigerator, uncorked it and poured them each a glass. "A sip or two." He grinned, as they clicked glasses. "We don't need those martinis you made for us last week. I was hung over for two days," he said, laughing.

"So was I," she admitted. "Now what is it you have to tell me, Emmet?" She tried to hide her impatience. What she wanted was to go to bed, now. Even here. But she would listen first. She didn't want to seem *that* eager.

"When I first heard the partners talking about you and Mrs. Holachek, I wasn't sure who they meant. But then I placed her—she lives just a block and a half from here. I had once offered to speak about traditional desserts at a chef's seminar and she chose someone else, so I guess I was already irritated with her. And when I heard she was causing trouble for you, I was very upset. As you know, Claire, you've been my idol for fifteen years. Even when your husband was alive. There was always something about you."

C.G. reached over and squeezed his hand as he went on. "Now, the man who lives next door," he continued, "is Andrew Merritt. He's a religious nut. I've known that for a long time. He says a prayer before he cuts the grass so God will bless his lawn. And one time a few days before the business with Mrs. Holachek, I had given him a lift to a meeting and some of his papers had fallen on the floor of my car. He didn't miss them and I didn't notice them until days later. They were warnings, like those they found on Mrs. Holachek's door. So when I saw the thing in the paper about her husband and realized that she was upsetting you so, even though the story in the paper was very sympathetic to her, I figured there was probably another side to it, too. One of the waiters at the Sky Club had bowled on a team with her husband once and hadn't found him so terrible.

"So I figured I'd put a note on her door. I often take a walk after work. I just kept one in my pocket with a thumb tack and I figured if no one was around I would do it and otherwise I wouldn't. I thought it would just be irritating. I really didn't think anyone would take any of Merritt's silly signs seriously and be frightened. You wouldn't if you knew him."

"Then it was you?" breathed C.G. in shock.

"Yes. I felt like I was getting back at her, for you. I did three of them, and then I stopped. I realized it was stupid. I've never done anything like that before. Never wanted to. It was just that I wanted so much to help you. I didn't realize you or anyone else would consider it despicable. And now, even though I'm still upset at the trouble Mrs. Holachek caused you, I feel like I should write a note and explain and apologize. Or would that only make it worse? I don't know." He refilled their glasses and they both took long, thoughtful swallows. What was it that made them so thirsty when they were together, C.G. wondered. Maybe what they thirsted for wasn't really alcohol. It was each other. "I need your advice, Claire. What do you think?"

She reached across the counter and squeezed his arm. "My darling Emmet, it was a silly thing to do, but we all do silly things. I'm so touched that you did it because you wanted to help me, or punish someone who had harmed me. When I said *despicable,* I meant someone who might do that deliberately to terrorize a person. But just to irritate them? That's a whole different picture. A small misdemeanor. But I am touched."

Emmet pulled her hand to his mouth and kissed the palm. He clicked her glass with his and they drained them. "And what to do about it?" he asked.

"I don't know. Let's wait and see. If the police aren't making much of it, why do anything? If they are, maybe an anonymous note saying you found the papers and put them up as a prank and now you've stopped. But unless there seems a need, I think you should do nothing. Don't you?"

He came around the counter and took her in his arms. "I was afraid this stupid business might upset you so you wouldn't want to see me anymore," he said. "I'm so relieved, Claire."

"My brother," she said, her face pressed against his, "tells me I should rethink my attitude to all this. He says I was taking advantage of her and only doing the part of the job I liked. I've thought about it. I'm afraid that—that maybe he's right."

"What's wrong with that?" Emmet cried in her defense. "Why should you do the part you aren't comfortable with?" He took her hand and led her into his bedroom. "It's early. My bed is not as big as your king-size," he said, "but it's big enough. Let me help you take your dress off, my dear." She went to pull the heavy drapes first to bring the light down to half-darkness. Bright light revealed too much. No need for him to see her bare body's sags and wrinkles yet. That could wait.

The two of them began removing their clothes. He helped her with her jacket and blouse. She unbuttoned his shirt. They finished disrobing, sneaking peeks at each other, until he was down to his shorts and she, down to her slip, with just a bra underneath. She slid under the sheet, knowing that in a moment he would be touching her and she would be touching him and it would feel so good. Emmet crawled in beside her, pulled her slip over her head, unhooked her bra, and pulled it off. He buried his face in her breasts. "Oh, Claire, Claire," he whispered passionately, as he began caressing her. "Darling, let me get your pearls. My secret dream all these years was to make love to you while you wore your pearls." He got up and carefully picked up the long ropes from the dresser, came back to lift her head from the pillow and slip them on. He tenderly arranged them, then pulled the pins from her hair. Then he slipped in beside her once more and buried his face in her breasts again, breathing a deep guttural moan of pleasure.

In his bed, as in hers, the quiet, tentative Emmet became the master—considerate, affectionate, but definitely in command. C.G. loved the way his touch made her feel sweet, then warm, then hot—then out of control.

"Oh, Emmet, Emmet! Oh, yes. Oh, now!" she cried as she reached down and felt him to be as ready as she. She couldn't wait. She climbed on top and pushed him inside her and clung to him with all her might. Ohhhhh, a man who could do this at their age, who adored her, who couldn't get enough of her, ohhhhh, and who aimed only to please? What difference did it make how big his bed was or what kind of a house he lived in? Ohhhhh, how could anything matter but this? She squeezed and squeezed him, again and again, delirious with joy.

If he wanted to live in a tent, by God, she'd live in a tent!

Thirty

The cozy little wooden enclosures they sat in resembled small jury boxes and were duplicates of those she had seen in the tapes of *Clues* shows that Mac had lent her.

They were being taped in the Fontainebleau Hotel's grand ballroom, where there was plenty of space for the equipment as well as the audience. She had been nervous about being on the show and sitting in this box with so many people watching—about 600, she guessed. But she found they didn't bother her a bit—she couldn't even see them once the spotlights were on, couldn't look out to try to spot Mac or the girls. She could hear them, but that was all.

She had followed the *Clues* producer Bart Neff's assistant's advice on what to wear—no distracting bangles, no dizzy prints. She had listened to the preshow briefing about the rules and met her teammates—a wedding consultant from Boca Raton named Sara Cardwell, and a lawyer from Miami,

Ron Hankerman. The three of them had been led to their box and seated, and the other three contestants had been led to the other box. Then the star, Perry Wales, walked out and the audience went crazy. Audiences adored Perry Wales.

He kidded with them for a few minutes. "They didn't tell me I'd have an audience of lobsters," he said. "Oh, wait a minute. That's sunburn? You're real people, only just a little overdone? Well, yeah. Me, too. Under this make-up I'm medium rare. Are you all staying here? Pricey, isn't it? Did you hock the kids? That's all right. Go ahead and hock them. Everybody should stay in the Fontainebleau at least once in their lives."

Perry Wales wasn't a great wit, but no one cared. He came across as corny, but warm and friendly.

Then suddenly a voice boomed over the mike. "Stand by, Perry." He stopped talking. One of the five cameras onstage moved in front of him and another to his side. The voice called, "Five, four, three, two, on the air." Nelly saw a small red light suddenly flash on the front panel of the first camera as Wales broke into a big smile. "Hi, folks. Glad you could join us. Welcome to *Clues!* We're coming to you tonight from the Fontainebleau Hotel here on Miami Beach. Got your thinking caps on? Good. Then let's see what answers we can come up with here."

The little red light went off, then flashed on another camera—the one facing their boxes. From Mac's tapes and the few shows she had watched,

Nelly knew what was happening. The cameras were quickly panning over the two sets of contestants and the little curtained stage between them while a voice-over explained what *Clues* was all about. Then a commercial and a short tape, also with a voice-over, flashing one scene after another from key previous shows, some with celebrity contestants. By now Wales had moved over to the other box and two cameras followed him.

The little red light came on again and Wales began talking to the contestants on the other team. As was his custom, he interviewed each of them briefly. Then he moved over to her team.

"And how are you all feeling tonight?" he asked, as he did every week to each team. Nelly and Ron Hankerman nodded and smiled, but Sara Cardwell said, "You really don't want to know." The audience roared. *Clues* audiences loved a saucy answer.

"Oh, but I do. What's the problem, dear?" Wales asked.

"Well, I don't want to say I'm nervous, but if it sounds like you've got an extra drummer in the band tonight, it's just my knees knocking." The audience roared again.

"And your name is?" he asked.

"Sara Cardwell. I'm a wedding consultant."

"Are you! Say, what kind of questions do people usually ask you?" Wales asked. "What do they want to know?"

"Well, I don't tell them how to find somebody to have a wedding with in the first place," she said. "But once they find someone, I can take over and run it all—from announcements to rice-tossing. The works."

"What a handy person to know," said Wales, whom everyone knew had been married five times. The audience guffawed and cheered. "Thank you, Sara." He turned to Nelly. "And you are . . ."

"Anyella Devin Lure," she said in deliberately soft tones.

"And I understand you're a matchmaker?"

"Well, yes, I guess I am in a way," said Nelly. "My agency, 1000 Words, matches up what we call bookees and bookers."

"Bookies!" cried Wales. "Oh, so you make it easy for people who want to play the horses?"

Nelly couldn't help but laugh. "Not exactly that kind of bookee," she said. "We match up speakers and engagements, using retired or amateur entertainers."

"Oh, now I see," said Wales. "Another handy person to know. I mean, if I'm running a bachelor party and I want a girl to jump out of a cake, do I call you?"

"No. Not unless you want that girl to give a lecture on tax deductions, or some such," said Nelly. "Or unless you want to ask me out to dinner."

The audience tittered and Perry Wales hooted. He looked at Nelly again, and said, "Forget the cakebuster. I'll call you for dinner." And he moved on to

403

Ron Hankerman. "OK, so Anyella makes the match, Sara helps tie the knot, and you—you help untie it?"

"If they insist," said Hankerman. "Though I'd rather handle their property sales and leases."

"Oh, one of those," nodded Wales as the audience roared again.

Wales turned to the camera. "There you have them, folks, our contestants for tonight. We're ready for our little playlet packed with clues. But first, a word of advice."

Another commercial, Nelly figured. Two cameras moved to face the small curtained stage between the two contestants' boxes. After a minute, the curtain opened and two *Clues* actors performed a short, inane skit about a couple visiting Miami and calling home about what they had done and seen. Not one of their better productions, thought Nelly. Then again, most of their skits were usually plot-free. The phone conversation was packed with errors, as intended.

The curtain fell. As the audience applauded, the cast took a curtain call and Wales began asking the other team questions. "The skit made three glaring mistakes about places in Palm Beach County, Broward County, and Dade. Can you name any two of them about Palm Beach County?"

"They said the Kravis Center was on the ocean and it's in West Palm," said Sally Valdez, a dental hygeinist. But neither she nor her teammates could come up with another.

Nelly nudged her teammates. "The Trump Plaza is in West Palm, not in Palm Beach," she whispered.

Hankerman raised his hand and repeated her words and they scored. Wales came over to their box—now they had the ball. "Can you give us two of the three mistakes they made about Miami or Miami Beach?" he asked. Hankerman said, "Biscayne Boulevard is in Miami, not on the beach."

Nelly added, "This hotel, the Fontainebleau, is on Collins, not Harding."

Wales nodded and beamed approval. "OK, now Fort Lauderdale. Any mistakes there?"

Sara Cardwell's hand flew up. "The elephant you take rides on at the circus at the Swap Shop is Carol, not Susan. I know because my niece had her picture taken on her once."

"OK," said Wales. "Anything more about Fort Lauderdale? You just need one more answer to win this round."

Neither of her partners raised a hand, so Nelly did.

"Ah, yes, Anyella. What did we say wrong about Fort Lauderdale?"

Nelly grinned. "It's a good thing you're down here in Miami Beach. You called Fort Lauderdale a suburb of Miami. It certainly is not. If you said that up there you might get lynched."

At the reception later in a suite upstairs Perry

Wales pecked Nelly on the cheek. "Darling, I appreciate your warning. I won't venture into Fort Lauderdale until I make a public apology."

He and Mac slammed each other on the back and slapped each other's arms. "Damn, Mac, good to see you. And thanks for getting us this classy contestant." He turned to Nelly. "You know, dear, while I was taking off my make-up, the hotel desk called to tell me they already had five people from the audience today asking for the number of your agency. My secretary will call New York tomorrow to say that when this runs they must have your number and address up there, too. Give me your card. And listen, stay and have dinner with me. Some friends are coming by—" He put his arm around Nelly.

But Mac was shaking his head. "Gee, I'm sorry, Perry, but I've got a commitment tonight I can't get out of. And watch it there, fella. I saw her first."

Perry laughed and pulled his arm back. "'Nuff said, buddy. Let me call you at the office tomorrow. We'll work something out. I'm gonna be here all day tomorrow, too. Maybe lunch."

Minny pulled into the Carter Bowling Center and parked. She grabbed her bowling bag from the trunk and headed toward the entrance. Albert came out and met her halfway, taking her bag. "Boy, you sure have changed, too, Albert," marveled Minny. "I never saw you take anything Nelly was carrying from her. I've seen you just sit there while she lugged in five bags of groceries."

"Yeah, I know, but I'm finding out a lot of stuff now. From the counselor and the A.A. meetings. I woulda done some of that, maybe. I just never thought of it. And no one told me." He held the door for her, too.

"Will miracles never cease?" Minny cried.

"I got us all set up," he said, leading her toward lane five.

"I called Allison, Nelly's new manager, and told her I'd come in later today after she was gone," said Minny. "She didn't ask why. She said she'd leave a whole stack of stuff in folders for me. The agency is going great guns. We can't keep up with all the new bookees. Nelly's gonna start looking at office space. Or if she moves to a condo, she may get another condo in the same building for the agency, if that's allowed."

"She's moving?"

"Yeah, selling the house."

Albert picked up his ball angrily. He wanted to throw it right through the side of this damn building and then gulp down six beers and take this place apart. Selling their house? But it wasn't *their* house. It was her mother's. He stared down at his ball, breathing hard. He would handle it. He would handle anything, now. He had to. Anything, no matter what.

Even the divorce. It would be granted, the lawyer said, in just a few days. He threw his ball down the alley and watched it swing smoothly into the pocket. Wham! A strike. He turned around to Minny, who was picking up her ball. "So hey, Min—what do you hear about the girls?"

"Oh, isn't this just the most *darling* little place you've ever *seen?*" cried Joanie Jackson when they entered the LaRezza restaurant. "I mean, it surely doesn't look like anything on the outside, but I just don't *believe* what I'm seeing in here! It's Disney! It's a wonderland!" She gaped at a glassed-in Christmas tree at the entrance, every inch covered with pink and aqua ornaments, lights, pink snow, strings of pink pearls, little angels, and pink-and-silver-wrapped packages. She looked up at the boxes in Christmas wrappings, hanging from the ceilings and walls, the wreaths and teddy bears, the swags of pine branches covered with cones and holly, the twinkling lights, the dozens of dolls, many of them mechanical, with heads and arms moving. "I mean, I *love* it! Everyplace else has their Christmas decorations taken down by now."

"Those weren't put up just for Christmas, Joanie," explained Reb. "This is the way the place looks all year long."

"We're here every week or so," said Reb's girlfriend, Angel. "You have to make reservations ahead, because you can see how small it is. And anybody we ever bring here wants to come back."

"Is the food Christmassy, too?" Joanie asked. "I mean do they serve roast turkey and Christmas cookies?"

Mac winced, but Reb laughed. "Nah! They got some of the best Italian-continental stuff you ever dug a fork into. I'm crazy about this place. I try to keep it down to once every week or two because otherwise I start gaining weight. I can't resist."

Joanie turned to Mac. "Isn't this *fun!*" she cried eagerly.

He nodded politely, wondering why he'd let Reb rope him into this. Why was it that everyone assumed that if you were single you must be lonely? And they kept trying to get you to meet friends of theirs, the way Reb and Angel had been trying, until you finally let them do it, just once, to keep from hurting their feelings. And you were always sorry.

"I just *love* places that have their own thing going," said Joanie after they were seated at a table for four. "Places with their *own* personality."

She had been that way during cocktails at Reb's place, too. Joanie Jackson was certainly attractive—a model's figure, a model's well defined features, with full lips, a perfect nose, thick brows and lashes. And a halo of teased red hair. But she was boiling over with enthusiasm at everything, everybody, every moment. Wasn't there anything that turned her off?

She was the exact opposite of the Nelly Holachek he had first met. But when Nelly had decided to emancipate herself, she hadn't, thank God, gone to the other extreme. Nelly didn't think the world needed her comments, opinion, and approval on every person, place, or thing.

"Oh, will you *look* at this menu?" exclaimed Joanie after flipping through it for at least fifteen seconds. "All named after celebrities. Look at this Frank Sinatra—veal cutlets with tomato, mushrooms, pepperoni, and eggplant. And baked with cheese on top. Can you believe it?"

"Anything you want to know, ask us," said Reb. "Angel and me—between us we've pretty well tried everything on the menu."

"When I can't make up my mind I get the John Wayne—veal, chicken, and shrimp all in one dish," said Angel. "Or if I know I want seafood but I'm not sure which kind, I get the Joan Collins. Snapper, clams, and shrimp."

"If you like something a little heartier but you don't want steak, that Burt Reynolds is good," said Reb. "Veal and sausage."

"I'll take that," giggled Joanie. "I never thought anyone would *ever* offer me Burt Reynolds."

The hostess came back. "Now, tonight's specials," she began . . .

Mac barely listened. He didn't care what he ate, he just wanted to get it over with and get out of there. Sometime maybe he should bring Nelly here—she'd get a kick out of it. Damn, here he was out with another woman so stunning that everyone in the room was turning around to look at her, and all he could think of was going home. He certainly wasn't being fair. She couldn't help it if she suffered from chronic acute enthusiasm, and he was allergic to it. He could at least pay her a little attention. He turned and gave her what he hoped was a respectable smile. "So you like this menu, do you?"

"Oh, yes. Only there's so much, it's like reading a telephone book. But more tempting." She smiled again and ran her tongue over her bottom lip.

"It's always more fun eating out when the menu is tempting," he said.

"Always more fun when *anything* is tempting," said Joanie, leaning toward him and looking at him in a very friendly way. She left no doubt about what she meant.

Despite his irritation at her enthusiasm, her boldness, and her air of absolute confidence—Mac felt the smallest familiar tingle of sexual awareness. Oh, well, might as well enjoy the view, he thought, looking down at her cleavage. The night couldn't last forever.

Thirty-one

"I guess you really meant it when you said you were really getting into this real estate stuff," said Evan Gumbel. "Don't you even come up for air? Not a word, not a clue for three weeks. And now—big deal—you finally found time for breakfast."

"Don't feel bad, Ev. I haven't seen anyone else the last three weeks, either—just customers and teachers. I've sold five houses and two warehouses already. I've found what I've been looking for. Hell, I didn't find it—I tripped over it. It's something I can really get into and be super-good at. It's almost like I know what they're teaching me before they say it. Maybe I was a realtor in another life. I can't get enough. I've got tons of stuff I want to read stacked all over my place. I need more space, but I don't have time to move."

"Shit, man, there's more to life than real estate."

"That was my problem, Evan. That other part was my whole life. Thrills, sex, partying. Hell, it was all so much fun, I didn't want to miss a trick. I'm a damn addict. I could never tear myself away long enough to do anything else. I've never worked at anything I wasn't doing for the thrills. Even the Amazon and Kuwait and the Antarctic—those were paying jobs, but that's not why I took them. And I certainly wasn't worth my salary."

"So now you've reformed. You know there's nothing more obnoxious than a reformed sinner, don't you? Will you ever have any time to buddy around again, Rocky?"

"Yeah, in a few months. I gotta get some of this stuff behind me first. You know, Evan, I've got something to tell you. And after I do, you may not want to buddy around with me anymore."

"Christ, what could be so heavy? You're not telling me you're gay."

Rocky laughed. "Not that I've noticed."

"Well, man—what is it?"

"Just this. When we took your boat out, Ev, you thought you were getting three pretty expert sailors. But you weren't."

"Yeah, I know. The girls weren't as experienced as we thought."

"Not the girls, Evan. Me. As a sailor, I'm a goddam amateur. The twins were ten times better qualified. Emma took the helm because I asked her to. I couldn't have. I watched you closely that first day and memorized everything you did. I can do that, and then later play it back in my head like a video. That's how I got us out to the buoy. And then I put Emma in charge. It was what my dad calls totally irresponsible. He's right. I conned you, like I've conned a lot of people in the past to get to do things I shouldn't have been doing in the first place."

Evan stared at Rocky, pulled his glasses off, and peered at him some more. "Why the hell are you telling me this now?"

"Because it's old news, I think. I hope. I'm trying to straighten up and fly right. You know the twins' mother? She changed. Overnight she went from an invisible little nobody to the knockout she is now. The girls told me how she planned it like it was Desert Storm. Every detail. I figure if she could, I can."

"But why did you suddenly—?"

"The way I was, I was driving my father right into the nuthouse, Evan. Right into the goddam dirt. And I guess, inside, I've been pretty disgusted with myself for a long time, too. And here's the papers making me sound like a damn hero."

"Well, you were."

"No way. The girls were the heroes. I was trying to tell that reporter, only I was so sick I could hardly talk. She thought I was being modest, and the twins didn't tell her how I lied to them. Just about me organizing things on that sandspit."

"The boat sinking—that wasn't your fault, Rock."

"But the whole *thing* was my fucking fault, Ev. Don't you get what I'm saying? I use people and I lie and after a couple of times, people I want to stay friends with catch on and chill out, and people who're just as nuts as me and as useless want to stay friends. I don't want that anymore. I don't want to lose you as a friend. Or the twins."

"Hey—I don't know what to say," said Gumbel.

"You could crunch me for losing your boat."

"Listen, that wasn't all your fault. I shouldn't have let you guys go. Bad decision. I knew it had engine trouble. I'd had work done on the radio. It was listing sometimes. I just wanted to go on that damn race myself enough that I made myself think positive. I should have taken it out on a long one myself first. And that storm was a lollapalooza. I don't know if anyone could have gotten through it with that Briny. The other boats got knocked apart pretty good, too. Every one of them had damage."

"What I'm saying, buddy, is I'd still like to be pals if you think you can stand me. I may be so straight now, I'll be a bloody bore, and all I can talk about these days is real estate. But it's just something I've gotta do, Ev. Now that I've gotten started, I just gotta see where I can go. It's as exciting to me as anything I've ever done."

Evan shook his head. "OK, tycoon, when you wanna take a break, call me. I thought maybe the four of us could take a spin. Or maybe just go to dinner."

"Sounds great to me. Let's talk to them and see what they say."

"When do you think you might be able to spare the time?"

"Anytime after next week. Next week I'm jammed. Any night the week after would probably be OK."

"You nail it down and let me know," said Evan. "You take Emma. I'll take Jane."

All the way up to Jupiter, Mac talked about Rocky. Nelly wondered what she had done wrong. She knew she looked very smart, very feminine. She was wearing a black linen suit with gold buttons, a black blouse with gold and beige fleur-de-lis, and matching matte-finished gold earrings and necklace. She'd even had her nails done, although she usually felt that a home job and clear polish were good enough.

But he hardly seemed to notice. He was too full of his son and his son's sudden leap into a new career, to be able to register anything else. Now what was it her mother had said to do in such a situation? Ah, yes. *Very subtly attract attention from other men. Then he'll notice and take another look at this fascinating creature.* So far, her mother's advice had scored A-plus. At the seminar, she would give it a try.

But meanwhile, she just listened. She *was* interested, after all. This was a young man who had intrigued both of her daughters. He was bright, handsome, and charming—almost charismatic—despite his rather condescending attitude that seemed to have lessened lately. And he was the central concern of this man who attracted her so and who seemed to be equally attracted to her—when his attention wasn't completely taken up by his son's antics. She sat quietly and listened.

"I talked to your daughter Emma and she says it's all true. He's sold a bunch of houses, one-two-three. And two warehouses. That first one fell into his lap when one of the buyers mentioned he was looking for a warehouse in the area. Rocky picked up on it right away, even though your girls don't do that much commercial stuff. He asked the man exactly what he needed, and said, 'Give me two days, and I'll have it for you and save you a lot of looking.' He pored over every listing in the county and gave the man three choices at the end of forty-eight hours. I think he's somehow lucked into his niche."

"I think he's sold my mother's house, too," said Nelly. "The house I live in."

"I've hoped for so many years that this might happen that I'm almost afraid to believe it has."

Nelly kept nodding sympathetically and letting Mac talk. He looked happier and more animated than she had ever seen him. Enjoy it, Mac, she thought. By tonight, you're definitely going to focus that energy on someone else. Like me, for instance.

At the seminar, two of Nelly's people lectured before the luncheon. One of them, Jason Picanno, was far better than the other. They might be able to book him for really high fees. Mac's speech was the same one he'd given at the brunch. It provoked the same enthusiastic response and another barrage of questions. She slipped up to the podium the same way, thanked the audience, and wound up the questions as she had at his brunch.

During the break before lunch, Nelly smiled a friendly smile at everyone who so much as glanced her way. When she was introduced to anyone, she gave them Lauren's treatment, looking intently into their eyes with a subtle smile. When they shook her hand, she squeezed theirs warmly in return. She listened with obvious interest and fascination to their comments and laughed heartily at their puns and quips.

When the crowd moved into the dining room for lunch, five different men invited her and Mac to their tables. When they finally accepted one offer, other men kept coming up to talk to them, sometimes just to Nelly. Several asked for her card and gave her theirs. Two of them boldly told her she was the most beautiful "businessman" at the seminar. Had she overdone it?

Mac was smiling at the luncheon's start, beaming proudly and holding her arm possessively. Lauren's advice had worked.

They listened to five more speakers. She asked for cards from those she didn't know in case they might want to be listed. By dinner time, Mac hadn't mentioned Rocky for hours and he was hardly taking his eyes off her. During dinner, a combo played dance music, and several men came over and asked Nelly to dance. She deferred to Mac each time and each time he waved her onto the floor, but when the sixth man came by, he shook his head. "I'm sorry, pal, but I haven't had a dance yet and my feet are itchy." He guided her out to the floor and into a fox-trot.

After one easy turn around the small floor, he pulled her so close she could feel his chest against hers, his thighs, his—? Nelly blushed.

"God, I like dancing with you," he said, sniffing her hair. "How can anyone who looks that good, and feels that good, smell that good, too?"

He had her out on the floor for every dance after that, except a cha-cha. "I hate the cha-cha," they said at the same time, as he led her off the floor. They laughed. "I've been taking a few lessons," said Nelly, "but I refuse to learn that one. I hate dances where I have to count."

"My sentiments exactly. I never like to see those dance school virtuoso numbers and that's what most cha-chas are. I never want to work that hard on a dance floor."

"Great minds," nodded Nelly. For the dances that followed, he wouldn't let anyone cut in. She had rarely danced during all those years with Albert. He had two left feet and couldn't be coaxed out on a dance floor. But with Mac it was fun. It felt like they'd been dancing together for years. And from all the touching—her arm around his neck, his hand holding hers, their bodies locked sensuously during the slow numbers—she was melting.

On the drive back, Rocky was not on Mac's mind. His attention was totally focused on her.

"Well, Nelly, or Anyella, was the belle of the ball again," he said. "I felt like I'd brought Marilyn Monroe to the prom." She laughed. "No, really," he said. "But don't change any more. You're perfect now and you don't want to go too far."

"When I started this, I didn't think I could."

"Listen, Nelly, there's a proper range for anything. Last night I went out with Reb Stepit and his girl on a kind of blind date that he insisted on setting up. I couldn't really get out of it so I figured, what the heck. It was the most miserable evening I've ever spent. She was a liberated woman—nothing wrong with that. And beautiful. But she was trying so hard, being so damned animated about everything but the salt shakers, you got tired just watching.

"She was *so* enthusiastic, *so* eager. Everything was *so* wonderful, *so* funny, *so* fascinating. By the time we got to the restaurant I was worn out. She made it clear that she was interested and it was awkward, because I wasn't. I don't know what I'm telling you this for. I really don't want to say, 'Don't get like that,' because you couldn't. You look a little different from most women. You dress differently. But you're still for real."

Nelly listened, openmouthed, to this confession. Because that's what it was. *When a really nice, moral man feels very interested and kind of committed to a woman, even if they haven't talked about it yet,* her mother had once said, *he'll feel guilty if he has to be with another woman. And he'll find a reason to tell her about it and let her know it was nothing to him. It's a confession. So he won't feel guilty.* And here it was!

"You're still sweet Nelly," he was saying. "You're still smarter than all those eager ones."

At that, she shook her head. He was so wrong. "Oh Mac, I'm not smarter. There's so much they know that I don't know. I'm thirty years behind them. I don't know anything much about love and sex. It's only these past few weeks that I've ever been kissed in a way that made me want more, that I've begun to think that maybe it could be something

421

wonderful. Like in books or the movies. With Albert it was a horror. So I'm a novice, a beginner. And I hate being clumsy and new at things.

"I read in a magazine the other day," she went on, "that one thing men like about older women is that they know what it's all about. But not me. If all those men coming up to be introduced because I'm a new face—if they made a date with me, they'd probably be pretty disappointed when they found out how inexperienced I am. Goodness, I don't even know what happens when someone tries to kiss you and make out in the back of a car. It's never happened to me."

Mac chuckled. He reached for her hand and patted it. "Nelly," he said, "worry no more. We can take care of that one tonight. I've got a brilliant idea." He turned on the radio, patted her hand again, and hummed as they sped down I-95, ticking off the miles south. "What I propose," he said as he pulled off the highway north of Boca Raton, "is a stop at my place before I take you home. Our parking is divided into those little alcoves for six cars each. You've seen it. We bought a whole alcove. It was only three extra places. The penthouses get three anyway. That was one reason I bought the place. Unless you strongly protest, I'll take you up to my parking alcove and give you a kiss there in the back seat of my car. I won't try to lure you upstairs. Unless you insist, of course. And you'll see that necking in back seats is vastly overrated. It's a lot of trouble," he said, grinning. "But if I can help you with this long-overdue part of your education, I'm pleased to do so."

Nelly grinned back and said, "How terribly kind. I accept your offer."

Driving up to his parking floor, Mac pulled into his alcove, parked, turned off the motor, and came around to help her out of the front seat and into the back. Then he crawled in after her. "Now we don't just sit here," he explained. "I have to kind of hold you. I get back here and pull you into my arms." He grunted, struggling to push himself back into the corner and pull her with him. "I think it's easier when you're seventeen."

He put his arms around her, held her close, and kissed her on the lips, a friendly kiss. "That's all there is to it?" asked Nelly. *"That's* what they made all the fuss about?"

"Not exactly. Sometimes they went further." He kissed her again, this time gently sucking on her upper lip, to open her mouth to his. Tasting. Until she started tasting back. When he raised his head, she grabbed his face and pulled it down to hers again, and as he kissed her harder she kissed him harder, too, their tongues talking a language unhampered by words, telling of their need. When they finally broke apart, she pressed against him, whispering into his ear, "And then what, Mac? Then what? I have to know. Tell me, show me."

"Nelly—I better not—I—"

"Hold me. Touch me. Somewhere. Everywhere. I want to feel you touching me," she cried, taking his hand and pressing it to her breast, against her cheek, running it down her side.

"Jesus, Nelly!" He reached inside her jacket, and inside her blouse to touch her bare skin. He slid his fingers inside a cup of her bra to touch the nipple and squeeze it gently, and squeeze it again. He kissed her neck, murmuring hungrily, pushed her down onto the seat and maneuvered to get on top of her. She strained to press back eagerly against the rock pressing against her as he reached under her to pull her closer, and then pushed against her hard and fast, again and again. He caught his breath in a rush, groaned loudly, caught his breath again, pushing—pushing—and then slumped on top of her, breathing heavily into her neck.

Not again, thought Nelly in a daze of confusion and sensual delight. Had he come? Without even being inside her? Mac, too?

"Oh, Nelly, no!" he cried. "I didn't mean to—Jesus, how could I do that? Goddamn, Nelly, you are the sexiest woman I've ever—"

"Mac, the movies are right," she breathed, frustrated yet ecstatic. "It *can* be wonderful."

"It's better if you finish," he groaned. "Even like I did. Like a goddam teenager with no brakes. Now what? I should make love to you. I want—. Oh, God! Do the right thing, Mac. Damn!" He shook his head. "Come on, Nelly. We're getting out of here."

On the way to Plantation, he was silent. Until she finally reached over and stroked his hand on the wheel. "It's all right, Mac," she said. "I learned what I wanted to know. I never found out when I was younger, but I know now what all the shouting is about. I wouldn't have missed a second of this. Now I know what happens."

"Sometimes. It didn't always go that far. And hopefully, if it went far enough that the guy made it, the girl did, too. But tonight was kind of nostalgic for me. I haven't come in my pants in almost forty years. Not bad," he chuckled ruefully, "if I'd only—. You know why we left, don't you, Nelly? Because I would have taken you upstairs and taken your clothes off and—it would be taking advantage of you. You don't know what you want and what you don't want. You didn't come up there to get laid to-night."

"I don't know. Maybe I did."

"Until you're sure—. All I lured you up there for was a kiss."

"But it was *my* fault that it was more. I'm the one that wanted you to go on," Nelly said. "It was too nice to stop. I felt soooo wonderful. I'm learning,

Mac. I'm learning. I'm pretty sure now that making love, when it's with the right person, can be every bit as good as they say."

Lauren was awake, made up, and dressed when Emma and Jane, yawning sleepily, staggered into the kitchen. "Nana, what are you doing up?" they cried.

"You two tycoons are so busy, I thought I'd better catch you early, because I need your help with something and we have to move quickly."

"Mom's not going to be on another TV show, is she?" asked Jane. "Telling Perry Wales he'll get lynched! When she changed, she didn't fool around. I think he had eyes for her."

"No, something more important, I think." She poured them each a cup of tea. "I think I see a way out of your mother's tangle with C.G. but I'll need your help. First of all, I must tell you I have ulterior motives. I'm doing this partly for Barton, C.G.'s brother from Montreal. You met him at the New Year's party. I've been seeing him when he's down here and he's been supporting AT&T when he's not."

"What ever happened to Donald Brandt?" asked Emma. "I thought he was really hot after you."

"Well, yes, I guess he was. But I told him I'd call him in a couple of weeks. I'm stalling. I'd rather try to help Barton with this, just now. He's such a dear!"

"Oh yeah, dear enough that you ran off to Canada to visit him last week," said Emma.

"Don't tease. It wasn't that kind of running off, girls, although it just might get to be. It was because he's been a good friend to your mother, and because he's rather quickly become a friend of mine. And now he needs a little help with his sister, who, as it turns out, is perhaps a bit spoiled and pretentious, but is not, at heart, quite the bad egg she has seemed. He's been on Nelly's side throughout this falling out, and still is, but he says the picture has changed."

"What picture has changed?" snorted Emma. "She pushed Mom around for two years and she's still pushing."

"But who didn't, girls? Face it. Your mother seemed to invite it. She was more comfortable being pushed than asserting herself."

"And then when Mom got a bellyful and fought back, she's been bad-mouthing her ever since."

"No. Only at first, then she stopped. She couldn't let herself keep it up. And it was a kind of self-defense, in a way, the only defense she had when her whole world started falling apart."

"So what's changed?"

"Well, Bart says she's a different person overnight. Kinder, uneasy about what she's done, but with no idea how to undo it."

"Excuse me. That's not so complicated to figure

out," said Jane. "You apologize. You say you're sorry, that's all."

"Even the Woman of Our Time project doesn't seem that important to her anymore, Barton says. She was going to go to the nominating luncheon and take her new assistant, who could then nominate her. But now all of a sudden she doesn't care about it anymore. She's not so sure she wants so much spotlight, and she's beginning to realize what an utter asshole she would look like if her assistant nominates her."

"It's probably just a big act, Nana," said Jane. "People don't change that much."

"Look at your mother. Look at Rocky."

"Mother, yes. But I'd give Rocky a few months before jumping to any conclusions." Jane insisted. "And why would C.G. suddenly change? Now that she's been given notice, I'd expect her to be angrier than ever."

"But there's one other thing that can make people change, and almost always for the better," Lauren reminded them.

"Nana," cried Emma, "you don't mean—"

Jane finished the question for her, "—C.G.'s in love?"

Lauren nodded. "Exactly."

"But, who? When? It must have been awfully fast—"

"Someone who's been in love with her for years

but never dared approach her. A waiter at the Sky Club."

Emma snorted. "I can see why he never dared approach her," she said. "I can see her falling for an Argentinian cattle baron, or a Greek shipping magnate. But a waiter?"

"Well, he happens to own 15 percent of the club, and he happens to own a restaurant supply company in Miami and a couple of pieces of real estate. He once owned a popular restaurant in Chicago. But he started out as a waiter and he has no pretensions at all—except he's had this thing for C.G. for years. He seems to adore her."

"No accounting for taste," sniffed Jane. "She's damned lucky."

"And Bart says she's suddenly like a young girl in love. Kinder. Sweeter. The spotlight is no longer so alluring."

"That's a fairy tale ending for someone who didn't really deserve it," said Jane. "But where do *we* come in?"

"I want you to help me with your mother. Nelly needs C.G. No one could do all those parties and meetings better. And no one would be happier doing them. It's the ideal solution. It would automatically cancel anything bad C.G. has said about your mother in the past, and you can bet she wouldn't say anything more. Not against the company she's promoting and the person she's working for. She'd look like a jackass. And she'd do her best. She wouldn't want to lose a job so perfect for her."

"You know, Jane," said Emma thoughtfully, "as wacky as it sounds, it makes sense. But how do we get them to see that?"

"I think it'll take more than a meeting—perhaps a gesture of some kind. I told Bart he should get C.G. to nominate your mother for Woman of Our Time at that luncheon. There will be open nominating at one point—most people don't realize that. They expect the slate is all figured out and confirming the nominations will just be a formality, as it usually is. But when C.G. was helping get this thing started, she pushed for open nominations, probably just so she could be sure *she* got nominated. But several of those on the committee agreed, that that's the way to truly reflect *all* of the community's choices. If she nominates your mother, and your mother already knows that C.G. would love that job and wants to ask for it—"

"But Nana, Mom doesn't want to be Woman of Our Time. She's not into that stuff."

"She's not going to be named Woman of Our Time. There are too many really qualified people who will be nominated. Your mother doesn't chase after such rainbows. She can graciously decline, but it would be a great compliment from C.G. It would be featured in whatever coverage the luncheon gets. It would be a public sign to anyone who knew about their scrap, and not all that many people do, that the feud is over. And it's got to be wonderful for Nelly's business."

The girls looked at each other, grinned, and clicked teacups. "You know, Nana, as usual, you've seen right through all this so clearly. I think it would work," said Jane.

Emma nodded. "OK Nana, tell us what you want us to do."

Lauren arrived at Emmet's address at nine, carefully following the directions he had given her on the telephone. She was totally unaware that C.G. had driven off in her old, much-repaired Mercedes just twenty minutes earlier—a blissfully happy and fulfilled C.G.

It was a small house, compared to others in the area. Stucco, with a red tiled roof and a one-car garage. Almost identical to the one next door. Both were nicely landscaped, well-kept, and clean. And the lots, she noted, were quite large. At the door, she rapped the brass knocker, and a wiry, brown-eyed, nondescript man who she guessed could have been anywhere from fifty to sixty-five years old, opened it.

"Oh, Mrs. James. I'm Emmet Mathias. Thank you so much for coming," he said, backing away to allow her inside.

The interior walls were stucco, too, and the furniture simple but solid. Some of the pieces were fine antiques. He had two chairs pulled out at the round antique oak dining room table which was set for two. A coffeepot was plugged in. "Please sit down," he said. "I'll be right back." He ducked into the kitchen, returning quickly carrying a serving platter of eggs and bacon and a basket full of toast, muffins, and tiny Danish, which he placed on the table. "Please," he said, indicating a chair. He pushed the platter toward her, poured their coffee, and then moved the cream and sugar within her reach.

"This was very nice of you, but wholly unnecessary," said Lauren. "Barton told me you're the gentleman seeing his sister, and that you wanted to talk to me."

"Yes," said Emmet. "I'm very serious about C.G. and she's serious about me. That's why I know about the misunderstanding between her and your daughter and how much it distresses C.G. That's not the real C.G.—she hasn't been herself since her husband died. She felt like her back was against the wall and the enemy was closing in. That's why she didn't have a very good relationship with your daughter. But she's more herself now. And I was hoping that perhaps you and I, if we put our heads together, could help the two of them get past what happened and become friends."

"What a coincidence," said Lauren. "I've been

working on the very same thing the last couple of days. As I told Barton, C.G. would be perfect in a job my daughter needs to fill in her new agency. But I don't—"

"Her brother mentioned that to her. I think she would be perfect, too. Better than anyone else. She has class, that elegant way about her. She loves socializing. That's why she's so good at it."

Lauren nodded agreement. "So what do you suggest?"

"I don't know. But there's one other reason I called you. Something it's very difficult for me to talk about because I've never in my life done anything so cruel and hurtful. But I can only say I was very frustrated at the time, and I didn't realize that what I was doing would be anything more than a nuisance."

Lauren ate her eggs and listened, puzzled. In halting tones Emmet began to explain about the notes he had put on Nelly's door. "They're such silly messages. I didn't think they would frighten anyone, much less terrify them."

"They probably wouldn't have if Nelly's husband hadn't just tried to kill her. That could leave anyone a little paranoid."

"I want her to know, though, that the man they caught was telling the truth. He made one phone call and put one note on her door, if that's what he says. He's my tenant, and he's a religion freak, true. But scrupulously honest. I put the other notes on the door—when I was taking walks. I walk a mile or two every night after work, just around here. As you see, I'm only two blocks from Mrs. Holachek's house."

"But why Nelly?"

"Because I was so upset for C.G. when I heard that Mrs. Holachek had left her in the lurch. To me, it seemed that your daughter was hurting C.G., and I could do nothing to protect her. Andrew had left those notes in my car by accident, so I put them up. One, then two more. Then I felt rather stupid and quit.

"When I found out that the police were concerned and someone was putting notes on other houses, it really began troubling me. I don't want Andrew blamed for the ones he didn't put up. And I don't want you to think C.G. had anything at all to do with it. She didn't. It was after I stopped that we suddenly found each other. We're very happy. We don't want, in any way, to make anyone else unhappy. Mrs. James, I don't know what to do next. Should I tell Mrs. Holachek and apologize? I think I would feel better. But aside from that, how can I help get her and C.G. to heal the rift?"

Lauren took a bite of her muffin and chewed thoughtfully. "Well, I think you're right, Mr. Mathias—"

"Just Emmet, please—"

"And they both, I think, would like to have this nonsense over with. Hmmmmm . . ." And then she said, "May I have another cup of coffee? I think I'm coming up with a plan."

When Lauren arrived at Nelly's, her daughter hugged her tightly and pulled her into the bedroom. "If anyone calls, take the message, Allison," she called out before closing the door.

"What's up, dear?" asked Lauren. "Why are you so agitated?"

"Mom, I'm so confused. First of all, I have to tell you, I have been—uh—making out a little. Getting kissed and—and—things, by three men—Mac, Ben, and Boz Richter. And—uh—two of them have gone a little further."

"Darling, what are you blushing for? People have been doing things like that since time immemorial."

"Well, I haven't. Not like this. And Mother, each time has been just lovely. Oh Lord, compared to Albert—but you can't compare them to Albert. You have no idea what a lout he was at such things."

"Oh, I think I know, Nelly. After all, I was married to your father. They were two of a kind."

"Oh, Mother, I've been so curious about sex, and love and all that, since I first started getting attention from all these men. I think I've encouraged them.

Each time I got in a situation where they wanted to kiss me, I just tried to kiss them back the same way."

"I'm sure they loved it," said Lauren. "What's the problem?"

"Well, I haven't gone—you know—all the way with anyone. But two of them have—have—you know—with their clothes on, while we were—uh—just kissing and—"

"Making out a little?"

"Yes."

"Well, they can't help it, dear. Men's sex equipment isn't as well designed as ours, somehow. Not just that it's not as indestructible, but they can't always control it too well, either. Their response is sometimes too fast or too slow. Too much or too little. Sometimes, even when they have the best of intentions, they get so swept away they go off when they didn't intend to. It's easier for us. It wouldn't matter, but they expect perfection of themselves all the time. I mean except for oafs like Albert or your father, who don't even know you're there, really. All they actually need is a handy knothole. But when men really want to treat you right, you have to be understanding."

"The problem is, Mother, I liked it all so much, I could probably have done everything with any one of them. Am I some kind of tart? I was so eager each time. It was so wonderful. With Albert it started

436

out unpleasant and then got worse. He was so rough."

"I was so sure of that, Nelly. You don't know how I've grieved for you about that. But you wouldn't even talk to me about it or let me talk to you."

"I know. If only I had. But, Mother, how can I be so eager with three different men?"

"Because you've been starved for love for so long, darling, and you have normal instincts. You're basically a very affectionate person. And now, it's like you've just discovered chocolate. Three very nice men are all attracted to you at once. But doesn't one of them attract you more than the others?"

"Oh, yes. Mac. But that didn't stop me from wanting Ben when he started kissing me. Or from responding to Boz when he did."

Lauren gave Nelly a hug. "I'm basically monogamous, Nelly. Not necessarily one man forever, but certainly one at a time. But that doesn't mean I never respond to someone. Some people just turn you on. There's a chemistry. A rapport. Pheromones or something. Of course we respond. But we don't do anything about that response if we're committed to someone. Nothing wrong with chemistry. It's how you handle it that matters."

"I want to be monogamous, too, Mother. I think. I scare myself."

"Well, on the other hand, dear," advised Lauren, "there's nothing wrong in doing a little research and getting some experience and a kind of idea of what it's all about. Not to go to bed with every man who attracts you, but to sort of test the waters. And then you settle on one. You'll be happier that way."

"Mother," sighed Nelly, "isn't it funny that for so long, I didn't appreciate what an outstanding, first class person you are? That I never thanked you for being my mother?"

"I thank you, too, my little chick," said Lauren. "And now let me tell you what's been going on with C.G. lately and how I think you can heal that breach and solve a couple of other pesky problems at the same time."

Thirty-two

Morganthau called just after Lauren left. "Mission accomplished, Nelly," he said. "Your divorce. When can you come in to sign a few papers?" There was a pause. "Nelly? Are you there?"

"Oh, yes. Yes, I'm here. I heard you. I was just—uh—a little stunned. It's all done? Just like that?"

"Just like that. You did the right thing, Nelly."

"Yes, I know. I'll talk to your secretary and see if there's any time today or tomorrow that you're free and I'm free, too."

After hanging up, she stood there for a moment. She felt like singing. Laughing. Crying. She did a little jig. "I'm free. *Free!*" she cried aloud. When she had put Albert out, she had felt like a butterfly crawling out of a cocoon. But right this moment, that butterfly was soaring where only eagles fly. She was free!

The phone rang again. She swooped down from the heights to grab it. It was Mac.

"Good morning, my sweet and sexy delayed teenager," he said. "This is your tutor, Quick Draw Britton, calling to check if there are any other subjects you'd like to study. I offer a broad curriculum—making out in closets, making out in the *front* seat of a car, under the boardwalk. This tutor is volunteering to teach you anything you'd like to know, whether I'm qualified or not."

Nelly laughed. "That's a very generous offer. You sound more lighthearted than you have in weeks."

"I think maybe things are looking up, Nelly. I think my worries about Rocky are over. That is a heart-lightener if ever there was one. The other thing I called about—I talked to Evan Gumbel this morning, of all people. He and a friend at Coral Ridge are hosting a dinner outing on the friend's yacht tomorrow night for about thirty-five people. Your daughters and my son, me and whoever I'd like to bring, so long as it's you. I won't try to make out with you in a lifeboat, unless you insist. That *is* one of my subjects. But no classes. Tutoring only."

"I'd love to come," Nelly said, giggling. "I'll check my calendar." She found nothing filled in for the next evening. "I'm free," she said. She wanted to say, "That's not the only way I'm free, Mac. I'm legally free, too, now. I'm divorced," but she couldn't think how to put it. It seemed the wrong moment. She let it pass.

"I'll call Evan. But I have to tell you something

else that absolutely floored me—Rocky voluntarily confessed to him that he doesn't know beans about sailing. He insisted that it was all his fault—what happened He told him all the stunts he's pulled before and said he's determined to change now and accomplish something. I really think he means it. Your girls think so, too, apparently. They've asked him to stay with them. He told them he'll stay for one year, if they want him to, and then he might open his own office. I'm walking four feet off the ground."

"That's wonderful, Mac. I'm so happy for you."

"And I'd be even happier if you'd have dinner with me tonight. Just to show you I can restrain myself sometimes, if I try very hard. And if I keep out of the back seat."

"Oh, dear. I can't tonight, Mac. I have a commitment."

"Let's see, the boat thing is the next night."

"And the day after is the luncheon."

"And we're going to that together. Well, I guess you won't forget what I look like too quickly then. And we're pretty much in the same boat in one way. Even though you've lived here most of your life, you're trying to establish your agency in this community just like I'm trying to establish our law firm. Attending a few of these things is important to both of us."

"I'm afraid so," said Nelly. "Oh, and guess what,

Mac? Two other bits of news. Your son is the salesman who's showing me a couple of apartments later. And his clients who bid on the house? My mother accepted the bid."

There was a knock on the door at eleven. When Allison answered it, calling through the door first as Nelly had instructed her, the voice on the other side answered, "Emmet Mathias, a neighbor. I would like to talk to Mrs. Devin Lure."

When Allison let him in he introduced himself to her and Nelly. "I'm a friend of Claire Clemency-Graves," he explained.

This must be the man Lauren had told her about, thought Nelly. C.G.'s new friend. "I'm very glad to meet you," she said. "What can I do for you?"

He took a deep breath and plunged in. "Mrs. Holachek—Mrs. Devin Lure, C.G. doesn't know I'm here. But I did want you to know that she's looking forward to meeting with you again. She was very stressed when you left the firm and she felt threatened. Her job security suddenly went sour and she lashed out. But that's not the real C.G. and she's hoping the two of you can get past that. She will be leaving Raymond, Schlesser soon, and if she can ever be of use to you, I know she would love to."

Nelly had been studying his face. She had met him before, but where? And then it came to her. "I know you," she blurted. "You're the waiter at the Sky Club who offered to do a lecture a while back. On—what was it? Elegant restaurant desserts? Only they didn't use you. I thought you were far more qualified, but they chose someone else."

"You thought I—? I didn't know that. Yes, that's me. And I know more about art-form desserts than the man they chose. By far. I make them three times a week for a couple of top restaurants."

"Would you like to be listed?" asked Nelly. "We're growing so fast. And we get calls for everything."

It was Will Raymond who came to tell her. C.G. knew the minute he stepped in her office. She read it on his face. That determined, uncomfortable look. This was it. Melissa was out, thank goodness. "C.G.," he said wearily. "We're letting you go."

She nodded. "How soon do you want me out?"

"You can stay until you find something, but I hope that would be within a couple of weeks. Do your job-hunting on our time, if you like. You really don't have a lot to do here, now that we're transferring all the booking business. Guidance isn't your thing."

She nodded. He was right.

"You haven't been with us long enough for a pension or anything, but we voted you severance pay. Four months salary."

"That's more than generous," she said.

"I talked them into it. It wasn't hard. We felt we owed you, too, in a way. This was just the wrong job for you."

"Yes," said C.G. "Don't feel bad, Will. It may be the best thing that could happen."

"You gettin' a cold or something, Minny? You sound snuffy."

"No, no cold. I guess I was crying a little."

"Whatsa matter? You hurt yourself or something?"

"No. I broke up with Freddie last night, and it got to me, I guess. I kept waking up and crying all night. What are you calling so early for, Albert? I'm getting ready to go to work."

"Yeah, but I figured you get up early. I just wanted to tell you my Rag Tag league—the one that bowls at a different place each week? They need a woman sub tonight. You'll bowl free, if you wanna sub."

"Where are they bowling?"

"You know those lanes in Hallandale near the dog track? No point in taking two cars. I could pick you up."

"Yeah, that's all Nelly needs is to see *you* picking *me* up at *her* house. No. I'll do it, but I'll meet you

444

there. Maybe keeping busy is the best thing to keep my mind off Freddie."

"Yeah. Well, sorry about that. But you're right—it's probably the best thing."

"Yeah. Nobody's gonna make me take up tennis. I tried it. It's the pits. Running around in the damn sun getting sweaty is fun?"

"Naw, you're a bowler, Minny. Find someone that likes bowling."

There was an awkward silence on the line. And then Minny said, "OK, what time do I have to be there tonight?"

Nelly met Ben at Wan's. "OK," he said as they settled in a booth, "now you've had a couple of days to digest what happened, Nelly. How do you feel about it?"

"I told you I don't have much experience with such things," she said. "But I talked to my mother about it, in sort of general terms. I guess it was a lovely compliment, in a way."

"I've never heard it called that before," he said with a grin.

"And I think I'm kind of sorry in a way that we didn't take our clothes off and do the whole thing."

Ben's mouth dropped open. "You say the damnedest things lately, Nelly. Do you have any idea how provocative you are when you're being that frank?

445

You make me want to leap over the table and sweep you into my arms and squeeze the breath out of you."

Nelly shrugged. "Maybe just because you like me. I know you do. And I like you, too, Ben. More than *like* you. You've been the best friend. I want to leap over the table sometimes, too. But I can't give in to every urge. I have to think about what I'm learning and who I want to learn the rest of it with. I'm free now, Ben. I'm divorced. All I need is a little time." She reached over and put her hand on his, and they looked at each other—feeling close and distant at the same time—happy, but unsure. "Will you be at the nominating luncheon?"

He nodded. "Yes, with Will and Danny. Maybe Jack. And, of course, C.G. and Melissa. C.G. had a lot to do with putting it together."

"A lot? She had everything to do with it, Ben."

"Starting today or tomorrow, we're directing all booking calls to your agency, Nelly. We'll be sending you a letter asking you to sign up a couple of our people who do that kind of thing. We're getting it all smoothed out."

When Ben brought her home after dinner, he said, "I think I'd better not come in, Nelly. I think I'll just kiss you good night out here. If I take you inside, I'm going to make love to you."

She smiled. "You're right. If you come inside that's exactly what will happen. I wouldn't let you leave until you did."

"You say the damnedest things," he said again, looking at her with open longing. He helped her from the car and pulled her close, then held her gently and kissed her cheeks and her forehead. "Nelly, dear Nelly," he said, his voice husky. "I said it before. I'm too old for you. I'm crazy even to think of you that way, but I would give anything to be the one who helps you learn what making love can be. We'd have the bed smoking, honey. But if not, I still care about you. No matter what. Please think about that."

And this time he kissed her with passion, holding her tightly. Nelly wanted so much to pull him in the house with her and to hell with trying to make a rational judgment. Ever so slowly, he released her, as if it hurt to let her go. "Good night, my Nelly," he whispered. And he quickly got back into his car.

Jane pretended to balk at boarding the *Coyote Kid*. "You promise we won't go out on the ocean?"

"I promise, I promise," said Evan.

"And you swear the radio's working?" said Emma.

"Sea Scout's honor."

"And you promise no waves? Not a ripple?" demanded Rocky.

"The Intracoastal will be a sea of glass," said Evan, looking heavenward. "And if you believe that, I've got a bridge to show you."

The four of them boarded the luxurious 80-foot yacht and shook hands with its owner, Win Erhardt. "Wasn't easy to talk these three into boarding," Evan said. "I think they lost their sea legs out there somewhere near Freeport."

"We'll try and keep her so steady you don't need them," laughed Erhardt, a compactly built, weather-beaten man of perhaps 55, who was greeting his guests and directing them to the main salon. "After your wild adventure a couple of weeks ago, I don't blame you," he said. "Sailing's no fun when things go wrong, but I hope you'll enjoy this tonight. I've got a local historian who's going to talk over the loudspeaker later and point out some of the historic places as we pass them. We've got a couple of people kind of new to the area with us tonight, like your friend Rocky here and his dad, who might find that kind of interesting."

Fred and Florence Brown, who belonged to the Sea Rats Yacht Club and had competed in the race to Freeport, too, boarded next. Then Nelly and Mac. "I'm so glad to meet you again, Mrs. Devin Lure," said Erhardt. "I met you at that Chamber of Commerce thing last month. Ben Schlesser introduced us."

"Oh, yes, of course," said Nelly, looking into his eyes and half smiling. He *did* look familiar, but she had met so many people that night. And that name. Where had she seen it lately? "Didn't I receive—"

"Yes, we've sent you invitations to a couple of parties we've had since then."

"Oh, that was so nice of you," she cooed. "But I've been chained to my new business the past month or so. Not a moment for anything else, no matter how much I wanted to."

"Yes, I know all about your agency. I've booked entertainers from you twice, now, and the historian tonight came from you, too."

He turned to Mac. "And you're Mac Britton. The new lawyer in town from New York. And Rocky's father. Your son is already on board. And your daughters are, too, Mrs. Devin Lure."

"Anyella, please," said Nelly.

"Anyella," he repeated, giving her a crinkly smile. "Beautiful name. They're probably in the lounge or they might be taking a look at the boat. My sister Pat and her husband Rex are showing the first-timers around." He took Nelly's hand and squeezed it. "I'll catch up with you later," he said. Nelly felt a little tingle when he touched her hand. Was it her imagination?

She and Mac made their way toward the door to

the salon. Inside it was cool and comfortable. A combo played in one corner. One couple was dancing on the small circular dance floor, and Jane and Gumbel were playing backgammon in another corner with Emma and Rocky coaching. Next to them a bartender tended the bar and a buffet offered appetizers—canapes, shrimp, and snacks. An artist sat on one of the bar stools, sketching the guests. He was capturing Jane as she concentrated on the game.

Nelly felt a faint tremor beneath her feet. "I think we're moving out," she said. They watched the docks recede as the yacht eased away into the Intracoastal and headed north.

"I want to talk to Rocky about something for a minute, Nelly, if you don't mind," Mac said. He went over to his son and said, "You have a minute, son?" Rocky nodded and the two of them went out on deck to talk.

And they were no sooner out the door when Erhardt was standing beside her.

"You know why I ran this little shindig, don't you?"

"No," said Nelly, innocently. "Are you celebrating something?"

"Not exactly. Unless it's trying for six weeks to get a certain lady to have lunch or dinner with me or to come out on a little boating party. And batting zero. Did I say anything that night we met that bothered you?"

"Oh, no, no, nothing of the sort," Nelly said quickly. "I'm so sorry. That's terrible of me but I guess I just didn't connect the name with the person I met." That was the tactful way, Lauren had instructed her, to cover the fact that you don't remember meeting someone. "And I really have been so swamped. You can't imagine. I *am* sorry."

"Good. Because I'd still like to if you would. I know you're with someone else tonight. I discussed this guest list very carefully with Gumbel and he figured I could get you here if I invited Mac Britton, whom he says you've been seeing."

"I'd say that was rather ingenious of you," laughed Nelly. "There are a couple of other men you might have invited, too. I'm not sure why you went to so much trouble, but if you haven't given up yet, I'll have to find a free evening."

"That'd be great. We could go boating, or we could just go to dinner or lunch. Or you could come to my place out west and we could have a little rodeo. Whatever suits you."

"A rodeo?" repeated Nelly.

"Yep. I'm probaby the only boating nut in the club that's also a horse nut. I've got a place out on the edge of the 'Glades. I had a real ranch in Colorado until two years ago. Love it out there but it's just too damn much trouble commuting. This one's handier. I've got my own ring here, and I've put on mini-rodeos for the charities a time or two. I live out there. I just keep a little place in town to bunk at when there's a lot going on at the club. Do I call you at the same number?"

Nelly dug out a card and scribbled another number on it. "That's our new line. One just isn't enough anymore. I'll tell my manager to put through any calls from you."

"Great. Who haven't you met yet?" he asked, pocketing her card and walking her around the salon, introducing her to his sister Pat and her husband Rex, both of whom looked like simple country folks. He introduced her to the Browns. To the artist, who handed her a sketch of herself. To a couple named Cundiff, from Colorado. To the Hopewells. To a couple of young men who turned out to be the Browns' sons. He brought her to the bar and helped her onto a stool.

He took her hand again in both of his, which were gnarled and sinewy like a rancher's. And again she felt that little rush of warmth where his strong fingers pressed her palm. He studied her frankly, a long, almost quizzical look—was he blushing slightly?—and let her hand go. Grinning, he went back out on the deck.

Nelly looked down at her hand, half expecting to see a mark where he had touched her. Good grief, was she responding to him, too? There was something very male and strong about him. He was a man of determination. He seemed amused by life.

She couldn't help but like him. What would happen if she went out with him and he kissed her? Would she want more? Probably. Damn! Was this thing with Mac ever going to head toward something serious? Or was she going to get involved with someone else first, just because she was surrounded by temptation? And because she was so ready.

Mac and Rocky returned to the salon just then, looking pleased as punch. "Well, this is a very happy party," Nelly said. "Everyone is grinning their heads off. Did I miss a joke here?"

Rocky returned to the backgammon game and Mac climbed onto the nearest barstool. "That was a very rewarding conversation," he said.

"How so?"

"I think he's actually done a complete turnaround. I can't get over it. I think it's time I showed him a little support. There's a bunch of real estate bigwigs down here this week for some kind of informal information exchange. Rocky has somehow managed to get an exclusive on a chunk of Key Biscayne that he's heard a couple of them might be interested in. So I said I'd run a little cocktail hour at the apartment, and we'd have a few locals, a few people from my office, and whoever can come from the New York bunch. I know several of them. Rocky wants to invite the girls, too, and Evan. He says he's not so sure Emma will go out with him alone yet and he wants her and Jane to be there. He says it can't hurt them to know these guys and you never know when it might help."

"That makes sense," said Nelly.

"And I need you to give it a little class. Will you come?"

"Oh, Mac, why don't you do this one without me? I'm—the elevator—I kind of—"

"Nelly, you said you were trying to get over that."

"I am. I've got these tapes I'm playing. But I—"

"Please, Nelly. Try. I'll come down to the lobby to bring you up, if you like. And I'll go down with you when it's time to go home. Please?"

She looked at him helplessly. She could see he really wanted her there. "Well, all right. I'll try."

The evening passed pleasantly enough, Nelly thought. Erhardt certainly ran an informal, relaxed get-together. No schedule. Half an hour after the boat left the club, the caterers moved the appetizers to one end of the buffet table and put out a dinner with several choices of hot and cold entrées, salads, vegetables, pastas, desserts. People could eat when and what they liked. They could play billiards, darts, cards, or other games in a cabin set up as a game room. Or watch TV from the oversized screen in the main salon, another large one in the game room, or the smaller set on the stern. The local historian who spoke over the loudpeaker only did so now and then, for a minute or so. "This is the home on the right here, of Blockbuster CEO Wayne Huizenga and his wife, Marti." His commentary was interesting and it didn't interrupt anything for too long. Erhardt and his sister and brother-in-law moved around chatting with this one and that, seeing that everyone was comfortable and enjoying themselves.

At one point when *The Coyote* had turned around and was heading back to the club, he came over to Mac and said, "I hate to do this, Mac, but I've got a big favor to ask. I have a couple here from Boca Raton who need a lift back up. I thought they could borrow my car but my sister's going to need it. Could I impose on you? Could I ask you to take them back with you after we dock?"

Nelly didn't miss the instant flash of disappointment in Mac's eyes. And did she see a flash of triumph in Erhardt's? "Of course. No problem. Be delighted," said Mac quickly with an overly jolly grin. "Which ones are they?"

"The Hopewells. They've pretty much stayed on the upper deck. They're up there now. The historian needs to talk to me for a minute, but I'll introduce you right after that. Or maybe you want to run up and introduce yourself before we get in so there won't be any confusion when we dock."

"Good idea," said Mac.

"We'll all look after Anyella until you get back," Erhardt assured him.

"Oh, I'd better go with—" began Nelly. But Mac was already charging across to the door and as she stood up to follow him, Erhardt took her hand and pulled her onto the dance floor. The combo was playing a ballad she loved, "Memories." "I thought your historian needed you," she scolded.

"He can wait. This is more important," he said, twirling her easily around the small floor. He was surprisingly light on his feet. Maybe it was the music that moved her. He held her lightly but surely. They only danced the one number, but she felt the same warmth as she had when he'd touched her before. I don't have any dead spots, she thought. Just touch me anywhere. She could have danced with him all night. The grin he gave her as he led her from the floor when Mac returned was almost wicked.

Nelly was flattered but not pleased. Erhardt had maneuvered that chauffering chore adroitly. It meant that Mac could only drop her off at the house; he couldn't come in to take up where they'd left off two nights before. He couldn't very well tell the Hopewells to wait a minute when they got to Plantation—he had to make out a little with his date first and then he'd be glad to take them home. The other option was to take them to Boca and then come all the way back down to bring Nelly home. Too obvious.

She'd better forget about Erhardt. He was certainly likeable, and clearly interested. But far too manipulative and clever. He'd have her jumping through hoops before long. And her hoop-jumping days, she told herself, were over.

Then again . . .

* * *

Mac couldn't even kiss her good night when he dropped her off—not with the Hopewells watching. The phone was ringing when she came in the door. It was Minny. "Nelly, I'm glad you're home, I just gotta talk to you."

"Are you coming over?" Nelly asked. "Should I put on the teakettle?"

"No, I can tell you by phone. It'll probably be easier."

"Tell me what? You sound upset. You and Freddie?"

"We broke up. A few days ago. But it's not about that."

"Well, what is it, Minny? Do you want me to come over there?"

"No. I—I—it's Albert."

"Oh, Minny! What's he done? Are you all right?"

"No. Nothing like that. He's been nice as can be. You wouldn't know him. He's trying so hard to get it together. I been keeping him informed, like we said, about you and the girls and all. And he's been going to A.A. and getting therapy and working so hard, like I told you. He's going to start a business again. Repairs."

457

"Good for him. But he's a closed chapter in my life, Min. Morganthau called. It's all over. We're divorced."

"Well, good, I guess. But I've had dinner with him a bunch of times now. And I've bowled with him a couple of times. He's a new person, Nelly. I can't get over it. He's trying so hard. He's even carried my bowling bag in from my car."

"Albert? That's amazing."

"I just wanted you to know—no big romance or anything like that, but I'm seeing him now and then, more than just to tell him what's happening. He needs a friend right now, Nelly. Someone to talk to. I don't take any crap from him. I call a spade a spade and tell him all he did wrong. But he's trying so hard. I gotta help a little if I can. Is that OK, Nelly? You understand? We're still friends, even if he's my friend now, too?"

Nelly didn't know what to say at first. Albert and Minny? But Minny was a grown-up. She was no intellectual. She didn't aspire to sophistication and elegance. She was down to earth, simple, dependable. And lonely. "Minny," she said, finally, "you're my dear friend forever. I hope you're not getting into anything that will cause you trouble. I love you like a sister. You know that. And whatever you do, whomever you pick, I'm on your side. Just like you've always been on mine."

After another pause, Minny said, "Thanks, Nell.

I feel the same way. It couldn't make any difference to me, but I just thought I should tell you. Especially since Albert and me even talked about him maybe renting a room in my house. He'd feel more at home in this neighborhood. I told him don't even think of it until you move into your apartment. Anyway, talk to you more tomorrow, kid."

Nelly could hardly hang up the phone. She saw her makeover notebook and checklist next to it on the table, but didn't pick it up. Not tonight. No Retin-A. No tapes. Tonight, she just needed to sleep. Minny and Albert? Sometimes life was stranger than fiction.

Thirty-three

The Panorama Room at Pier 66 was ready. The tables were topped with soaring bouquets of soft pink roses and baby's breath—donated by Flowers and Found Objects—with scrolled pictures of clock faces and calendar pages tucked in.

It was not set up for a large crowd as charity luncheons go. But most of the 80-plus people attending were influential, effective community activists, including representatives from several organizations which might sponsor the award luncheon the next year—Hospice Hundred, the American Cancer Society, Salvation Army, and the Urban League.

The reception area was already swarming by the time Nelly and Lauren arrived with Mac and two younger members of his firm, Rob Levin and Bruce Dangerfield. Ben Schlesser drove up a minute later with McKinnon and the Raymonds. And three cars behind them were C.G., her brother Bart, and Emmet, in C.G.'s Mercedes.

Mac headed for the bar to get Lauren and Nelly each a diet soda, while Rob Nevin and Bruce Dangerfield went to check them in. "I wish this whole business was over and done with," said Lauren. "Maybe I've made mountains out of mole hills here. What difference will it all make 100 years from now?"

"What table are we at?" asked Nelly when the young lawyers returned.

"You and your mother and Mr. Britton are at table two," Nevin said. "We'll be at table three, right next to you. They said they don't have a head table—just a podium and a mike over there."

When Ben, McKinnon, and the Raymonds came in, they spotted Mac and Nelly and hurried over. Ben gave Nelly a hug and a kiss, and then Lauren. Danny gave Nelly a hug, too. "Well, that witch will get her comeuppance today," said Danny. "You know what? I think all the time she was supposed to be working on guidance and bookings, you were doing her work, and she was pushing this thing. At least eight different people have told me she was the one who first brought it up to them. Why? Because she wanted to be named Woman of Our Time herself. She was planning to bring her new assistant Melissa along, so I had Will tell her that if she came to this thing and nominated C.G., she'd get fired. Will didn't think C.G. would pull anything that brassy. Sometimes men are so blind."

461

"You're right about her starting the whole thing herself," Nelly agreed. "But it's a good idea. We *should* honor people who really work for the community."

"*If* it's someone who really works for the community and not just someone trying to promote herself, like a lady we both know," said Danny.

"We don't have her at our table," said Will Raymond. "We just decided to wash our hands to that extent. She'll be gone in a few weeks at the most. We showed up. That's enough for now. We'll support it more after she's no longer associated with it."

"Which I'm sure she won't be after today," added Danny.

Nelly smiled uneasily. Danny and Will, Ben, and McKinnon all seemed so friendly today. But by the time this luncheon was over, she knew they might feel a lot differently toward her.

Lauren took in their conversation with obvious interest. But when the partners moved on, she said, "Don't listen to anyone, darling, not even me. Whatever you do, I'm on your side. Oh, look, dear. Here come Bart and C.G. and her friend."

The trio was headed right toward them, Bart forging eagerly ahead, C.G. looking uneasy and being guided firmly by Emmet's hand at her back. Lauren sprang to her feet. "Oh, Bart, I'm so glad you could come down for this," she said as he swept her into a bear hug and planted a big smack on one cheek and then on the other.

"It's wonderful to be Canadian," he chortled. "You get twice as many kisses." He hugged Nelly and shook Mac's hand. "Nelly, Mac, Lauren, this is Emmet Mathias. Emmet, meet Mac Britton, Nelly, and Lauren." Emmet nodded. Lauren and Barton stepped aside and C.G. and Nelly were suddenly left facing each other.

C.G. stared at Nelly, stunned by her transformation. "I—hello, Nelly," she said, finally. "I—I'm glad you came today." She put her hand out hesitantly. Nelly reached out, also hesitantly. Then they clasped hands. Lauren looked on, beaming approval.

"I wouldn't have missed it," Nelly said. "I think you've started something important here. It's good to say thanks for what some of these people do."

"It's always important to say thanks," said C.G. "And every time I've forgotten that, I've—I've been sorry."

Nelly blinked at that, surprised. It was like an apology. She didn't know what to say. Lauren nudged her. "Oh—uh—C.G., maybe after the luncheon we could talk. There's something I'd like to discuss with you—about a job."

"I'd love to," replied C.G, fingering her pearls. She looked over at Emmet and smiled. "If we don't catch up with you here for some reason, I'll call you, if you'd like."

"Perfect," said Nelly.

Danny and Will Raymond, watching the exchange, frowned at each other. Why the hell was Nelly being so nice? A little of the old, timid Nelly peeping through? Will poked Ben and Jack McKinnon on the arm. "Did you see those two being absolutely civil, even pleasant, to each other? No fireworks? Go figure."

"It's easy," said Ben. "Nelly Holachek is just a bigger and kinder person than most of us will ever understand."

"I can't believe what I just saw," said Mac, standing beside Lauren. "You couldn't have been nicer."

"Isn't it better this way?" asked Lauren. "Having a scene wouldn't accomplish anything."

"She seems so different," murmured Mac.

"You're right," Lauren said. "I guess getting fired, no matter how you look at it, knocks the pins out from under you. But falling in love can do even more. And she's in love, you can see that. She's not so angry at the world, not quite as snooty."

"But that doesn't change what she did to Nelly," said Mac. "If neither of you ever talked to her again, who could blame you?"

The eighty-plus guests dined on salad, grilled chicken breast, and miniature veggies. A one-man band supplied music and Nelly's agency had found them a singer and a magician. The nominations were opened during dessert, a white chocolate mousse in a dark chocolate shell. Sally Forbes Lipski guided the proceedings from the podium. "It's not usual to take nominations from the floor," she said, "for an award such as this. And the Woman of Our Time committee reserves the right to add names to the list. But those who put this project together felt that this way we'd run less chance of overlooking someone without a high profile, who still ought to be a nominee."

At various tables, people nodded agreement. "The voting, however, will *not* be public," Sally went on. "A group made up of ten members from every organization involved will pick the winner, or winners, if we honor more than one nominee. And now we open the nominations. Explain briefly why you are suggesting a nomination. To become official, they must all be seconded from the floor."

Two dozen hands were raised. Alma Yockey, Lisa Butler, Sharron Navarro, Fern Mayhue—one by one they made their nominations. One by one Jan Amis Jessup, Bobbe Schlesinger, Mimi Bauer, Pat Du-Mont, and others seconded them. Melba Urbanek, Rosemary Zenobia, Sue Gencsoy, Miriam Oliphant, Norma Horvitz, Lillianne Fines, Kitty Oliver, Donna Casto—the list grew quickly.

After the twelfth nomination, Lauren bent toward Nelly to whisper, "Now. Don't wait too long or they'll close the nominations before you get a chance." But just as Nelly started to stand, C.G. stood and raised her hand on the other side of the room.

Sally recognized C.G. Fingering her pearls as she spoke in the deep, throaty voice that could carry throughout any room, C.G. said, "Madam Chairwoman, I would like to recommend a lady who has supplied entertainment and great speakers to so many charity and community events the past two years, enabling them to sell more tickets and thus make more money for their causes. Which certainly makes this community a better place to be." Nelly caught her breath and held it. "I would like to nominate Anyella Devin Lure, whom many of you have known by the name Nelly Holachek."

"We have the nomination of Nelly Holachek, alias Anyella Devin Lure," reported Sally with a grin.

Ben Schlesser jumped up and cried, "I second the motion."

Nelly quickly stood up and raised her hand. Ben and his table started a round of applause. "Madam Chairwoman," she said. "Please. I appreciate this honor, this kind gesture more than I can say. But I must decline. The service I have performed free in the past, I am now performing for a fee through my new company. And I will be so busy with it, I won't be doing as much as I would like for community projects next year. However, we must not close the nominations until there is one more important name on that list, Madam Chairwoman. And that is why I'm nominating Claire Clemency-Graves, who is the one person, if you all compare notes, who put this whole wonderful idea together, and got so many of you committed to it. People who work so hard for their community betterment, as all of you in this room do, should be appreciated. Sometimes we forget to do that. That's why this idea is such a good one. Thanks to Claire Clemency-Graves."

Barton couldn't second her nomination, being from out of town. Lauren couldn't—she was from Miami. Nelly poked Mac, who quickly rose to his feet. But Emmet beat him to it. "I second the nomination," he called out simply.

C.G. looked stunned. Her mouth fell open. Emmet whispered a few words to her and she closed it and blinked her eyes several times.

Many people in the room knew her but some had no idea who she was. Sally closed the nominations. Lauren hugged her daughter. "You did it. And beautifully," she said. "She'll never win, of course, but it's a thrill just to be nominated."

"You're right," said Nelly. "There were too many other people who have done so much, and any one of them could win. Any one of them *should* win. But they might put her in a special category by that time—honorary nominee, founding nominee."

"It'll warm the cockles of her heart forever," predicted Lauren, smiling smugly. "Give her that job. She really does have an elegant look about her."

Sally Forbes Lipski wound up the luncheon business with a short speech. "We'll send you all updates on how we're progressing, and we welcome your suggestions and input. That's all the business for today. We thank you all for coming and for supporting this project."

The crowd didn't clear out immediately. Guests began moving to other tables to share comments with friends, congratulate and hug the nominees, about half of whom had attended the luncheon, and talk with Sally and the other committee members.

At least a dozen people rushed over to C.G's table—friends and those she had urged to get involved in the project—to shake her hand or hug her.

She was wiping tears one moment, flashing ecstatic smiles the next. Emmet kept holding her hand and patting it.

Mac watched for several minutes, then turned to Nelly. "I guess I'll never understand women. I can see why you're being civil to her, but why on earth nominate her? I can understand her nominating you. Smart tactic. She's realizing that if she tries to smear you, nobody will take it kindly. Too many people have learned how good a person you are and how useful your agency is, so she's trying to change her tune in one grand gesture. But you? You owe her nothing."

Nelly didn't know how to explain. She turned to her mother.

"Mac, sometimes there really is more to a situation than meets the eye," said Lauren. "I urged Nelly to nominate her. C.G. used to be a nice enough person, I'm told. A little pretentious, but generous and reasonable. Until her husband died. Since then, she's been lonely and depressed, fighting for her place in the order of things. But now she's in love and she's changed. The bottom line is, she and Nelly need each other. C.G. needs a job, but her talents are limited. And Nelly just happens to need someone just like her to attend all those events. Whatever else you may think of her, you must admit she is a very classy lady."

"Well—I suppose—"

"And in the fine print somewhere, there's the fact that C.G.'s brother, Barton deLys, and I have become rather close friends. We find it extremely awkward to have the two of them feuding."

Mac shook his head. "I still don't believe it."

"Whatever the reason, Mac," added Nelly, "isn't it better to have two people who were furious with each other become friendly? To have them try and understand why they acted the way they did, and forgive and forget? And even help each other?"

"Now you sound like one of those fanatics who

puts notes on people's doors," he said. "Oh, look! They're all heading here."

C.G., Barton, and Emmet were approaching the table. Nelly and Lauren stood up. Barton rushed ahead, and Lauren gave him a high sign which he returned; when he reached her he swept her into his arms and twirled her around. "You're a genius," he said, kissing her again on both cheeks.

"And you're very brave," laughed Lauren. "You could get a double hernia with a trick like that."

Barton turned to Nelly. "Your mother can solve anything," he said. "She should run for president."

C.G. came up to Nelly. The two of them reached out tentatively, and then hugged each other, something they had never done before. "Oh, C.G, that was so nice of you. I'm so glad we're working it all out. I feel so much better."

C.G. nodded emphatically. "A weight has been lifted."

"And the job. You'll do it better than anyone else could."

"I'll certainly try," C.G said. "I never was any good at all that guidance business."

"And you won't have to worry about files. Just attend a lot of social functions and report on them, check out speakers and so on. We're working out of my house now, only it's just been sold so I'm getting a new place. My mother wants me to find a condo on the ocean. I saw that yours was for sale."

"It was but we took it off the market. Emmet won't let me sell it. For now, we're keeping both places. We'll mainly live at the apartment, but not all the time."

Emmet took Nelly's hand and kissed it. "I'll be forever indebted," he said. "You made this a wonderful day for C.G. I can't thank you enough."

After C.G. and Emmet left, followed by her mother and Barton, and Mac's junior lawyers came over to see him, Ben stopped by on his way out with the Raymonds and McKinnon. "Damn kindest, craziest thing I ever saw," he growled. "Danny thinks you've flipped your lid, Nelly. That was more than turning the other cheek—that may be asking for trouble. Sometimes I think you're too nice for your own good, but I think I understand you."

Several of the columns and society publications mentioned the luncheon that week, listing the nominees, including Nelly and C.G. Emmet had two sets of them framed—one for C.G's apartment, into he which was moving and for which he was now paying the maintenance, and one set for his house.

Thirty-four

Nelly jumped as the thunder crashed nearby. Would this gloomy weather never let up? Yesterday. Today. The streets were flooded. The canals were up. Powerlines had been hit. Telephone lines were down in places. Parking lots at the shopping centers were almost empty.

Nelly usually loved the rain. She liked to snuggle in bed and hear it pounding the roof and splatting on the window. She loved to walk in it, and let it clean her face—except when it was blowing and thundering like this. Two days was enough. She almost hoped Mac would cancel his party. But no, he called to say it was still on. "I thought you didn't have hurricanes in the winter," he teased.

"This isn't a hurricane. We have several other varieties of nasty weather, too, once in a while, and this is one of them. The good weather most of the time more than makes up for it."

"Says who?"

"The tourism bureau. And anyway, when it gets a little feisty, it can be a marvelous spectacle to watch. Skies have an eerie light, or they turn strange, vivid colors. The palm trees whip in the wind. Big trees are uprooted and blown down. Sometimes we have savage twisters or tornados. Your apartment is a box seat."

"That's comforting," said Mac. "If this building blows over, I'll find that thought very comforting. I can feel the damn thing swaying in the wind."

"It's supposed to sway, my mother says. She says then it won't break. Think of it as nature pushing your swing. My mother always says you have to think positive."

"I'll try. Oh, listen, Rocky said to tell you the girls will be late. They're showing a warehouse he was supposed to show. He couldn't change the time, so they insisted on doing it for him. They'll get here as soon as they can. That's really nice of them, Nelly. They're terrific young women. If this thing with Emma and Rocky ever jelled, I couldn't be happier."

"I'd like to see the girls find someone, too, but they're very independent They were dating two brothers, Rod and Royal Carpenter, for almost a year, but now I haven't heard them mention either brother in weeks. Then again, Rocky and Emma seem to be sparring more than romancing at this point. They're showing a warehouse? I didn't think they did warehouses."

473

"Apparently after Rocky sold one almost by a fluke, he knew so much about what's available that he started mentioning them to every client. Lo and behold, he sold another one. So your girls decided to let him take any that come their way for a while to see where it goes."

"Well, I'll try to be on time," said Nelly. "Right now, I've got to play my *Overcoming Fears* tape. And hope it'll help with your elevator."

"Go to it. See you at seven."

"I'll be there if I have to come by canoe. And by the looks of it out there, I may have to."

Thunder shook the house again. She said to Allison, who seemed completely oblivious to the weather, "Take any calls for me. If C.G. calls, tell her to come in here Monday morning. I'm going to my room to play my tape."

"Is it helping?" asked Allison. "I'm terrified of spiders. Maybe I should try it."

"It's supposed to help with all kinds of fears, but I don't know if it's working yet. I haven't been up past a tenth floor since I bought it, and I've only listened to it a few times. But give it a try sometime, if you like." She retreated to her room and closed the door.

* * *

The tape certainly was comforting—she could say that much for it. Like the hypnosis tape she had played to boost her courage and determination when she first kicked Albert out, this one almost put her to sleep, but it summoned her back to wakefulness at the end. Like the other tape, it spent a lot of time at first telling her to relax and let all her body parts grow very heavy. Somehow that never worked too well for Nelly. She was too slim to feel very heavy no matter how she tried. "Listen to my voice, and do what I tell you and you will take all of my suggestions to heart, and you will overcome this fear, forever. *You* will be in command, instead of the fear."

By the end of the tape, Nelly was—as she had been every time she had played it—so nearly asleep that she wasn't consciously registering much of what the hypnotist was saying. Until he instructed her to come out of her trance and wake up.

She didn't feel any different. Refreshed, of course, as if she'd had a nice little nap. Would it work? Going up to the party in Mac's penthouse—that would be the test.

She switched on her closet light and ran her eyes over her growing collection of pretty clothes. What should she wear tonight?

Emma and Jane sat in Jane's car outside the warehouse, watching the rain. Occasional flashes of light-

ning illuminated the sign over the door. NELSON EN-
TERPRISES. They had the right building.

Their client, Mr. Grabel, was late. "Maybe we
should just go inside and turn on a light," said Jane.
"And make sure the key and the alarm code work.
We don't want to be struggling with anything in front
of Mr. Grabel." She pulled her car up as close as
possible to the entrance overhang. "Got the flashlight?"

Emma nodded and patted her purse. "Check."

"The alarm code?"

"Check."

"The keys?"

"Check."

"Floor plan?"

"Check. I've damn near memorized it. I know
how we get back to the warehouse rooms and there
is a strip of offices in the middle and one down each
side. You can get through to the warehouse space
through the hallways or certain middle rooms. The
place is a maze. But to Grabel, we'll just point out
how nice it is to have all those offices plus the warehouse space."

They grabbed their umbrellas, flipped them open,
jumped out of the car, and sprinted to the overhang.
Emma shoved the key in the lock. It turned too easily. Had it been locked at all, she wondered. They
pulled it open, slipped inside, and let it close behind
them.

Emma switched on the flashlight. Yes, there on the right—the alarm buttons panel. "But look," Jane whispered. "No lights." Emma moved the flashlight over the wall and spotted the alarm control box up near the ceiling above the wall panel.

"That's the battery and stuff up there," she said. "Let's go find something we can climb on to see what's wrong. Where's a light switch?" She found one next to the doorway into the rest of the building, and flipped it, but no lights went on. "Oh, damn. We'll have to find the circuit breakers."

They passed into the next room, which was large with corridors leading off on either side. Against the wall were several desks, chairs, and filing cabinets, some tipped over on their sides. Jane tried the light switches that Emma found with her flashlight. They didn't work either. So the two of them tugged an empty file cabinet and a chair back into the reception room.

There they turned the flashlight off and tried to let their eyes adjust to the faint bit of light coming in from the two small windows high on either side of the door. But with the dark storm outside, it was minimal. They tugged the file cabinet across the room and pushed it beneath the control box. Emma used the chair to climb up on top of it. She stood up, clinging to the wall, turned on her flashlight, pried open the control box, and inspected its insides. "I think the fuse is dead. No alarm system. Great."

"Come down from there and let's get out of here, Emma," said Jane uneasily. "That Grabel guy isn't coming. He must be half an hour late by now, and this place gives me the creeps. All this rain—" She was interrupted by a crash of thunder that shook the walls. And then another. "We'll contact the office and have Erin call and say we gave up on him."

Emma nodded and lowered herself to a squat, then climbed down from the cabinet. As she did so, Jane reached the door and pushed. Nothing happened. She grabbed the doorknob and turned it. It would only turn so far. "The key," she said. Emma fished the key from her purse and hurried over to try it. It wouldn't go in. Jane grabbed it and tried. The same. Emma inspected the lock with her flashlight, then held a light on the lock while Jane tried again. Finally Jane said, "It just won't work, Em. We're locked in."

Emma gasped. "But let's not panic," she said. "We'll just call the office and have someone run up here with the other key to let us out. You call, Jane. I don't have my phone in my purse."

Jane groaned. "Oh, no. Mine's in the car, too. I thought you—"

Emma sighed. "Well, no matter. Those doors at the other end—one or the other will open. I guess we're going to have to tackle that maze of rooms back there, like it or not." She pulled the floor plan from her purse and turned on the flashlight.

"We better conserve that thing," said Jane, "unless you have more batteries in your purse. We might be in this damn cave longer than we think."

"Yeah. I guess our best bet is to take the corridor to the left." Emma said. She gripped Jane's hand and led her back into the second room. "I'm going to be groping our way here so hang onto my jacket, Sis." She flicked the flashlight on and off to get an idea of just where the left wall and the corridor leading from it were. Step by careful, tentative step, they began working their way toward it. God only knew what junk might be on the floors—this place had been empty for almost a year. And all they needed now was for one of them to trip and fall. In this room and down the corridor, they could hear the rain pounding the roof more clearly.

The corridor was lined with doors. Jane tried the first one and it opened easily. Emma flicked on the flashlight and they peeked inside. On the floor were two pallets and several blankets in disarray. A chair was piled with clothing. Shoes and several boxes littered the floor and a grocery cart stood against the wall. They stared at the scene in shock.

They hurried from that room and into the next and saw only packages and boxes on the floor. But behind the third door, more pans and dishes, a sleeping bag, two stained pillows, towels, clothes, boxes, a hot plate on a desk, and two Styrofoam coolers.

Emma turned the light off. "People are living in

here!" Jane whispered. "My God, suppose some of them are in here now!"

"I don't know," Emma whispered back. "We'll let the police worry about that. All we want to do now is get out of here."

The storm seemed to be easing up a bit, but a crash of thunder swallowed up the sound of the phone. Mac didn't hear it until the second ring. It was Erin McBride, a clerk at the twins' office. The girls didn't like using answering services. They kept at least one clerk on duty from seven until midnight every day. "A Mr. Grabel called for Rocky Britton," she reported. "He can't make the appointment at the warehouse. His parking area is flooded."

"I'll tell him when he comes in," said Britton. "He should be here any minute." No one had arrived except the caterers and bartenders who were busy setting up.

Rocky showed up about ten minutes later. "God, Dad, that's a real deluge out there. Half the streets are under. They say there's some beach erosion likely. Any calls for me? Anything from the twins?"

Mac grabbed the memo pad he'd scribbled on minutes before. "From your office. A Mr. Grabel can't make the appointment at the warehouse. His parking area is flooded."

"Damn!" Rocky socked a fist into his other hand.

"I'm uneasy about those girls showing that place anyway. It's empty and you never know what happens to a place that's empty. I've heard all kinds of horror stories since I started showing them. Furniture being stolen, addicts breaking in and using them for crack parties and such. But they pulled rank and insisted on going. I shouldn't have let them. I'll call and tell them and they'll be up here in thirty minutes." He dialed Emma's carphone number. No answer. He dialed Jane's. Again, no answer.

He dialed the office. "Erin, hear anything from the bosses?"

"No," she said.

"Call both of their carphone numbers every couple of minutes until you get an answer on one of them," he ordered tersely. "I'm not sure which car they took. And then call me back here in about ten or fifteen minutes whether you get an answer or not and let me know." He hung up, paced the floor up and down a couple of times, and then looked up to see his father watching him.

"I don't like this at all. I knew I shouldn't let them go. Last week I was looking at a warehouse in that area and some stoned guy just came walking in the front door, carrying a bag of his things. I chased him out. I think he just tried one door after another until he found one open so he could spend the night there."

The phone rang again and Rocky dove for it but it wasn't Erin. It was the gate downstairs. "Three cabs full of people for you, Mr. Britton," said the guard.

"Let them up," said Mac.

"Yes, sir!"

"Nelly's late, too," Mac said. "So much for my plan to have attractive hostesses to greet them. The party's starting anyway, ready or not."

Mac knew Howard Reiner, Jacob Schinder, and Hal Novac from up in New York. They introduced him to the other ten realtors, developers, and entrepreneurs in their group. And Mac introduced them all to Rocky, who charmed them easily as he always seemed able to do. "I didn't intend this to be a bachelor party," said Mac. "I invited a few women, including the two young women realtors Rocky's been working with. But this storm is messing up the best laid plans."

Five local guests arrived within the next few minutes, and Mac introduced them to the New York bunch. The phone rang and Rocky grabbed it on the first ring. It was Ace Mentor, another local realtor, calling to beg off because of the deluge. Two more calls for the same reason from Oscar Jayes and Paul Lechstonoff. Rocky called Erin and found out she'd been trying to reach him. Trouble getting through. No word from the twins. "Which is funny," said

Erin. "They usually call in every twenty minutes or half-hour or so. You don't suppose anything's wrong?"

The New York bunch looked out over the wondrous view, chatting about it, about the weather, and about how they always enjoyed their yearly rendezvous in Florida. They ordered drinks and settled into chairs and sofas.

Then they got down to the reason they were there, and began asking Mac and Rocky and several local guests a stream of questions. "Is it still as much trouble to get on and off Key Biscayne as it was?" "Any new restrictions, limitations, or requirements peculiar to the island?' "'How many people live there now?" and so on.

Downstairs, Nelly stepped into the elevator. Think of it as going to the tenth floor two and a half times, she told herself optimistically, pressing ten. Tenth floors are easy. Don't panic. You've broken it up into manageable parts.

But her breath was coming faster already. What was it the tape said again? Darn. She couldn't remember a word. At ten the doors opened and she had to hang onto the rail to keep herself from running off. But if I do, she thought, I'll never get back on again.

She sucked in a deep breath, moved her hand toward the panel, and ordered her finger to press the penthouse button. She clung to the rail to keep from darting out as the doors began to close. Dizzy, frightened, her knuckles white against the rail, she flew upward, trying to push from her mind's eye that vision that plagued her in elevators. She saw herself on a small, open platform strung on a slim wire and soaring up into the sky, with space and clouds below. By the time the car stopped and the doors opened, she was trembling so with fear that she almost fell scrambling off the elevator.

She was standing in the small, lobby-like space next to the elevator doors. Chairs, sofa, reading lamp. She collapsed into a chair and leaned back, eyes closed, until her heart stopped pounding and her breathing slowed. She fumbled in her purse for a Kleenex to blot her face, then found her compact and repowdered. With a hand trembling only slightly now, she reapplied the lipstick she had bitten off. The ride was over. She'd be all right, if she didn't think of the inevitable ride down later. She got up and headed toward Mac's door. It was open, so she let herself in.

He saw her, came over with a finger to his lips, and took her hand in his. "They're talking business," he whispered. "You made it upstairs without help. I'm proud of you." They waited until Doug Kurlin, a local banker, finished answering a question about Florida thrifts' problems, and then said, "Ah, finally, we have some female company." He introduced her briefly and then led her into the dining room.

"Forgive us, Nelly," he said quietly. "We're right in the middle of a groundbreaking discussion here. Get a drink, and something to eat, if you like. The girls will be late, and quite a few people couldn't make it because of the storm. But these tough New Yorkers can handle anything." Nelly nodded and did as he Suggested. A Diet Coke from the bar. But the lavish buffet turned her off—she couldn't yet manage any food. Rocky emerged from the den, saw her, and beckoned her to follow him back in.

"I was about to send for the Coast Guard again. Nasty out there, isn't it?"

"The water table certainly won't be low after this," she said. "The girls are late?"

"Yeah. Looks that way. I may just have to go and get them."

Nelly frowned. "I hate to think of them out in that. Rather than try to drive up here in this storm, I think they should skip the whole thing. Have you talked to them?"

"Got a little trouble with the phones," Rocky said.

Rocky led her back into the living room. Mac caught her eye and patted the sofa next to him. She went over and sat down. Rocky waited until Doug Kurlin finished making a point and then he said, "Listen, folks, this storm has turned everything into a muddle. I have to go pick up the two women I work with—Nelly's daughters. It won't take me long. Before I go, let me tell you briefly about this property you might be interested in, the restrictions, possible uses, one kind of deal that might work, and so on."

He spoke quickly. Nelly watched him. The same charm, the same almost brooding good looks. He did indeed resemble a taller, leaner John F. Kennedy, Jr., but he was quite different now than when she had first met him. Far more down to earth. Eager. Energetic. That almost condescending tone was gone. Would Emma like him enough now to actually get involved with him seriously?

She looked out the floor-to-ceiling windows onto the terrace. Everything was tied down. Several plants had washed out of their planters. Another crooked stab of lightning was followed by a crash of thunder. What a perch from which to watch the storm. But why this tight squeezing in her stomach? Was danger hovering? Or was it just sensations left over from the elevator ride?

She turned back to see Rocky pull a raincoat from the front closet and tug it on. He said, "I can't tell you how sorry I am, everyone. But sometimes you don't have a choice. My only problem now is deciding whether to take my car or borrow a motor boat." And as the group chuckled, he ducked out the door.

"It won't take him long," Mac said. "And meanwhile, let me tell you something about this pretty lady and the amazing new company she has started."

Thirty-five

In the car on the way down he dialed Evan's number. "Hey, Ev, you heard from the girls, yet?"

"Not a word. What's up? They should have been here over an hour ago. I called their office and they haven't heard zip. I tried you and your carphone didn't answer."

"I've been up at my dad's and I left my phone in the car."

"Did I get this all wrong? I thought they were gonna pick me up here and take me to your dad's, and we'd meet you there. They're not the kind to screw up. They'd at least call. What's going on?"

"I'm on my way to pick you up. They never got to the party and their office hasn't heard a word. They were going to show a warehouse for me so I'd be on time and meet all those New York big shots. They insisted. I shouldn't have listened. And now, what the hell's happened to them that I can't get hold of either one of them? Their carphones don't answer. Nothing."

"I'll be at the door," said Gumbel. "Where we headin' for?"

"Well, they're not at the office or at home. We better go check out that warehouse. It's only five or ten minutes from you."

They didn't have to use the flashlight in the large warehouse spaces in the back of the building. In each section, a low-wattage, battery-powered emergency fixture up near the ceiling gave off a dim, eerie light. But each of the three outside doors was secured with a heavy padlock, and none of the light switches they had tried while groping their way back to the warehouse space had worked either. In several rooms and in two warehouse sections they had discovered wall boxes containing switches that looked like circuit breakers, but flipping them accomplished nothing.

"Boy, are we dumb!" Jane whispered suddenly after they tried the last one. "It just means the power is out. It's probably been out since we got here. I don't remember seeing any spotlights on outside, do you? And these places always have spots on at night."

"My gosh, you're right," said Emma. "Well, that's a relief. At least now I don't think there's some kind of diabolical plot going on here." They tried the last door Emma knew of in the warehouse section, but it, too, wouldn't budge. "I give up. We're stuck in here until someone comes to get us."

"Oh, Lordy," Jane said with a muffled giggle. "Evan's going to tell me I'd do anything to get out of going on a date with him."

"Let's go back to the entrance. If someone does come, we should be up there where they can find us. Wait! Did you hear something?" They froze and held their breath for a moment. "Did that sound like people in here somewhere?" Emma whispered. "Talking and stomping around? Or was it just the rain and the wind?"

"I don't know. Oh, God, what do we do if it *is* someone in here?"

"Now, don't panic. It won't necessarily be a mass murderer."

"You're so reassuring."

"Probably just a harmless street person who comes in to sleep."

"And does his murders and mugging somewhere else. Oh, well then, it's OK," hissed Jane.

"Maybe it's the rain. Come on, we're heading back up front. Then if someone does come in that door, we can be right there, ready to shoot out, knock them over if we have to, hop in our car, and drive off."

"Emma, I think you see too many movies. You're sure the car is unlocked? If not, we'll have to unlock it. And if we didn't lock it, will it even still be there?"

"Wait! Did you hear that?" They froze again. "If that wasn't voices, my ears need checking."

"I don't know," whimpered Jane as they began retracing their steps, groping along as silently as possible toward the front of the building, pausing every few moments to listen.

Rocky and Evan pulled into the lot and immediately caught Jane's Lexus in their headlights. And beyond it, a beat-up '78 Honda, with a crunched hood and a piece of plywood replacing a back window. "Jesus, I don't like this," Rocky said grimly. "Why are they still in there if Grabel didn't show? And what's that other car doing here? That wreck sure isn't Grabel's."

He grabbed his carphone and dialed 911 and explained where the warehouse was. "I'm not sure what's going on here, but two women realtors went in that building over two hours ago and haven't come out yet. They can't be reached in there by their portable phones and they were expected elsewhere, a firm commitment, about an hour and a half ago. I think someone else may be in there—may have broken into the building. There's another car here and no reason for it."

He pulled a chain of keys from the glove compartment and selected the warehouse key. "Wait out here for the police, Evan. I'll leave the key with you, once I go in." The two of them leapt from the car and ran through the rain to the entrance. Rocky tried to insert the key in the lock. It wouldn't go in all the way. He tried it again, jiggling it furiously.

Trying to conserve the flashlight batteries, they bumped into walls and doors several times and tripped over books and boxes, but they finally passed through the doorway leading to the lobby, and in a flash of lightning, saw the by-now-familiar pair of high windows flanking the entrance door. Several times on the way they thought they might have heard voices, but with the rain pelting and the wind howling they still weren't sure.

"Should we try that other corridor?" whispered Jane. "Maybe there are doors to the outside over there."

"No way. There weren't any on the floor plan. And if someone else *is* in here," Emma said ominously, "that's where they are. They sure weren't on our side. And we don't want to confront them, Jane. There could be a whole bunch of bums over there, for all we know. Let's try that key again."

But just then they heard the metallic scraping of a key being inserted in the lock from the other side. They heard it again. Someone was trying to unlock that door from the outside!

"Plan A," whispered Emma. "When the door

opens, we dash out. Run for your life. Through whoever's there. Into the car, fast!"

"Didn't we lock it?" whispered Jane.

"I've got the car keys in my hand. But if it's locked, just run for your life. You go left. I'll go right. If they have guns, run in a zigzag. Look for someplace to call the police."

They stared at the lock. For a moment it was silent. They could make out a muffled voice on the other side. They held their breath, facing the door, bent over like track runners at the starting line, ready for the gun. They heard it again, the metallic scraping, a jiggling. The door swung open, and Emma and Jane charged through it like Olympic sprinters, crashing with a double thud into the two men outside, the four of them tumbling into the water that by now had submerged the parking lot.

The girls flailed desperately against the strong hands grabbing them. Then they heard Rocky's voice shouting, "Emma, Jane, it's me—Rocky. And Evan yelling, "Hey, Jane, stop! It's me, Evan."

They stopped fighting and sat perfectly still in the water for a moment, peering through the pelting rain at the faces next to theirs. Then Emma threw herself into Rocky's arms, crying, "Oh, Rocky, I've never been so glad to seen anyone in my whole life!" He crushed her to him and kissed the top of her head. Evan held Jane in front of him as the rain sheeted down. "It's OK, it's OK," he shouted. Jane started to sob, "We—

were so—t-t-terrified," and he pulled her to him and patted her clumsily on the back.

Just then another car careened into the lot and screeched to a stop and the four of them, sitting in the water, were caught in the beam of police headlights. They helped each other stand up and squinted into the lights. Officer Wendal Carver stepped out of the car, gun in hand, and shouted over the rain, "OK, folks, what's this all about?"

"Let's go inside to talk," Rocky called to him.

"No, you *can't* do that!" cried Emma and Jane together. "The door locks once you're inside," Emma explained. "Someone's really jimmied it and the key won't open it from the inside. That's how we got stuck in there for two hours. There's no power, no air conditioning, no lights. It's spooky. And I think there are people in there."

Carver came over to them and they all ducked under the overhang in front of the entrance. "Why do you think that?" he asked.

"Because we saw bedding and clothes inside," answered Jane. "We're realtors. We were supposed to show the place to a Mr. Grabel tonight, but he never showed up."

"He called your office to say he couldn't come, but you were probably here already," said Rocky. "Erin kept trying but she couldn't reach you on your carphones."

"Yeah, we both left them in the car," said Emma.

"So anyway, Officer, we went inside. And then we couldn't get out. We saw things in two of the offices, like people have been camping out in there. And we kept thinking we heard voices. We were so frightened that someone in there would find us and do God knows what to us." She noticed the car next to Jane's. "And look, that car. It wasn't here when we got here. I bet whoever drove it is inside."

Rocky dug out his driver's license and broker's card and handed them to Carver, and the others did the same. "Hey, you're the guy that was on the boat that went down near Freeport a few weeks ago," said Carver, after turning his flashlight on Rocky's license.

"Yes, and so were these girls. In this man's boat," said Rocky.

Carver put his gun away and shook their hands. "Let me get numbers where we can reach you if we need you," he said. "Hang on a sec My partner will call in for help, here." He peered over toward the Honda. "Oh, yeah, I think I know the car. Those nutty Harper brothers. They never change. But don't you worry. We got 'em."

He went back to his car and talked to his partner for a few minutes, then returned. "Gee, good to meet you all. I'm into sailing myself. We can handle this from here. Help's on the way. We're pretty sure who's in here, but you don't want to hang around while we find out. You got the owner's number handy? Better let 'em know there's something wrong with his locks. The Harpers probably rigged them. They're pretty handy that way. We'll call if we need you but you guys can go."

"Do you have a card?" asked Evan. "Sometimes I need help in a race. Most of the races I'm in, the boat doesn't sink."

"Yeah, dullsville," laughed Carver.

The four of them turned toward their cars. "We'll take you to your mother's," said Rocky.

Emma nodded wearily. "Can't go to a party looking like this. Mom is expecting us to stay tonight, anyway. We have a key. We just want to call and tell her we're OK, and what happened." She climbed into Rocky's car, clumsy with fatigue. Evan helped Jane into the passenger seat of her car and then he took the wheel. The two vehicles pulled out of the lot, Rocky's car first, and headed for Route 84, I-95, and Nelly's house. Emma picked up Rocky's carphone and dialed his father's apartment.

Up in Mac's penthouse the rain was splatting at the windows with fury. The lightning and thunder had resumed after an hour's respite, so his guests had to talk between bursts of noise. They seemed to be growing more and more uneasy, jumping at the crashes, cringing at nearby lightning, looking frantic when the lights flickered. They could feel the building's sway as the wind gusted. Someone had turned on the TV for the weather report, and they saw Bob Soper explain what was going on. Then in a very sober tone, he offered sensible advice for listeners whose power failed.

"You know, I hate to cut this short and leave before Rocky gets back," said Hal Novac. "But maybe we'd better. It's only getting worse out there. We may not be able to get cabs if we wait much longer. And if the power goes out, I'm not too keen on the idea of climbing down twenty-some flights of stairs."

Mac started to nod in understanding when the phone rang. He grabbed it, talked for a minute, and handed it to Nelly. "That's my son and Nelly's daughters," he explained to the assemblage. "I think you're right, Hal. They say it's still a mess in Fort Lauderdale and getting worse. Some streets are impassable. They found Nelly's twins accidentally locked in a warehouse all this time. Now we know why they didn't get here. Some thieves had broken into the building and were apparently in the other side of the warehouse at the same time. They're pretty shaken up. Rocky and his friend are bringing them home and then heading up here. The friend, Evan Gumbel, was supposed to be here tonight, too."

"My gosh, I knew it," Nelly was saying into the phone. "I had this awful feeling. Oh, no, honey— don't give this party a thought. Yes, I'll tell them you apologize, but everyone will understand. Have a cup of tea or a brandy or something and get ready for bed. I'll be home soon." She turned to the guests. "They were locked in for more than two hours. No lights, no air-conditioning. Rocky and Evan got them out safely and the police took over. They all got soaked in the parking lot. The boys are on their way up, but they said to tell everyone the same thing—get out while the getting's good."

Mac flipped through his desk phone book for cab companies. The first one couldn't send even one car. The second could send three, but one at a time. The first would be downstairs in a few minutes. "He says be down there when they get here," said Mac. "They won't wait. Not enough cabs and too many calls."

As though an air raid siren had sounded, the guests all stood up at once and headed grimly for the door. Mac opened it and with Nelly beside him, shook hands with the rapidly departing company. "We sure picked a great night for the party," he called as they paraded out into the hall.

"Say goodbye to your son for us," said Jacob Schinder. "He seems to make a habit of being a hero. That boat thing and now this."

"So sorry about the weather," Nelly murmured as they passed.

"It wasn't a total loss," said Schinder to Mac. "We met your friends and your son. He's quite a guy. He's put a bee in our bonnets. That was a clear, concise rundown on the Key Biscayne property. And we've had a real experience with your weather that we'll damn well never forget!"

"Well, Nelly," said Mac, closing the door after the last of them, "just you and me. Rocky and Gumbel should be here soon."

"Time for me to go, too," said Nelly.

"No, you're not riding that elevator down alone. I promised. Let's just get the caterers out first, and I'll take you down."

Nelly nodded. "Fine. I'll help them clear out." She went into the kitchen and oversaw the storing of leftovers. The dismantling of the caterers' equipment went quickly. They opened their folding cart in the dining room and stacked the warmers and coffeemakers on it. They and the bartenders carried two large bags of trash to the chutes and hurried back, clearly in a hurry to leave. Mac tipped them all as they pushed their cart out the door and departed.

The phone rang. He answered it and passed it to Nelly. It was Emma again. "We're home, Mom. At your house, safe and sound."

"I knew something was wrong tonight," Nelly told her. "I got that feeling."

"We're OK now. Just muddy and beat. It was so hot and scary in that place. Our dresses are ruined. And we all fell in a puddle."

"Well, I'm leaving now. On TV they're warning about power outages and the lights keep flickering. Mac's guests all left."

"Mom, I want to tell you, I was never so glad to see anyone as Rocky. I wanted to eat him up alive. He was such a stuck-up ass when we first met him, but I think he's turning out to be the greatest guy. And Mom, he cares about me. I mean really cares!"

As she hung up the lights blinked again.

She and Mac looked at each other, then up at the lights. If they went, so would the elevators.

He could feel her fear and tried to lighten the mood. "How *not* to give a party," he said, forcing a laugh. "Could anything else go wrong? Come on. Let's get you out of here."

She managed a smile as he drew her to him. "It was a perfectly lovely party," she said. "Who could predict the weather?"

There in his arms she felt safe. "You know," she said, "if it weren't that this storm is about to get to me, if it weren't that I know I've got to face that elevator, if it weren't that I'm eager to see that the girls are all right, I'd stay for a while and enjoy the rain with you. I love being indoors when it's pouring, just listening and watching the sky."

"So do I," he said.

"But not twenty-five stories up. It's better on the ground."

"Didn't your tape help?" he asked, reluctant to let her go.

"Oh, it was marvelously relaxing. If I had any other fears, I'm sure they'd have been cured. But I can't see that it helped much with this one. Maybe it takes a few tries."

"Or maybe I'm going to have to move to a lower floor if I ever want to lure you into my place to continue your education."

"That is a problem, isn't it?" said Nelly with a naughty grin. "And I do so want to learn everything you have to teach me. Well, let's get this over with."

Mac locked the door and they hurried down the hall. The lights flickered again. He pressed the button and she began to tremble. "It's OK, Nelly. I'm with you. I'm not going to let anything happen."

She nodded quickly. "I know. I'm trying to think positive."

The elevator doors opened. He almost had to push her inside. As the door closed, Nelly immediately started gasping and her heart began pounding. She grabbed Mac's hand and pressed it to her breast so he could feel the heavy throbbing as the car began to move. He wrapped his arms around her. "Nelly, I'm here. I want to help you."

Just then the light flickered and went out and the car stopped abruptly, started, then stopped again, bouncing sickeningly a few times before coming to rest. Nelly wailed, eyes wide open, shook her head frantically in alarm, and tried to climb up Mac's body as if escaping from some tunnel. She flailed her arms in a frenzy, grabbing for support that wasn't there.

"Nelly, please, don't be afraid! Nothing will happen. The power will come on any minute," he said, trying to soothe her. "Nelly, please, honey, listen to me." He held her squirming form close, stroking her back. He kissed her forehead, her cheeks, her neck.

"Oh, Mac, Mac!" She suddenly seemed to realize who it was there next to her, whose body was pressing hers, whose lips kissing and comforting her. "Don't let me go," she wailed, lifting her blouse and reaching to pull his hand under it onto the bare skin of her back. "I need you there, inside, on my skin—don't let me go!" she begged. He slipped his other hand under her blouse, too. Now both of them pressed against her ribs, trying to still her as she writhed against him in her terror. Mumbling, nodding, she pulled at his shirt and her hands found his bare skin too and frantically clutched at him, as if pulling herself to safety.

He tried to hold her as she flailed. He moved his hands around on her warm flesh. God, what she was doing to him. His fingers, of their own accord, reached around her middle, and under her bra as he breathed comforting sounds into her ear.

She began kissing him fervently, running her hands erratically up and down his back and tugging at him as if trying to lock her body onto his. Then with a whimper, she suddenly began slipping downward. At first he supported her, trying to hold her upright, and then began to drop with her, slipping down until they were both prone on the elevator

501

floor. "Oh, damn, Nelly, I want to help you. And here I feel—I feel—oh, Christ!"

Nelly's moan turned to a kind of crooning. "I know, I know. I feel it, too." She reached and touched him as if to confirm that she knew that what he meant was what she meant. "Hold me, help me, touch me, love me. Please, Mac!"

He quickly pulled off her jacket and his. He yanked down her skirt and pantyhose, tugged down his own pants as she clung to him, rubbing against him, kissing, biting, sucking at his face and neck as if she would swallow him whole, filled with fear and this sudden intense sexual craving. At first it tore her in two directions at once, then fused into the same headlong rush.

For Mac, the need to comfort and the need to love pulled him along with Nelly to the same irresistible pitch of emotion. As if every sensation, every touch were magnified 100 times. He lifted the front of her blouse, pushed her bra up above her breasts, and fell on them with a passion as intense as hers. Groaning, wailing, they tore at each other, lavishing delight and a comfort as intense as their pleasure and her panic—absorbing it greedily—reaching, touching, and kissing.

"It's swinging. We're swinging," she shrieked in terror. "I feel it . . . Oh-h-h-h!"

"Feel *me*, Nelly," he shouted back. "Let it swing. Its only makes it better. Feel *me*, honey!"

She reached up to pull even closer, to pull him

into her even further, to surround him and wrap around him, every part of her clinging to every part of him with a frenzy that finally pulled her taut and flung her high into an almost spastic joy she had never imagined. Again and again with Mac digging deeper into her body and soul.

Up there, between the twentieth and twenty-first floors while the rain and winds played their fervent, erratic love song, while the thunder rolled majestically, Nelly suddenly learned everything she had been aching to know about making love.

They slumped on the elevator floor, smiling, panting together triumphantly, as if they had just scaled Mount Everest. Gasping, grinning, floating weightlessly on a cloud of elation. Breathing in time, more and more slowly.

"Nelly!" cried Mac, suddenly clambering to his feet. "Honey, Christ, put your clothes on!" He quickly pulled up his pants, tucked in his shirt, and yanked up his zipper. He helped her to her feet, reached inside her blouse and pulled her bra down where it belonged, and slipped each breast inside. She bent over and stepped into her skirt. He pulled it up, turned her around, zipped it, and tucked her blouse in, then picked up her jacket and helped her into it. She picked up his jacket and did the same for him. They stood brushing each other off, chuckling inanely. He pushed her hair back off her forehead and she patted his in place. She dug lipstick and powder from her purse and freshened her face.

"We might be here a while," he said. "Or they might get the power in two minutes. No way to know. I don't want you to make the papers again, this time with your clothes off." He hugged her. She hugged him back. "But we might as well sit down," he said. "God, I need to sleep." They sat on the floor. "Too bad we didn't bring along a pillow and a deck of cards to distract ourselves."

"We can always play twenty questions."

"OK," he said. "I've got one."

"Animal, mineral, or vegetable?" asked Nelly. But just then the elevator lights flickered on. Flickered off. Flickered on again. The air came on. The elevator shook. He stood up and pulled her to her feet and pressed the "L" button. The car began descending. He held her hand tightly, but neither one of them noticed that Nelly didn't seem nervous at all.

Downstairs, they found a large crowd waiting in the lobby, including Rocky and Evan Gumbel. "Dad!" cried Rocky, all but lunging at him, and hugging him again and again. "You're OK. I *knew* you were in that thing. I couldn't get an answer upstairs and they said the caterers were the last ones to come down before it got stuck. They couldn't get the generator working at first."

"We're fine, son, but I think Nelly here needs to get home. She's ahh—she's been through a lot." Nelly did not look as though she had been through a lot. She looked beatific. She was glowing. "I don't want her driving alone," Mac said. "I'm going to follow her, and come back."

"In this?" cried Rocky. "No way. You go in Nelly's car with her and Ev and I will follow. Then the three of us can either stay at your place, Ev, or go down to Miami to mine."

"You can all stay at my house, if you can manage in just two rooms," said Nelly. "The girls are staying over."

"That'd be great," said Rocky.

"We'll manage," said Mac. "And we'll be out of there early. I'll drive Nelly in my car. Evan can drive Nelly's."

They hardly said a word until they were halfway to Plantation. Mac just kept patting her leg. And she patted his. When they pulled off of I-95, he said, "You'll have to call and cancel all those dates with other men now, Nelly." She nodded. "And you know, it may not be that fantastic every time."

She reached over to kiss him softly on the cheek. "I went from nothing to everything," she said.

"I'm not sure who's teaching who at this point."

"I don't want any other teacher," she said.

"We'll move to a lower floor," he said.

"I'll live on the moon if you want me to."

"It'll seem so funny to know you're sleeping a room or two away tonight. Soon, we'll be in the same bed every night."

"I don't want you to feel lonesome in the middle of the night—"

"Nelly, listen. We'll just stay until the storm stops. I'll call you either from my place or the office. We have so many plans to make, but I don't want five other people doing it with us."

When they arrived, the other cars were already there and Rocky and Evan were sitting at the dining room table with the twins, drinking Cokes and eating homemade cookies. "No more talk tonight. If we get started, we'll all be up until dawn," said Nelly. She walked the men down the hall to the room next to hers, Albert's old room. "You take this one, Mac." Then she walked Rocky and Evan out to the Florida room and the guest room that opened off it. You two take this one. There are towels and things in the bathrooms. Now everybody kiss everybody good night and get to bed."

The thunder crashed and rolled as Rocky kissed and hugged Emma, and Evan kissed and hugged Jane. The girls went to their room. Then Rocky and Evan went to theirs and the two doors closed.

Mac walked Nelly to her door where he pulled her to him and nestled her head in his neck. "Go to sleep, honey," he said. "We're both knocked out. This will be the last night we'll spend apart."

"No, I need you to hold me tonight. I want to sleep with you while it's raining outside. I'll chase you out in the morning before anyone's up." She led him into her room. They pulled their clothes off, climbed wearily into bed and curled up, like two spoons, deliciously close. In two minutes they were fast asleep.

Thirty-six

"Nelly. Nelly." It was the softest whisper in her ear. "I'm getting out of here, honey." She rubbed her eyes and opened them. The room was still dark but she could make out Mac, next to the bed, crouching over to whisper to her. "I'll be at my place if the power's back on. Or at my office. I'll call you. Decide whether you want to spend tonight at my place or here. We're never going to sleep apart again, honey. I love you." He kissed her and slipped out of the room. Nelly heard the front door open and close. He was gone. And he had said, "I love you." That wasn't a dream, was it? He had really said it. She slid over to his side of the bed, and snuggled into the warm pillow that had held his head. And she drifted back to sleep.

Emma and Jane knocked on her door at 7:30. "Hate to wake you, Mom," said Jane, "but we have to go back. And we're dying to talk to you first."

Nelly sat up. "It's 7:30.? Where are—"

"They're all gone. Mac left about six—I heard his car pull out of the drive. The rain had stopped by then. Rocky and Evan just went, but we made them breakfast first," said Emma. "I hope the neighbors don't think you're running another little business here. Anyella's Bordella?"

"Come on," said Jane, handing Nelly her robe. "The oatmeal's ready. The teakettle's on and there's even a pot of coffee. You and Nana think tea makes the world go around but the rest of us need a cup of coffee once in a while."

"Especially after a night like last night," said Jane.

"After last night, I need one, too," said Nelly "Could I?"

"You? Coffee?" cried Jane. She turned to her twin. "Well, Emma, I don't know why I keep letting these things shock me. When Mom said change, she meant change. We'll come up here one day and find she's put a diamond in her nose."

"So now," said Nelly, "you've got me up. Tell me what happened. I was getting some strange vibes, but I thought that was from the horrible elevator ride. That hypnosis tape didn't help me a bit. Rocky knew where you were, so I wasn't too concerned. When he said he was going to get you, I thought it was because of the weather. And then you called and said you'd been locked in a warehouse?"

The girls quickly related the tale of their spooky ordeal and rescue. "Nothing really happened, Mom, except that we got scared out of our wits and drenched in the rain. And ruined our dresses."

"Well, I hope you learned something. Let Rocky handle the warehouses."

"He didn't want us to do it. We insisted—gave him orders," said Jane. "It was our fault, not his."

"By the time you got here with Mac, we were back to normal," said Emma. "But Mom, *you* looked so different. Your eyes were shining. *You* were shining. We figured something had happened."

"Well, yes, something had happened," said Nelly. "We got stuck in the elevator around the twenty-first floor in Mac's condo. For about twenty minutes. It was—uh—an experience," she finished lamely.

"But you didn't look like you'd been through an ordeal. You looked like you'd just been crowned Miss America."

Nelly decided to quit while she was ahead. That incredible, heavenly happening in the elevator was her secret and Mac's. You didn't have to tell your children everything.

"And then when you came in you just hustled us all off to bed," said Jane. "You didn't keep us up for hours to talk. And you always keep us up to talk about what happened to us, Mom. Even when nothing has. So we just figured some thing must have happened to you. And then you told Mac he could have Dad's bedroom—"

"But we know he didn't sleep there," said Emma with a sly grin. "The bed wasn't touched. We peeked in this morning after he left."

Nelly blushed. "Well, I—well—he—that's none of your—"

"I knew it," said Emma. "I just knew it."

"Now, wait a minute. If you think we—we—"

"Oh, Mom, we're not asking for a detailed report," said Emma. "We just think it's wonderful you've found somebody so nice."

Nelly blushed again. "Yes, it's wonderful. Worth waiting for."

"Mom," said Emma, "maybe this time I've got to come to you for advice. I always thought it was so easy before, but now it suddenly starts looking complicated."

"What looks complicated, darling?"

"She's in love, Mom," said Jane. "Rocky. Is that some fancy kind of incest or something?"

"Well, what's so complicated?" Nelly asked. "I mean, it's obvious he likes you, too."

"Likes, sure. But does he feel more? Or will he? As much as I do? It just about swallows me up, Mom."

"Tell me," said Nelly. "I know just how you feel."

"And if so, what then? Do we move in together, get married? His whole attitude's changed so. He's so careful not to mislead anybody about anything. He's dumped all that thrills-and-danger business. But is he ready to give up all the other women for me?"

"Are you ready to give up all other men for him?" asked Nelly.

"Boy, *is* she ready," laughed Jane. "Especially after last night when he rescued us. I thought she was going to hug him to death right there in that damn puddle in front of the building."

Nelly ignored Jane's teasing. "Are you, Emma?" she repeated.

Emma thought for a minute, then nodded. "Yes, I think I am."

"I now pronounce you man and wife," giggled Jane.

"Well then, girls, there's just one thing to do. That fellow who caused me to break out, Talpano, the one who writes all the self-help books—he says you can make anything happen. Just lay it all out. You want to get from point A to point B. Carefully figure out a plan, a strategy, and then follow it. Don't get discouraged. Don't give up. Don't wait for it to happen by itself. It never will. You make it happen and you'll get to point B."

"That's just what you did, Mom."

"And it worked," said Jane.

"So all you have to do now," said Nelly, "is figure out how to get from A to B. What does he like about you? Why does he need you? How can you spend more time with him? How can you make him want you so much he can't even consider the possibility of not having you? Figure out a very careful, complete plan, exactly like I did. Give it a name, just like I did. In fact, you can use the same name. Call it the Holachek Strategy."

She hugged Emma and then Jane. "Actually, I wouldn't be surprised if Rocky isn't doing the exact same thing at this very minute—plotting a way to win you forever. But whether he is or not, it doesn't matter, as long as you get *your* plan worked out. With Jane and me helping you, he hasn't got a prayer."

512